Praise for Luan Goldie

'A sharp, funny, wonderful writer'
Diana Evans, bestselling author of *Ordinary People*

'A timely and powerfully told tale . . . a new
and exciting voice in fiction'
Mike Gayle, *Sunday Times* bestselling author

'Luan Goldie is one to watch. Her writing
is heartfelt and sublime'
**Abir Mukherjee, author of *A Necessary
Evil* and *Smoke and Ashes***

'Compelling . . . finely crafted, compassionate'
Guardian

'A warm, confident writer with the lightest of touches'
Observer

'Pacey and powerful'
Mail on Sunday

'The type of story that will stay with you
long after you've read the last page'
Closer

'Brilliant . . . touches on race, mental health
and community in a fresh way'
Good Housekeeping

'A story of hope, a cheer to the strength and importance of
community and resilience. Beautiful, assured and sincere'
Platinum

'Flawlessly portrayed ... A riveting read'
Candis

Luan Goldie is a primary school teacher, and formerly a business journalist. She has written several short stories and is the winner of the Costa Short Story Award 2017 for her short story 'Two Steak Bakes and Two Chelsea Buns'. She was also shortlisted for the London Short Story Prize in 2018 and the *Grazia*/Orange First Chapter competition in 2012, and was chosen to take part in the Almasi League, an Arts Council-funded mentorship programme for emerging writers of colour. In 2019 she was shortlisted for the h100 awards in the Publishing and Writing category.

Her debut novel, *Nightingale Point*, was longlisted for the Women's Prize for Fiction 2020 and the RSL Ondaatje Prize. It was also a Radio 2 Book Club pick. *Homecoming* is her second novel.

Also by Luan Goldie

Nightingale Point

HOME COMING

LUAN GOLDIE

H Q

ONE PLACE. MANY STORIES

HQ
An imprint of HarperCollins*Publishers* Ltd
1 London Bridge Street
London SE1 9GF

This edition 2020

1
First published in Great Britain by
HQ, an imprint of HarperCollins*Publishers* Ltd 2020

ISBN: HB: 978-0-00-831462-0
TPB: 978-0-00-831463-7

MIX
Paper from
responsible sources
FSC
www.fsc.org
FSC™ C007454

This book is produced from independently certified FSC™ paper
to ensure responsible forest management.

For more information visit: www.harpercollins.co.uk/green

This book is set in Sabon

Printed and bound in Great Britain by
CPI Group (UK) Ltd, Croydon, CR0 4YY

For Mum

CHAPTER ONE

COFFEE SHOP

September 2020

Yvonne

The coffee shop is one of a chain but this particular branch seems to have lost its way. The tables are filthy, the pleather seats are burst in places and two men sit closest to the counter openly making their way through a six-pack of supermarket croissants.

Yvonne finds an empty table, next to the toilets. The armrest is spotted with dried milk; it's the kind of dirt that signals neglect, it unnerves her. The walls are lined with photographs of generic Italy, wicker baskets of tomatoes, mopeds, skinny women in large sunglasses drinking espressos at pavement cafés. The door opens and a homeless woman emerges, bulging carrier bags at her side, smelling of urine.

Yvonne doesn't want to be here.

Deep down she hoped he would cancel, was almost waiting for it. But when he texted her in the morning it was to confirm this address and time.

He's late.

Maybe he won't come at all.

Then she sees him on the other side of the glass door, taller than she imagined, far from the gangly eight-year-old he was when she last saw him. His hair is long and sits in a curly mass on the top of his head. He's wearing a pale pink sweatshirt with the sleeves rolled up, his arms marked with random tattoos. He's a man now, completely unfamiliar. But as he spots her and squints, she sees it's him, it's Kiama.

Her hand goes up but she feels too stunned to smile as he makes his way over.

'Hi,' he hovers near the table.

She stands up, 'Hello Kiama.' It's awkward but she feels grateful that the furniture blocks the hug the situation requires.

He scratches at his hair, 'Wow, this is crazy.'

'Yes,' she laughs. Nervous.

'So weird to see you again.'

They stand like this, locked in the act of looking each other over, before he snaps out of it. 'I'm getting a coffee.'

'Okay.'

He backs away then pauses, 'Sorry, do you want anything?'

Yvonne gestures to her cup before sinking back into the chair, relieved to be able to return to poking her Earl Grey teabag with a wooden stirrer.

Kiama joins the small line at the counter, he dives for his phone, not content to wait and waste the moment. Yvonne knows she's in the minority of people without such a habit, without the need for continuous entertainment.

As he reaches the front of the line there is talk between him and the pretty barista, definitely more words than it takes to order a coffee. The stud in his nose catches the light and his face breaks into that smile, his dad's smile, it's uncanny. The barista beams too and lowers her reddening face as Kiama returns to the table. His knees knock Yvonne's as he slides into the seat opposite. He was always a lanky child, all elbows and knees; they used to call him a baby giraffe. It makes her smile.

'What?' he asks.

'Nothing.' Yvonne looks down at the smudged table and flicks away the crumbs of previous customers.

Steam floats from his takeaway cup. Why takeaway? Is what he has to say to her so short? He catches her eyeing it, 'I get fed up of spelling out my name.'

She's confused, but then notices the scrawl of *Kev* on the side. It's sad that he's not proud of his name. But it was simple for her, growing up with a name like *Yvonne*, something everyone could spell and pronounce without a second thought.

'Kev?' Yvonne says.

'It's an easier name.'

'But Kiama's a beautiful name. You know it means—'

'Course I know, *light of life*. But most name meanings sound poetic when you look them up. Here,' he takes his phone back out of his pocket and types something in. 'See, Yvonne means *Archer*. I don't know what that is.' He furrows his thick eyebrows and reads on, 'Ah, listen, *people with this name are dynamic, visionary and versatile*. Any truth in that?'

Then despite the pink clothes, the tattoos, the hair, the nose piercing, Yvonne says, 'My God, you're so much like your dad.'

'Lucky me.' Kiama puts his phone on the table and sits forward in his chair. His eyes seem a darker brown now

3

than when he was a kid, but he's still never quite grown into them. 'Dad asked me if I'd found any photos of you online.'

'Photos? Why?'

He shrugs, 'I don't know. Maybe he wanted to see what you looked like after all these years. You do look quite different though. Especially your hair.'

Her hair? She'd had it cut last week, but has worn it in this bobbed style for as long as she can remember.

'Funny,' he says, 'I can't remember it being so ginger.'

It breaks the tension and makes her laugh.

'Sorry,' he says. 'Is that rude? I didn't mean it.'

She rubs the back of her neck. 'I know I'm a redhead.'

He holds his palms up, 'I just remember it being lighter that's all.'

'It was. But I don't dye my hair anymore. Except to get rid of all the grey.'

Kiama stares at her hair as he takes the lid off his drink. 'I like it,' he says. 'The red. It suits you more than blonde.'

The way he looks at her, surveying and watching, it's too intense.

Her tea is stone cold, unappetising. She raises the cup then puts it straight down. 'Your arms,' she says, 'you really are covered, aren't you?'

He stretches them out across the table, and under a tangle of festival wristbands and beads, they're a mess of tattoos: feathers and roses, playing cards and Kanagawa waves.

'My best mate is training, so I'm sort of like his guinea pig. He's done all these in the last six months. A few of the crappier ones I had done when I was sixteen.'

'That's surely not legal?'

'Course not. But it's free.'

'What did your nana say when she saw them?'

'She cried. I stopped showing them to her after a while. When I find a good portrait artist, I want one of her face right here,' he slaps the left side of his chest.

'How is she?'

'She um,' he looks away and Yvonne knows what's coming. 'She passed away earlier this year.'

'I'm so sorry, Kiama. I didn't know.'

'Nah nah. You wouldn't have.' He rolls his sleeves back down and adds four packets of sugar to his coffee. Noticing her watching he says, 'I used to be mad into the energy drinks, but they were giving me heart palpitations, so I gave up. But you got to replace it with something.'

'Sounds logical.'

He smiles back at her, then his face changes. 'I'm glad you were up for meeting me.'

She takes a breath; she's not yet ready to hear the reasons he got in touch with her, why he wanted to meet in person and talk. 'How is your dad? Does he… ' she pauses, searching for how to frame the question, 'I don't even know what he does for work these days.'

'I don't want to talk about Dad.' Kiama leans forward again, he's staring at her and she can feel his energy, his nervousness. This was a mistake. She should never have come. Should never have responded to his original message, but she couldn't ignore him.

'Obviously, I asked you here for a reason. I need to talk to you about something.'

'Okay.'

He moves his coffee to the side of the table and fidgets with his bracelets, rolling them up and down. 'I'm going back to Kenya.'

It's not what she expected to hear from him. Though, what did she expect? 'Why?'

He wraps an empty sugar packet around his thumb and purses his lips. 'I don't know,' he says quickly.

'You don't know?'

'No, I *do* know.' He puts a hand over his face, as if embarrassed. 'But I don't know how to say it.'

She waits for him to compose himself, to explain, but he stays hidden. 'Kiama?'

'I'm not okay.' He removes his hand and looks straight at her. 'I need to go back so I can deal with things properly. I can't keep carrying this.'

'Carrying what?'

'What happened there,' he says, 'don't you ever think about it?'

There's no response that will do.

'Don't you ever think it would help to go back?'

'I'm not sure what you're—' she stops. She looks away, at the men polishing off their croissants, the barista who glances hopefully at Kiama, the glass door she wants to escape through.

'Yvonne, I have so many patchy memories about what happened. I can't even tell the difference between what I saw and what I heard from others. What I've read online.'

'Why would you read anything online?'

'Because I wanted to know,' he says quietly. 'I was only eight. It's hard to trust my own memories. And I think that's

6

why I'm stuck, like not able to move forward. No one ever talks to me about Kenya. About what happened there. We came back to the UK and everyone just got on with things.'

'Got on with things?' she almost laughs, it's a ridiculous way to describe those months which followed their return from Kenya, the months in which Yvonne 'got on' with nothing.

'I can't talk to Dad about this. I used to talk to my nana but... ' His face falls.

Yvonne lifts her hand to put it on his arm, but pulls back. She hasn't seen him in a decade, she can't suddenly step in and start comforting him. It's not her place.

'I don't want to do this alone.' His voice cracks slightly. 'I can't. I can't do this alone.'

She knows what he's about to ask.

CHAPTER TWO

SNAKEBITE

May 2001

Yvonne

The middle step is prone to squeaking, so Yvonne carefully avoids it as she heads downstairs. She tiptoes past the downstairs bedroom. Though she doubts a little noise will be enough to stop Emma and her latest fling doing whatever it is they're doing.

Emma squeals from behind the sky-coloured bed sheet stapled in the doorframe. The door fell off weeks ago. The hinges, like everything else in their dump of a student house, rotted, and one night Emma drunkenly slammed it too hard and it swung from the frame with a crack.

It was Yvonne's idea to put up the sheet.

There's a growling noise from behind it now, followed by laughter, delight. It's too intimate, Yvonne shouldn't be listening to her housemate having sex, but it's that car crash thing. How can she not?

The bed creaks and someone groans, guttural, she's not sure if it's Emma or *him*. Him being SWEETBOY76, his screen name on MSN Messenger. Over the last month, Yvonne has wasted so much time in the library, helping Emma to become her sexiest, smartest self, which has mostly consisted of correcting spellings of words like *risqué* and *licentious*.

The groans die down to light laughter followed by whispering, and in a way it's more intimate. They really need to get the door fixed.

The kitchen looks worse than usual this morning, past messy and dirty, now firmly in the realms of filthy. Fairy lights twinkle around the whiteboard, Christmas every day, the board itself is covered with doodles of lecturers doing inexplicable things to each other and Box Room Bethany's complaints about people using all her tampons.

If someone would have asked Yvonne years ago, back when she was living in the cramped terrace house of her childhood with her three older brothers, what she imagined it would be like to live with girls, she would probably have used the word *clean*. But here, in this house, there is only grime. A saucepan of congealed pasta rests on the hob, surrounded by dried white froth from where it was allowed to boil over. And there, on the counter, amongst the crumbs, empty CD cases and dirty dishes sits an open takeaway box from California Chicken, a few brown thigh bones and a smear of ketchup left in it.

So, Sweetboy's not a vegetarian then. That would be Yvonne's deal breaker. She could never bring herself to share saliva with someone who had dead animal on his breath. She lifts the gaudy box, its slogan proclaims it to be '*Hot and Tasty. Just the way you like it*'. The smell disgusts her, but the bin is full, close to overflowing. She should take it out really, like she always does. But instead she drops the box back on the counter and grabs a whiteboard pen, scrawls a note on the board.

Clean your shit up! I'm not your slave. Y.

Yvonne dumps her notepad in her rucksack, checks for a working pen and refills a Poland Spring bottle with tap water while rereading her whiteboard message. It's a bit strong. She drops her rucksack to wipe it off with a sleeve and rewrites.

Please can whoever cooked last night, clean it up.
Thanks. Y.

The male voice in Emma's room says, 'Not now.'

He doesn't sound how she expected. But then, what did she expect? That he 'sound black'? Her mum always says you can tell on the phone, but Yvonne doesn't think so, or at least, she would never admit it.

Are they coming out of the bedroom? This will be awkward. She doesn't want to meet him. Quickly, in the hallway she kicks off her slippers and grabs a battered pair of pink Dunlops from a pile by the front door. They smell. Emma's been wearing them without socks again.

'Dude?' Emma whispers as she comes into the hall, a short towel wrapped around her like a toga. She grabs Yvonne's wrist and pulls her into the kitchen. 'Did you hear us?' She drops open her bottom jaw and fakes a silent laugh.

'I think I would have heard you if I was in John o'Groats.'

Emma laughs. But Yvonne doesn't. 'You're ridiculous,' she says. 'No one likes sex that much.'

Emma pushes her black fringe from her eyes. 'Shush, he'll hear you.'

'Don't *shush* me. You're the one with no volume control.

And I'm fed up of this,' she points to the sheet. 'Call the landlord and tell him you need a proper door. No, tell him you need sound proofing.'

Emma laughs, then mouths overenthusiastically, 'I've not slept all night.' Her chest is red and her mascara is smudged making her green eyes look liquidly cold and pale. 'Seriously, like, seriously,' she says with the international school twang she's never quite managed to shake, 'I love a guy so open to trying new things.'

Yvonne fake gags, 'Please, stop talking.'

'Wait till you meet him.'

'I don't want to meet him. It's bad enough I'm talking to you post-sex.'

Emma covers her mouth to stifle a laugh. 'Why are you going out so early anyway?'

'I've got my final tutorial at eleven. Surely, yours is today as well?'

'Urgh, for what? So they can tell me how unreadable my last essay was? I know that. Stay home today?'

Yvonne thinks about the cost of truancy, all that student debt she's racking up to sit on the sofa and watch *Diagnosis Murder*. 'Nope. I'm going in.'

Emma frowns, 'Well, he's going to work so I should, like, drag myself in as well. Wait for me.'

'No. You'll make me late.'

'I'll be quick. Talk me up to him,' she whispers.

'No. I'm leaving.'

But Emma's already halfway up the stairs pulling off her towel, 'You know me, three minutes and I'm done.'

Three minutes to shower followed by an hour pottering

about the house. Yvonne steps outside and closes the front door. There's a car parked on their usually empty drive, a Volvo Estate, not the kind of car a young guy would drive. A crucifix on a purple beaded chain hangs from the rear-view mirror. Surely it's his parents' car, she thinks as she walks towards the bus stop at the end of the road. But then, stops, she's left her rucksack. She runs back to the house and looks in the hall, but it's not there. A tap is running in the kitchen, and as she goes in she sees him there by the sink, bare back and a pair of black jeans.

She averts her eyes and grabs the bag from the floor.

'Morning,' he says brightly.

'Morning.'

'I know you,' he says.

She looks up. He leans against the kitchen counter and narrows his eyes at her.

It can't be.

'No way,' he says loudly.

It can't be. There are over eight million people in London. How is it *him*? The odds are impossible, they have to be.

'There's no way.' He smiles widely, the smile that got her the first time around. 'I can't believe it's you.' He drops his head forwards and laughs, then stops to look up and confirm it. 'This is messed-up. Emma's going to freak out.'

He can't be serious. He can't tell her.

The shower water runs loudly through the pipes, Emma will be downstairs any minute, ready to deliver her patter about quick showers and water efficiency.

He pulls back. 'What are the odds?'

Yvonne is aware of all she hasn't said, but right now, she

doesn't know where to start. 'Emma doesn't need to know we know each other. I mean, we don't really know each other, do we?'

He cocks his head to one side and smiles, 'Actually, we kind of *do* know each other.'

The water thumps off. The time ticks.

'Please, don't say anything,' she rubs her head.

'Calm down, Evelyn.'

'It's Yvonne.'

He puts his hands up in mock defence, 'Don't get like that. It was months ago. You probably don't remember my name either.'

But, of course she does. She remembers everything about him. How he smelled, how he danced, how he wrote down her number on the back of a travel card the next morning. How he never called. Emma can't know about any of this. 'Please, don't tell Emma.'

'I only just started seeing this girl and you're asking me to keep a secret from her?'

'Yes. Well, no. Not a secret, it's not worth mentioning, is it?'

He nods. 'Sure. I can keep a secret if you can?'

The bathroom door opens upstairs.

'I need to go.'

When Yvonne gets home later that evening she's greeted by the sound of the television coming from the living room. She puts her head around the corner but no one's in there. She walks towards Emma's room and pulls back the bed sheet from the doorway, 'Em?' The sheets are still ruffled and she wishes she'd never seen it.

'Hey,' Box Room Bethany shuffles past holding a plate of potato smiley faces, a fleece blanket thrown over her shoulders.

'Oh, you're in. Where's Emma?'

'I don't know where that little cow is,' Bethany says as she walks through to the living room. 'What was she playing at last night?'

Yvonne follows her and checks the time, it's late. This is a bad sign. A sign that Sweetboy's maybe not kept his mouth shut.

Bethany forks a piece of potato into her mouth. 'I don't want to hear all that moaning and shit. And to be honest, it sounded like she was faking it. Was it the guy she met in a chat room?'

Yvonne nods.

'So, basically, he's a complete random? Some stranger she met on the internet, home to the world's paedophiles and serial killers.'

'He's not a stranger. She was talking to him for weeks.' But really, it was Yvonne talking to him, typing all those witty, flirtatious lines while sharing a chair with Emma in the library.

'People aren't who they say they are on the internet. He could have been anyone. Can't believe she let him in our house. Oh,' Bethany suddenly shouts, jabbing her fork in the direction of the TV. 'I bloody hate this guy. He needs to get evicted.'

'How can you keep losing so many hours of your life to this?'

'I know. I know. It's trash.' She whoops as some of the TV contestants start dirty dancing with each other.

The front door opens, Emma's home. This is it. Yvonne

goes out into the hallway but Emma has already run upstairs to the loo. Yvonne waits for a minute, before returning to the living room, where Bethany explains in depth which contestant is her favourite, which one is a slag and so on.

Emma takes ages. Then finally, when she comes into the living room she sits in the armchair, rather than next to Yvonne, like she usually would.

He's told her. Shit.

'Well, look what the cat dragged in?' Bethany shouts.

But Emma's expression is far from the proud smirk she usually sports after subjecting everyone to one of her noisy sessions. 'I've had the worst evening.' She glances at the TV. 'Oh no, not this. Why is everyone watching this?'

'Because it's amazing,' Bethany says licking ketchup off her knife.

'Emma? You okay?'

'No. Not really. Just had a really intense session with my therapist.'

'Can this story wait till the ad break?' Bethany asks.

Yvonne sinks further into the sofa, ready for a long night. She had forgotten Emma had an appointment with *Sympathetic Sally* this afternoon.

'Anything you need to talk about?' Yvonne asks, because she always does and Emma is always happy to share what she worked through during her session, which most of the time is stuff about her parents. Yvonne thinks that if she went to therapy she would struggle to say anything of interest about her mum and dad other than that they were hard-working and big-hearted, but she knows she's lucky.

'I'm all talked out,' Emma says.

'Cup of tea then?' Yvonne asks.

'A cup of vodka? Yes, please.'

'I'll make you a tea.'

Emma lifts her head. 'I need a cigarette.'

Yvonne goes to the kitchen to make the tea, and clean up the huge mess Bethany managed to create while oven cooking a few potato products. The security light in the garden flicks on as Emma walks across the overgrown grass and sits in a cloud of moths and cigarette smoke. She definitely doesn't know about Sweetboy then, and there's no way Yvonne is going to tell her. He's just some guy after all. He doesn't matter. He didn't call Yvonne after sleeping with her and he probably won't call Emma either. It makes sense to forget about the whole thing.

Yvonne takes the tea out and sits next to the paddling pool bought last month during the heat wave. Both of them could just about fit in it, their knees bent, the water flowing over the side each time one of them moved.

Yvonne offers Emma the packet of chocolate digestives stolen from Box Room Bethany's cupboard.

'I'm really anxious about going back to Kenya this summer,' Emma says.

'Why?'

'Because my parents are going to drive me mad. My dad's already giving me a hard time about getting a job. He even suggested I do a Master's. As if it's a guarantee that I'm going to get my degree.'

They both laugh. A phone beeps from within the over-grown grass.

'Urgh, is that mine?' Emma says through a mouthful of biscuit. 'I think I dropped it somewhere.'

Yvonne finds the small square of light next to a pile of burnt-out disposable barbecues and hands it over, trying her best not to look at who the message is from. But it's clear from Emma's smile that it's him.

'Can you believe Sweetboy is trying to invite himself over again?' she says.

'He's coming over? Now?' Yvonne panics.

'Course not. I'll get cystitis if I have another night like last night. Such bad luck to meet someone right before I go away for the summer.'

'So, you like him then?'

'Yeah. He's so fit.'

'I know he's fit. You've said. Several times actually. But do you *like* him?'

Emma looks up and smiles. 'Yeah, I think I do. But I'm not sure how much he likes me. He sort of runs hot and cold. But this,' she holds up her phone, 'the fact he got what he wanted and is still messaging me is a good sign. Right?'

Yvonne attempts to formulate a response, a confession of sorts, but all she can do is nod.

The phone beeps again. 'Ah,' Emma says, 'he's being quite persistent.'

Then, despite herself, Yvonne says, 'Maybe it will cheer you up to go out tonight, take your mind off things.'

'He can wait,' Emma hops up. 'You fancy dinner at The Plough? It's two for one?'

'You're choosing me over Sweetboy?'

Emma pulls Yvonne to standing. 'Always. Are you okay? You seem distracted?'

Yvonne wants to stay in this moment and tell Emma the

truth, for them to have a laugh about the coincidence and their scarily similar taste in men. But it's embarrassing, so embarrassing that she slept with him after a few drinks, that he never called her and that this morning he struggled to remember her name. Besides, Emma's relationships always fizzle out to nothing. What would be the point in telling?

May comes quickly and despite everyone being busy securing jobs and internships for the summer, they all make an effort to meet at the final Pound-a-Pint Night in the student bar. Yvonne and Emma have attended it religiously ever since they met at one during Freshers' Week almost three years ago. It's hard to believe that this will be their last. That soon they will no longer be students. Yvonne looks at her group of friends and suddenly feels nostalgic for something she still has.

Emma jumps as her phone vibrates in her lap, she squints at the screen then her face breaks into a smile. She starts finger combing her hair roughly and wipes at the corners of her mouth in that self-conscious way she sometimes does. Sweetboy has been invited along tonight to meet Yvonne, for what Emma thinks will be the first time. Hopefully he will cancel. He's already cancelled several times before, and the one time he did show up Yvonne made sure she was on a train back to her parents' house in south London for a fabricated family birthday.

But now there's no getting out of it.

Of course, Yvonne should have come clean that night in The Plough as they sat drinking shitty house ale and reminiscing about all their past flings. She should have light-heartedly said, 'Here's a funny coincidence,' but she didn't. She kept silent each time Sweetboy was mentioned and prayed nothing would come of it.

Box Room Bethany is talking about the topic they can't seem to escape at the moment, their post-university lives. The group go round and round with it, bragging about the securing of internships and further education until Emma declares loudly, 'I'd rather fucking die than endure a Master's degree.' She's tipsy. They've all been down here since lectures finished three hours ago and it doesn't take much with her.

When Sweetboy arrives, it's almost like the crowd parts for him as he swaggers over to their table. A man has never looked more pleased with himself.

Emma bounces up from her seat to kiss him. 'Dude, where have you been?' He pulls off his jacket and gives Yvonne the briefest moment of eye contact.

'Everyone,' Emma says, 'this is Lewis.'

He slumps into the booth and slings his arm around Emma. His property. Yvonne hates that. Hates him.

Panjabi MC comes on over the speakers and everyone in the bar cheers, except Box Room Bethany who mouths, 'How many times?' and mimics hanging herself.

A tacky big-faced watch glints on Lewis's wrist; he looks like one of those ridiculous American rappers. It's exactly what Yvonne needs to see to prove her impression of him is right. 'Love this track,' he says while bopping his head.

'Finally,' Emma shouts as the barman puts down a paper boat of chips in the middle of the table. 'I ordered these fries ages ago. Shit, this is a big portion. Guys, help me out, save me the hassle of puking it all up later.'

Stools are pulled from other tables as more people join and

it quickly becomes one of those group conversations where bits and pieces get lost in sound, where you catch some of one topic, none of another. Lewis stifles a yawn and coils Emma's hair around his fingers till she turns to him.

'So, Lewis,' Box Room Bethany says. 'Are you studying?'

'No. Studying wasn't really my thing.' He explains how he could never have afforded it and didn't need it to set up his men's fashion label anyway. The label. Of course. Yvonne's heard some of this spiel before. 'Street fashion for the modern man', 'limited-run T-shirts with a message'. They'd been standing outside The Troika bar that night surrounded by ravenous drunks demolishing kebabs, and he had stunned her with his ambitions.

'I'm all about doing something for real, you know,' he says. 'I'm not one of those people who sit around talking about how to change things. I'm more about making it happen.' Everyone nods along even Box Room Bethany whose sole purpose in life *is* to sit around complaining about not being able to change things.

'T-shirts are hardly going to revolutionise the world,' Yvonne says.

'Yeah, well, no, course not. But it's a start. My label's like a stepping stone to other things I want to do. Music. Art. Marketing. I like to have my fingers in lots of different pies.' He holds her gaze steady, challenging her and she can't rise to it.

'Well,' Emma shouts, 'Yvonne and I are also going to change the world.'

Yvonne cringes, she doesn't want Emma telling him their plans, the things they discuss when it's the two of them, their bright-eyed ideas to save the world. She tries to get Emma's attention from across the table.

'Oh no, is this your Crayons for Kenyans company idea again?' scoffs Bethany. 'As if anything is ever going to offset your parents drilling oil from the ocean floor.'

'Whatever,' Emma laughs, but it's a sore point, the fact that despite her self-righteousness she can never win an argument on ethics because her parents work for an oil company.

Lewis smiles, 'So, tell me about this idea then?'

'Backpacks for Africa.' Emma drops her jaw as if to say, 'wow'. 'Yvonne and I have been trying to work it out ever since we met.'

He pulls himself up straight and smiles across at Yvonne. 'Really? Keep talking.'

'So,' Emma explains, 'remember how at the start of a new school year your mum would take you to Woolworths to buy you a pencil case and stationery, ready to start fresh? Remember how great it was? How it made you excited for school? Well, the kids where I grew up—'

'You mean the kids of your maids,' interrupts Bethany.

'Fuck you, Beth. Everyone has help in Kenya, okay? It provides jobs. It's nothing to be embarrassed about.'

'Everyone? Were you seriously that cocooned in your privileged little expat bubble to think that's true?'

'Look, my parents aren't rich. They're not these oil tycoons or whatever you think. My dad's a normal hardworking man, he just happens to work in—'

'A former British colony,' Bethany laughs.

Lewis steps in. 'Let's talk about something else. This is a bit heavy.'

Emma looks relieved. 'Yeah, you're right. Proper vibe killer. Back to fashion talk.' But since when did she care about fashion? Her wardrobe mostly consists of things she's borrowed from Yvonne and never returned and even the suggestion of going shopping causes her to start quoting passages from *No Logo*. It's as if, with him, Emma's a completely different person. There's nervousness in her voice, an exaggeration in her laugh and the way she keeps packaging up whatever he says and giving it back to the group with an excess of enthusiasm is pathetic. She must really like him. A lot.

His phone rings several times and cuts out. 'The reception is terrible down here.'

Yvonne wonders if her name and number ever made it into his phone. If he ever intended to call her.

He stands and makes his way out of the bar. She considers following him, but for what? Her stomach lurches at the thought of being alone with him, away from the eyes of everyone.

'So?' Emma slides in next to Yvonne and wriggles her eyebrows comically, like a children's TV presenter. 'What do you think?'

'That you need to stop drinking.'

'I'm talking about Sweetboy.'

'Yeah. He seems nice.'

'Nice? Is that all?'

'What do you want me to say? He's not what I expected.'

'How comes?' Emma's eyes fall down to the now crushed paper boat, smeared with grease, she pushes it back and forth with a finger. 'You knew he was black.'

'I didn't mean that. But, I am surprised by how all over him you are. Do you even know his last name?'

'Dude, I've only just found out his first name. We're taking things slowly. And I like having an older man, he's so focused too. Not like boys our age.'

They both look up at Lewis as he makes his way back through the crowd.

Emma pinches Yvonne's thigh under the table. 'He's fit, isn't he? Look at that body. He told me he goes to the gym five times a week.'

'Yeah and he probably wears his T-shirts a size too small on purpose.'

'And for that, we thank him.'

'You're drunk.'

'No, I'm not. I've only had two pints. Small ones,' Emma holds up a thumb and forefinger.

'A pint comes in one size.'

'Urgh, you're in such a mood at the moment.'

'No, I'm not.'

'Yes, you are. I'm trying to cheer you up. Maybe have a drink and loosen up a little.'

Yvonne sighs, careful not to invite Emma to probe her moodiness further. 'Fine, I'll get us a drink.'

The stickiness of spilt drinks pulls at Yvonne's thin rubber soles as she makes her way to the bar. 'Can I have a snakebite and black please,' she drops the hot pound coin from her pocket into the bartender's hand.

Lewis brushes against her arm. 'Are you buying me a drink?'

She glances at him. 'I've already ordered.'

He waves over the bartender. 'Can I get a Pepsi, please?' He pulls a note from a money clip. A money clip? He's ridiculous.

'Your girlfriend wants another pint.' It comes out childish, snarky.

'I think she's had enough.'

Yvonne is pushed nearer to Lewis as a few drunken girls jostle close by. She feels her face flush as she steps back, away from him.

The drinks are set down and the cold liquid runs down the side of the plastic pint glass.

'You look pissed off, Evelyn.'

This thing with her name, he's doing it on purpose. As if she doesn't already get it, that she was a mediocre shag, forgettable as a human being.

'Emma says you want to go into public relations when you graduate?'

'That's the idea behind studying communications. Why are you discussing me with Emma?' It makes her nervous, anxious, the thought that her name has passed between them.

'You guys are best friends, right? She talks about you a lot. She talks about *everything* a lot.'

Is there some scorn in his voice? Some hint of boredom?

'I'm really interested in advertising. Marketing. Branding.'

'Hmm, good for you.'

He laughs. 'It's competitive though. Emma knows she doesn't stand a chance of working in that kind of field. But then, she's going on about training to be a teacher. As if. The kids would eat her alive.'

'And you'd know, would you? Emma's quite tough actually.'

'Look, my mum's a secondary English teacher. It takes a lot more than liking books to be good at it. My mum had me reading Wordsworth in primary school. Can you believe that? I used to perform poetry at family barbecues.' There's a dimple on the right side of his cheek, it gives him a warmth she couldn't see before, almost boyish.

'Why are you telling me this? I'm not interested.' But she can see him, as a child, up on a stool in front of his whole family.

'*She was a phantom of delight, when first she gleamed upon my sight. A lovely apparition sent.* Why are you laughing?'

Her mouth needs to do something other than encourage him, so she takes several mouthfuls of her drink. 'I don't want to insult your mum so I can only assume you were a horrible student.'

He straightens up, 'I can't be good at everything, can I?'

'You're unbelievable.'

'You said it. What's that you're drinking?' he nods to her cup.

'Snakebite,' she answers shortly, wondering how much longer she needs to keep up the farce of talking to him before she can go back to the table, back home even.

'What? You're drinking something called snakebite? Can I try it? It's always good to be reminded of why I don't drink beer.' He takes the cup from her hand and slowly raises it to his lips, watching her sceptically as he has a sip. His face snaps into a wince.

'Not to your taste?'

'No,' he chases it with his drink, 'that's foul.'

'How much longer do I need to pretend I'm enjoying talking to you?'

'That all depends, doesn't it?'

'On what?'

He sidles closer, his arm hot against hers. 'How much longer will it take me to get back into your good books?'

CHAPTER THREE

JUMP? HOW HIGH?

September 2020

Yvonne

The phone on her desk rings and Yvonne stares through the glass of her office at her new intern, a tall dumb girl with an unpronounceable name. Yvonne thought her instructions this morning were quite clear, that she didn't want to be disturbed unless it was really important. But maybe it's her mum. Again. Since she retired every little thing has become something important enough to disturb Yvonne's work for. Or maybe it's her brother Claude, maybe his divorce has finally come through, she told him to call her straight away.

She tuts and picks up, 'Yvonne Olsson.'

There's a pause at the other end and then he speaks. The sound of his voice throws her back two decades, to being that twenty-one-year-old girl blinded by hormones.

'Lewis? How did you get my number?'

'I looked in Kiama's phone.'

'I can't believe they put you through.'

'I just told them I was one of your brothers.'

'What do you want?'

'So, it's like that? No small talk?'

'I haven't heard from you in a decade.' Her voice shakes as she slips her feet into the unlaced running shoes under her desk.

'Time flies, eh?' He sighs and she imagines the feel of his breath on her neck. The warmth of it.

'Why are you calling me?' But ever since her meeting with Kiama she has thought of nothing other than this inevitable conversation with Lewis, his slow approach as he rises back into her life.

'You know why. But I want to talk face to face. You're still based in London, right? I could get the train in—'

'No. You can't do that. What do you want?'

'To talk about Kiama. I know you met up. What did you speak about?'

'What do you *think* we spoke about?'

'What did he say? Did he ask you questions?'

She laughs, 'I don't need to report back to you.'

'This is serious. You can't start going down memory lane with him, there's lots of stuff he doesn't know.'

Stuff, Lewis makes it sound so casual, so throwaway. Maybe it was, to him.

'Is there something in particular you're worried about?' The insoles of her trainers feel damp from this morning's run to work in the rain, but she accepts the discomfort, a distraction, as she waits for his answer.

'Did he tell you my mum recently passed away?'

'Yes, and I'm sorry, Lewis.' She feels herself soften. 'I really am sorry.'

'They were close. Since she passed, he's been a bit of a mess.

Doesn't know what he wants. He's all over the place. Job to job. Girl to girl.'

She laughs bitterly, 'That sounds familiar.'

'No, he's nothing like me. When I was young and being wild it was just that, being young and wild. But Kiama, he's different.'

'He's only eighteen. You were still *wild* at thirty.'

'And I could afford to be. He can't. Not with everything he's been through. He's not that sort of kid.'

'He seems fine.'

'You don't know him.'

It hurts because it's true, she doesn't know Kiama. She's not the one who has been there for him through these years; she's not had the privilege of watching him grow up.

'Why did he want to see you again?'

'I don't know.' And it's half true; she's still confused about why he thought to call her after all this time.

'You must know. He won't tell me. But he must have said something to you.'

She's getting stressed, losing her strength. 'I think he was curious, about me, wanted to see my face after all these years. And he wanted someone to talk to about Kenya. I think he's getting nervous about going by himself. But—' Lewis takes a breath on the other end of the line and the silence which falls after is heavy. 'You didn't know,' she says, 'did you?'

'Please tell me he's not thinking of going back there?'

'He's talking about it. He sounds serious. He's got a plan. He wants to see his grandparents and Purity—'

'His grandparents? You know how hard I've tried to protect him from those two over the years?'

'I can imagine, but maybe they'll be different now. Maybe

now he's older they can build a relationship. It'll be good for him.'

'You don't know what's good for him. They have no interest in Kiama whatsoever. He can't go there. I won't let him.'

'Whatever happened to not wrapping him in cotton wool?'

That was how Kiama's nana put it the last time Yvonne spoke to her. She had said that even though she was terrified each time Kiama left her sight, she knew she had to let go so he wouldn't be scared of the world, she wanted him to have as much freedom as any other child.

'I've never told him what he can and can't do,' Lewis says. 'But that's part of the problem with Kiama. He wants to drop out of college after three months? I let him. He wants to piss about in Barcelona all summer? I let him. He wants to do some nonsense courier job? I let him. For the last ten years I've let him do whatever the hell he wants. But I won't let him do this. And why is he talking to you? I'm his dad. I'm the one who has been there for him.'

'Because I was there, Lewis, in Kenya.'

They both fall silent.

'Please,' he says.

She presses the phone against her ear with a shoulder, filling her head with the sound of his voice. 'Yvie, I'm begging you.'

Why does she still shiver when he says her name? Why does he still have such power over her?

'Talk him out of this.'

'Lewis, you shouldn't have called me.'

'Let's talk face to face. Let me take you out for a drink or something and we can—'

'No. I don't want to see you.'

But she's curious. What does he look like now? How would it feel to see him again?

'He's my only child. You can't imagine how hard it's been. How much I worry about him.'

But what about her? Who was there to worry about Yvonne? Her entire world crumbled and she was required to get on with it like nothing happened and then, a decade later, be happy to drag it all back up again.

'I need to go.' She puts the phone down and lays her head on the desk. The residual heat of his voice tickles her ear. She should have hung up straight away. She should never have listened to him.

'Ms Olsson?' The intern never knocks. 'Are you okay?'

Yvonne flicks her head up. 'Yes, fine. I have a headache.'

'You need a paracetamol?' A look of genuine concern etches its way across her young face.

'No. No, thank you.' Yvonne turns to the window, to the dull blanket of drizzle.

'I'm sorry about the call. Your brother said it was important, so I wasn't sure,' the girl rambles. 'Did I do something wrong?'

Yvonne needs to get out. She grabs her bag from the floor, jacket from the back of the seat and brushes past the girl without another word. On the street outside she is grateful for the chill, for the way it clears the build-up of tension in her forehead. She walks away from the office towards a little park tucked between groups of council blocks.

Yvonne finds a damp bench, partly sheltered by a tree, opens her bag and takes out her phone. After their meeting ended so abruptly last week she never expected to hear from Kiama again, but then last night there was one message after another. Each one detailing some vague plan for the ten days he will spend in Kenya, from visiting his grandparents in Nairobi, to eating at a particular beach bar in Mombasa. He also wants to spend time with Purity, the woman who cared for him so closely during the six months he spent there.

When he first mentioned Kenya at the coffee shop Yvonne never even thought to ask him where Lewis stood on all this. It never crossed her mind that he would have been kept in the dark about the trip. Why wouldn't Kiama have told him?

But Kiama's reasons for going back to Kenya are so unclear. It has to be about more than filling in the gaps from his memory and meeting up with his grandparents. When Yvonne questioned him he briefly mentioned a book he'd read about someone who got over a childhood trauma by returning to its source as an adult. But he seemed embarrassed by this and shrugged it off when Yvonne probed him. It was only later that evening she realised he was talking about one of Lord Mountbatten's grandsons who survived a terror attack. But it wasn't the same thing, not at all.

She rereads his last message, the one confirming that he would book his flights this weekend. The flight numbers included in the hope that she would change her mind and join him. How can he expect her to do this? To drop her life and follow him to Kenya? To relive all those memories?

Her hands shake. She's not strong enough to revisit the past.

But maybe she doesn't have a choice.

*

A week after the phone call with Lewis, Yvonne walks down the high street of betting shops, tacky boutiques and vape-bars towards The X-Treme Jump trampoline park. It's flanked by empty lots on both sides, so stands alone and proud. She turns her nose up at the Day-Glo orange awning, the steps which alternate green and orange, the tarpaulin branding cable tied to the fences still shouting about a Late Night Valentine's Special, months after the fourteenth of February.

Inside the trampoline park, two girls in bright orange polo shirts stand behind the counter scrolling through their phones.

'Good morning,' Yvonne says and both of their flawless blank faces turn to her.

'Morning.' The girl's spider eyelashes flutter as if too heavy for her lids. 'Are you booking?'

'Oh no. I'm here to see Kiama.'

'Did Kiama say a woman's coming to see him?' the girl asks her friend, who is busy balling orange grip socks and stacking them into the shelves behind the counter. 'Yeah, he's in the café.'

'He's in the café,' the first girl repeats. 'I'll take you through. Hope you're not from Health and Safety.'

'Why? Would that be a problem?'

The girl stops, spins around, her long plait swinging with her. 'No, I was kidding. We do all the proper checks here and that.'

Yvonne follows her into a huge dark hall with a carpet of various sized trampolines. They head upstairs to a dim mezzanine café. Hip-hop thumps through the speakers and spotlights dance around the near empty arena.

'He's over there,' the girl says. Yvonne makes her way

across, again going through what she wants to say before she reaches him. This is it, her chance to talk to him properly.

'Kiama?' she says.

'Hey. You found it alright?'

'Yeah, I got a cab.' She slides in the booth opposite him. 'So, this is your work,' she says, 'it's very loud.'

'Yeah, bit much on a Sunday morning, isn't it? I'll get them to turn the music down.'

'No,' she shakes her head. 'It's fine, really.'

He rubs the side of his face where a small amount of stubble has grown since she last saw him. 'Guess this isn't the sort of place you usually hang out?'

'You'd be surprised actually, how many weekends I've lost to places like this.'

'Oh, you have kids?' he asks cautiously.

'No. But my brothers have seven kids between them.'

'Right,' he says.

His ever-present phone sits blinking on the table between them, along with his laptop.

'Busy?' she asks.

'Looking into a few things,' he says business-like. Lewis had said something on the phone about Kiama quitting college, but she can't remember what for.

Another polo-shirt-wearing girl comes over, the X-Treme Jump logo stretched across her boobs. 'Kiama, did you want to try one of those new vegan burgers?'

He considers it. 'Yvonne, are you hungry?'

'No. A coffee would be great though.'

'I'm going to be honest with you, the coffee here is a little sketchy. I'll have a slushie, please.'

The girl laughs and puts a hand on his shoulder. 'One coffee and one slushie. You want me to mix the flavours for you?' She wriggles her hips as she says this.

'You know how I like it, Tina.'

'Trina,' she corrects before walking off.

They both watch her go and Yvonne struggles to think of what to talk about next. 'It's cold in here,' she notes. 'Are you trying to save on a bill?'

'Always. Plus, it keeps the kids from overheating, lets them jump for longer. More jumping, more money,' he laughs.

'Sounds like you've got it all worked out.'

'Hardly, this place is a money pit. I don't know how much longer we'll be able to keep it open.' He speaks like he owns it.

'How long have you worked here?' Yvonne asks, keen to find out his link to the place. Maybe he's more driven than Lewis made out.

'Too long.'

Trina returns, staring at Kiama, who doesn't have the sense to flatter her with anything more than a nod as she puts down his drink.

He notices Yvonne looking. 'You think you won't like it because it's a kids' drink.'

'And because it's bright blue and purple.'

'I don't even know what we put in here, but it's so good.' He takes a sip then slaps his hand against his forehead and squints. He looks goofy, like eight-year-old Kiama.

They drink and Yvonne finds herself tuning into the music, there's a line about asking girls in the club to 'rub their titties'.

Kiama laughs, 'This is obviously not my playlist.'

'I would hope not.'

'Dad plays this crap seven days a week at home. He doesn't listen to anything made past 1996.'

Of course, it was always the type of music Lewis liked. He tried tirelessly to get her into hip-hop, but she only ever pretended to like it.

'Lewis owns this place?'

He looks surprised by her question. 'Yeah, doesn't he bombard you with voucher codes for it online?'

'I'm not online.'

'Oh yeah, I forgot. Apart from that one page on your work's website, you're a ghost. How can you keep up with what's going on?'

'I don't need to know everyone's business. Is he here?'

'Who Dad? Nah, he's never here on a Sunday.'

'Does he know *I'm* here?'

Kiama shakes his head. 'He knows I've found you. Spoken to you. He's been a bit off about the whole thing. Made me not want to bring it up with him again.'

She shifts in her seat.

'When was the last time you saw him? Years, right?' Kiama suggests.

What were Lewis's reasons for keeping their call a secret? She doesn't want to start lying to Kiama, but also knows better than to get in the middle of their relationship.

'Yes,' she says trying to rub some warmth back into her fingers. 'Years.'

Kiama looks down at his drink and squeezes the straw to dislodge a build-up of ice. It's so hard to know how to treat him, how to talk to him. He's not a kid anymore, but there's something about him that makes her feel like she has to hold back, to treat him with kid gloves. 'I brought something to show you.'

His big eyes flick up to hers and she breaks away, going in to her bag to get the envelope. She holds it against her chest and the contents suddenly feel too precious to share. 'I don't know how many photos you have of her, of your mum.'

Yvonne lays the envelope on the table and he places a hand on it and pulls it towards himself. But he doesn't look at them straight away, instead stares at Yvonne, as if for permission. She nods and he pulls the photos out. His face softens as he studies each one. 'Wow. I've never seen these. My grand-parents hardly have any photos of her. Except a few from birthdays and Christmas.'

Yvonne is surprised they even had that, yet she feels com-pelled to defend Emma's unsentimental parents. 'It was differ-ent back then. People only took photos on special occasions. Now, everyone seems to take them constantly. Though your mum was a fan of those disposable cameras you used to get. She was always snapping away when we were out drinking.'

While she rambles on, he carefully lays each photo on the table in a line. He taps the one of Emma hugging a large Kenyan woman in a garden. 'She looks so pretty here.'

Yvonne bites the inside of her cheek and looks away. 'Yeah. She does.'

He tips his head to the side, 'Where is this place? With these kids?'

'I don't know.' Yvonne lifts one and stares at it, as if seeing it for the first time. Emma stands in front of a rural Kenyan house, surrounded by about ten children. The same round woman is there too, this time holding a baby. 'I think, but

I'm not sure, it's a school. She helped out at one once when she went back for the summer.'

'Are these your only copies?'

She nods and his face falls. She should have thought about this before. 'But you can have them.'

'You sure?' he asks, already pulling them close, 'I appreciate that.'

She looks away, doesn't want to cry. 'I kept some of your mum's things. They're in my attic. Photos of us on nights out, wearing too much make-up and bad fancy dress. Also, her collection of botanical postcards, her books, they're mostly on ethics, feminism and that sort of stuff. Silly I kept them but she's annotated almost every page in some. I've had all this stuff for a long time. You should have it now. If you want it, of course.' She treads carefully. 'I never got round to giving any of it to your dad.'

He pulls a few papery napkins from the silver dispenser at the end of the table, hands them to her and looks away as she wipes her eyes. 'This is exactly what I thought of when I contacted you.'

'What? That I'd be this blubbering wreck.' The tears are so unexpected. The last time she cried was almost a year ago, when her dad was cured of prostate cancer. It was from relief more than anything. 'I'm sorry,' she says, embarrassed.

'For what?' He holds the photos inches from his face and smiles again. 'This is amazing. That already you're showing me photos of Mum I've never seen before. Telling me stuff I've never heard. Like, I didn't know she collected botanical postcards or that she was really into ethics.'

'She wasn't,' Yvonne says. 'She fancied the lecturer.'

Kiama laughs. 'Now it's getting good.'

'I shouldn't have said that.'

'No one ever tells me anything of interest about her. I like that she had an inappropriate crush on a teacher.'

The music stalls as an announcement calls time on the session. Yvonne fully dries her eyes and tucks the napkins into her bag.

'I still don't understand it,' she says. 'Why go back there? It sounds like such a bad idea.'

'I have to,' he says.

'But what's behind you wanting to go? Has someone recommended it to you? A therapist or something?'

Kiama pulls back. 'I don't have a therapist, Yvonne. This is from me. It's what I want. And honestly, I don't fully know why, I just know I have to. That it's what I need to do.'

Another song starts, which Yvonne recognises as Dr Dre. It makes Yvonne think of the crap house party she and Emma went to one Christmas break, it took three buses to get there and when they finally arrived everyone was already drunk. They danced with Two Minute Terry then Emma cut off the music to lecture everyone on how wrong it was to use the N word, even in the context of a rap song. These are stories Kiama would love to hear and only Yvonne can give them to him. Yvonne is his closest link to his dead mother.

She tears at the damp napkins under the table and for once allows her mind to block out all logic. 'Kiama?'

When he looks up at her this time she doesn't see a reflection of Lewis or Emma, but the vulnerable eight-year-old boy she left when he needed her the most. 'I've decided to come with you.'

CHAPTER FOUR

PUMPKINS

September 2020

Kiama

'So who was that lady earlier?' Tina asks Kiama as he unlocks his bike from the railings. Or is her name Trina? He can never remember and feels bad asking now, especially after what happened on the last staff night out.

'Family friend?' he answers, noticing his voice lift at the end, as if he's asking her a question.

She puffs out smoke and laughs. 'You don't sound too sure.'

That's because he's not. What is Yvonne's link to him really? She's not just some friend of Mum's, it's more complicated than that. He takes his phone and EarPods from his pocket then sees a message from Dad.

Special K, you eating here this evening?

Then.

I'm making lasagne, says serves 6 on the jar.

Kiama sends back the thumbs up emoji and waves bye to Tina/Trina. By the time he wheels his bike round the front there's another four messages from Dad.

You need anything from the shops?

Doritos

Quinoa?

Opioids?

Kiama laughs and messages back, Should go without saying. He cycles off towards Nana's house, taking the long way across the rec grounds, allowing a bit more time to clear his head and think about what he's going to say, how he's going to phrase it.

It's only ten days he's going for. It's nothing in the grand scheme of things. After Nana died he went off travelling for three months and Dad was cool with it, encouraging even. Though he knows deep down that it's not so much the length of the trip, it's the destination that's going to cause the kick-off.

Kiama jumps off the bike as he nears the drive and wheels it down the side alley, finding Dad in the garden.

'Old Man?' he calls, 'Why aren't you in the kitchen already?'

Dad looks up, his face etched with stress as he pulls at a tangle of stubborn plants. 'I'm sick of these pumpkins,' he says. 'The vines are swallowing up everything.'

'But they're not big enough yet.' Like barbecues and water fights, Nana's pumpkin patch was a staple of Kiama's childhood. 'You've got to leave them till Halloween.'

A splattering of damp compost flicks up Dad's shirt as a vine snaps. 'Aren't you a bit old for pumpkin carving?'

Kiama huffs, insulted, 'No.'

Dad throws a little green pumpkin, but it slips from Kiama's fingers before he can get any grip on it. 'Why are you chucking stuff at me? You've got muck on my sweatshirt. This is *Supreme*.'

'I'm three feet away from you. How'd you miss that?'

'Because it was wet. It's cold, I'm going inside.'

Dad laughs, 'Make yourself useful first. Get the shears and cut away some of these vines for me.'

Kiama stands above the toolbox and looks over the array of tools.

'The giant scissors,' Dad calls.

'Yeah, I knew that.' Kiama says as he holds them out.

'Cut some of that frizzy hair off while you're at it.'

'I'm definitely going inside now.'

'Oh man up.'

'No one says *man up* anymore.'

It's clear Dad wants to make another smart comment but settles instead for a roll of his eyes. Kiama kneels next to him and they tidy up the patch of garden in silence, cutting the thick vines away until they can see the bare compost again.

'How was work today?' Dad asks.

'Good.'

'Good?'

'Quiet. For a Sunday.'

'I really need it to pick up soon.' He chucks a handful of greenery onto the leaf pile.

Kiama puts the shears down. It's always fun to make digs about Dad aging but this year is the first time Kiama can actually see it, the greying beard, the slowing reflexes, the damn Crocs.

'I need to start earning again.'

'Dad, you don't need to worry about money.'

'I'm not worrying. I'm thinking ahead.'

'But we've got money,' Kiama says.

'No. *You've* got money. There's a difference. I need to make some plans. I can't stay in this house forever either.'

Why does he keep bringing this up? They've both lived in Nana's house ever since Kiama was a kid, but it's become this huge issue since she passed away. No one in the family wants to sell the place, but it no longer feels right that the two of them are living here inhabiting it like it's their own, without her.

Dad sits back on his heels. 'Why'd she plant so many pumpkins?'

It keeps hitting him like this, completely out of the blue. He's fine for weeks then gets mad upset about the fact that the upstairs bathroom hasn't been redecorated in years or that there's too many tins of ackee in the larder, which neither of them will ever eat.

'I don't know, Dad.' They gaze towards the end of the garden and watch as a train passes beyond the fence. 'It's cold out here. Let's go inside.'

Dad stops at the back door to kick off his Crocs and slap his muddy gloves against the wall. 'Sorry, I didn't go to the shops yet. I got distracted.'

Kiama removes the envelope from his pocket before propping himself up on one of the breakfast bar stools, 'No problem. I know you got lots on your mind.' Dad washes his hands at the sink and with him turned away it seems like the right time to say it. 'So, I saw Yvonne again today.'

Dad's back straightens, then he carries on, moving about the kitchen, silently peeling and chopping onions until Kiama can't handle it anymore. 'I know you're not happy about this.'

'Nothing good ever came from digging up the past.'

'But she's the one person who knew Mum.'

'Plenty people knew your mum.'

'Not like Yvonne.'

Yvonne, who was in all of his birthday photos, who often spent Boxing Day with him and Mum at their flat in Stratford, Yvonne who was always there, offering to babysit and take him on the types of day trips Mum couldn't afford or be bothered with, Yvonne who was always there, until one day when she wasn't.

Dad finally looks over and his eyes drop to the envelope. 'She gave you a letter?'

'No. They're photos.' Kiama takes a breath knowing this is the moment, his opportunity to lay it all out. 'I'm going to Kenya.'

Dad's face betrays nothing. When it comes to hiding emotions, he's the absolute master. At least when Nana was around it was clear when Kiama had put a foot wrong as he'd hear about it loud and clear, but with Dad it's always dealt with like this, a few vague comments and then complete shutdown.

'I want to go for ten days, it's long, but then I can spend a few days at the end in Mombasa. Mum took me there once. There's a beach bar that does the best masala chips.'

Dad says nothing.

'And I can see my grandparents again.'

'You don't even talk to them on the phone. Why would you go all that way to spend time with them?'

'Because,' Kiama stalls, remembering the phone calls, how cold and stilted they always were, how he used to dread that routine check in with them, 'because, I want to. I want to see them again. On the phone is always awkward, but if I got to spend real time with them, it would be different. And Purity, she must be getting on, I'd love to see her.'

'Who's that? Your mum's old nanny?'

It's annoying, the way he's being so dismissive. 'She was a bit more than that. She practically brought Mum up. Looked after me when I was out there too.'

'Yeah, cause your grandparents didn't. I'm not sure about you spending time with them. Have you told them your plans yet?'

'Not yet. But I'm going to email them.'

The little bottles in the spice cupboard rattle as Dad rearranges them. So that's it then. That's all he's going to say?

'Yvonne's coming with me.' It makes it real, saying it out loud. 'Dad? Please say something.'

The cupboard door slams as he takes out the frying pan. 'Why?'

'Because I need to know how you feel about this. But you're not saying anything.'

'Why have you asked her to do that with you? You don't

know her. You haven't seen her since you were eight and now you're meeting up with her, going off to Kenya together. What next?'

'I'm not trying to exclude you. But Yvonne was there. She understands.'

'I'm worried about you. This has been a hard year, what with your nana passing and you turning eighteen.'

'And that's why I need to do this. I'm an adult now.'

'You're also still my son.'

'I really need to do this. I think it'll help. It'll help me see past—'

'See past what?'

'This block I have. When I worry. When I can't see past things.'

Dad steps forward and puts his hands on Kiama's shoulders. 'We can arrange some counselling for you. It's normal. Especially with Nana, I knew it was going to trigger something.'

'You're not listening to me.'

'No, I'm not, because this Kenya plan is crazy.'

His hands feel heavy and the oil in the pan starts to burn. *Crazy.* Is that really what's going on here? Is he unravelling? Kiama stands up. 'Maybe you're right. Maybe I'm getting carried away with things.'

Dad nods, but there's nothing behind it, like he scored a victory he doesn't even want.

'I'm going upstairs for a bit, okay?'

'Okay, son.'

*

He wakes up a few hours later, fully dressed and lying on his bed. From downstairs he can hear music, Dad's playing Wu-Tang, again.

'Alexa,' Kiama shouts as he enters the kitchen, 'play something made in the last decade.'

Dad jumps and turns around, 'Boy, don't address my woman. Alexa, play *Enter the Wu-tang (36 Chambers)*.'

Kiama yawns. 'How many times do we need to hear this?'

A huge lasagne sits covered in foil on top of the hob. 'Did you eat already?' Kiama asks.

'No. I was waiting on your lazy arse.'

'I'll get the plates.' As he does he notices the envelope has been moved to one side. Maybe it was moved while Dad was cleaning the kitchen.

'Do you want to eat in the—' Dad nods towards the dining table, to where they used to eat every dinner, but Kiama can't remember the last time they sat there. It feels too weird without Nana. Her chair, at the head of the table, still has the little purple cushion on it, the one she kept for her back.

'Here's fine,' he says.

'Good.' Dad looks relieved.

'This smells amazing. All I've had all day was a vegan burger at the jump park. It was rank. Whose idea was that?'

'Yours,' Dad laughs while piling food onto the plates.

They sit side by side and start, but the atmosphere is heavy. They can't go on acting like nothing was said earlier, like nothing's changed.

Dad shifts forward on the stool and nods towards the envelope. 'I can't believe how young Emma looks in those photos.'

'You looked at them?'

He nods and pushes the food around on his plate. 'I can see a bit of you in her face. Weird. It's not something I ever saw before.' He puts his fork down. 'You should get reprints. Your grandparents might like copies.'

Is this it? Dad's way of giving his blessing to the trip? 'What are you saying?'

Dad gets up and goes to the fridge, but shuts it and returns empty-handed. 'You know, the last time you went out there you almost didn't come back.'

Kiama tips his head back and huffs. 'This isn't what I need to hear.'

'Of course not, but for me, it's all I think about, that I could lose you.'

And as much as Kiama knows he's got to do this trip for his own peace of mind, he suddenly feels the pain of what he's putting Dad through.

'But I understand what you're trying to do. Why you need to go.' Dad raises his hand and rubs Kiama's shoulder. 'I understand.'

CHAPTER FIVE

TRUST

June 2001

Yvonne

Yvonne shuffles in her seat as they make the bus journey from one dreary side of Harrow to the other. 'I can't believe I let you talk me into this.'

Emma checks her reflection in the window and swipes the lip gloss wand across her mouth. 'Dude, what is wrong?'

'Nothing.'

'So, why are you so down? I know it's not your time of the month.' Emma throws the gloss into Yvonne's open bag.

'I'm not down.'

'You are. Talk to me.'

'It's nothing. I'd just rather not spend my Saturday third-wheeling with you and Lewis.'

'It's a barbecue, there'll be loads of people there. We'll have fun, okay.' Emma puts her feet on the seat opposite, carelessly kicking the box of cupcakes she brought along. Her toenails are neatly painted in the dark shade of purple they share. 'It's the next stop by the way.' Emma pulls a tissue from a pocket and wipes the lip gloss off. 'This is way too shiny. Proper blow job lips.'

Yvonne reaches for the tissue and wipes at her own mouth.

The sky looks overcast as they step off the bus, but it's humid and sticky. Yvonne prays for rain to fall in the next five minutes, a huge storm and an excuse to return home or back into the town centre. She would much rather waste the day browsing clothes she can't afford and eating a baked potato in the depressing food court than this.

'Fuck knows where it is from here,' Emma says. 'Let me check the address he sent.'

'Your sense of direction is terrible. I don't want to be wandering around the suburbs for hours,' Yvonne complains.

'He said it's like a five-minute walk. Here,' she points her little ski-jump nose in the air and sniffs, 'just follow the smell of burning animal flesh.'

Emma near enough skips the whole way, the box of cakes bouncing against her legs. They turn off onto a tree-lined street of semi-detached houses, each one covered with pebble dash and accessorised with a Volvo Estate or campervan.

'Do I look like a Plain Jane?' Emma asks.

'You look great.'

'Urgh, give me that gloss again?' She wipes it over her lips before hitting the doorbell and turning to Yvonne. '20p to whoever spots the first other white person.'

And for the first time that day, Yvonne laughs but before she has a chance to turn back and scold Emma, the door flies open.

'Whoa, you actually came,' Lewis says. 'Hey,' he looks at Yvonne awkwardly.

'Dude, we're still in that student mindset, we're hardly going to pass up free food.' Emma stands on her tiptoes to kiss him.

'Course. Come in.'

Yvonne wants to run, but instead she stands there as Lewis wraps his arms around Emma. He pulls away and slaps her arse as she walks into the hallway, 'Go through. Get a drink.' Momentarily he fills the doorway and blocks Yvonne's entry. By coming here she's agreed to whatever it is he's trying to do. It's too late to change her mind now.

'Good to see you again,' he says.

She follows him through the hallway, the walls on each side are covered with family photos of Lewis and his brothers, each one a little older and wider than him.

'Look, Mum, I told you white people would start arriving soon,' he calls into the kitchen.

His mum looks up from behind the fridge and shouts, 'Behave yourself.' She lifts out a tray of meat skewers and searches for somewhere to put them but every surface is packed with marinating meat, burger buns, drinks and bowls of salad. Lewis takes the tray and shoves it on top of the microwave. 'Mum, this is Emma and Yvie,' he says, without effort to differentiate which one is which.

'Yvonne,' she corrects.

'Hi, nice to meet you. I'm Julie.' The woman stretches out her hand to them both.

'I baked,' Emma says as her eyes cast over the three plates of luridly coloured cupcakes on the table. 'Sorry, they got a bit squashed on the journey over.'

Julie cradles one of the shabby cakes in her hand. 'Look

at that. How kind.' She peels off the paper wrap with slender fingers, 'Mmm, so much nicer than that additive-filled crap the boys bought from Costco. Always better to make it yourself at home, then you know what's in it.'

'Exactly,' Emma says. Though her cakes came from a Nisa box mixture she panic-bought in the off licence last night.

'Lewis, get these ladies a drink,' Julie says as she adjusts her head wrap.

'Course. Though, I'm not sure we have anything to suit Yvonne's exotic tastes.' He nudges her arm and while the touch is teasing, almost childish, it's still a touch. She shouldn't have come.

There's RnB playing, something old and smooth with a woman faking an orgasm in the background. Emma laughs and Julie looks up, embarrassed. 'Lewis? Switch off this nasty baby-making music.'

'Yes, Mum.'

Yvonne wishes she didn't like him so much.

They are directed outside into the sprawling, messy garden, filled with children wiping down plastic furniture with dish-cloths and an old man too immersed in painting planks of wood to acknowledge anyone. They sit, drinking wine and watching as the sky darkens over the barbecue.

'Emma, what time did he tell you to get here?' Yvonne asks.

'I'm sure he said three.' There's noise from inside the kitchen, laughing and talking. 'See, other people are starting to arrive now.'

Two men with paunches and unfashionable dad clothes

come outside. They say hi then struggle to put up a cheap-looking plastic marquee over the barbecue. More people filter into the garden, yet Lewis never comes over or introduces Emma to anyone.

Julie struts about kissing people, absorbing compliments on how good the spread looks and the crack of her laughter can be heard over the music. It's obvious where Lewis gets it from, this easy charm.

At one point, Lewis's brother, Danny, the one who was with Lewis at the club that night they met, catches Yvonne's eye and frowns, as if trying to place her. Eventually he must realise, as he covers his mouth and laughs.

'Yvonne?' Emma pokes her in the side to get her attention. 'I'm talking to you and you're—'

'What?'

Emma wide-eyes her, 'You're on another planet today. Are you listening to me at all?'

'Sorry, it's this weather. This humidity gives me a head-ache.'

'So, drink something other than wine,' she pulls the cup from Yvonne's hand. Emma looks across at Lewis, as he chats with his friends. 'He's hardly even spoken to me.'

Of course he hasn't. It's too awkward with Yvonne there. What was she thinking coming along?

'I thought he was going to introduce me as his girlfriend.'

'Really?' Even she can hear the mild panic in her voice.

The corners of Emma's lips are going purple from the wine. 'No. I guess not girlfriend exactly, but you know, at least a special friend.'

Yvonne laughs. '*Special friend?*'

Emma sticks her tongue out to one side and slaps one hand with the other.

'Stop it. That's not funny.'

Emma looks over again at Lewis. 'I feel like he's ignoring me, like he's changed his mind.'

'About what?'

'About me,' Emma snaps, 'about liking me.'

'Why do you care so much?'

'Because,' Emma starts then stops to finish the contents of her cup. 'Forget about it.'

Why is she acting like this? Yvonne's never known a guy to hold Emma's attention for so long. And she's definitely never wanted to be anyone's 'girlfriend', not in the three years they've been friends.

Yvonne shifts in the plastic chair, it's humid and her skirt sticks to her thighs. 'You really like him, don't you?'

Just then Lewis turns in their direction and begins to walk over. Emma smiles as he kneels down in front of her. 'And how are the students doing over here?'

'Good. Except I'm worried about having to eat a bowl of coleslaw for dinner,' Emma says as she flicks her hair over a shoulder.

He smiles and rubs his hands along Emma's thighs. 'It's a strong possibility. We're not used to having to feed your kind.'

'Lewis, you're joking, right? Your brothers literally sprinkled bacon on every salad over there.'

He pulls her to standing, 'Course I am. My mum's put some stuffed peppers in the oven. You can eat that, can't you? My dad grows them himself up at the allotment. So they're organic too. I know you posh girls like that.'

'Actually, there's something I don't really trust about food grown in people's gardens,' Emma says. 'With the grocery store you like know it's gone through all the proper checks and stuff.'

'Surely you were growing food when you lived in Africa?'

'Actually, we just went to the supermarket like everyone else.' She turns to Yvonne and rolls her eyes playfully.

'And what about you, Snakebite? Did you also grow up in colonial splendour?'

'No. South London.' She finishes her drink and wonders how to get away from him.

Emma nudges her, 'Your dad has an allotment too, right?' she says, keen to bring Yvonne into the conversation.

'Yeah.'

'You know how to garden?' Lewis asks.

'Not really. I have three brothers, so it was more their thing.'

'I've got three brothers as well,' Lewis says.

Emma sighs, 'You guys with your unusually large families.' She wipes the corners of her mouth. 'So, Sweetboy, aren't you going to congratulate us?'

'On what?'

Emma puts her hand in the middle of his chest and pushes him gently, 'On finishing university.'

'Oh, it's done, is it? You've given back your library books and everything?'

They nod.

'So what now?' he asks Emma.

'I told you, I'm going back to Kenya to see my parents for a bit.'

'Yeah, but after your holiday? When reality sets in? And your parents want to see some pay-off for all that private education.'

Emma shrugs. 'I don't know.'

'What happened to your idea to teach? You were all over that idea a week ago. If you're serious you could ask my mum about it today.'

'Oh, teaching was just a passing thought,' she says. 'Plus, I've been studying forever, I need a break.'

He shakes his head. 'What about that volunteering thing you were going on about? Some women's refuge or something?'

'Oh yeah, that, but they make you commit to like four weeks in a row and I didn't want to start then go away for the summer and let anyone down.'

Lewis raises his eyebrows at her, boredom creeping across his face. 'There really is nothing you want to do?'

'Why do you keep asking me about this?'

'I know you don't *have* to do anything, but there must be something you're interested in.'

Emma has no shame in her complete lack of ambition, but it's wearing on her, the way everyone keeps asking.

'Lewis,' his mum calls.

'I'll be back in a minute.' He walks off.

'Do I look alright?' Emma whispers.

'Stop drinking red. Your lips are going purple.'

'Shit. I'm going to run to the loo. If he comes back, talk me up, alright.'

Lewis steps away from his mum as he sees Emma walk off into the house, perhaps he's going to follow her, seize his moment to finally get her alone without the complication of Yvonne there. But instead, he makes a beeline straight towards her. 'Where's the Princess gone?' he asks.

'Toilet.'

'Good. I need your help with something.'

Her heart beats.

'My sister-in-law wants to make mojitos. I need to find mint in the greenhouse. Walk with me?'

She follows him down the path which leads to the greenhouse.

'I need to thank you,' he says as she steps in behind him.

'For what?'

'For not telling Emma.'

'I was never going to tell Emma.'

'It must have been awkward for you these last few weeks.'

'Yeah, it has been.'

'But you know what's funny?' he asks, smiling slightly. 'Last night, I found something I've been looking for.' He pulls a travel card from his pocket and holds it up, her writing scribbled on the side. 'After we first met I looked everywhere for this. I even went back to The Troika the following Friday night but you weren't there.'

'Why are you telling me this?'

'Because I need you to know that I would have called you. That I wanted to.'

'You're full of shit,' she laughs. How can he stand in front of her and say this? How can he think this is okay?

'It's not working out with me and Emma. It's fun but she's not really my type.'

A train thunders behind the fence and rattles a loose pane of glass overhead.

'And have you told *her* this?'

'She doesn't care.'

'She *does* care, Lewis.' And that's the real problem. It's not that he lost Yvonne's number or that he's not told Emma they know each other. The real problem with this situation is that Emma is starting to like Lewis, really like him.

'She's not going to be around this summer,' he says. 'For her I'm just someone to fill the time with. We have nothing in common. I don't know what I was thinking when I asked her to come here today. I'm surprised she turned up. But I'm glad you did.' He takes a step closer and she smells the smoke of the coal on his shirt. 'I'm going to break up with her.'

No. He can't. It will hurt Emma too much. And what would be the point? Wouldn't it be better to just let the long summer holidays happen and for them to fizzle out?

'But,' Lewis raises his hands, 'I want to know if you'll still let me call you?'

Is he serious? He can't be. 'No,' Yvonne snaps. 'Just no.'

'Why not?' he touches her hand.

It's unbelievable that he's even asking this, that he can't see why this is all so wrong. 'Because you're with my friend. My friend who happens to like you. Who happens to think you're a nice guy.'

'But if I wasn't with your friend?'

Then yes, of course he could call her, he could call her every day and they could spend the whole summer together.

'I know you like me, Yvie.'

'That's irrelevant.'

'I'll break up with Emma, we'll keep it quiet for a few weeks and then you can tell her.'

It sounds so easy when he says it like this, but then Emma isn't *his* friend. So it doesn't matter how much she likes him, she's not going to a let a guy come between three years of friendship.

'You're ridiculous,' she says as she backs out of the greenhouse.

It's cooler outside, a light drizzle has started and Emma is squeezed under the lopsided marquee with Julie and a gaggle of women holding plastic cups of wine.

Yvonne's usually good at hiding her emotions but feels flustered by Lewis, by how he ambushed her. There's nowhere to go, he's still at the end of the garden and between her and the house are too many people, too many faces.

He got what he wanted, from both of them. Why drag it out? Surely there are hundreds of other girls he could hook up with over the summer.

Yvonne grabs Emma by the wrist. 'You're right. I've had too much wine. I feel really sick.'

Emma looks confused. 'What happened?'

'Nothing. I just overdid it.'

Lewis is walking back up the garden, he glances at them both and stops. Is he thinking about coming over? To say what?

'Can we leave?' Yvonne asks.

Emma looks back at the group of women she was previously speaking to, 'Now?'

'Yeah, my head is spinning.' It's not much of a stretch to say this, because her head does hurt from the wine, the situation, the humidity in the greenhouse and then from the way he held her hand and looked at her.

'But dude, I'm getting in there with his mum. And Lewis is a total mummy's boy.'

'Em, how many times have I near enough carried you home this year? Let's go.'

Emma doesn't move, but looks back at Julie and then down the garden to where Lewis is. 'I really like him,' she says, her face flushing. 'And it means something that he's asked me here today, to his actual home, to meet his mum and brothers. It shows that he feels the same way about me too.'

Yvonne shakes her head, 'You don't know that.'

'I'm even thinking about cancelling my trip home and staying here over the summer.'

'Don't do that. You shouldn't do that.'

The rain gets heavier and the women cackle from under the gazebo. 'Girls, come under,' Julie shouts.

'I'm sorry, Em. I've really got to go home.'

Emma looks put out but nods. 'Okay, I'll come with you. Just let me say bye first.'

Later that evening, Yvonne receives a text message from an unknown number. There's no name, just the words, **After Emma leaves for the summer, call me.**

CHAPTER SIX

PACKING

September 2020

Kiama

'You want me to iron anything for you?' Dad asks as he comes into Kiama's bedroom. He looks at the open rucksack on the floor and shakes his head. 'You really have just chucked it all in, haven't you?'

Kiama balls up some underwear and throws it in the bag.

'You've got to roll them so they don't get crushed,' Dad says.

'No one cares about me having crushed boxers.'

Dad picks up the purple microfibre towel from the bed and holds it up, 'What the hell is this?'

The last time they went to Barbados Nana had kicked off at Dad for being way over the luggage allowance and delaying them. It turned out his case was full of towels, trainers and bottles of aftershave. He knows nothing about packing.

'Have you done your liquids? I left one of those kits for you; you know, where all the bottles are 100ml.'

'Yeah, I found that in the bathroom. Didn't realise it was for me.'

'Good job I'm thinking ahead.'

'We're not flying EasyJet though. We're going to check in our bags.'

Dad nods. 'Cool. Good idea.'

This seems to be his way of dealing with the trip, to keep giving useless but thoughtful crap, like swimming shorts, compression socks and the *Rough Guide to Kenya*, which Kiama gave straight to the charity shop.

'So,' Dad says as he sits on the bed.

'So?' Kiama sits on his desk chair, rolling back and forth on it. He sniffs the back of his hand, where earlier he sprayed some Avon product Nana used to swear repelled mosquitoes. It reminds him of her.

'Will you stop moving?' Dad says. 'You're going to wear holes in the carpet.'

Neither of them speaks for a few minutes and Dad peers down into the rucksack again. 'Have you packed condoms? You've got to be careful with the girls out there. Actually, maybe stay away from the local girls.'

'Boundaries,' Kiama shouts. This has been going on since he was about fourteen; long before he even kissed a girl Dad was stuffing his wallet with condoms.

'I'll be having nightmares about little Kiama's running around Africa. It's already bad enough I don't know what you were doing in Barcelona all that time. I'm too young to be a granddad.'

'Actually, you're not,' Kiama laughs.

Dad shakes his head, but smiles a little.

'And, how are you going to keep yourself occupied while I'm gone?'

For a second Dad looks kind of lost, but then his face flicks back to neutral. 'What are you talking about? I'm going to be too busy *living my best life.*'

Kiama laughs, 'Old Man, you're making me cringe.'

'I've got a deep clean lined up for next weekend. I might even hire a carpet cleaner. Also, I'm looking forward to opening the fridge and finding food in it.'

Kiama winds up a laptop cable.

'You're taking your laptop?' Dad asks and Kiama shrugs.

'I don't think you should take any valuables. I've got an old handset somewhere too, so you don't have to take your phone.'

'And what do you expect me to do in the evenings?'

'Hotels have televisions. There's no point taking something that might make you a target out there.'

They had argued last week after Kiama caught him looking up the crime statistics for Nairobi. It wasn't helpful and it wasn't what either of them needed.

Dad leans forwards and grabs the arm of the chair to stop it moving. 'Have you got your antimalarial tablets?'

'Yep.'

'And the stuff you bought, for your grandparents?'

'Yep.'

'How? How did you fit everything into that tiny little rucksack? Especially for ten days. You're going to run out of T-shirts.'

'Stop stressing.'

'I'm not stressing, I'm trying to be organised for you. To make sure you're ready. You know it's cold out there too, I checked the forecast and the temperature drops at night. Have you got sweatshirts?'

Kiama goes over to his chest of drawers to find another sweatshirt. There's a photo of Mum on the wall there, most days he barely notices it, but recently he finds it keeps grabbing his attention. It used to be in the hallway downstairs, along with all the other pictures of the family. But as Kiama got older he started to feel self-conscious about people seeing it, this image of his mum who was no longer alive; it made him feel kind of exposed, so one day he took it down and brought it up to his room.

'I can't believe you're going tomorrow,' Dad says. 'It feels like you've only just come back from travelling and now you're off again.'

In the photo Mum's sitting in a garden or park somewhere, she's wearing a lot of make-up and a nice dress, like she was done up to go out.

'How did this picture get here?' Kiama asks.

Dad glances up it, 'You put it there. Remember? It was down in the hall with the others and you moved it. I can put it back if you want?'

Kiama shakes his head. 'No, I mean, where did we get it from?'

Dad carefully rolls up the microfibre towel and squeezes it into the rucksack. 'Nana must have got it from your grandparents. Or maybe we took it from the flat.' His voice lowers and his head drops. Kiama won't push it more as he knows how uncomfortable Dad gets talking about anything from that time. 'I'm not sure. Sorry.'

Kiama looks again at Mum and imagines how close to her he'll feel once he's back in Kenya. It's the place she loved best in the world; it was 'their home'. She said it to him once and he's never forgotten it. She had taken him for pizza at the local food court. At first, it was fun, going out for junk food straight after school, but then he started to miss his old life, his friends and afternoons running around at the local adventure playground.

'When are we going back?' he moaned.

'Back where?'

'Back home,' he said.

'Baby, this is our home. Our home is wherever we are together.'

And even though he continued to pine for the friends he left and his bedroom back in Stratford and weekends at Nana's, he understood, even at that age, that she was right.

Now that he looks at the photo properly, there's something about the light in the background that doesn't look like the UK.

'Maybe this was taken in Kenya,' he says. He turns back to see Dad removing T-shirts from the bag and rolling them.

'Sorry, son, I really don't know. But I can try and find out. Maybe your Uncle Danny will remember.'

Kiama takes a snap of the photo with his phone and smiles. 'Nah, it's fine.'

Because after tomorrow he's going to be in a place where all his questions will finally be answered.

CHAPTER SEVEN

PACKING

June 2001

Yvonne

Yvonne sits on Emma's bed, watching drops of water flick across the room as she combs her hair roughly in front of the mirror. 'So, I tried talking to my dad about Backpacks for Africa.'

'You actually told him about that?' Yvonne knows that Emma's parents see her as the 'sensible friend', the good influence, so it's a bit embarrassing that Emma's been spouting this half-baked idea to them.

'Yeah and he was his usual unsupportive self. He bombarded me with a hundred questions about logistics and how I would fund it, as if I had a business plan. I wasn't even asking him for money, just advice on how to get some.' Emma chucks the hairbrush into the open suitcase on the floor and sorts through a pile of T-shirts on the bed, some dirty, some clean. 'If I had money I could start the project up myself this summer. Wish I was eligible for one of those student loans. Then I wouldn't have to justify every penny of my allowance to my parents. Do you have any of your loan left?'

'No, because I spent it on food and rent. Remember?'

Every argument they've ever had has been because Emma left on the lights, turned up the heating or spent their joint kitty on M&S mayonnaise and double-quilted toilet roll. Money, and Yvonne's lack of it, has always been the topic they tried to steer clear of.

'Purity said I could help out at an orphanage she knows this summer and my dad said if I commit enough to that, he'll help out with the project. It's something, I guess. How much is your student loan anyway?'

'Don't ask.' The truth is, Yvonne doesn't know. For each time a white envelope with that dreaded Glasgow postmark arrives on the doormat she places it unopened into a wallet marked '*Debt*'.

'This is why we should both move abroad,' Emma says. 'The government will wipe all your debts clean after four years.'

'That's untrue and I wish people would stop saying it.'

Emma sits on her suitcase and zips it shut. 'No one's going to break your kneecaps for that money. Plus, when I'm someone's trophy wife I'll pay it off for you. Fuck. I think I'm way over baggage allowance. How are you meant to weigh your suitcase anyway?'

'Kitchen scales,' Yvonne says.

'Really? Do we own kitchen scales?'

Yvonne laughs and Emma throws a T-shirt at her. 'You're taking the piss out of me?'

Emma comes over and lays her head on Yvonne's shoulder. Her hair smells like the miracle shampoo they discovered in the pound shop. After three years of living with Emma, sharing everything and always having someone to talk to, Yvonne knows she's going to struggle moving back home.

'I'm a bit anxious, you know,' Emma says.

'About what?'

'About the orphanage. I've never really seen that side of Kenya.'

'You'll be great at it.'

'I still wish you would come with me. You do know I'm going to email you every day?'

'Which I'll ignore, because I'll be working sixty hours a week at Sainsbury's and the other sixty at my internship.'

Emma grabs Yvonne's wrist to check the time. 'I need to go.'

'Where to?'

'To see Terry. He's got a discount voucher for the cinema so I said I'd go.'

'Two Minute Terry? Again?'

'Stop calling him that. It sounds so wrong. He's shy, that's all. Also, he's much closer to ten minutes,' Emma winks as she pushes her purse into her pocket.

'Please tell me you haven't slept with Two Minute Terry?'

'No, course not. I'm not *that* easy. But it's not like there's anyone else calling me, is there?'

After the barbecue, Yvonne had watched Emma leave Lewis a voicemail explaining that she could stay in the UK over the summer. She had followed up with a text, then another voicemail the next day. But it was clear, at least to Yvonne, that he was pulling away. Emma had sulked around the house for a few days, her phone close by at all times. Then, once, she burst into tears and handed the phone over to Yvonne. 'I can't keep waiting like this,' she said, before slamming the front door and disappearing for an afternoon. Yvonne had sat there with the old brick phone in her hands, waiting for the screen to flash with a message from Sweetboy, but it never came.

Emma rattles about in a jewellery box. 'Why can I never find a matching pair?' She holds a few up then throws them back in. 'Fuck it, it's going to be dark anyway.'

'Do you even like him?'

'Who?'

'Two Minute Terry.'

Emma wobbles her hand. 'I'm not looking to get serious with anyone. I did that with Sweetboy and ended up getting hurt.'

'So you're only going to go for guys you *kind of like*?'

'I'm only going to go with guys who like me back.' Emma sighs. 'Though you can't always tell, can you? I thought Sweetboy was into me. I thought, this is it, he's the one.'

'The one?' Yvonne hears the surprise in her voice and looks away, down to the jewellery box. 'I didn't realise you felt that strongly about him.'

'Neither did I,' Emma says, 'until he didn't call me back.'

Yvonne hands Emma a matching pair of earrings.

'But when I think back, it's obvious what kind of guy he is; a proper player. A few times I felt like he was checking out other girls when I was with him. He was even kind of flirtatious with you.'

'I don't think so.'

Emma laughs, 'Are you serious? You didn't notice? You're so oblivious.'

Yvonne clears her throat, desperate to change the subject. 'Do you really have to go out now? The landlord is on his way over. I hate being alone in the house with him.'

Emma sprays a cloud of Tommy Girl and walks into it. 'Merv the Perv? He's harmless. Besides, he doesn't need to know you're here alone, tell him Bethany is upstairs sleeping.'

'He gives me the creeps. I hate the way he's always jangling those keys. Remember the last time he came I caught him touching my bra as it dried above the bathtub.'

Emma leans down and kisses Yvonne on the head, 'You do have some pretty sexy bras for someone not putting out much. You'll be fine, but keep the rape alarm close.'

Merv stands on the doorstep and jangles the keys in his pocket. He rings the bell for the third time. Yvonne really doesn't want to let him in. Not while she's alone in the house.

He rings again.

'This is ridiculous,' she tells herself then opens the door. 'Sorry, I had my headphones on,' she rattles a pair, the wire hanging unconnected to anything.

'I told you I was coming round.'

'Sorry.'

'In the old days, before all these tenant rights, I would have used my own keys. But now it's the law, you can't. Got to be invited in. Like a vampire.' He bares his slightly yellowed teeth and laughs. As he walks through he stalls at the sight of the blue bed sheet stapled into the doorframe of the downstairs bedroom. 'What have you done?'

Yvonne grimaces. 'It just fell off.'

His face reddens. 'Fell off?'

'It was loose anyway, I think.'

He walks ahead of her to the kitchen and takes in the piles of dishes in the sink and the overflowing bin.

The kettle knocks the dishes as Yvonne tries to fill it. There's so much limescale, she tries to scoop some of it out with a spoon, as it rises to the surface. 'Would you like a cup of tea?' She lifts two mugs from the draining board and out of force of habitat sniffs them.

'Think I'm alright for tea,' Merv says.

'My housemate is upstairs sleeping.'

Merv makes an exaggerated gesture of shuffling up his sleeve to check his watch. 'It's gone three o'clock.'

'Really? Already? You know what students are like.' She tries to laugh.

'Students? No, you can't hide behind that anymore. Have you got a job lined up?'

'Yes. Two actually,' she says proudly.

'Good for you. And where are you going after you move out of this place?'

'Home. To my parents'.'

He nods at her. 'Sensible thing to do. Right, I'll do that upstairs tap first then have a look at the bedroom door.' He puffs, then stamps his way up.

Yvonne busies herself cleaning the kitchen, sorting the crockery she brought from home from the old chipped plates that were already in the cupboards. It's sad the way everything now has to be wrapped in newspaper and dragged back to her parents' till she can find a house share cheap enough to rent again.

The sound of Merv clanging his tools and singing Jennifer

Lopez songs fills the empty house. The doorbell goes and Yvonne walks through to answer it, expecting Emma, finally having come to her senses about wasting time with someone as dull as Terry. But it's Lewis.

'Emma's not here,' she blurts.

'I didn't come to see Emma. That's done.'

'So, what do you want?'

'I came to get some stuff I left here. My sketchbooks. Got a meeting with a manufacturer later and need them.' He starts to come in and she steps back so she won't have to be close to him. Close enough to touch him or smell the aftershave he always wears far too much of.

'They can't be that important if you left them here all this time. It's been three weeks.'

'But who's counting? Besides, I've kind of had other stuff going on.' He looks at her, 'My mum's been unwell.'

'Oh, I'm sorry. I—'

Singing floats down the staircase.

'Who's that?'

'Landlord,' she mouths.

'The pervert? You here alone with him?'

'He's fixing a leak.'

'Bet you're glad I came by then.' He kicks off his trainers and walks past her into Emma's room. 'This place is such a mess.' He gestures to the unmade bed, the suitcase on the floor and carrier bags of clothes. 'How can she live like this?'

'She's flying out Monday.'

'Oh yeah, back to Africa.' He picks at things on the desk, lifting piles of papers and books, copies of *National Geographic* and *Time*, the magazines Emma talked her parents into getting her subscriptions for yet never reads. Lewis scratches his head, as if about to give up, 'How can she get anything done here? Disaster. A-ha.' One by one he pulls the sketchbooks from the depths of the mess.

'The blueprints for your fashion empire?' She's trying to sound smart. Not that he takes much notice; too busy flicking through his books smiling, happy to be reunited with them.

'Yeah, something like that. Where is the Princess anyway?'

Should she say that Emma is out with someone else? That she's moved on? 'She's got a job interview,' she lies. 'For an internship in the autumn.'

Lewis laughs. 'Really?'

'Yes.'

Merv has stopped singing upstairs and is now talking on the phone; his booming voice fills the awkward space between her and Lewis.

'So, you've got your stuff and I need to get ready to go out, so…' she trails off, the way he's looking at her is unreadable. 'What?'

'I sent you a message,' he says. 'I called you, but you never answered.'

She takes a deep breath and leans back against the wall, 'Emma's my friend.'

'I know that—'

'I don't think you're worth it.' The line has been well rehearsed in her head, but it loses conviction as it leaves her lips, even she doesn't believe it. 'It was a one-night thing,' she adds weakly, like one-night things were a common part of her life.

'Harsh, but okay then.' Lewis crosses his arms over the books and looks at her. 'Though I don't see what the issue is. Emma's not going to care what you're doing here, while she's in Africa.'

'And you're certain about that, are you? Is this a game for you?'

'No. It's not a game.'

'Then why are trying to play two friends off against each other?'

'I'm not.'

'I shouldn't even have let you in.'

'But you did.'

'I'm not doing it, Lewis, I'm not like that.'

'Listen to me. I'm sorry I lost your number.'

She didn't even know if this was what she wanted to hear. 'You're lying.'

'I swear. I really wanted to call you. I only found your number again the night before the barbecue. We had fun together, Yvie. And I'm not just talking about sex. I'm talking about you. I like you.' He's close enough to take her hand in his. 'Of course I would have called you.'

She shakes him away. If only things weren't this complicated. If only Emma didn't like him so much. If only Emma had never met him at all. 'I can't, Lewis.' She feels him lean closer and knows she shouldn't look up at him, that she's not strong enough for it. She squeezes her eyes shut and puts a hand over her face. 'I can't. I can't do it to Emma.'

But as he leans in to kiss her she doesn't stop him. Doesn't stop herself. Because, it's *him* and despite everything she likes him more than she's liked anyone before, so when he kisses

74

her she lets it happen. But, no, Emma is her friend, her closest friend. She steps away, embarrassed.

'What's wrong?' he asks.

And this is the problem, that to him it's nothing, Emma's nothing, her feelings are nothing. But to Yvonne it's everything. 'You should leave.'

It's hard to tell if the disappointment on his face is because she's saying no, or because he's never been knocked back before.

'You really want me to go?' he asks.

More than anything she wants to lean into him, put her head on his chest and tell him to stay.

'I get it. You're loyal to your friend. But Emma and I,' he shakes his head, 'it was nothing.'

'Is that really what you think?'

'Emma was never looking for anything deep with me. She's a good-time girl, right? She's probably already moved onto another guy.'

Two Minute Terry. The consolation prize. How could Lewis not know or feel how intensely she liked him?

'We didn't even get on that well,' he adds and it hurts Yvonne how little he cared for her friend. 'But with you, Yvie, we click on so many things. We're so similar.' Again, he moves closer.

'No, we're not. You don't know me.'

She can feel his eyes. He opens his mouth to stay something but then decides against it.

'Lewis, just go.'

CHAPTER EIGHT

ARRIVAL

October 2020

Yvonne

The airport pub smells of beer-soaked carpet and fried food. The football highlights play soundlessly in the background and the white wine is terrible. Yvonne feels oddly calm. Kiama eats a double burger, side salad, chips and onion rings, stopping frequently to read the incoming messages on his phone.

'You're popular,' she says.

'It's my dad.'

Lewis made Kiama out to be some emotionally unstable wreck, but the way he rolls his eyes as he reads the texts makes him look like any other sulky teenager.

'Not much of a portion, is it? Are you going to eat that?' He points his fork at the extra bowl of chips he ordered, despite her protests.

She pushes it across the table. 'Are you one of those annoying people who eat whatever they want and never put on weight?'

'What can I say? I got good genes. Though when I look

at Dad I can see how it catches up with you. You're probably picturing him still all buff, but I'm telling you, he's eaten pasta every day since Nana passed. He's like this,' Kiama puffs his cheeks out and Yvonne laughs. 'He says he's going to get back down the gym. But he never does.'

'And you? What are you into?'

'Definitely not the gym, that's for sure.'

'Are you thinking of going back to college? Or,' she trails off, waiting for him to fill in the blanks. Surely, he's not just working at the family business.

'I'm not very academic so college didn't really gel with me. Since I came back from travelling I've been helping out at the trampoline park. But I'm also working on my music.'

'Your music?'

'Yeah, I do a bit of producing. I'm really into nu-Jazz at the moment, but still making a lot of funky minimal. Why are you making that face?'

'I didn't make a face.'

'Yes, you did,' he looks bruised. 'What's funny?'

'I never know what to say when people talk about making music or art. The average age at my company is twenty-three and they're all at it.'

Kiama puts down his chips and frowns. 'Nothing wrong with a creative side hustle. What do *you* do?'

'Work,' she replies. 'I work.'

His phone vibrates against the table. 'He's doing my nut in with these messages.' Kiama types something back, his thick eyebrows knotting together. He chucks the phone on the seat next to him and lets out a kind of groan.

She feels bad for making fun of him and wants to ask

a question about his music but is interrupted when the phone buzzes again and Kiama growls comically as he lifts it to his ear, 'Dad? Why are you bombarding me? Yeah, I'm fine. Course, I'm fine. Yvonne's here.'

She looks at him and Kiama takes it as an acknowledgement. 'She says hi,' he smiles. 'No, we're through security already. We're flying in an hour. You got my flight details, read them.' He picks another chip from the bowl and listens. The sudden loud snap of his laughter reminds Yvonne of him as a kid. It's still loud enough to turn heads. 'Course they let me through… No they didn't make me take my piercings out… Actually I put the heroin up my arse.' He laughs again. He talks to Lewis like a friend, not a parent. It makes it hard to see him as she's been trying to, as an adult with a middle-age spread. 'Why are you asking me stupid questions? Okay. Okay. Okay. I'll send you her number.' He's getting ratty. 'Talk later. Message me.' He hangs up. 'Jesus. I'm sending him your number.'

'Why?' she asks.

'Because soon I'm going to stop answering these ridiculous messages from him.'

Kiama doesn't know that Lewis has been trying to contact her, calling her work and filling her voicemail with messages. She had listened to each one several times, amazed at how many different ways Lewis could word 'get your story straight'. It's all he seems to care about, that Yvonne not divulge the past to Kiama.

But surely the whole point of the trip is for him to find out about the past. Though she's unsure exactly what it is he wants to find out.

They walk out of the pub and towards the gate. He stretches and groans, 'I ate too much. I'm also so regretting these jeans.' He hitches them up. 'I was going for that DJ-on-a-world-tour look.'

'Please tell me you don't DJ as well?'

'No,' he side-eyes her, 'not anymore.'

They step onto the escalator and he faces her. 'When was the last time you went away?'

'I don't go abroad much.'

He nods. 'Surely you earn enough doing your... whatsit you do again?'

'I'm a partner at a comms agency.'

'Yeah, that. Bet you jet off every now and then?'

'Not if I can help it. Though I did go to Abu Dhabi last year for the Grand Prix.'

'Cool.'

'My family are big into racing so I took my brother for his birthday. But it was such a long flight for a short trip. Also, I work long hours and when I get a break the last thing I want to do is this.' She nods ahead to the twisting hordes of people.

'Fair enough. I got the travelling bug hard. Tried to do Europe this summer, but I only managed like four cities before I got stuck in Barcelona. You been?'

'No.'

He throws his head back, 'Ah, you should go. It's the perfect city. It's got nightlife, the beach and the mountains. I didn't want to come home.'

The queue moves slowly and as they make their way towards the gate, he keeps talking. 'Really want to do the States next. Few of my friends are thinking of hiring a car and doing the Route 66 thing. I can't drive, but I really want to go along.'

She tiptoes to look ahead, but the queue seems to merge into a crowd, it's as if there's no way out.

'Besides trainers and ketamine, travelling is the only thing I'm genuinely interested in.'

'What?' she asks.

'Oh, so you are listening?' Kiama laughs.

'Yes. Sorry.' She wrings her hands and wonders how much small talk he'll need and if he'll insist on catching up with her for the whole of the journey.

'You look like the spa break type,' he says. 'Country hotels, that sort of thing. Am I right?'

'I love being outdoors. Running mostly.'

He scrunches his nose. 'Really?'

'Yes,' she answers, bringing to mind the utter serenity of her favourite spots, places where she can run for hours without having to interact with anyone. Places so far from here, this too-busy, too-bright space.

'I never get people who run for fun. Have you done the marathon?'

'No, because that pretty much represents the complete opposite of everything I like about running.'

The air-hostess smiles as he checks their passports and tickets and they walk on and find their seats. Yvonne takes the window. She fastens her seatbelt and closes her eyes, hoping Kiama won't continue to talk the whole journey.

Once airborne he undoes his belt and pulls out two Toblerones. 'For you,' he hands her one. 'Can't fly without.'

He puts in his EarPods and settles into watching something,

but he's still distracting, laughing out loud at his screen and nudging her to look at the things he finds amusing.

She takes her water from her bag and downs a Zopiclone, the sleeping tablet her doctor prescribed as her anxiety around the trip began to surge.

The last thing she remembers is Kiama snapping off triangles of chocolate.

Then his hand on her shoulder as he tries to wake her up. 'We're landing in five minutes.'

'Already?' she asks rubbing her eyes.

'Yeah, it's been eight hours.' He lets his hair out and it sticks up around his head like a fluffy mane. 'You were out of it. What did you take?'

'Zopiclone.'

'Jesus,' he laughs. 'That's no over-the-counter stuff, is it?'

'I hardly ever use them. Only when I've got a lot on at work. I thought they would be good for the flight.'

'You don't need to explain, I'm the last person to judge when it comes to taking pills. Trust me.'

'Haven't you slept?'

'No. I never sleep on a flight,' he yawns.

'Do you want one for the next leg? Or maybe half?'

He laughs again. 'I can't believe you're offering me prescription drugs. Is this what Dad was worrying about when I got in touch with you?'

'Sorry, I don't know why I said that.'

'I'm not a good sleeper,' he says, almost apologetically. 'Nana and Dad never believed in medicating me, so I've learned to deal with it over the years in my own way.'

'Insomnia?' she asks.

'Nah, everyone gets that. More like night terrors and stuff. I've not had them in a while, but any little thing can trigger it. I definitely don't sleep easily.' He zips his EarPods in a little case and looks out of the window at the dark night. 'Right, we've got two hours to kill, let's go.'

They walk around the glittered floor of the Duty Free at Dubai International Airport browsing cosmetics, premium alcohol and gold lamps on key chains. She allows him to buy her a large green smoothie which she sips until it gives her a headache and then throws away while he's distracted by a yellow Porsche parked in the lounge.

'Have you started lessons?' Yvonne asks.

'No. I never really had a need for it. Nana used to drive me everywhere. I could call her at 2 a.m. and she'd come and get me.'

'That's ridiculous,' Yvonne says as they walk on.

'I know, right. I miss her.' He stops at a stand filled with stuffed toy camels and starts rearranging them.

'She used to spoil you. You always used to come back from her house with something new; trainers, toys, whatever you wanted.'

'Maybe I deserved it.'

'Ha,' Yvonne says. 'Though I think I was probably the same with you.'

He adds a final camel to his display and takes a photo of it before he walks off. When Yvonne looks he's posed them in a lewd sex act, which she dismantles before following him.

The flight to Nairobi is announced and hearing the destination causes her stomach to drop. She's kept herself busy going through the motions of travelling, of listening to Kiama, but now it hits her.

'Excuse me.' She ducks into the nearest toilet and sits on the closed lid as she tries to calm down. *I can do this*, she tells herself, *I have to do this.*

It's fear she feels, pure fear for what's going to happen next and how little she can control it. Outside the taps run, hand driers blow and doors slam. She unrolls the tissue and wipes her tears. This is hard. It's too hard. How can she do it? How can she open herself up to so many possibilities like this?

Outside the cubicle two women have a conversation about their joint fortieth birthday afternoon tea at the Burj Al Arab. Emma would have turned forty this August. She would have hated the extravagance of doing something so opulent.

As the women's voices withdraw, Yvonne emerges from the cubicle. She splashes water on her face and reapplies her make-up. She has to remind herself that even if Emma was still alive, it's not a guarantee that they would still be friends. They would probably never have been those middle-aged women going on holiday together. The thought hurts her, because it opens up too many *what ifs*, all these parallel things which might have happened had Emma lived.

Kiama sits on the floor outside, his long legs in the skinny jeans straight out in front.

The departures board announces the last call for flight EK225 and a shrinking crowd makes its way through the gate.

He turns over the luggage tag on Yvonne's bag in his hand. 'Your name wasn't always Olsson, was it?'

'No.'

'You were married?'

'Yes, for three years. But I liked having a name different from the one I grew up with, so never bothered changing it back.'

'Bet the press couldn't find you so easily then either?'

'No. But they mostly left me alone.'

'Wasn't that easy to disappear with my name. Some journalist came to the school once, walked into the playground at home time as if to collect me. Completely freaked me out.'

'I'm sorry. They weren't supposed to do that.' A national paper had published Kiama's picture a week after Emma's death. Yvonne's brother Claude had seen it first and brought it over to her flat. It was terrible to know that people were reading about what happened, looking at Kiama's little face and feeling sorry for him. But this, the idea that someone would actually try to seek him out, was worse.

Yvonne should have been there when this happened; she should have been able to stop it.

One of the air hostesses makes another call, shooting Yvonne a look. 'Last call for Flight EK225,' she repeats, '*Very* last call.'

Kiama sighs, 'I know this isn't your idea of a holiday, it's not mine either.'

He looks like that little kid again, the one who sat on the stairs at his nana's house, down on himself because, after living in Kenya for six months and only wearing only flip-flops, he had forgotten how to tie his shoelaces.

'Kiama, I'm going to find this hard. I can't hide that.'

He looks away from her.

'She was my best friend.'

'Yeah and she was my mum. My mum who no one ever talks about.' Again, he growls in frustration. 'I know I'm not meant to say this but I can't be sad about Mum anymore. I don't want this to be some sad trip where I walk about Kenya feeling miserable about her all the time. Crying and sitting in this big hole of grief. I need to feel something else.' He looks up at Yvonne. 'I want to remember her and be able to feel something other than sadness.' He draws his legs up, sitting cross-legged. 'That's why I called you, because you knew her the best. You can tell me stuff.'

Is that all? Is that really the reason he wants to do this trip? They could have done this at home? Why travel to Kenya for it?

'Kiama, I'm not sure what you want to hear from me.'

'You just need to tell me something other than that she died. Because I already know that.'

'Okay,' Yvonne nods. 'I get it.' She reaches down her hands to pull him up from the floor.

CHAPTER NINE

TEAL TIE

October 2020

Kiama

They emerge into the arrivals hall of Jomo Kenyatta Airport after nine at night, shuffling slowly through passport control and onto baggage claim. He yawns again, it's hard to stop.

'You really should have tried to sleep on the plane,' she says.

But it's alright for her, popping a pill and being knocked out for hours, the odd snore escaping. He had nudged her a few times and she smiled in her sleep before turning her head the other way. Yvonne doesn't seem to be much of a smiler so it was kind of funny to see her with her guard down. He doesn't remember her having such a serious vibe. She was fun back when he was a kid, always the one up for taking him somewhere; cinema, park, farm, it was always with her. He remembers he could make her laugh too, that she used to call him a 'baby giraffe' and slip him a fiver whenever they passed a shop.

'The arrivals hall is this way,' she says the second after lifting the bags from the belt.

Is she going to manage every second of the trip like this? It's kind of tiring. Originally he was going organise the whole thing himself. But once Yvonne agreed to come it felt like her taking over the organisation was one of the conditions. She mapped out everything for the days they would spend together, updating him with detailed emails about a local driver, the best hotels and what time they would be meeting his grandparents for lunch. She even asked if he wanted her to book his hotel in Mombasa for the extra days he would stay after she left, but he'd already booked the same budget hotel he'd stayed in with Mum. It was easy to find online, a bright pink building with a roadside café, famous for serving the best tamarind juice on the coast.

The arrivals hall is filled with men holding placards, but none of them say their names. They walk past and stand between giant potted plants and posters for safari tours. This is it. They're really here again.

'I'll call the driver,' she says as she pulls out a mobile phone and plastic wallet filled with papers.

'Which museum did you steal that handset from?'

'They're great for travelling with.'

He watches over her shoulder as a slow pixelated image of two hands shaking lights up the screen. 'Can you even take pictures with that?'

'Why would I want to take pictures? I'm not one of these people who feel the need to photograph my every move and meal.'

'Like me?'

'Yes, like you,' she says.

'I'm not addicted to my phone. I could easily go without.'

'I'd like to see you try,' she mumbles.

He takes off his rucksack and chucks his phone in it. 'Check me out,' he says doing jazz hands. 'I'm living in the moment.'

She smiles slightly, 'I give it ten minutes.'

It's hard to get any kind of banter going with her, sometimes she seems up for it, but then just as easily shuts down and goes quiet. So quiet, she hardly said a word on the last leg of the flight, just gazed in front of her, refusing to eat any of the plane food or watch anything. But he gets this must be hard for her as well. She and Mum were good friends, almost like sisters.

'The reception is terrible,' she says. 'Wait here, I'll go closer to the doors.'

He nods her off and sinks into one of the spare metal seats, pulling out a packet of Minstrels, the last of his snacks. The sugar should keep him going for a while longer, though his head is starting to feel fuzzy and all he wants to do is lie down and pass out.

A white girl with a rucksack sits down opposite, pulls her giant bag onto her lap and wraps the straps around her arms, she looks mad nervous.

'First time in Kenya?' he asks her.

She nods. 'How can you tell?'

'No one's going to steal your bag at the airport.'

She relaxes her grip. 'It's my first time travelling. Have you been here before?'

'No,' he says, now full of regret for initiating conversation, he's too tired for small talk.

'It's so exciting, isn't it?' she says. 'I'm doing a gap-year project at an orphanage.'

'Sounds life-changing.'

The girl recoils slightly, like she's trying to work out if he's making fun of her or not.

Yvonne clears her throat. 'Sorry to interrupt, but I'm having issues with my phone.'

He takes the Nokia from her hand and tries holding down the off button but the screen remains frozen on the logo. 'I would offer mine but I've switched it off and put it away, because I'm all about having real-life experiences.'

She huffs and stares him down until he goes in his bag and takes it back out. 'Nice chatting,' he says to the girl as he stands. 'Enjoy your orphanage.'

'What was that about?' Yvonne asks.

'Nothing.'

'I heard you tell her you've never been here before.'

He didn't realise she'd been standing there that long. 'So?'

'So, why lie?'

'You expect me to start rolling out the *real* story to some random girl?'

'No,' she says, 'I guess not.' She holds the phone out towards him, 'It's locked.'

'170880.'

Her eyes flick to his, obviously recognising Mum's date of birth, she hands it back. 'I hate iPhones. Can you do it, please?'

Eventually they find Joe, a short, tired-looking man in a crushed teal-coloured suit and tie. He walks them out into the car park, the whole time complaining about his newborn twin daughters and how little sleep he's getting. It's cold and the dark outside, the opposite of what Kiama had expected. But why? He and Mum used to stay out late on cold dark nights like this, sitting on the balcony drinking hot chocolates in their coats. He hasn't thought about that in years. It's amazing, they're not even out of the airport and already the memories are coming back.

'Kiama?' Yvonne puts her hand on his arm. 'Are you okay?'

Joe walks ahead and opens the car, a 4x4 the same colour as his suit. The boot flies open breaking Kiama's train of thought.

'Give me your bag,' Yvonne says.

He recognises the look on her face, pity. Sometimes he feels like he's received more pity from people than anything else. It used to make him angry, but now he understands it's just one of those things that comes with losing a parent when you're a child.

'I can carry my own bag,' he snaps. He slides it from his shoulder and throws it on top of her case. Yvonne looks away from him and he instantly feels bad. 'I'm tired,' he says, hoping she'll take this as an apology.

'I know. Me too.'

Inside, Joe locks the doors and puts the radio on, filling the car with fast-paced voices which switch between Swahili and English. It all feels like noise to him. The heat is on too high, it dries his throat and lips, or maybe he's getting sick. Plane journeys do that to him. He needs to sleep whatever it is off; this trip is too important to be wasted being ill.

Another yawn.

Yvonne leans over and whispers, 'Are you okay?'

'Yeah.'

'It's a forty-minute drive. I'm not going to sleep again, but if you want to… '

'I'm fine.' He wishes he could lay his head against the window and close his eyes, that he could allow the motion of the car to help him drift off. But what would be the sense in that? For him to sleep now and miss any other triggers, any other smells or sights that will remind him of something he's forgotten?

They never spent that much time in Nairobi when he lived here, only occasionally coming in to meet up with Mum's other expat friends who lived in the city. But he recalls this, the traffic, the way it thickens as you edge closer towards the centre, how the air gets dirtier and the streets more cluttered and claustrophobic. 'Reminds me of London,' Mum used to say, because she would always relate anything slightly crappy back to London.

They slow for the lights and he jumps as a hand slams on the window by his ear. 'Fuck.'

On the other side of the glass a man slaps his pink palm several times on the window and Kiama slides away.

'Money, please?' the man asks.

'You okay?' Yvonne asks for the hundredth time.

'Yes. Fine.' His voice sounds harsh. 'Made me jump, that's all.'

At least it stopped him from dozing off and he spends the rest of the drive feeling wide awake. Finally, they pull up at the hotel, some high-end chain, modern and European-looking. The type of place he usually only ever goes in to use the toilet.

'Thought you said it wasn't fancy?'

'It's not,' Yvonne replies. 'It's a standard hotel.'

Her standards are obviously a bit higher than the average

person's. Dad's idea of splashing out on accommodation is getting the premium cabin at Center Parcs.

The car doors are opened by doormen on both sides, then they're greeting them and grabbing their bags and waving Joe off and it all feels too quick, going from the dark streets cocooned in the hot car to this, the bright yellow lights of the hotel drive and cold air.

Yvonne takes the passports and checks in while he sits in a big armchair yawning and feeling confident that he'll be able to fall asleep once in the room, that he won't lay wide awake with his mind running for hours. This last part of the journey has felt so long, so drawn-out.

He takes out his phone; he's had five messages from Dad in the last hour, all of them questions he doesn't have the energy to answer, so instead types back.

In hotel. Yvonne splashed out on 5 stars.

The replies shoot back.

Did you get my other messages?

How are you feeling?

Did you guys talk much on the journey over?

Yvonne walks towards him, key cards in hand.

'Come on,' she says handing back his passport. 'You look absolutely shattered.'

He stays silent in the lift and as they walk along the plush carpets of the hall. 'I'm only next door if you need anything,' she says.

'Cool.' He nods towards the key, still in her hand.

'Really? You don't seem cool. Your shoulders are up by your ears.'

Does he really need this? Now? He makes a conscious effort to shake out his shoulders and slump. 'I'm tired. That's all. Tired.'

'Okay,' she hands him the key. 'Goodnight then.'

He goes into the room and they both shut their doors at the same time. The lights are all ablaze and again the heat is up too high. He turns it off and lies on the bed, knocking over the towel twisted into an elephant. He should shower and change, but can't gather enough energy to get up now he's down. This is good though, this is what he needs. Eyes closing. Silence. But without the drone of the heating system everything sounds so loud, the traffic on the street outside, the squeak of a room service trolley going past, doors opening and closing.

Warm milk, that's what Nana would suggest; even up until last year when he was far too old for it, she'd still make him a mug and bring it up to his room. What he would give for that kind of pampering right now. He sends Dad a message.

Do you think room service will judge me if I order warm milk?

But he's probably fallen asleep now he knows Kiama is safely at the hotel.

Kiama checks the minibar for familiar Kenyan snacks, but it's all American stuff and sugar will only perk him back up. He pops open the packet of complimentary slippers and tries on the fluffy white robe but the arms are too short and it looks ridiculous.

'Now what?'

He can't sleep. He just can't sleep. Yvonne's door opens and there's talk outside, before it closes again. She's up. Maybe she's gone out. But where? He takes his key and gently taps on her door.

'Kiama?'

'Sorry. You still awake?'

'Yes, I am very much awake.'

He looks past her to the trolley in the middle of the room. 'Ah, it was room service. Finally got your appetite back then?'

'I thought I better eat something,' she pulls back. 'Come in, you'll probably like it.'

He sits on the bed and pulls the trolley over. 'Jesus. Why did you order so much?'

'I didn't know what I fancied.'

'This is enough for three people. Are you one of those secret binge eaters?'

He's embarrassed her. But what's this about? Maybe she's got some eating issues, refusing food all day, then ready to pig out like this alone at night.

'I didn't realise the portions would be this big,' she says as she sits next to him. 'All I wanted was a snack. Why are you not sleeping? I thought you were exhausted.'

He kicks off the hotel slippers and puts his feet up on the bed. 'I am.'

'But you can't sleep?'

He shakes his head and rubs his eyes. 'Maybe filling up my

stomach will help.' He feels her watch as he makes a sandwich of falafel, pineapple chunks and chips. 'You want me to make you one?'

'No, no thanks. Just don't get that all over my bed.' She puts a piece of falafel on a napkin and picks at it. 'How are you feeling about tomorrow? About seeing your grandparents?'

While seeing his grandparents was one of the main reasons for returning to Kenya, it's also one of the things that has been stressing him out the most, especially after Dad reminded him of how distant they had been in the past.

'Hmm, I'm kind of nervous. The last time they came to England was five years ago and it was weird. Nana offered to put them up at hers and they sort of refused. Plus, they were always a bit off with Dad.'

She leans back and looks away. It's so obvious that she's thinking about what to say next, so he fills the silence quickly. 'I know my grandparents and Dad never got along. I remember that, from when Mum was alive. But I'm sure it felt worse after I moved in with Dad. Do you think it's because they thought I should have stayed here with them?'

Again she looks away, this time down to her napkin, which she's shredded into thin strips.

'Yvonne, please?' he laughs. 'Tell me what you think.'

She wipes the crumbs from the bed. 'They were already well into their forties when they had Emma. Neil was never the most patient man in the world and Cynthia used to find it quite hard looking after you when you stayed out here.'

He doesn't remember this. 'Why? Was I difficult?'

'Not particularly. But little boys are energetic.'

It sounds familiar in some ways, that feeling he often had around his grandparents of not really doing the right thing or being as good as he should be. Mum used to reassure him, tell him it was fine to make mess and noise but whenever Neil was home Kiama knew he had to almost shrink down.

'So, you don't think they wanted me to stay here with them?'

'No,' she says slowly, almost like she's apologising. 'Everyone knew at the—' she stalls, takes a breath, '—time, that it was best for you to go home to the UK and live with your dad. But I don't think it was because Cynthia and Neil didn't want you. I'm sure they really, really wanted you, would have loved to have—'

'It's okay. I get it.' Of course they didn't want to be saddled with a grieving eight-year-old. 'Still, I don't get why it was always so strained between everyone. It made me feel bad about contacting my grandparents. So I didn't that much. I guess I chose my side, didn't I?'

'You were a kid. Also, I don't think it was as simple as picking a side. I'm sure they would have loved to be more involved with you growing up, but it's a big distance.'

He shrugs.

'Anyway,' she says, 'you're here now.'

'Guess so.'

He twists his hair around his fingers causing it to stick up.

'Why do you keep it so long?' she asks.

'Can't be bothered to cut it.'

'Your mum liked it long too.'

'Dad hates it.'

'He always did. But then he's the type of man who spends every weekend at the barbers, isn't he?'

Kiama laughs, it's true. It's weird that Yvonne knows him as well, Kiama never thought of that before. Dad didn't go to university with them, but they must have all hung out together when they lived in Harrow.

'It will be nice to see Purity,' she says.

'Ah, yeah, I'm really looking forward to seeing her. You know she Skyped me a few times?'

'Really?'

'Yeah. One of her kids moved to the US so she used to go to the internet café and call me after calling him, but not in ages, probably like a year. It was always hilarious, she'd be chatting to me, but at the same time eating her lunch and running like three other conversations with the people sitting either side of her. I miss those calls.'

'Why did the calls stop?'

'She always seemed so busy and I didn't want to keep taking up her time. Plus, I think that was around the period I was busy failing my AS levels.'

'She must have been so excited when you told her you were coming.'

But he hadn't even thought of that. Just assumed his grandparents would pass on the message. Though maybe they haven't and tomorrow will be a surprise for her; he can't wait to see her face.

He feels another yawn coming, but doesn't want to go back to his room. 'Should we put on the TV?' he suggests. 'I was surprised they've got all the American and British channels.'

'I don't watch that much TV.'

'For real? No social media, no side hustle, no TV. You must do something other than work?'

'Of course. I told you, I run. I go to events. Plays. Readings.'

'You really are middle-aged, aren't you?'

'Ha ha. I'm only recently forty.'

It's weird to think that Mum would have been forty too. He had thought about it on her birthday this year, imagining how big her party would have been. How he would have surprised her with some amazing gift. But what? He can't imagine what she would have liked at this age. And it would be a weird question to ask Yvonne.

'You really don't like TV?'

'No.'

'But what about series? What about true crime?'

She lifts a chicken skewer and takes two bites before putting it back down.

'What about sci-fi? Fantasy?'

'Definitely not.'

'Well, we've got six evenings together and we're not going to spend them watching a play.' He gets up and heads to the door.

'You're going?'

'Back in a minute.'

His room is dark and now slightly chilly. He grabs his laptop and takes it back through to Yvonne's. 'I downloaded some series before I left.'

'Shouldn't we be having an early night? Especially you.'

'Why? We're not due in Kilimani till one. You don't need to get up early.' He flips the lid open and Yvonne smiles at his screensaver, a picture of him and Nana.

'That's such a nice photo of you both.'

'It was New Year's Eve. Originally, she wanted to go to

Barbados, but she wasn't well enough to go abroad. So we went Center Parcs instead.'

It was kind of depressing at first, hiding out from the bad British weather in those big chlorine-smelling spheres. But after they got over not being on the beach, it was one of the best holidays ever, because they were all together, all the uncles and cousins, and Nana seemed so happy.

'I didn't realise you went back to Barbados,' Yvonne says.

'Yeah, a few times. Though, getting Dad to leave Harrow is like pulling teeth. He hates going abroad.'

Kiama mirrors the laptop to the hotel screen and jumps back on the bed. 'You're going to like this show. Trust me.'

He takes a few pillows and lies down, closing his eyes while the opening titles run.

CHAPTER TEN

BLACKFACE

August 2001

Yvonne

As Yvonne walks into the house party at Emma's new place, she realises she didn't get the memo. Almost everyone is dressed in full school uniform, like the trend for the club night her and Emma went to in their first year. They had travelled all the way from Harrow to Hammersmith, spending £12 each on a ticket, only for Emma to declare it sexist and creepy.

Yet, tonight, every woman is in a pleated mini-skirt and rolled-up shirt. While men are made up like seven-year-olds wearing shorts, caps and comprehensive school ties. And then there's Yvonne, dressed simply in jeans, and a top she deemed flashy enough for a house party. She makes her way around the ground floor looking for a familiar face until she spots Emma in a long white shirt covered in felt-tip doodles, including two smiley faces over her boobs. It's the first time she's seen Emma since she arrived back in London three weeks ago. Her hair is pale pink and she has that post-holiday tan which always makes her look older than she is.

'Dude,' she squeals, running towards Yvonne and grabbing

her for a hug. 'So happy you came.' When she finally pulls away she says, 'Where's your outfit?'

'You didn't tell me it was school disco themed.'

'It's not. The theme is *adolescence* and I texted you about it.'

'No, you didn't, because I would have remembered that, because that's a stupid theme.'

'I'm sure I did. Let me get my make-up bag, I'll draw freckles on you.'

Yvonne shakes her head. 'Don't worry about it.'

'I'm an idiot. I feel bad now. Here,' Emma undoes her tie and puts it around Yvonne's collar. 'You look hot regardless.'

Yvonne pulls a bottle of wine from her handbag and hands it over.

'Thanks.'

They look each other over, while thinking of what to say next.

'Your hair looks different,' Yvonne says, 'the pink, it—'

'Yeah, so dead, right? I was trying to look like Gwen Stefani. I'm going natural once this grows out. So,' she cocks her head, 'welcome. Can't believe it's taken so long for you to come up to my humble abode,' she laughs, but there's some scorn in it. Yvonne had been invited over several times, but between her job and internship she was putting in long hours most weeks. Plus, living back at her parents' she was conscious of spending too much time out socialising, especially after her mum accused her of treating the family home *like a hotel*.

'This is place is huge,' Yvonne says. 'How many people live here?'

'What now? Like, seven. Cool building, right? It's a decon-secrated pub.'

Yvonne laughs.

'What's funny?'

'You can't deconsecrate a pub.'

'No? Anyway, let's find Geoff. He's so excited about meeting you.' She takes Yvonne by the wrist through to the kitchen, which looks out directly onto a brick wall, six feet away. The windowsill is covered with books on method acting and crinkly copies of the *Guardian*, there's also a stick of IKEA lucky bamboo in a red jar.

'Who's Geoff?'

Emma finds a single plastic cup and then pulls a mug from the sink, emptying it of inflated Rice Krispies and giving it a quick rinse. 'Geoff. Dude, wait till you meet him. He's so fucking beautiful.'

'You've been back five minutes, how have you managed to meet someone already?'

'No, I met him *before* I flew to Kenya. Thought I told you? Talk about cure for a broken heart.'

Yvonne winces. Is that really what Emma thinks? That Lewis broke her heart?

'I came to a house party here one night,' Emma says, 'can't remember much of it, except ending up in Geoff's bed. Didn't think I'd see him again, but then a room came up and what can I say,' she tucks a pink wisp of hair behind an ear, 'it was meant to be. Seriously, like sharing a house with guys is so fun.'

Is that a dig?

'You know, he's not my usual type, but I thought about

it a lot when I was away and I've got to choose better when it comes to guys. Anyway, why did you come alone? You're seeing someone, aren't you?' Emma stares until Yvonne recoils. 'Ha, I knew it. I can always tell with you.'

'It's nothing. Nothing serious.'

Emma nods. 'Who cares about having something serious? You know Box Room Bethany is engaged to some freak she met while travelling?' Emma hands over the plastic cup. 'She called me earlier to drone on about true love. But I'm not interested. I want to hear some smut.'

'Can we talk about something else? Tell me about Kenya. How were your parents?'

'Oh, they were fucking awful.'

Yvonne instantly regrets asking about them. 'How was the orphanage?'

Emma's face lights up, 'Life changing. Seriously, life changing. It's really made me think about things, you know. And this backpacks idea, I'm completely over it. Those kids don't need pencils, they need therapy.'

'Therapy?'

'Yeah, the level of mental suffering I saw out there was shocking. They're just little kids and they're dealing with all this shit and have no one to talk to about it.'

Yvonne gasps. 'Yes, I can imagine you as a child therapist. You would be great at it.'

Emma's care for others is her best quality; she would be amazing in a role like that.

'Come on, I'm hardly going to stick out seven years of psychology training,' Emma says, 'I'm talking about setting up a project that puts therapists into orphanages.'

There's some cheering from the other side of the room as two people dressed as Bill and Ted enter, each carrying a box of Stella.

'What do you think?' Emma asks.

'You told me before the kids barely eat two meals a day, is therapy really a priority out there?'

Emma's eyes widen, 'I can't believe you just said that. Especially when you know how important therapy has been to me.'

'Sorry,' Yvonne says, 'I didn't mean to belittle it.'

'Just because they're poor, it doesn't mean that they don't have feelings too.'

'Yeah, I know that. I'm sorry.'

It's still hard for Yvonne to understand something like therapy, the idea of paying someone to listen to you talk about your problems, but then Yvonne has never been short of people to talk to.

'Shit, Yvonne, I have so much to tell you. Can't believe this is only the first time I'm seeing you.'

'Sorry, but Sainsbury's have loads of extra shifts at the moment so I'm taking advantage. I've almost halved my overdraft already.'

'You're still at Sainsbury's? Quit already.'

'My internship is unpaid.'

'Oh, I didn't know that.'

They each take a sip and wince, commenting at the same time, 'This is horrible.'

Emma nudges Yvonne with a shoulder, 'When you start earning those big PR bucks you can buy me a decent bottle. Still, I'm so glad you came.'

'You know, you could come and visit *me*. My mum's always asking after you.'

'I know, I know. I will. But I've been busy too, you know?'

'Yeah. With what?'

'With Geoff and this Therapy for Kenya idea.'

'That name needs work,' Yvonne says and Emma laughs.

'I'm so happy to see you again.'

'Me too.'

'Geoff has heard me go on about you so much. You need to meet him,' Emma looks about the packed kitchen. 'You're going to love him. He's hilarious. Hang on, let me find him.' Emma shoves her way through the crowd, leaving Yvonne with two crap drinks and a roomful of strangers.

'There's some bean chilli on the hob,' an over-accessorised-model-like girl with a plummy accent says. 'It's Hugo's speciality.'

'Oh, I don't know Hugo,' Yvonne says as she tips the wine down the sink. 'I only know Emma. We went to university together.'

'I don't know Emma,' the girl says as she snaps a bread-stick. 'But Hugo always has so many people in and out of here. When I came back from travelling last year, I lived here for a month. Can't remember a single day of it,' she laughs.

'Is he the landlord?'

'No. It's his parents' place. They let him rent it out to friends. You know, *mate's rates*.' Her bracelets jangle as she makes air quotes.

The house is split over three floors and while it's a bit of a ruin, it's beyond Yvonne's comprehension how anyone could give such a thing to their kid.

The model girl is pleasant enough and also sober enough to make small talk with and eventually she pulls Yvonne into the living room to join more pleasant but slightly drunk people. They lie across futons and exchange stories about how they all know each other.

'So,' the girl asks, 'how do you know Hugo again?'

Yvonne excuses herself and heads into the dim hallway to find Emma, who's been gone for almost an hour. The house is a maze, each room filled with smoke, batik-covered walls and yet more futons. The Strokes 'Last Nite' comes on for the fifth time and a group of men dressed as Nineties TV characters mosh about, pushing Yvonne into a small but quiet marijuana-filled room.

'Careful,' she shouts at a tall guy wearing a cloak and full blackface. He apologises and lifts his white palms in defence.

'Arseholes,' Yvonne says as she sits down next to a black girl dressed as Dolly Parton. 'Everyone here is so drunk. It's not even late. How do they manage it?'

The girl laughs then offers Yvonne a beer from under the chair. 'Are you a Drama graduate as well?' she slurs.

'Er, no. I'm a friend of Emma's.'

'Chinese Emma?' the girl asks.

'Chinese? No. Brunette Emma, well, pink-haired Emma.'

'Oh yeah, I know her.' Dolly recentres her wig and frowns, 'Do you mean blonde Emma or the other one?'

Yvonne checks the time. She should leave. She didn't travel all this way to spend time with these people. Just then the blackface comes into the room, the whites of his eyes dart about. He looks over at Yvonne and Dolly and bites his lip.

'So,' Yvonne says, 'it was nice to meet you. If you see

pink-haired Emma, could you let her know—' But Dolly's not listening, too occupied staring at Blackface. He comes over and kneels down in front of them. 'You're not offended by this, are you?' he says as he waves a hand in front of his face.

'You're asking me because?' Dolly says.

He wipes the sweat from his forehead, smudging paint onto the purple bandana around his head. 'I'm not trying to be a black person,' he stretches his arms out and proclaims, 'I'm Papa Lazarou.' The paint makes his teeth appear a weird colour, like he's given them a once over with Tippex.

'Actually, *I'm* offended,' Yvonne cuts in.

Blackface's shoulders dip and he puts his palms up again. 'Calm down. Can't you take a joke?'

'Look up the definition of joke.'

'What does it matter to you anyway? She's not bothered,' he says, pointing at Dolly, whose eyes are now closed.

'You're an idiot,' Yvonne says.

Blackface begins to back away.

'Geoff,' Emma calls as she walks in the room. She grabs him for a kiss. 'Oh, you met Yvonne?'

'What the hell, Emma?'

'Sorry, I got talking. So glad you met Geoff. Do you love him?' She squeezes herself onto the end of the futon.

'That's Geoff?'

'Yeah and trust me, he's not that colour all over.'

'I can't believe you're going out with the kind of person who thinks it's okay to come in blackface to a party.'

'He's not in blackface. He's Daddy Lazarou. I don't know what that is, but everyone thinks it's really funny.'

'Are you serious?'

'I didn't live in the UK through the Nineties. I don't get most of these pop culture references. I don't think it's a racist thing though.' There's a black smear on her cheek. 'Did you try that bean chilli? Gross. I've literally been on the toilet for twenty minutes.' Yvonne sighs and Emma pokes her in the ribs, 'I forget how moody you are at parties. Is it because of the theme? Because you're too cool to do fancy dress now?'

'No, it's not because of the theme.'

'Then, it's because you're not drunk yet. Drunk Yvonne is so much fun.'

'I don't want to get drunk. I've got work tomorrow.' For effect she adds, 'Early.'

'You've got the rest of your life to work. Have a drink.'

'No. And anyway, you're not drunk. You're not even tipsy.' Yvonne takes the cup from Emma's hand and confirms she's right. 'Lemonade? Bit of out of character. At your own party?'

'I got fucking dengue fever in Kenya. I'm still trying to wean myself off antibiotics. You're the only person who's noticed.'

'That's because I know you too well.'

Emma bumps her shoulder against Yvonne's. 'I think in this situation, you need to drink for both of us.'

'Em, if I don't leave now, I'll miss the last tube.'

'So? You can stay over. Crash with me. We haven't even hung out properly yet. My room is on the top floor, the noise won't travel up.'

It would be nice to hang out like that, to stay up all night with Emma sharing a bottle of wine and talking. But this isn't uni anymore and Yvonne's priorities have changed.

'You can be late in one day,' Emma says, 'it's not going to kill—'

'No, I can't be late,' she says, too abruptly. 'My job is important to me. I told you I was only going to show my face tonight.'

'Okay,' Emma says deflated. 'I was so happy that you came anyway. The last few times I've invited you out you've shown zero interest. I was starting to get a complex.'

'That's definitely not true. What have you invited me to?'

'Last week, I invited you to a picnic on the Heath.'

'On a Monday afternoon. Plus, I hate picnics. All that warm hummus and sitting on the grass. Also, I told you, I'm working seven days most weeks.'

'Okay, so no house parties, no picnics and no hummus.'

The sound of someone attempting to play 'Last Nite' on a guitar interrupts the conversation.

'Right, that's definitely my cue,' Yvonne says as she stands up.

Emma stands too and they loop arms as they make their way through the hallway. A couple sit necking on the bottom step and Emma shakes her head, 'Urgh, everything looks so graphic when you're sober.' She pulls a blue pleather biker jacket from the overflowing coatrack and puts it over Yvonne's shoulders. 'Here, the temperature's meant to drop tonight.'

'Thanks.'

'I still have so many of your clothes anyway.'

Yvonne bats a hand away like she doesn't care, but even as she got dressed for this party she felt the loss of all the items Emma had borrowed over the years and never returned.

'Let me know when you're free. I'll come over to your mum's place. I'll bring a pie or something.'

Yvonne smiles at her. 'Good. Also, I'll see you at graduation. Have you ordered your tickets yet? You can't leave it last minute.'

'I don't think I'll go. They should have done it straight after we left. Why have they dragged it out all these months? Plus graduation is for parents really, to feel proud about their kid. And there's no way my parents are going to travel all this way to see me get my 2.2.'

'They might surprise you. But even if not, I'll be there and I'm proud of you.'

They give each other a tight hug and Yvonne pulls away to open the front door. 'Graduation,' she calls over her shoulder. 'You worked for it. Order your gown.'

'Maybe.' Emma blows her a kiss.

Yvonne should never have come tonight. She knew it would feel like this, somehow dishonest. She's not even at the end of the road when she takes her phone out and checks to see if he's sent her a text. She smiles as she opens it, reading his brief message. **Call me when you're done.** It's only just gone half eleven, she should make him wait, at least until after midnight. But then if he's going to invite her over she needs to know before she gets on the tube and loses reception. She loiters outside the station, watching the pickpockets and tipsy office workers, her finger poised on the call button.

Emma was right, it is cold. She zips up the jacket, which smells of cigarette smoke and Tommy Girl, and hits call. The phone rings several times and she prays it doesn't go to voicemail.

He picks up. 'Hey.'

'Hey.' She blushes at the sound of his voice. It's always like this with him, she's not sure if it's because they never see each other enough to get fully comfortable, or if it's something more than that. The way she feels about him is so much more all-consuming than she's ever felt about anyone else.

'How was the party?' he asks.

'It was okay. But I didn't really know anyone there.'

'And how was the Princess?'

Never before has he asked about Emma. She was the subject they both happily avoided.

'Fine,' she answers, her voice small; she doesn't want to talk about Emma with him. It was weird enough telling him whose party she was going to in the first place.

'Did you guys talk?'

'About what?'

He sniggers. About him, that's what he wants to hear, that they compared notes. 'I don't know. Girl stuff?'

'Lewis.'

'No, you're right. It's none of my business.'

'I didn't tell her, if that's what you're asking me.'

There's a silence.

A group of drunken women in tights and trainers ask a station attendant the times of the last tube. She can't stand around here for much longer. She needs to make a decision.

'So,' he says. 'What time do you think you'll get here?'

'I didn't say I was coming over.'

He laughs. 'But my brother's gone out. I'm alone and don't know what to do with myself.'

She sighs. She shouldn't go there. Not now. She shouldn't play it so easy. 'I have work in the morning. At eight.'

'You have work every morning. Come over, you know I always wake you up on time.'

'I've been at a party, I'm tired. What makes you think I want to come all the way up to yours?' She's not even convincing herself.

'You can read a book on the tube.'

She feigns indecision for all of five seconds. 'Lewis, I'm—'

'Give me a missed call when you're close by, I'll pick you up from the station.'

Yvonne sweats under the polyester black gown, while her dad encourages her to pose in various parts of the Barbican. He splashed out on a digital camera especially for graduation and has spent the entire morning directing her, then viewing and retaking almost every picture. 'It's dark in here,' he complains. 'Why is it so dark in here?'

'I think you've taken enough,' Yvonne says firing her older brother a look. 'Nick, please tell him to stop.'

Without taking his eyes from his paper Nick says, 'Dad. No. Stop.'

Why did her brothers bother coming today? All they've done all is look bored and slightly put out by having to take a day off work to celebrate her. It's not like she insisted either.

'I know,' her dad says. 'How about I take one from down here with you all standing up on that balcony? But where's Claude?'

Finally, her mum puts her foot down. 'Enough. Leave them alone. Go and take some photos of the art or something. There is art here, isn't there? Not that I'd be able to spot it. I'm assuming it's all modern. Not to my style, love a bit of Jack Vettriano.'

Yvonne searches for her beeping phone within the folds of her gown. She's been waiting to hear from him all morning. But it's just another auntie congratulating her. Perhaps Lewis has forgotten it's today. Between setting up his new business and caring for his mum, he's got so much going on.

Yvonne sighs and her mum puts an arm around her. 'Is there a particular reason your eyes light up every time that phone goes?'

It's as if everyone stops to stare at her.

'No,' Yvonne says, but she sounds too defensive.

Nick laughs, 'We all know you're seeing someone. Is he here?'

'No. It's nothing, there's no one. I was checking in case it was Emma.'

'Is she the stuck up one?'

Mum squeals. 'What are the odds? We were just talking about you.'

'Look who walked into my shot!' Yvonne's dad calls as he pulls Emma through a sea of black cloaks.

Yvonne moves towards her. 'Weird. We really were just talking—'

Emma pulls away quickly. 'Don't get too close.'

'What's wrong? You're ill?'

'Yeah, don't anyone kiss me,' she says.

'Sweetheart, hangovers aren't contagious.' Yvonne's mum pulls her in for a hug, while her dad drops to one knee and starts taking shots of them.

Emma tips her hat at him, 'We do look stunning in these outfits, don't we?'

'Dad, enough. Where are your parents, Emma?'

'Oh, they're not here.'

'Guess it's a long way to come, isn't it?' Yvonne's mum says. 'Still, I'm sure they're very proud of you.'

'You look so pale,' Yvonne says. Maybe it's her hair, the pink now gone and back to jet black, or maybe she is genuinely sick. 'Is this still from the dengue thing you made up?'

'No, more like a stomach bug.'

Yvonne nods at the acceptable answer, recalling how often Emma got food poisoning, gastro-flu, head colds, rashes and even once, in the first year, impetigo which saw the skin on her hips blaze red and her parents check her into a hotel for a week.

Yvonne's parents become embroiled in a row with Nick about something in the newspaper, the perfect time to move away from them. 'They're driving me mad today,' she tells Emma. 'We're going for a walk,' she calls back, taking Emma's clammy hand in her own.

'God, look at everyone here with their parents,' Emma says. 'I shouldn't have come.'

Yvonne has never met Emma's parents, but often heard their voices on the phone, her dad's short, clipped way of cutting down everything Emma said, while her mum ummed and ahhed in the background.

The tannoy sounds signalling five minutes till the start of proceedings.

Emma straightens Yvonne's cap and gown. 'You better go. Your family look super keen to see you walk across that stage.'

'Are you alright?'

'Yeah, just feeling a bit rough today.' She plucks a leaflet for a rock opera from a stand and fans herself. 'I'm going to look like shit in every photo.'

'What exactly did you eat last night?'

She turns her head away and flaps the leaflet more furiously. 'I need to sit down.'

'What's going on?' Yvonne follows Emma over to a low sofa and kneels on the ground in front, her gown gathers around her legs like an oil spill. Something isn't right. Emma has always been prone to dramatics but this is different, she really isn't herself. 'Talk to me?'

Emma bursts into tears. The last time Yvonne saw her cry like this was while watching footage of the Gujarat earthquake. Emma was inconsolable for days, but then mobilised the student union, through a slave auction, to fundraise almost five hundred pounds.

Yvonne pulls out the packet of tissues she brought in case the day got emotional. 'Are you sick sick?' She braces herself for bad news.

Emma looks up at the crowds as they move slowly into the main hall.

'Em, you're scaring me.'

'I'm pregnant,' she whispers. 'It's my graduation and I'm fucking pregnant.'

Yvonne sinks further down to the floor. 'Shit. No.'

'Yeah. Nightmare. So now you know why my parents aren't here. I told them the other day. Went down like a cup of cold sick.' She plucks a tissue from the pack and blows her nose. 'Sorry, can you move back, the smell of your perfume is making me nauseous.'

Yvonne doesn't move, her concern for her friend's health suddenly turns to anger, 'Pregnant? What were you thinking?'

Emma glares at Yvonne for a few seconds as if gathering the strength to fight back. 'Clearly, I wasn't.'

How could Emma get herself in this situation again? The last scare, in the second year, had been sorted by a quick trip to the chemist. But it really shook her up, the idea that her life could be thrown so far off track by being too drunk to remember to use a condom.

'Sometimes the moment just takes you.' She says it like it justifies everything, like she has some excessive amount of passion that prevents her from being safe.

'But don't you ever worry about other stuff? STDs? AIDS?'

'No. Geoff's a nice guy, he told me he was clean. And when was the last time you met anyone with AIDS? You worry about everything.'

'Geoff, the guy in blackface?' Yvonne pictures a baby in blackface. 'Have you told him yet?'

'I'll tell him when I'm ready. He's not living in the house at the moment, so I haven't seen much of him. Also, I'm not even sure how pregnant I am. My periods have always been crazy.'

Yvonne throws her hands up. 'You must have a rough idea.'

'A couple of months maybe? Three? Though, possibly four.'

'Four months?' Yvonne looks down at her friend's stomach, hidden under the gown.

'It's not even noticeable.'

'Let's just say, this outfit is really working for me. I found out last month.'

A few laughing graduates run past them and into the hall. The proceedings must have started, one of the biggest moments of Yvonne's life, yet here she is, sitting on the floor, feeling guilty that Emma has had to deal with this all alone for weeks now. 'Why didn't you tell me?'

'I tried. I called you like ten times last week. You're always too busy.'

Yvonne gets up from the floor and takes the seat next to Emma, turning to look at her. She doesn't only look ill but also tired, fed up, she looks worn out. Yvonne puts her arm around her friend's shoulders and pulls her in for a hug. Ten times is an exaggeration, but there were definitely a few missed calls from Emma. However, when Yvonne is lucky enough to have time with Lewis, the last thing she's going to do is take a call. 'I'm sorry I haven't been around much recently.' She wants to blame her work, it's the get-out clause no one can argue with. 'But I'm here for you now.'

'Thanks,' Emma pulls away and blows her nose.

Again, a baby comes to mind, all rolls of fat and a blacked-up face. Yvonne tries and fails to hold in a laugh.

'What the hell could be funny right now?' Emma asks.

'I'm sorry,' she says, but can't stop.

'Dude, what the fuck?'

'I keep picturing this little baby in blackface.' She laughs again and Emma throws the balled-up tissue at her.

'This is so not the time for jokes.' But Emma now laughs as well, through her tears until they stop.

'You've got to tell him.'

Emma sighs. 'I know.'

'What are you waiting for?'

'The birth?'

'Em, this is a huge. If you're really going through with this—'

'Of course I'm going through with it.'

As much as Yvonne wants to ask why, deep down she knows, Emma's lonely and has absolutely nothing else going on. Maybe this isn't the worst thing in the world to happen to her. After all, her own mum had Nick when she was twenty; she always says it was the making of her.

Yvonne hands Emma back her mortar board and says, 'I think you'll be a great mum.'

Emma smiles weakly. 'Really?'

'Yeah.' Yvonne can see it then, Emma would be a fun mum, a cool mum, someone who would be more like a friend than a parent. And Yvonne would be there too, buying the kid the best presents for their birthday and taking it to the park when it could walk.

'I thought I'd be a bit older when this happened,' Emma says, 'and also, not alone.'

It's always the issue with Emma, this almost paranoia that everyone is off having a great time with their families while she's by herself. It's even more of a reason why becoming a mum will probably be such a good thing for her.

'You're not alone. In fact, you'll never be alone again.' Yvonne nods down to her friend's stomach.

'You really think I'll be a good mum?'

'Yes. This kid is going to be so lucky to have you.'

A few weeks pass before Lewis gets round to celebrating graduation with her. She was excited in the morning when she received his text message and invite for lunch. But now, as she sits in a high street chain, famed for a food she doesn't even eat, she feels annoyed.

He walks over to the table, and shares out the cutlery and napkins. 'What?' he asks. 'Is something wrong?'

'I feel like I've hardly seen you recently.'

'It's been busy, for both of us. It's a good thing it means we're both working hard.'

It's true that they shared a kind of satisfaction in being busy, in her coming up to the flat he shared with his brother after a long day working.

'You're still upset about the cinema last week?' he asks. 'I'll ask the DVD guy to get it.'

'No, I just wish you would let me know in advance. At least then, I could make other plans.' And stop keeping her evenings free on the off chance he's going to be around.

He places his hand on her knee under the table, 'You're right and I'm sorry. I'll make it up to you. You staying over tonight?'

She tries to hide her smile, 'Maybe.'

'Maybe,' he mimics her laughing. 'Though, I'll need to call you when I'm on my way back. Got to meet some guys in central first; they're really interested in the T-shirts, think this could be it Yvie. They seem really keen and they've got money too.'

'I took a day off work to come and spend time with you.'

'Yeah and we are spending time. But I'm talking about later.'

'When?'

'About four this afternoon.'

Maybe this is how it's always going to be with him, she's so low down his list. She shakes her head, frustrated with herself for jumping ahead and imagining that she'd have the whole day with him.

'I can't get it right with you, can I?' he says.

'I can't believe you think you're trying. Or do I need to learn to be grateful for whatever I get? Some days, not even a text message.'

'I'm sorry I forgot your graduation. I can't keep saying it.'

'Actually, that's the first time you've said it.'

He takes his hand from her knee and looks around the restaurant as if seeking an escape. 'I'm trying to juggle so many different things here. Work. My mum. Give me a break.'

She's pushing him away. Why? Because his business is doing well? Because his mum has sickle cell? 'Sorry. I didn't mean to snap at you.'

'No. I deserve it. I can't expect you to sit around waiting for me all the time.'

But he never really asks her to, she just does it. Can she really blame him?

He leans forward on his elbows. 'Feels like you left uni ages ago. Am I allowed to ask how graduation was?'

'Gowns, speeches, lots of proud parents taking photographs.'

'And was everyone there? All your old crew?'

'Most of them. It's graduation, you only get to do it once.'

He takes a bottle of sauce and screws up his face at the stickiness of the lid.

'I saw Emma. She's pregnant.'

He nods slowly then says, 'I know.'

'What?' Her stomach plummets. How would he know? Is there maybe someone back in Harrow who knows both Emma and Lewis? Someone who would have gossiped?

The food arrives and he thanks the waiter. Then, rather

than looking at her, he dumps the chips on each of their plates.

'I don't get how you know that?'

'Because she called me.' He looks at her, his expression so neutral. 'A couple of days ago.'

'Why would she call you?' Why would he answer?

'I don't know why,' he laughs and looks at the food, as if he expects them to carry on as normal.

'Lewis?' It's embarrassing, the way her loud voice sounds over the generic world music, the way the eyes of others turn towards her.

'You know what she's like. She's a drama queen. She was probably calling up every guy she slept with in the last year to freak them out. Get a bit of attention.'

'But why would she call you? She's been with Geoff, he's her boyfriend, he's been on the scene since before she left for Kenya. And even before then, there was another one.'

Lewis looks up at her, and frowns and Yvonne feels like she's throwing her friend under the bus. But it's the truth, there were other guys. So why did she call Lewis?

He pushes a plate towards her, the chips falling off. 'She's four months pregnant.' He pulls his shoulders up and closes his eyes. 'She's four months. So that's why she called me.'

Yvonne stops and tries to count back the months in her head, but at this moment she can't even remember what month it is now, when they left uni, the last time Lewis and Emma would have been together. Surely it doesn't add up. Yvonne tries to compose herself, to explain to Lewis why he doesn't need to worry, and now that she looks at him properly, he does look worried.

'She never even mentioned you, Lewis. When she told me she was pregnant she said it was Geoff's. Of course, it's Geoff's.'

Lewis sighs. 'Let's hope so. But, I don't know, Yvie.'

'How could you two do this? How could you be so stupid?'

'You think I need to hear this right now? You think I'm happy that one stupid mistake with some random girl could be about to fuck up my life.'

'Your life? What about Emma's?' Poor Emma, crying her eyes out at her own graduation, terrified of becoming a single mum. Yvonne had been calling her often since, letting her know that she wasn't alone and also pushing her to tell Geoff. Now, it's clear why Emma didn't want to.

'What about us?' Yvonne asks, but of course there is no 'us', and Lewis shows this by turning away from her and putting his face in his hands.

It's too much to think of the baby as being Lewis's, but even the idea that Emma thinks there's a chance it is, well, it's enough to make Yvonne stand and step away from the table.

'Please sit down. Yvie, please.'

'I should have known this would end badly.'

He looks up and reaches across the table for her hand. 'It's not ending. It doesn't need to end.'

'It does.' She pushes between the tables and out onto the street.

'Yvie?' he calls behind her.

She walks on, quickly towards the tube station, taking a breath deep enough to make herself dizzy, anything to stop her crying, because if she starts, she won't be able to stop. He grabs her by the arm, 'I get it, okay. I get why it's awkward for us to see each other now. So why don't we wait it out? See what happens?'

'Then what?' she snaps. 'If the baby's not yours we pick up where we left off? But what happens if *it is* yours?'

He squeezes his eyes shut for a second. 'I don't want us to stop seeing each other.'

'We have to. Surely, you can see that?'

He says nothing, but she knows him well enough to recognise each little flinch of his face, she knows he feels it too, that this is the end for them.

'I'm sorry,' he says.

'About which part?'

'All of it.'

And a little part of Yvonne imagines what it would be like to never see Emma again, to cut the friendship off completely and choose Lewis instead. It's a terrible thought, one she wouldn't even consider for any other guy, but Lewis is different, *being* with him is different. She had talked to her brother Claude recently about 'a guy she was seeing'. And as much as she tried to keep it vague, Claude had laughed, put his arm around her shoulders and said, 'I can't believe my little sister has fallen in love for the first time.' It was embarrassing and of course she and Lewis had never said anything of the sort, but she could feel it when she was with him, she knew Claude was right. And now it was all over.

As she walks down to the train station, wiping her eyes, she tries to picture Emma and Geoff's blackface baby, but the image no longer comes to her.

CHAPTER ELEVEN

WAGON WHEELS

October 2020

Yvonne

Kiama stares out of the car window and bites his thumbnail.

'Are you okay?' Yvonne asks.

'Yeah.'

What else can she say? He's obviously nervous; she can feel it in his one-word answers and the way he keeps fidgeting. But then, she's nervous too. Maybe she said too much last night about Cynthia and Neil, or maybe she should have said more. It's so hard to know if she's saying the right thing at all.

Kiama was so self-assured about this trip when they first met, so straightforward about what he wanted to do here and why, but less than twenty-four hours in and he looks unsure, he looks exhausted.

She hadn't even realised he'd fallen asleep last night until she turned to ask him a question. She couldn't bear to wake him, especially after he had spoken about his troubles with sleep, of easily triggered night terrors. She threw a blanket over him and eventually fell asleep down the other end of the bed.

'This area looks quite different to where they lived before, doesn't it?' she asks emptily, because really it looks exactly the same. Neat, well-kept, gated.

'Hmm.'

'I liked their old house. It was quite decadent in a way.'

'Guess so.'

Yvonne's strongest memory of Cynthia and Neil isn't of their shell-shocked faces at the hospital when they were told about Emma's passing, nor of the last time she saw them at Emma's flat bagging her things for the charity shop, but of a dinner at their house in Kilimani. It summed them up, sitting at the dining table, everyone pretending to enjoy stringy rhubarb crumble and small talk about current affairs back home. All this while Kiama tried to suck up his tears at the other end of the table after being scolded for playing football in the corridor. They weren't bad people, but they were terrible parents and even worse grandparents.

'So, what did you end up doing with them the last time they came to England?'

He turns to face her, his big eyebrows knot together, 'What did we do? Erm. We had lunch at their hotel. It was a short visit.'

Like the posting of birthday cash but no card, the hotel lunch was a speciality of theirs. Each time they visited England they always insisted Emma travel into central London to eat out with them, not once taking an interest in seeing where she lived, where she was studying, who her friends were.

The car slows and Joe points up at a series of sandy orange high-rise apartment blocks. When Yvonne originally asked Kiama if he minded them staying in a hotel rather than with them, the relief in his voice was palpable.

'I really liked their old place too,' Kiama says as he looks out of the window. 'It was so big you could always find somewhere to hide.'

Was he scared of them? It's something she's never considered before, something Emma never alluded to in all those phone conversations they had after she moved back here.

'But you got on well with your gran, didn't you? She was always taking you to clubs and swimming.'

'Yeah, she enrolled me in loads of stuff. But what else was she going to do with me?'

The area seems peaceful, serene, yet it's hard to ignore the way each block is peppered with CCTV cameras and warnings of armed patrols.

Joe stops the car and double-checks his phone. 'Yes. It's this one. Phone me half an hour before you want me to collect you.' He hops out to open the door for Yvonne. There's a stain of milk, or perhaps baby vomit, over the right shoulder of his bulky suit.

'You've got a little—' she indicates the stain and Joe's face falls. Inside her bag is a packet of face wipes, she hands one over and smiles. 'See you later, Joe.' She quickens her step after Kiama, who is already inside the block and speaking with the doorman.

In the lift he cracks his neck on each side and Yvonne winces. 'You're too young to creak like that.'

'Huh?' he looks at her blankly.

'Don't be nervous.'

'I'm not. I'm fine.' As the lift doors open she hears him take a deep breath before walking towards his grandfather,

Neil, who is waiting. They shake hands formally and look each other over.

'Welcome,' Neil says. He's older, of course, but also shorter than Yvonne remembers. 'Please, come inside,' he gestures grandly and they take the few steps required through to the small dim sitting room. Cynthia stands by a glass dining table. She is, as always, well put together, her slim body in a patterned dress, face made up and earrings glittering. Neil stands by her side and they take each other's hands; a united front.

'Hi, Grandma,' Kiama says.

She leans forwards to kiss him on the cheek but he takes it as an invitation to hug her. She doesn't quite reciprocate though her arms lightly touch his back before she pulls away and says, 'Come through and sit.'

Despite the brightness of the day, the heavy, floral curtains are partially closed making the room dull. The flat is pokey and modern, the walls white and dominated by Patrick Kinuthia prints of Maasai women. But the furniture, the roll-top armchairs, heavy oak dining table and clunky grandfather clock is the same stuff they had in the big house. *Hoary shit from England* is how Emma used to describe her parents' taste, it was one of the things that annoyed her about them, how outdated and traditional they were.

The clock chimes and everyone laughs nervously.

'Exactly on time for lunch,' Cynthia says. 'Please, sit down. Excuse me, I'll start bringing it through.'

They take their places at the table but Neil stands, switches on a lamp and lights a cigarette. The last time Yvonne visited, he and Emma stood out on the terrace facing each other as they puffed away, their profiles almost identical.

Cynthia lays out several plates of sandwiches and cake and serves tea from a pot. They're so old-fashioned, so English and proper. They must have found it strange to have a daughter like Emma, with her American twang, loud politics and scruffy clothes. They gave her so much to rebel against.

'It's ready now, Neil,' Cynthia says. 'Please, come and sit down.'

He looks at his cigarette and tightens his lips before stubbing it out on an ashtray and joining them at the table.

They quickly flick through all the conversation starters; finding the flat, the flights over, the ease of Dubai as a transfer spot. Then, there is silence.

'I hope you like madeira cake,' Cynthia says, a blush rising across her cheeks. 'It's so hard to find good cake here. The Kenyans over-ice everything.' Her hand slightly shakes as she hands Kiama a small slice.

'Thank you.'

She stops and stares. 'You look very different. Doesn't he?' she asks the room.

'It's been a few years since we last saw him,' Neil says.

'Five. It's been five years. You look more like your father. But then, you've always looked more like his side.'

Kiama nods. 'I get that a lot.'

'There's not much of Emma in your face,' she stops herself. 'Except the odd expression and—'

'So,' Neil interrupts, 'what are you going to do while you're here?'

'We really want to drive up to Lake Nakuru to see the

giraffes. Mum used to take me there, so I wanted to see it again.' He looks down at his plate, 'And Yvonne's never been. You should come along too?'

Neil laughs, 'No, we're a bit past doing that kind of tourist stuff. I never understood why Emma liked it there so much. And there are no flamingos left anymore, global warming put an end to that.'

Kiama laughs in a dry way Yvonne hasn't heard before. 'I guess it is quite a corny thing to do. We also wanted to go up to Hell's Gate and hire bikes.'

Neil laughs. 'Bikes? Have you finally learned to cycle?'

For the first few months after she emigrated, Emma used to moan about her parents. About how seemingly uninterested they were in bonding with Kiama, this loud, sensitive child who turned up on their doorstep. This child who struggled to do any of the things they expected a little boy to do, like ride a bike or swim. But he was a city kid plucked from the only life he knew. He wasn't like Emma either, he hadn't grown up spending a year here and a year there, he had been nowhere and his experiences of the world didn't stretch further than London.

'We don't have firm plans though,' Kiama says attempting to fork a piece of cake, but it crumbles and falls off before meeting his mouth. 'Obviously Yvonne needs to go back for work at the end of the week, but I can change my ticket if...' He looks up.

Neil and Cynthia pass a look as if knowing they should complete his sentence with an offer to spend time together, but they don't.

'So, it's a holiday?' Neil asks.

Kiama puts his fork down and takes a breath. 'No.'

She wants to help him out. But isn't sure herself what the purpose was of him coming back here. Everyone but Kiama returns to sipping their tea, nibbling at the dry cake and pretending the weight of the atmosphere isn't suffocating them. Why isn't there more to say? To catch up on? To ask?

'More sandwiches, anyone?' Cynthia says, piling the crustless bread onto everyone's plate.

'So,' Yvonne tries, 'what made you move from the old place? This is all quite,' she looks around and gestures the room, 'different from the house you had before.'

'We didn't need all that space,' Neil says. 'All those bedrooms. It's only the two of us.'

'What about Purity?' Kiama asks.

'Purity hasn't worked for us for a few months now.'

'You didn't tell me that,' Kiama says, loud enough to get everyone's attention.

'I'm retired. We don't need that kind of live-in help anymore. Also, we're not entitled to a pension out here so we needed to cut unnecessary expenses.'

Kiama sits straighter in his chair. 'Unnecessary expenses? She's been with you since Mum was a kid. She's family.'

'No, she was an employee and she did a bloody great job, but we no longer need her.' Neil returns to the cake, squashing the crumbs onto his fork with a finger.

'So who does she work for now?' Kiama asks to which Neil shrugs. 'How can you not know? She lived under your roof for years and then one day you send her packing.'

'That's not what happened,' Neil laughs. 'She got another job. I just don't know where.'

'Well, why not?' Kiama raises his voice. 'Why aren't you bothered about keeping in touch with people?'

Neil looks at him over his glasses, 'This isn't about Purity, is it?'

The clink of teacups against saucers stops. Yvonne desperately tries to think of a subject change.

'She's gone full time for the charity her sister was involved with,' Cynthia says.

Neil turns to his wife. 'Really? Well, there you go then, Kiama, mystery solved.'

'Which charity?'

'It's a big one. They link people on gap years with local hospitals and schools. You know the sort. She runs one of the houses where the volunteers stay, but I don't have a clue where. I could find out for you?'

Neil laughs, 'Why? It's irrelevant.'

'No, it's not,' Kiama says. 'Maybe I want to know. Maybe I care about what happened to her.'

Neil throws his fork on the plate. 'You think you're the only one who lost something? That you're the only one finding all this difficult?'

Yvonne tries to catch Cynthia's eye, but she stares down at her ruined lunch.

Kiama rises from the table. 'Excuse me,' he says and walks off into the hallway.

Everyone looks at each other and Neil mumbles, 'He's still the same, always so quick to judge, to tell us what we should be feeling, how we should be acting, who we should employ.'

'I think,' Yvonne says, 'that he's still a bit jet-lagged.'

'You don't need to make excuses for him. We know what

he's like. We get it on the phone too. Whenever we talk, he's always in a huff about something. It's hard to know how to speak to him. And that's why we don't bother.'

'But this isn't like when you talk on the phone,' Yvonne says. 'He's made a big step coming all this way. He really wants to reconnect with his life here, with both of you.'

'I can't believe how much he looks like Lewis,' Cynthia says again.

Why does she care so much about who he looks like? It doesn't make him any less Emma's child just because he doesn't share her features. 'He's your grandchild,' Yvonne says, 'can't you at least try and be a bit more understanding?'

No one speaks.

'Why did he ask you to come with him?' Cynthia asks finally.

Yvonne looks to the hallway for Kiama's return. 'For moral support, I guess. He was scared.'

'But we're here. We've always been here for him. We could have offered him all the support he needed,' she says, now tearful.

Neil stiffens. 'He hardly knows us, Cynthia.'

'He hardly knows me either,' Yvonne says. 'I've not been in his life for years. But he asked me for help and now he's asking you too. He's still so young, don't you think we owe it to him to try and find out what he needs from this trip, why he's chosen to come back here?'

Kiama appears in the doorway and they all watch him, waiting to see what he'll do. If it were Emma, she would have probably shouted and sworn, or fled, but Kiama simply stands there and says, 'Yvonne showed me some photos of

Mum, at a school or orphanage. She was surrounded by kids and she looked,' he stops and shakes his head, 'she looked really happy. Do you remember where she worked when she used to come back for the holidays?'

'Emma? Work?' Neil says with a laugh, his Yorkshire accent seeping through.

Cynthia puts a hand on her husband's arm. 'No, she never worked. But she did spend time helping out at an orphanage. Don't you remember it, Neil? It was one of the countryside ones Evivo used to support through its outreach scheme, I can't remember where exactly. It was right after she finished university.'

'Oh,' Yvonne says, 'yeah, she looks about twenty-one in the photos, so that makes sense.'

'So she was pregnant with me when she was there?' Kiama says.

Yvonne had never thought of that. 'Yes, I guess so, in the first few weeks of it.'

'Yes, *that* summer,' Neil says, as he stands up and opens the small glass door on the grandfather clock. 'And what about you? I know you're not studying, so what are you doing?'

Kiama attempts to stand tall. 'My dad runs a business, so I spend a lot of time helping out there.'

Neil winds the clock then shuts the window. 'And?'

He seems to physically shrink under his grandfather's scrutiny.

'Well, I wanted to do this first, come here, and then, when my head's a bit clearer I can really think about what I want to do.'

'And how long are you expecting to think for?' He sits back at the table and holds his empty plate in Cynthia's direction.

'I,' Kiama stalls, 'I can't answer that. I don't know how I'll feel when I get back.'

'And I guess you don't feel the urgency because you have your money now.'

Kiama looks at Yvonne quickly and then turns away.

He'd never mentioned any money to her. But she was aware that things didn't quite add up. He readily admitted the trampoline park was doing bad business, yet he was able to go on countless holidays and pay for his own flight here. If Kiama had a trust fund Emma would have told her. Perhaps there was a life insurance payout when he turned eighteen? Or a compensation payment of some kind?

'It's for your life, you know?' Neil says over his glasses, speaking to Kiama as if it were only the two of them.

'I know.'

'Not to be pissed up a wall.'

'I know,' he says more firmly this time.

'Do you? Because, ever since you turned eighteen you just seem to be spending it on nonsense. Your own dad said the same to me. Your mother died for that money, Kiama.'

'I know,' he shouts.

Cynthia jumps and her teacup clatters on the saucer.

This is the Kiama Yvonne remembers, quick to fly off the handle, to shout or burst into tears. 'Sensitive' is how Emma used to describe him, claiming she didn't know where he got it from. Surely Neil remembers this too, so why provoke him? Why be so brutal? He had a mean streak, Emma said so herself many times and now Yvonne was getting to see it.

She tries to catch Kiama's eye, to give him some reassurance that she's on his side, but he doesn't look at her.

'I'm struggling to understand why you've come here. Why you thought it would be a good idea?' Neil says, his voice sharp and abrasive, the same way it would sound when Emma put him on loudspeaker.

Yvonne wrings the napkin in her lap. This has all gone so badly and she's not sure how to fix it. Kiama looks tearful; she needs to get him out of here, away from this situation.

'I want to go to the place,' he says. He looks at Yvonne and she nods slightly to encourage him. 'The place where Mum died. If you would come with me I think that would really—'

'No,' Neil says. 'I honour my daughter by remembering all the places she loved and lived. Not where she died.'

'I don't need this,' Kiama grabs his bag from the floor and leaves.

The front door slams a few seconds later.

'It's so much for him to deal with,' Yvonne says, 'being back here, seeing both of you again.' It feels too much for her also.

'He shouldn't have come,' Neil says. 'I don't know what he's trying to prove.'

'He's not trying to prove anything,' she snaps. 'When he approached me about coming to Kenya, I couldn't think of anything worse. I didn't understand why he wanted to do it. But I get it now. I get why he needs to do this. Why can't you?'

Their silence says it all.

How can they not jump at this chance to build a relationship with him? He's the only part of Emma they have left.

The clock ticks loudly, marking each second of silence,

each second Yvonne continues to sit with *them* rather than go after Kiama. 'You know what? I'm going.' She rises from the table and throws her napkin to the chair, suddenly desperate to find Kiama, to make sure he's okay. It's part of her role here after all, to protect him. 'I'll leave you two to enjoy your lunch.'

Outside the sun is oppressively bright and burns the back of her hand as she uses it to shield her eyes. On the other side of the street he sits on the kerb, his back curled, head in hands. He doesn't look up as she approaches, nor as she sits down next to him.

Two security guards in khaki slow on the other side of the road and stare at them curiously before moving on.

'It must be hard for them, Kiama. She was their only child.'

He keeps his head lowered.

'I'm on your side,' she says.

'Really? Cause it didn't feel like it back there.'

He's angry with her.

'They're always so hard.'

'They were hard on Emma as well.'

'I don't want to talk about it. I don't want to talk about any of it.' He unzips his bag and pulls out a multipack of Wagon Wheels. 'That cake was disgusting.' He rips open the packet and says, 'Five items British expats miss.'

'What?'

'I was racking my brains about what to bring my grand-parents when I read this expat blog about the five food items Brits miss when they live here.' He passes her one and she experiences a moment of nostalgia as she smells the fake chocolate.

'Don't know why I even bothered,' he mumbles. 'I should have just brought myself more T-shirts.'

'You bothered because you're thoughtful.' It's a trait in him she wasn't quite expecting, maybe because her own teenage nephews are all narcissists, or because of how self-centred Emma could be. 'I don't know where you get it from. Emma was such a typical only child, no offence. She would do things like eat my favourite flavour of crisps and decide they were disgusting. Or use up the last of the milk in her cereal and waste the cereal. She would give me her last pound if I asked for it, but that's the thing, I would have to explicitly ask for it.'

He laughs a little, out of courtesy perhaps, and she wonders if she read the situation wrongly, if this is maybe exactly the opposite of what he needs to hear. She can't eat anymore of the chocolate. 'Did these always taste like this? It's like eating a Styrofoam cup.'

He pulls the Wagon Wheel from her hand and finishes it off.

'Emma used to tell me how much her parents wanted a baby, about how they tried for years before getting pregnant with her. I always thought they never deserved her. They don't deserve you either.'

He tries to smile at her.

'I know today wasn't what you were hoping for.'

'No. But, if I'm honest, it's exactly what I expected. I should have known from how they were on the phone.'

'It's easy to say that now. But look, we don't have to stay here. Let's say goodbye and leave.'

He doesn't budge, except to get another chocolate.

'Kiama, you can't sit here eating a six-pack of Wagon Wheels.'

'Is that a challenge?' He stops eating and presses his palms into his eyes.

Yvonne pulls a tissue from her bag and hands it to him. 'Look, fuck them.'

He mock gasps. 'Did you just say *fuck*?'

'I'm annoyed for you.'

'The fiery redhead is coming out.'

'I know you wanted to build some sort of relationship with them again, but you don't need this. You don't need *them*. If you want to go back to the hotel now, I'm fine with it.'

'Thanks,' he says, 'yeah, I want to go back.'

The sun is the hottest it's been since arriving, yet Kiama refuses to put sunblock on while they wait for Joe to drive back to Kilimani. They sit on the kerb for twenty minutes bickering about whether Wagon Wheels are a cake or biscuit, and then see Cynthia running from the block of flats.

'I've been watching from the window,' she says, her face flushed. 'I didn't know if I should come down or not.' She looks back up at the block, for Neil maybe. 'I'm sorry about how things have gone today.'

Kiama stands opposite her.

'This is not how I wanted it to be with you. But here,' she presses a piece of paper into his hands. 'I'm sure Purity would love to see you.' She kisses him on the cheek. 'Take care. Bye, Kiama.'

CHAPTER TWELVE

BIRTH

January 2002

Yvonne

The pub is empty and Yvonne spots her straight away, scooping a slice of lemon from her drink to eat.

'Wow,' Yvonne says as she gets closer.

'Dude,' Emma says as they hug.

'Wow,' Yvonne says again, 'you are so… '

'Pregnant? No shit, Sherlock. Here, I ordered you a house white. You should have seen the look that bitch barmaid gave me, as if I'm going to drink it.'

Yvonne slides in next to her and continues to stare. 'It's weird because from the back you look normal.'

'I am normal.' Emma picks up the wine glass and sniffs before handing it over.

'I don't think I've ever seen someone so pregnant before. Your boobs are enormous.'

'I'll take that as a compliment.' Emma adjusts her bra. 'My skin is itching like mad. No one tells you it's going to itch. Do you have any cream on you?'

Yvonne takes a bottle of hand cream from her bag and Emma hoots, 'Elemis? Someone's making money.'

'Hardly, I got it in a goodie bag at a work Christmas party.'

Emma pulls up her top and rubs the cream into her stomach. 'Ah, this feels good though. Can I keep it?'

Seeing her belly exposed and taut, with the red marks running up the sides, is shocking. This whole pregnancy thing feels like it's happened so fast. While they'd managed to catch up on the phone regularly, spending real time with each other had become rare as time went on. It wasn't only that Yvonne made excuses not to see Emma, it was also the other way around, with Emma constantly backing out of plans. 'She's embarrassed,' was Yvonne's mum's theory. She had told Yvonne to back off for a bit, but the months flew by so when she saw Emma at Box Room Bethany's engagement party last month, it was a shock. Emma didn't last long before getting fed up with questions about her pregnancy, plus she was never the kind of person who enjoyed socialising without a drink.

'So,' Yvonne says, 'I'm sorry about the party last month.'

'Why?' Emma asks, but it's clear from her expression she was expecting this apology.

'I felt like I should have left early with you.' Yvonne had watched Emma leave and known that a good friend would have left early with her, but it was Yvonne's first night out in ages and she was having fun.

'Don't be silly. It was a shit party anyway.'

There's no point going over it, Yvonne will only end up apologising for every night out she's not invited Emma to, for not shutting down the gossip from the others when they joked about if Emma's 'baby daddy' was Two Minute Terry or the new guy she lived with or some random she'd met in Kenya over the summer.

'So, where's all the baby shopping you were coming to get done?'

'They deliver it. I'm pretty much sorted now. Though I felt like a teen mum in there, everyone is so old.'

'I can't believe you're splashing out on John Lewis.' Yvonne looks at the Nursery catalogue on the table. 'Can't you get all this stuff from Argos or somewhere a bit cheaper?'

'Dude, the only way my parents know how to deal with this situation is to chuck money at it, so I'm letting them.'

'They're not being supportive?'

'They're being themselves.'

Yvonne pulls a box of reduced Christmas chocolates from her bag and Emma takes a handful.

'Where's your work?' Emma asks.

'Across the road.'

'And how's it going?'

'It's great. Really busy. But so great.' Yvonne checks herself. No one wants to hear her brag about her job. 'Of course I'm still only a junior publicist and the pay is terrible. Though this *will* be my last month at Sainsbury's.'

'Finally.'

Emma eats four chocolates in a row while explaining how many extra calories she can have a day. It's strange to see her like this, so pregnant and knowing. Also, the idea that inside her could be Lewis's baby makes Yvonne uncomfortable. It's strange to think how at graduation Emma had talked about Geoff as being the baby's father, but hasn't mentioned him or anyone else since.

'Stop staring at them,' Emma complains.

'At what?'

'My stretch marks.'

'Oh. I didn't even notice.'

'Lying bitch,' she says pulling down her top. 'Anyway, I've been covered in them since puberty. A few more don't bother me.'

'You didn't have stretch marks before.'

'What are you talking about? The backs of my legs are covered in them. I look like a cat scratching post when I've got a tan.'

Yvonne pictures Emma's pre-pregnancy body, her habit of leaving the bathroom door open as she took showers, the way she'd call you into her room for a chat then begin stripping off. Emma's complete lack of self-consciousness meant that everyone had seen her body a hundred times over.

'But then, you've never been the most observant person in the world.' Emma tips her head back and closes her eyes. 'Crazy how fast time goes, right? Old people are always saying shit like that. But now I realise it's true. Graduation was months ago. I feel like I blinked and missed Christmas and now I've got a baby coming.'

'Yeah, I guess so.' Again, no mention of Geoff, or Lewis. Why is Emma keeping so quiet about this? 'How have you been finding things? Being on your own?'

'I'm not on my own. I have friends.'

Friends. She means those on the large roster of names she keeps dropping, one of the many new people she's met since Yvonne began devoting all her time to work. Last night, on the phone, Emma wouldn't stop going on about Andrea and Cat and Frankie and Seb and Margot. All these people stepping in and following the pregnancy, in what should surely be the father's place.

'Friends can only help so much,' Yvonne says. 'What happens when it arrives?'

'*It?*' she laughs.

'The baby. You'll need more than a few friends to help raise a baby. And what about the birth? That's going to happen soon. You need someone with you for that? Will your mum will be there?'

'She's on holiday. Singapore.'

'How can she be on holiday when you're this far along?'

'Because I promised to keep my legs shut.'

'And she trusted you?'

They both laugh.

Emma opens the box again and picks out the strawberry heart, Yvonne's favourite. 'You're more stressed than me about this.'

'You don't even like having your blood taken and now you're about to give birth.'

'There's nothing I can do about it, is there?'

Yvonne feels her phone vibrate in her bag. She slips it out and reads the message from her boss, asking what time she'll be back at the office. She thought that by arriving an hour earlier for work this morning, it wouldn't matter if she actually took a lunch break.

'You need to get back?' Emma asks.

Yvonne has managed to stay away from Emma during this pregnancy, out of sight, out of mind. But now, seeing her like this, vulnerable, it's different. 'No, not yet.' She puts her phone away.

'What are you working on anyway?'

'Nothing interesting. Show me what you ordered?' Yvonne flicks through the catalogue, passing images of cots and pushchairs, searching for something to say. 'Are you going for one of these prams, with the big wheels?'

'Big wheels? Oh shut up, I'm not going to baby talk with you.'

'Why not?'

'Because it's boring. You're not interested. I'm not even interested. Tell me what you're working on.' Emma pulls the catalogue away and throws it behind them. 'Please?'

'Nothing really, it's all pretty standard stuff. Doing product launches, meeting journalists, going to networking events.'

'Why do you never invite me to any of these events?'

Yvonne nods towards the belly, 'Because you're eleven months pregnant.'

'Yes, pregnant, I don't have to be quarantined. I'm surprised you were even up for meeting me today.'

Yvonne offers Emma the last chocolate. 'I'm doing long hours at the moment. I hardly see anyone. It's just how it is.'

'How it is when one of you is up the duff.'

That's the reason she tells herself, everything else is stuff that doesn't register, no one needs to know about it. The whole Lewis thing was a mistake and she wishes she never met him. She thought after they broke things off it would get easier, but the very opposite happened. She found she couldn't stop thinking about him, missing him, wondering if there was a way 'around' the situation, if perhaps he was right and they could 'wait it out' to see if the baby was his. But Yvonne knew herself too well, she could feel how much she was getting attached to Lewis, how her feelings for him were growing stronger as time went on. The idea that they would carry on as normal only to then break things off when the baby arrived was stupid. They needed a clean break. And that's what they did. No calls, no texts, no cross-over friends reporting back on how the other one was feeling.

'Anything else going on with you?' Emma asks. 'You seeing anyone or are you becoming one of those women married to their work?'

Yvonne shirks away. 'No, I'm not seeing anyone.'

'Don't blame you. Most men are pigs. I'm going to make sure I bring my son up right.'

The idea of a son hits Yvonne, it humanises the pregnancy. 'Your son?'

'Yeah. I thought I told you it's a boy.'

'No. You never told me. Wow. A son. Do you have a name in mind?'

Emma laughs, 'Finally, you ask?'

'What's that meant to mean?'

'Let's be honest, you haven't taken that much interest in this pregnancy.'

'Didn't I just ask you about pushchair wheels?'

Emma smiles and shakes her head. 'You never ask me anything about the actual baby though.'

'Because it's not here yet. I'll get interested when it, sorry, *he* arrives.'

'Kiama,' Emma says.

'What?'

'Kiama. That's my son's name.'

Yvonne looks at her and squints, 'I'm sorry, what?'

'Key-ah-ma,' she says again slowly and loudly.

'Get used to repeating it.'

'Cheeky bitch. It's Kenyan. It means, *light of life*.'

Yvonne bites her bottom lip, 'Hmm, not sure about it.'

'Good job you don't have to be. Look,' Emma points to her stomach, at a bulge of movement under the stretched skin, 'he loves it.'

'Isn't it a bit weird that he'll have a Kenyan name, but isn't Kenyan?'

'I don't think so. He's going to spend time there. I can't wait to take him.'

'Yeah, I can imagine you, baby strapped to your back, boarding a plane to Kenya.'

'And why not?'

Yvonne looks again at the massive stomach. 'You really are huge. Is this going to be an unusually big baby?'

'I fucking hope not. Though, I think he's going to be really long. All knees and elbows. Like a baby giraffe. Can't believe I've got another four weeks, as if my stomach can stretch anymore.'

'Is Geoff tall? I can't remember.'

Emma rubs at the corners of her mouth and starts fussing with the empty chocolate box.

Why won't she just say it? Why won't she tell Yvonne that she called Lewis? That there's a chance, a small one, that he's the dad.

'Geoff's not been very supportive, has he?' Yvonne asks. This is it, Emma's cue, but she says nothing. 'Em?'

'Yeah?'

'Don't take this the wrong way, but how comes you're so

146

sure it's Geoff's? I mean, he wasn't the only one you were sleeping with in May. Was he?'

'I never slept with Two Minute Terry, if that's what you're insinuating.'

'I'm not talking about Terry.'

'Yeah, well of course there was Sweetboy too. But he can't stand me. I can't have a baby with someone like him.'

'You don't get to choose though, do you?' Yvonne wants another wine, no, more than that. 'I can't believe you slept with them both unprotected.'

'I know you're too perfect to understand, but sometimes people do get carried away. Geoff knows I'm pregnant. So does Lewis. You think either one of them has made any effort with me? Called me? Asked how I'm feeling?'

'You can't expect them both to hang around you waiting for the birth. This is life-changing for them as well.'

'You're taking their side?'

'No.' But she is, of course she is; Lewis looked terrified at the prospect of becoming a dad.

'Why are you mad at me?' Emma asks.

'I'm not.' But she is, she's raging and she can't tell Emma why, she will never be able to tell Emma why.

'I know having a pregnant friend doesn't fit into your new lifestyle, Yvonne. But you could at least support me a little bit.' Emma puts her coat on, doing up the top three buttons, leaving her stomach sticking out. 'I can't believe you're being so judgemental about this. You're meant to be my friend yet you're looking down at me because you'd never do something as stupid as sleep with two guys within a month of each other.'

'I'm not judging you. Em, please, sit down. We all make mistakes, I've made mistakes. If you knew—' She could tell her right now, she could blurt the whole sorry thing out and then it would be done.

'I'm about to have a son and I can't have someone around who's going to look at him like he's a mistake.' Emma shakes her head and walks off.

Yvonne stands on the street across from the flat Emma had moved to last month. The whole journey over she has thought of only one thing, what the baby will look like. It's stupid, but she wishes she could see Kiama alone first, at least then she wouldn't have to hide her shock at realising he's Lewis's or her relief that he's Geoff's.

Her phone rings and she answers immediately, glad of a distraction, especially from Claude.

'Hey, Sis. You at Mum's?'

'Mum's? No, I'm in north London.'

'Shit. I've locked myself out of the house.'

It's taken her almost an hour to get to this spot, but that includes walking at a slower than usual pace due to carrying the giant bean casserole her mum palmed off on her as she was leaving. And also Yvonne's been dragging her feet; of course she knows she should visit Emma and the baby, but there's also a part of her which is not quite ready to confront it.

'I could come back if you're really stuck, but it'll take me a while.'

'Where did you say you were?'

'Angel. I'm going to see Emma.' She looks up at the flat again and turns away. 'And her baby,' she adds.

'Oh shit, she had it?' Claude tuts. 'She's so young. Crazy.'

'She's twenty-one, it's not *that* young. You know Mum had Nick when she was twenty?'

'What are you trying to say, Yvonne? It's too young. Believe me.'

'You're preaching to the choir,' Yvonne says quickly. She doesn't even understand how people fit going to the gym into their lives, never mind children. It's definitely not something Claude has to worry about with her.

'Girls are always saying they don't want babies, until they hold one.'

'When have I ever been interested in babies?' Yvonne has always liked children, but never saw attraction of small babies; one was brought into the office last week and while she had a look and joined in with the coos she wondered when she could go back to her desk without being seen as rude. She simply didn't feel much around them, and didn't expect to with this one either. But say if he looked like, well, it was hard to think about. Would she be able to tell by looking at him? Probably not, every baby she had ever seen looked pretty similar. Of course it would help if she had seen Geoff without a coating of black paint on his face.

'Right, I'm going to call Nick.'

'You sure? I could come back and see Emma another day. There's no rush.' She wonders if Emma has already spotted her.

'Why don't you want to go? You two fall out?'

'No. Not exactly. But, well, it changes things when one of you has a baby.'

It was Claude who looked after her when she went home after breaking up with Lewis, Claude who brought her cups of tea and sat with her on the bed while she cried her eyes out. It was Claude who told their parents to back off when they kept asking why she was so sad. Obviously, he knew she'd had her heart broken, but he never asked for more information than that. She wants to tell him every little part of the story and has done for the last couple of months, but it still feels too raw, too painful and most importantly it's unresolved. Today could change everything.

'Yvonne, look, Mum's trying to call me. Go and see your friend but remember, don't go getting attached to that baby, alright?'

'Alright.'

'See you later.'

Yvonne walks across the road to Emma's new flat and presses the bell. She shifts the blue gift bag and juggles the weight of the casserole dish from one arm to another and tries to fix her face into a neutral expression. They hadn't spoken after their argument in the pub, Yvonne didn't know what to say, who was meant to apologise. But none of that mattered after she received the message to say Kiama had been born, early but well.

She presses the bell again and listens to footsteps on the other side.

'Wow,' Yvonne says as Emma opens the door, babe in arms.

'Hi.' She smiles brightly but her face is pale and even slightly gaunt.

'Hi. Oh my God. Look at him.' Yvonne walks slowly into the hallway. 'He's tiny. I thought he was going to be massive.'

'I know, I think it was just a load of water in there or something.' Emma kicks the front door shut, 'Can you hold him, please?'

She's wearing her striped fleece pyjama bottoms. The ones she used to wear when they didn't top up the heating in their student house. 'I really need the loo.'

'Oh hang on, let me put these things down first.' The flat is small, the front door opening straight into the living room and kitchen. 'I need to wash my hands. I've been on public transport.'

'No, don't worry,' Emma uses one hand to pull the gift bag and drops it in a pile with others, she then puts the casserole dish on the kitchen counter. 'Germs are good for him. He needs germs. Here,' she says passing him and running off to the bathroom.

'What the… ' Yvonne whispers as she stands in the middle of the room, her coat still on, trying to make sure she doesn't wake the baby, still as a doll. She sits on the slouchy sofa and manages to slide one arm out of her coat at a time. The baby doesn't move but at one point he yawns, which is the only way Yvonne knows he's even alive. He doesn't obviously look like anyone and she places her finger next to his cheek to check if he's white, but it feels a little wrong, so she stops.

'Sorry. Got a bit of a post-partum situation happening,' Emma says as she finally comes out of the bathroom. Yvonne's heard from others that this is one of the things that happen when your friends start having babies. All of a sudden, frank discussions about bodily fluids, functions and damage become regular conversation. This will be especially bad with Emma, who, in general, has no filter.

'Please, before you say anything, you know I'm squeamish. I don't want a birth story, okay? I just can't hear it.'

Emma laughs as she fills the kettle. 'Don't worry, he was C section.'

'Oh, okay.'

'So sadly, no horror story from me about ripped fannies or—'

'Emma, shut up.'

She laughs again and returns to the sofa. 'Dude. Your face, that's the first time I've laughed in days.' She kisses Yvonne on the head. 'Thanks for coming over. I wasn't sure if you would.'

Yvonne looks down, back to the baby, a slight whistle from his nose with each breath. She's overcome by a need to apologise for the argument, for everything she implied that day, for calling the baby a mistake. He's anything but.

'Kiama came the day after we met up. Weird, right?'

'Maybe it was all that reduced Christmas chocolate.' Yvonne strokes his head gently. 'The name actually suits him.'

The kettle clicks off and Kiama wriggles and stretches out his tiny arms.

'Here we go,' Emma says. But instead of taking him, she gets up. 'Do you want peppermint or chamomile?'

He's fussing now, emitting little cracks of sounds, a cough and cry at the same time. Yvonne bobs him up and down, humming till he stops and opens his eyes, which are a dark turquoise. 'His eyes are a strange colour, aren't they? Bit like yours? Greenish? Or are they blue?'

Emma comes back to the sofa with two mugs and a bottle

under her arm. 'Here, do you want to give him this? Don't judge me, I tried the breastfeeding thing and my nipples bled for days. I take back everything I ever said about Nestlé.'

He takes the bottle easily, opening his eyes fully to stare up at Yvonne. 'Oh, he's lovely,' she says, shocking herself by sounding like her mum. Is this what Claude meant? That even though you claim to not like babies along comes one particular baby who's so cute it kicks your clock into ticking. 'Look at his little hands and the fingers,' she says splaying them. 'How do you even cut these nails? And he's got such a wrinkly forehead,' she laughs. 'But these eyes, intense. Does Geoff have blue eyes?'

'Does it matter?' Emma snaps. She looks away then busies herself moving around the gift bags on the floor.

Maybe Yvonne shouldn't have come today. Perhaps Emma's not ready for visitors.

'He got a lot of presents then,' Yvonne says, keen to keep talking.

'Yeah, even Box Room Bethany and her boring fiancé sent something.'

Emma pulls up a little denim dungaree and sleeveless shirt set. She flips over the Tesco price tag with the red reduced sticker on it and they both laugh. It's good to see her lighten up. 'At least Kiama has an outfit ready for when he joins the Village People,' Emma says as she chucks it back in the bag. 'I'm getting fed up of all this blue shit everyone's bought. Look at it,' she indicates over to a clothes horse covered in tiny blue vests. 'I'll never buy him anything blue.'

'Glad I didn't either,' Yvonne says. 'Except for the gift bag.'

'Oh, sorry you brought something, didn't you?' Emma leans over and pulls out a stuffed giraffe.

'Sorry, my mum did say you're probably inundated with soft toys, but it's a baby giraffe and I thought it was so cute.'

'Thanks.' Emma smiles and holds the toy to her face. 'It *is* cute.'

The silence is heavy for a few moments and then Emma says, 'The midwife told me that mixed-race babies have this spot at the top of their bums, a Mongolian blue spot it's called.'

It is his baby then. Kiama is definitely Lewis's child.

'Don't make that face,' Emma says. 'Look it up. I checked him, it's true. He's light now, but the colour will start at his fingertips and spread.'

The idea of Lewis spreading across the baby is unsettling. The bottle is almost drained and this time when she looks down at Kiama, into his large unusually coloured eyes, it's obvious. Immediately she hands him back. 'Here, let me go to the loo.'

The windowless bathroom smells of mould and white vinegar. It's depressing. This whole flat is. She's never been here before but there are some familiar things. The pound shop shampoo they both swear by, a bottle of Tommy Girl perfume and the Hard Rock Café beach towel Emma has had since uni. But there are also a few drab beige bras drying over the shower rail, far from the lacy stuff Emma used to indulge in, and then there's the baby bath turned on its side in the main tub. How has so much changed so fast?

When Yvonne comes out, she puts the casserole dish in the freezer. 'My mum made you a kidney bean casserole.'

'She's so amazing. Thank for her me.'

'She says she'll come and visit you one day. You know how much she loves a baby.'

'I can't believe your mum did this four times. It's horrific. I already know I'm never having another one.'

'Really? After how much you've complained over the years about being an only child. How have your parents been by the way?'

'Obviously they got here late. Then, they refused to stay in the area as the hotels weren't good enough. But they come around every day, mostly to reiterate their disapproval.' Emma walks over to the kitchenette and hands Kiama back to Yvonne, shaking her arms once free of him. 'Are you shocked?'

'By what?'

'That he's Lewis's. I thought you would have mentioned it as soon as you saw him.' Emma's voice drops, 'I know it probably sounds stupid, but even when I was carrying him I knew. I could feel it.'

Yvonne exhales, it's almost too much for her. 'He's spewing up a bit. Do you have something I can cover my clothes with?'

Emma pulls a tea towel from a cupboard and tucks it under Kiama's chin.

'You remember Julie? Lewis's mum? I think you met her at the barbecue. She forced him to visit yesterday. But he didn't say anything, just stood off to the side looking shell-shocked. Though, Julie brought me a tub of beef stew. Said I needed to start eating red meat so I could build up my iron stores.' Emma rolls her eyes then heads back to the sofa. 'She means well, I guess. She actually caught me at a pretty rough time. It was embarrassing crying in front of her. But then, I'm crying in front of everyone at the moment. Lewis probably didn't even notice, not that he'd care either way. And you know what the worst part is?'

Yvonne's not sure she wants to hear anymore.

'That even after all this, how he treated me last summer, how he's ignored me the last few months, if he wanted to get back together and make a go of things, I would.' She leans her head back and Yvonne notices the thinness of her friend's skin, the darkness under her eyes. 'But he can't stand me. The way he looked at me yesterday was like I'd ruined his life. I don't think he's going to be much of a dad to Kiama.'

Emma carries on talking while Yvonne closes her eyes until the threat of tears passes. Only when she knows her voice will be normal enough does she ask, 'How can you be sure? Babies change so much. He's really fair.'

'Look at him, Yvonne, he's a mini Lewis.'

Yvonne nods and Kiama begins to fuss. She tries to hand him back but Emma doesn't take him, only holds out another bottle. 'Maybe he wants to eat again. I don't know.'

Yvonne switches position and he stops.

'I know he's a baby,' Emma says. 'It's what he's meant to do, but I didn't realise how much he would cry. Except when people are around of course, then he usually lies quietly like some sleeping angel, he must like you enough to let his guard down.'

Yvonne feels her arm going dead, not from the weight, but from the awkward way Kiama is lying. 'Is it okay that he's so curled like this? Don't you need to keep their spines straight or something?'

This time Emma says nothing. Her eyes are bloodshot and she looks as if she's about to doze off. Yvonne sits next to her and stares. 'Em? You okay?'

'You were right, Yvonne.'

'About what?'

'I shouldn't have tried to do this on my own.'

'You're not alone.'

'I am. I'm completely alone.'

'You're not. You've got your parents. Your friends.'

'They've all run a mile. Of course they have. I would do the same.'

'You've got me. Stop it. Stop crying.'

Emma dries her face on a sleeve.

The washing machine spins out. She looks at it and huffs. 'You okay with him if I pop out for a bit?'

Yvonne panics. 'To where?'

'Just on the balcony, for a cigarette.'

'I thought you gave up.'

'I did, but I need one vice.' Emma pulls on her big parka jacket and climbs out onto the small balcony; there she sits on a little plastic stool and smokes cigarette after cigarette. She's out there for so long that when pigeons land on the rail they jump down and peck by her feet.

Kiama purrs and falls asleep. Yvonne looks at a book titled *Your Baby and You, First Steps*. 'You've got a lot of targets to meet,' she whispers and he stirs slightly, his wide eyebrows wriggling. It's funny to think of him having Emma's overly animated eyebrows.

When Emma comes back in her eyes are red, she's been crying again.

'Should I be worried about you?' Yvonne asks.

'No. It's nothing. Hormones. It makes you go a bit crazy.' She washes her hands in the sink, but the smell of smoke sticks to her pyjama bottoms and coat. 'You want to give him back to me now?' She puts out her arms. Yvonne flexes her fingers; she can feel them prickling. 'No. He's fine, he's asleep. Let's not rock the boat.'

'I understand if you need to leave. You've got other things to do, right? Your work?'

Yvonne shakes her head. 'No, it's not important. I want to stay with you.'

'You don't have to.' Emma cries again.

'I know that. But I want to.' The washing machine beeps and Emma flops her head in her hands.

'He's got your eyebrows,' Yvonne says.

'You don't have to pretend to be enamoured. I won't be offended if you have somewhere else to go.'

'Stop it. Close your eyes for a bit.'

Emma nods, then puts her hands in the pocket of her coat and curls her legs underneath herself. Just before she closes her eyes she says, 'Sweetboy76, who'd have thought it would lead to all this?'

CHAPTER THIRTEEN

KINDRED KENYA

October 2020

Kiama

It's lunchtime and the streets are busy, Kiama keeps checking behind himself, slowing to allow those walking too closely to pass in front. Overly risk-aware, that's what Dad always rips him for. Even though they both know what it's rooted in.

'Why is it so busy?' Yvonne asks. 'Does no one here work?' She looks again at the directions to the Kindred Kenya offices she had taken down this morning when she finally managed to get through to the number Cynthia gave.

Kiama flips around quickly as someone bashes into his shoulder, but it's just a lady rushing for the bus, she doesn't even look back or apologise. He decides that he hates Nairobi, its crowds and dirt, its noise and traffic. Even the memories from before are crappy.

He remembers being here as a kid and sitting in a hotel restaurant with Mum and one of her expat friends. They spent a whole afternoon talking and laughing with each other while he sat in the middle, desperate for something off the dessert trolley, which Mum refused because he had been 'playing up' earlier that day. Then there were the few times he came into the city with Purity on errands. That was the worst, trying to keep with her as she weaved through the crowds, her little legs powering quickly through the streets she knew so well. He was always terrified of getting lost in such a big, unfriendly place and would grip the strap of her handbag.

In the first few weeks, before he began school, he spent a lot of time being dragged around with Purity. Mostly visiting family, the street children she called 'son' and women who looked a hundred years old and called her 'Auntie'. She seemed to know everyone.

'I can see the sign,' Yvonne says, 'there, at the end of the street. Finally.'

Kindred Kenya is wedged between a newspaper kiosk and a hairdresser's. They push open the door to a steep staircase, which smells of frying food and burnt sugar, and go upstairs.

A lady in a green head wrap greets them at the top. '*Habari Gani*,' she says.

'Hi, we spoke to Makimei on the phone this morning,' Yvonne says, putting on the voice she probably uses at work. When he first called her, it's the voice she used, one so bland and neutral he wasn't sure if he had the right person.

'Yes,' the lady nods. 'Through here, please.' She directs them to an office with a pin board covered in thank you cards, newspaper clippings and faded pictures of mostly white people in hospital scrubs. In the middle of the board is a large print-out which says, '*Imagine if you are heard each time you speak. Now live accordingly.*'

'I don't get it,' Kiama says. He picks a small easel up from the desk and reads, '*Imagine if you are watched each time you dance. Now live accordingly.*' He laughs. 'This is surely not her office?'

There's a poster sellotaped to the wall, a basket of fruit in the centre, surrounded by swirly writing. '*Imagine if God was to taste—*'

The door opens and they fall silent.

'Hello, guests. *Karibu, karibu.* I apologise for taking so long, I had an incident to deal with.' He introduces himself as 'Makimei, the CEO of Kindred Kenya'. He gestures towards the pin board, 'Have you seen?' he smiles, 'All the success stories from our work. Last year we placed many international volunteers at hospitals, schools and orphanages across the country.'

The head-wrap lady comes in and lays a tray of drinks and snacks in front of them.

Kiama gasps at the plate of deep-friend dough triangles, 'Mandazi.' He knew he recognised that thick, sweet smell. Purity never prepared them as Cynthia said they made the house smell for days after, but she'd often buy him a bag from a street vendor.

Yvonne slips out her anti-bac gel but Kiama goes straight in.

'Stop. Eating. That.' Yvonne mouths while Makimei speaks with the lady.

'I got a stomach of steel,' Kiama whispers before taking another bite.

The lady leaves and Makimei says, 'So, how can I help you? You want to volunteer? Perhaps, at one of our health clinics? Or the new clinic for the handicapped?' He sits in his chair and makes a full turn in it. 'We also have two orphanages under our umbrella, with over forty children.'

'We called earlier about Purity,' Kiama says.

'Oh? I misunderstood. Explain to me, please?' He leans his head back and closes his eyes.

'Purity worked for my grandparents. She helped raise my mum, who grew up in Kenya. Then when I was younger, we moved back and she looked after me as well. She's always been part of my family. We know she works for you now. And we're trying to find her.'

'Ahem, ahem,' Makimei says nodding.

'So where is she?' Kiama asks.

'I will show you something.' Makimei unlocks one of his desk drawers and removes a large laptop. 'Please, Miss, do eat the last one.'

Yvonne picks up the last mandazi and forces a smile.

Makimei leans close to his screen and squints while Kiama takes it from her hand and eats it in two large bites.

The laptop is turned to face them and when its screen finally loads it's crowded with icons over a distorted screensaver of Makimei holding a trophy, his smile stretched too widely. He opens a folder and shows them some photos of buildings in rural areas. 'Here,' he says, 'Purity runs the volunteer house in Kikuyu. It only has three volunteers this month, all from the United Kingdom. But there will be more in the New Year. And this is the hospital where they are working.' He flicks through more images, each one filled with more poverty than the last.

'Sorry,' Yvonne snaps, 'where is Purity?'

'In Kikuyu.'

'Great. And that's nearby?'

It would be amazing to show up at her work and surprise her. They could convince her to leave early and spend the afternoon together. On Saturdays when Cynthia would be out shopping Mum always used to talk Purity into leaving the housework and going for lunch with them. There was a little café at the end of their road run by locals. They'd sit on the plastic chairs roadside and throw crumbs to the giant cockerel that used to peck about. Maybe they could find that same place again.

'Kikuyu is two hours away,' Makimei says.

'Two hours?'

'Purity is looking after one of the young volunteers who is unwell. It is not possible for her to travel into the city today.'

Of course she is, she was always looking after everyone. She looked after him when he got sick during his first month in Kenya. Maybe it was from the water or change in food. Mum was ill too and sleeping all the time. So it was Purity who was cleaning the puke from his hair and stroking his head till he fell asleep.

'You should visit her in Kikuyu,' Makimei says but Yvonne shakes her head. 'Actually, I'm not sure we want to make that kind of journey. We can phone her instead.'

'Yes, of course.'

Makimei writes on a notepad and rips the page out, but it's only an address. 'There is no phone there at the house, not for many weeks now. But I will leave a message with a friend of mine who lives locally. He can get word to Purity that you are coming.'

'Thanks,' Kiama says. What's two hours anyway? They've already travelled over twelve to get here.

They thank him and head back out.

'What an absolute waste of time,' Yvonne says.

Kiama's mind immediately jumps to how he could help at the hospital; it's like kismet or something, they were meant to meet Makimei today, they were meant to hear about his work. Kiama can't wait to tell Purity that he's going to start supporting the charity she works for.

Yvonne backs into a shop doorway before taking Kiama's phone and calling Joe. 'He'll be ten minutes. He asked us to wait outside the mosque,' she says.

Kiama pulls his sleeves down over his hands; he'd rather not have to wait around in an area like this, it's got a vibe about it he doesn't quite like. 'Why can't he come and get us here?'

'He can't stop on this road, look at the traffic. I can see the minaret, it's not far at all.'

They walk towards the mosque only to find it's closed down, its yard filled with an old cement mixer and surrounded by metal fencing.

'This can't be right,' Yvonne says, calling Joe again and getting no answer. 'Perhaps there's another mosque somewhere. Let's ask someone.'

'No way.' Because that's the number one rule of being lost, you tell no one. He stares down at the paper Makimei gave, the messy scrawl of an address. Suddenly it becomes about more than just finding Purity, he wants to find the hospital too and the school or orphanage Mum worked at and the children in the photos, he wants to find it all.

'I knew this was a bad idea,' Yvonne says.

'You wish you never came?' he asks her. 'You wish I never called you?'

'No, I mean coming *here* today, to see some con artist.

And he could see you coming a mile off. Maybe he knows about your money too.'

Kiama turns his back to her and threads his fingers through the metal fence. He's surprised it took her this long to bring it up.

'Tell me what Neil meant about your mum's money?'

He leans into the fence. Of course he was going to tell her at some point, especially as he'll probably need her help to get rid of it, but he was biding his time and didn't want her to think it was the only reason for the trip.

'Kiama, what's going on?'

A car honks at them, it's Joe.

'I'll tell you on the way.'

'On the way where?'

'To see Purity.'

Joe honks again and Kiama heads towards the car, Yvonne follows behind.

'*Jambo*,' Joe says with a yawn.

The doors click and Kiama leans forward, 'Joe, can you take us to Kikuyu?'

He laughs. 'Kikuyu? You do not want to go there. There is nothing there to see.'

'This is ridiculous,' Yvonne says.

Kiama puts the paper in Joe's hand. 'How long would it take to get to get there?'

'It will be a two-hour drive, but not in this traffic. Maybe three.'

'You can't be serious? Why do you want to go there so badly?' Yvonne asks. 'You want to go and look at poverty so you can feel better about yourself?'

'I want to see Purity,' he repeats.

'So, we can arrange to meet her for lunch later in the week. I'm sure if we give Makimei a bit of cash he'd soon find a phone number for her.'

'Why wait? We can go and see her now. Or would you rather plod off to Lake Nakuru like a tourist?' Like the people his granddad hated so much, the ones who came to Kenya only to tick it off their bucket list. Is that what she wants?

Cars honk behind them and Joe clears his throat. 'Please, I must drive somewhere.' He adjusts his mirror and looks into the silent backseat.

'Two hours is nothing, Yvonne. You know how much I want to see her.'

'And what if we go all that way and she's not there?'

'Then, at least we can find out more about this charity. Come on. What would my mum do in this situation?' It's a cheap shot, but it's all he's got right now. Also, he knows the answer. He can almost feel Mum's hand on his back pushing him in the right direction.

Yvonne throws her arms up and sighs. But he needs to hear her say it, to confirm that she feels Mum as much as he does. 'Tell me,' he says.

'She'd go. She'd travel to see Purity.'

'Exactly,' he says, leaning back satisfied he's doing the right thing.

Joe was right, they hit traffic and over two hours later they are only just winding their way out of the other side of Nairobi. Joe yawns so often that Kiama leans over and asks Yvonne to take over the driving.

'There's been an accident,' Joe says. He steps out of the

166

car and talks to a group of other frustrated drivers, each of them shouting over the bonnets of their stationary cars.

'I knew something like this was going to happen,' Yvonne moans. 'We're going to be stuck here for ages.'

A bright orange minivan, packed with commuters, edges out from behind them and drives up onto the pavement. The other cars beep at it and the drivers shout abuse.

'The driving in this country is unbelievable,' she says as Joe gets back in the car. He turns on the radio, tuning in to a news station, and shakes his head. 'A coach has crashed. Up there, exactly where we need to go.'

It's another hour before they move again and Kiama feels his stomach growl, yet doesn't dare voice it. Finally, the city falls away and the roads become more rural; it looks more like the Kenya he remembers, the one he used to explore on weekends with Mum. There was a man back then who would drive them out to places like this and they would walk until his legs felt wobbly. Mum used to make fun of how little energy he had when the activity involved doing something outdoors. 'I'm doing you a favour,' she'd say, 'helping you burn off some of that energy.' Cynthia was always making comments about him needing 'fresh air' and 'a walk', like he was a pet. He wonders if Mum missed their pre-Kenya weekends as much as he did, the ones spent entirely inside, lying on her bed watching TV or sitting on the sofa filling reams of paper with sketches, while she chatted on the phone.

They pass a small night market full of stalls lit by oil lamps and bars with corrugated iron roofs. As they pass through the centre of Kikuyu the roads switch to smooth then to completely unpaved as they drive up a blackened hill. Joe stops the car at a set of duck-egg-coloured metal gates and honks the horn.

'Is this the house?' Yvonne asks. 'I'm desperate for the toilet.'

Kiama crosses his fingers, hoping for the best.

Joe gets out and tries the gate, but it's locked, although the house is ablaze with lights. 'Are they expecting you?' he asks through Yvonne's open window.

'No,' she says, raising her eyebrows at Kiama, 'they're not.'

Joe bangs on the gate several more times, but there's still no movement.

'Let's get out,' Yvonne says, 'I'll go behind a bush if I have to.'

'Classy,' Kiama says following her. Then the gate flies open.

'Hi,' a girl, probably not much older than him says. 'Sorry, we didn't know more people were arriving tonight.' She's got some sort of accent, Irish or Scottish. He can never tell.

'Hi. We're here to see Purity Collins?' he says.

'Purity? She's at the hospital. One of the volunteers has malaria so she's sticking with him.'

Another young white woman comes into the yard, this time English. 'Alice? What are you doing? Close the gate.'

'No, it's fine, he's a westerner,' she whispers to her friend. Noticing Kiama shift she explains, 'I only saw your driver and got a little scared, you know how it is.'

'Do you know when Purity's going to be back?' he asks.

'Not tonight, that's for sure.'

'Where is the hospital? Is it far?'

Yvonne takes him by the arm. 'No way,' she says, 'wherever it is, we're not going.'

'Oh, you can't get there at night anyway,' one of the girls says. 'You might as well come back in the morning.'

'I knew it,' Yvonne says.

Joe leans on the gate with his eyes closed, he truly looks like he's napping standing up.

'Do you want me to see if I can get a signal and call her?' the Irish girl asks.

'Please,' Kiama and Yvonne both say in unison.

They follow the girls through the yard and into the house. The front door opens into a large living space, full of sofas and armchairs flung with blankets on one side and a large dark wooden dining table on the other.

'By the way, I'm Delia,' the English one says, 'and this is Alice.'

'I'm Kiama. Purity used to work for my grandparents; she was my nanny so I'm really keen to see her while I'm back in Kenya.'

'Ah,' the girls both coo.

'Are you hungry?' Delia asks. 'Purity cooked before she left this morning and we were just heating it up.'

'Yes, please,' Kiama says, excited at the prospect of eating food cooked by Purity. He used to love her food, especially her desserts, rhubarb crumble being his favourite. 'We've hardly eaten today.' He sits at the long table while Yvonne excuses herself to use the bathroom.

'I've got reception,' the Irish girl says, hanging the phone slightly out of the window, 'this section of the house is like the magic circle,' she laughs. 'It's ringing, but you need to lean out here.'

Kiama balances on the chair and takes the phone. 'Hello? Hello Purity? Is this you? It's Kiama.'

169

There's a pause, filled with rustling on the other end then a voice answers, 'No, no, it's you.'

Hearing her voice again, it's like being punched in the chest. 'Yeah. It's me. I'm in Kenya,' he laughs.

She gasps, 'Where? Where? Tell me.'

Delia and Alice look on expectantly, smiling.

'I'm at your house,' he says, aware of his audience.

'In Kikuyu? No. I do not believe you are there. You should have telephoned me first, at the hospital.'

'Yes,' he says, feeling stupid, 'I didn't think of that.' She's right, he should have asked Makimei for the hospital phone number, but instead he decided to sit in a car for four hours, dragging Yvonne and Joe all this way and for what? To have a phone call with her?

'How is your grandmother?' Purity asks. 'Is she well? And your grandfather?'

'Yeah, good. They're both good.'

'And your father? Is he well? And your nana in England?'

It's suddenly too much, too many questions, too many people to account for. Yvonne comes out of the bathroom with her nose turned up. She flicks water from her hands then wipes them on her jeans. She's going to lose it with him. 'Purity, are you coming back tonight? I know it's late, but I'd love to see you.'

'Yes,' she squeals, 'yes, you will stay at the house and we will see each other tomorrow. Sarah will make you a bed. Bring her for me.'

'Sarah?' He's sure neither of the girls is called that.

Delia runs off to another part of the house.

Purity switches to a local dialect with someone on her side of the line, her voice sounds serious and direct.

'Kiama?' Yvonne steps forwards but he shakes his head and pretends to still be listening to Purity talk, but all he hears is a gabble of words and phrases that mean little to him other than to confirm he won't be seeing her tonight. A small Kenyan woman steps forwards and gestures for Kiama to give her the phone.

Kiama plasters a smile on and faces Yvonne. 'So,' he says, 'looks like we're staying here tonight.'

'We can't stay here,' Yvonne whispers.

'But we can't drive back either. Look at the state of Joe.'

Upon hearing his name Joe steps into the house, rubs his head and yawns.

'We can get a cab back to Nairobi.'

The girls, who have been listening in, now laugh. 'We only know one driver here but he's on an airport run tonight. And when we arrived, we were strictly advised to avoid using unknown local drivers,' the Irish one says.

'Okay, but we can't stay in this house,' Yvonne says. 'Not all three of us. Is there a hotel nearby?'

The other girl makes a chopping motion at her neck, 'Yeah, but I definitely wouldn't call it a hotel. It's more a place for *locals*.'

'Or for when you have a really heavy night and Purity locks you out. It's fine for your driver though.'

It feels wrong, but Joe actually smiles when Yvonne suggests he stay elsewhere. 'A hotel? What a blessing. I will sleep so peacefully,' he says while bringing in their bags and taking his leave.

'When Purity worked for your parents did she make you eat rice and beans every night too?' the prettier of the two girls, Delia, asks as they sit down to bowls of rice and lentil curry.

'Did Purity really cook this?' It's nothing like the food she would have made at his grandparents'.

'Yah,' the girl says. 'Why, what did she used to make you?'

'Pies, pasta, curries. English food.'

Delia drops her fork on the table, 'You're telling me she can make *normal* food?'

Sausage and mash, roast chicken, lasagne. Of course Mum hated it, she would sit there eating some grey meat replacement she got imported while Cynthia topped up Kiama's plate and delivered a lecture about how unhealthy it was to raise a child without meat.

'She used to make a greatest beef Wellington ever.'

The girls exchange a look.

'So why are we being subjected to this crap every night?' Delia says, looking down at her plate.

'Maybe because you're on a charity project,' Yvonne says, 'I can't imagine there's lots of money floating around to serve the volunteers a leg of lamb.'

She's being kind of rude to the girls, but then it's been such a weird day, a long one too, and now they're here, in the middle of nowhere and completely off plan.

'These girls,' Yvonne says through gritted teeth as they clear the table with Sarah, the house girl. 'They're completely vapid.'

'You're mean,' he says, because while he doesn't quite understand the word, he's sure it's something bad.

After dinner Sarah beckons them up the stairs to their room for the night. The room is large with three sets of bunk beds, stripped bare, a rolled-up duvet and pile of sheets at the end of each one. There are two small windows, covered in blue bars.

When she leaves, Kiama throws one of the sheets on the bed and roughly tucks it in.

Yvonne nudges him out of the way and takes over, 'Used to fitted sheets, are you?'

He shrugs, not about to expose himself as someone who let his nana make his bed. Ever since she died he's simply slept with the sheets hanging down. 'Thanks.'

'No problem.' She pulls out the huge toiletries bag she drags about and heads to the bathroom while he lies back on the bed and looks for something to watch on his laptop. The tiredness is there, but not yet overwhelming enough to knock him out.

Even though they had both complained of jet lag last night, they ended up staying up late again, eating room service pizza in Yvonne's room and watching local TV. He can't believe he fell asleep on her bed again, for the second night in a row. He doesn't even remember drifting off, just waking up and crawling back to his own room.

Yvonne comes out, 'The water's freezing here,' she moans, 'I've run out of face wipes and had to wash my face with a bar of soap. I'm going to look five years older when I wake up. I'm not sure I'll ever get to sleep here.'

'Me neither.' When he was little and couldn't sleep Mum would let him in her bed. She'd stay up watching TV or reading the papers, while he wriggled about under the sheets till he passed out. Is that why he's sleeping so soundly next to Yvonne? It's too weird to think about.

'And there are no towels,' Yvonne says.

'I brought my microfibre towel,' he says, happy that it's finally come in useful.

She waves him away then bobs about the room, lifting the curtains and checking outside, pulling the corner of the mattress up and the sheets away, going on about an article she read on bedbugs. He lies back on the bed and closes his eyes, but when he does his head fills with images from the last two days; the uneaten crumbly cake at his grandparents', the photo of the stained hospital beds, the oil lamps at the bars with corrugated iron roofs and Mum, everywhere. Mum telling Cynthia and Neil to 'back off', Mum pointing out the roadside shacks and smiling, Mum searching for ways to help the women forced to give birth on dirty beds.

She's everywhere here.

CHAPTER FOURTEEN

SOHO

March 2009

Yvonne

Yvonne rolls the desk chair into the bathroom of her flat and props her phone up against the taps. 'How hard can it be?' she mumbles as she plays the YouTube clip again, the one in which a useful-looking all-American man explains how to lay grout. It looks easy enough, it's just that it's a beautifully crisp Sunday morning and there are a hundred other things she would rather be doing. Such as returning to that Pilates class she swore she would attend weekly or exploring her new area or even lying in bed sleeping off her sixty-hour week. But this, wearing an £80 tracksuit while doing DIY, is the real homeowner experience.

Yvonne rubs her eyes with her wrists, her fingers already covered in grout. She doesn't want to have to do this. She wants to be able to call someone and have them sort it all out for her. But the bathroom smells of mould and there's no money left.

The clip pauses as her phone rings. It's Emma.

'Shit.' Why does Emma always call at the very worst

moment? Always, when Yvonne is on deadline, or being driven mad while babysitting her nephews or unable to pick up the phone because her fingers are covered in crap. She rubs a hand on the towel and moves the phone to the floor where it vibrates around in a circle. On and on it goes. But then, Emma has always been persistent.

Yvonne answers. 'Emma?'

'Babe. How long does it take to pick up the phone?'

'I'm busy,' she snaps. 'I'm doing DIY.'

Emma laughs. 'DIY?'

'Yes. Unfortunately.'

'How are you settling in? Housewarming on the cards yet?'

Yvonne picks at the duct tape holding the bath panel in place. 'No chance. I've got my family over later so let's see if I survive that first.'

'What, all of them?'

'Mum, Dad, Nick and Claude. I don't even have enough mugs for them all. But they'll only stay long enough to judge the place then head down to the pub. I was going to cook but—'

'You don't know how to?'

'Exactly. Why are you up so early on a Sunday morning?'

'Kiama has football. Can you believe I'm now one of those women standing on the side of a pitch freezing my tits off while he misses the ball?'

'Kiama? Playing football?' Each Christmas Yvonne contributed to his collection of expensive football kits yet she had no idea if he played or watched. 'Is he any good?'

'You have *met* Kiama, haven't you? He's not the most active seven-year-old boy in the world.'

Yvonne laughs as she tries to remember a time when she had even seen him run.

'He's so shit at this.'

'You can't say that about your own son.'

'This is not his skill set. He's too clumsy and he hasn't grown into his body yet. Why is he so much taller than every other boy his age?'

'Must be all that good home cooking you do.'

'Shut up. So, what's going on? You're hiding out in the flat, painting walls and stuff?'

Yvonne rolls back on her chair and checks the three tiles she's managed to lay. They look slightly wonky. 'This flat is eating up all my free time.'

'Free time? You've not had free time since 2001. When are we going out? I really want to have like a big night out.'

'How big?'

'I'm talking lining up the shots big, getting chucked out of an Addison Lee big, whose-house-party-is-this-anyway big.'

Yvonne shakes her head while Emma continues to list their past escapades. She's a bad influence, no matter how much Yvonne swears a night out will involve a meal, a few drinks then home it always ends up messy. It's almost like Emma makes Yvonne revert to the person she used to be, the one who existed before deadlines and projects and grout. Yvonne misses that person sometimes.

'So, homeowner, are you up for it?'

The tiles are definitely wonky. Yvonne drops the spirit level in the bath and admits defeat. 'Yeah, sounds good. Sort a babysitter and send me some dates.'

'Actually, Dickhead has stepped up his game a bit recently.

Kiama is staying over there most weekends at the moment, so I'm free whenever.' A whistle blows in the background and there's shouting. 'Fuck, Kiama just got hit in the face with the ball. I think he's alright though. No, hang on, I'm not sure. Shit.'

'I miss him. Tell me him he can stay with me when I finally get the spare room done.'

'Oh no, he's got a nose bleed. I've got to go. Say hi to your parents from me. Speak later.' Emma hangs up and Yvonne smiles, glad to have something other than work or family commitments to look forward to, then she realises the time.

Her family arrive en masse two hours later, bringing with them a plant she will fail to keep alive, a Nigella Lawson cookbook she will regift, and noise, so much noise. It doesn't feel this intense at the family home, where there's the space to sit in the kitchen or pair off into the garden but here, in her flat, it feels tight.

'This is wonderful,' her mum says. 'I'm so proud of my little one, finally starting to grow up.'

Yvonne takes the backhanded compliment and in an act of domesticity empties a packet of biscuits onto a plate.

'Though it is a shame that you're not actually *making* a roast,' her mum looks down at the oven, still uninstalled four days after being delivered.

'I don't even have worktops, so I'm hardly in need of an oven. But look, the cupboards are in.' Yvonne rubs a hand across a cupboard door then demonstrates opening and closing it.

'You know what you need?' her mum says and Yvonne,

knowing exactly what comes next, squeezes on a tea towel to stop herself from screaming. 'A man. Then you'd get all this DIY sorted. Why don't you get your new boyfriend to help you?'

'Why don't you go and sit down, Mum? I'll bring the teas through.'

In the living room her brothers complain about the lack of seating in the flat, but then what did they expect? That she buys a place big enough to accommodate all of them on the rare occasion they manage to coordinate a group visit.

'Good job Del's not coming with the kids,' Nick says as she hands him first a coaster, then a mug of tea. 'Don't think you could fit another person in this room. Is there any sugar with this tea, Sis?'

Yvonne sighs.

'There's still a bit to be done, isn't there, love?' her dad asks.

'Yes, but it all costs money. If only I knew a carpenter,' she says putting a hand on Claude's shoulder.

He pats her hand sheepishly, 'I will help, but I have so much work on at the moment and I can't say no to any of it. I promise I'll make time for it soon.'

He's just had his third kid, so she doesn't want to pressure him, but still it's frustrating the way he can't give her one evening of his time. Nick is the same, except he's too busy 'looking for work' to help her. He's wearing his battered, muddy trainers inside. Once she gets the wooden floors done properly she will insist everyone remove their shoes at the door. She might even invest in slippers for guests. Anything to ensure the flat stays perfect and clean, far from the worn grubbiness of the house she grew up in.

'Your phone keeps going,' her mum says.

Yvonne checks, it's a message from Emma with dates.

'Look at you smiling, is that Jaden then?'

It was unfortunate, that one of the first times Yvonne was out for the day with Jaden, she would bump into one of her brothers and his wife in Borough Market. It didn't take long for every member of the family to hear the news. Her parents have been pestering her to meet 'the new man' ever since.

'So,' Mum says with a smile, 'was it *him* then?'

'No, actually, it's Emma.'

'Oh, how is she getting on?'

'She's alright.'

'Has *she* met anyone yet?'

No matter what achievements Yvonne shares with her parents about herself or friends, the only thing of any real importance is if they're in a relationship or not.

'She's a single mum. She's not got time for that.'

Mum tuts, 'Is the dad a bit more involved now?'

'A bit, I'm not sure.'

'Is Emma the rich one?' Nick asks.

'Hardly, she lives in a council flat in Stratford.'

'But isn't she that white African girl? The stuck-up one?'

Yvonne ignores him and again relishes in how good her decision was to buy such a small sofa.

'I feel bad,' Claude says. 'I've got my tools in the van, I can do a few bits now,' he says standing.

'Don't be silly. I didn't mean it.'

But he doesn't sit back down and follows Yvonne as she goes in search of sugar.

'Claude, seriously don't worry about it. I know you're busy with work and the baby. My bathroom can wait.'

'I'll get round to it one day, I promise, alright.'

She finds a few loose packets of sugar in a drawer, 'Here, will you take this through to Your Highness?'

'Sure. By the way, why's Mum going on about meeting Jaden? I thought you broke up with him?'

'No,' she says, annoyed he remembered her saying that. She wasn't serious about breaking up with Jaden, simply exploring the idea. But things seemed a bit better now, especially since everyone at work found out about them.

'You're leading the poor bloke on,' Claude says. 'You said he was boring.'

'Did I?' She knows she did and sometimes he *is* boring. But in a way it's what she's been looking for, a serious, steady man who's not into playing games.

'You've been seeing him for months,' Claude says, 'if you were that serious I would have met him by now.'

'I'm a big girl, I don't need you to vet my boyfriends for me.'

'No, because I think you've already made up your mind about him yourself, haven't you?'

'Beer o'clock,' a voice shouts into the open office.

It's not even five. There's still work to be done, work which can't wait. But like ping pong and break-out rooms, finishing work early on a Friday to drink together is part of the 'culture' here.

Jaden sits on the desk, reaches over and switches off Yvonne's monitor.

'What do you think you're doing?' she asks.

He smiles at her. 'Work is finished.'

'No, it's not. I still have a few bits left to do.' It blinks back on.

Jaden sighs, but doesn't move.

'Can you not sit on my desk, please? It's so inappropriate.'

He snickers, but she's genuinely uncomfortable with it. They had kept their relationship quiet at the start, but it's hard to hide anything in this place, especially an office romance. Now it's out in the open, it doesn't matter how frequently they have lunch together, leave at the same time, or the fact that he likes to sit on her desk each time he passes, but there's a tiny part of her which wishes she could take it back. It has only been three months and now it all seems way too official and permanent.

Jaden stands as Hannah from accounts walks over and tuts, 'Now, now, Mr Slater, we have to work on those desks.'

'See what I mean?' Yvonne says. But Hannah has been the worst of the lot since they went public with their relationship, never missing an opportunity to taunt them.

'Yvonne,' Jaden says, 'it's Friday.'

She tries to focus on her emails, but it's impossible with him eyeing her like this.

'I think we should go for one drink with everyone and then head off somewhere together for dinner?'

What can she say? Of course she wants to spend time with him, but she also doesn't like the way it's becoming so regular, so expected. She thinks about the dust and debris waiting for her back home and compares it to an evening in a restaurant with Jaden, to another night at his immaculate flat.

'Okay, give me ten minutes to finish off.'

'Ten minutes,' he says as he joins the office exodus. 'I'm timing you.'

Almost forty minutes later Yvonne is switching off her computer and reapplying her make-up. She looks fine for after-work drinks, but not really for dinner, especially to the kind of place Jaden likes to go.

She walks across to The Endurance. It's busy outside, packed with crowds enjoying one of the first bright evenings of the year and pretending the cold isn't bothering them. She hopes they're not standing outside, as she's underdressed for the weather and her feet are already cold in their sandals.

'Excuse me,' she pushes her way through the entrance and towards the back of the pub where the work lot usually congregate and then she sees him.

Him.

Right there, in her pub. It can't be. But when she looks again she sees it's undeniably Lewis. He stands at the bar, nodding at the person in front of him. In his hand there's a glass which he raises to his mouth then stops and laughs at something the other person says.

Yvonne gasps and turns the other way. It's weird because he had been on her mind ever since her mum made that comment about him not helping Emma out and she hadn't known how to respond to it. It's been easy to push him from her mind and in the last eight years she's rarely thought of him, except in those moments when Kiama has made a certain expression or showed a touch of arrogance. But Lewis and that whole messy situation was such a long time ago.

'Yvonne,' Hannah shouts, 'I've been calling you. It's lovely outside, come on.' Her colleague takes her by the arm and leads her back outside to the group, who have lined up their wine glasses along the window ledge. Someone hands her a glass and Jaden makes a point of checking the time on his phone. 'That was a long ten minutes,' he says.

'Yeah, Yvonne,' another colleague says, 'Jaden was looking like a little lost puppy without you.'

Jaden turns down his bottom lip and she allows him to pull her close. She looks through the pub window, but from this point can't see all the way to the bar and Lewis.

She tries to enjoy her drink and small talk about everyone's weekend plans but it's impossible to concentrate. What would she say to Lewis again? Would she introduce him to everyone if he walked over right now? It would be awkward. She was a mess the last time they saw each other, crying and shouting, but she was also young, so young.

Her colleagues are getting louder, laughing enthusiastically about something she missed. Jaden tucks a loose strand of hair behind her ear and says, 'Can't believe she did that?'

Yvonne smiles and pretends to know what he's talking about, to have been listening all along.

Her own glass is still full, yet others seem to have run empty fast.

'My round. I'll get a bottle,' she says, keen to go back into the warmth of the pub and see him one more time. It's not that she wants to talk to him, more that if they're going to 'bump into each other' she'd rather it didn't happen in front of work friends and Jaden.

The crowd inside is denser now, as people realise how deceptive the sun is. An older version of Lewis, his brother

Danny, looks over at her. His face creases with recognition and also confusion as if trying to place her. She smiles a little and he nods back before saying something she can't hear. Then Lewis, who had been standing with his back to her, turns. He leans forward fractionally before smiling.

It would be best to pretend she hasn't seen him at all, but he's already making his way over. For her to get away now would mean she'd have to push through the crowd, to flee, almost run. She's not going to do any of these things so instead she stands there and watches him get closer and closer. He looks the same, softer maybe, the tight T-shirt and muscled arms gone, but when he smiles, that's it, her face flushes and she's that twenty-one-year-old idiot all over again.

'Yvie,' he steps forwards and kisses her on the cheek.

She squeezes her eyes shut for the seconds in which his face touches hers. 'Hi.'

'What are you doing here? Do you work in the area?'

'Yes, Wardour Street.'

He nods, 'Crazy, so does my brother. You remember Danny?'

The brother from the nightclub and the only other person who knew about their relationship all those years ago.

There's a silence, awkward would be too gentle a way to describe it.

'How have you been?' he asks.

'Good.'

He smiles again, revealing that dimpled cheek and she knows she needs to get away. 'Anyway, good seeing you again,' she takes a step away. 'Enjoy your drink.'

'That's it?' he calls after her.

'I'm with friends,' she says, 'and your brother is—'

'Entertaining himself,' he laughs. 'It's been ages. Let's catch up. What are you drinking?'

'No, I don't think so. I'm on my way home anyway.'

Two hands grab her shoulders from behind. 'Where's the wine?' Hannah growls.

'Sorry, the queue is mad.'

'Damn it, let's push in,' Hannah says as she drags Yvonne away from Lewis.

Jaden frowns when he sees her return with Hannah and two bottles of wine each. But she's done nothing, other than have a brief chat with someone she used to know. Though maybe, it shows on her face, how energised and jittery she feels, how excited and flushed.

'Looks like you're up for more than one drink?' he indicates the bottles under her arms. 'Thought we were going for dinner?'

'Yes. But there's no rush, is there?' And why should there be? This is *her* pub; she's not going to run from it because *he* happens to be here. So she drinks and joins in with the jokes and makes extra effort to enjoy every single anecdote. Jaden is unimpressed and hints several times about being hungry. Why does he always need it to be the two of them? They've already spent two evenings together this week. What's wrong with wanting to spend time with other people as well?

'I'm going home,' he says in her ear. 'You can call me in the morning if you're up for doing something.'

'Oh don't be like that.'

Tomorrow morning she will call him and apologise and he'll moan about always having to fit around her whims and plans. Though for now, he kisses her on the cheek and leaves.

The wine warms her but her bare arms goose bump and Hannah, who is very drunk, suggests they move inside now the crowd has thinned out. Lewis is still there, at the bar with his brother, both of their glasses empty.

'Actually, I think I've had enough,' Yvonne tells the group. 'I'm going to head off too.' They boo her as she slips away.

She's halfway up the road, hoping she won't bump into Jaden, when she notices Lewis. He walks alongside her for a few metres before she stops and faces him. 'What are you doing?'

'I've been watching you tip back glass after glass all evening.'

'So?'

'So, I'm not going to leave you to stumble home on your own, am I?'

'You've got so much front.'

He laughs, 'I also didn't see you eat anything. Maybe you should get some food, soak up some of that alcohol?'

'My God. You're seriously asking me to have dinner with you?'

'Actually, I was only offering like a bag of chips or something, but if you want a proper dinner—'

She walks on, shaking her head. He's the same, he's exactly the same. It's like stepping back in time.

'I'm kidding,' he calls. 'Wait.'

She turns to face him. 'How can you still be this arrogant?'

'Me? I think you mean confident. That's the word you were looking for?'

'No,' she squeaks, desperate not to laugh, 'it's not.'

She casts a look back at The Endurance and wonders how many times they've both been in there drinking and not seen each other.

'You look good, Yvie.'

She should thank him but knows that would only encourage him.

'Are you really going home now?' he asks, this time his voice is free of bravado.

'Yeah, I think so. It's a good idea if I go home now.' She nods to convince herself that it's the very best idea. 'It's late.'

'It is.' He nods back. 'I could drive you. My car's parked up on Goodge Street.'

'You drove into central London?'

'You know I don't like the tube.'

'That's ridiculous. Also, I'm not getting in a car with you.'

'Why not? I've been on the Pepsi all night.'

'I didn't mean that.' So what did she mean? That she wouldn't trust herself alone with him?

'At least let me walk you to the tube station? You're still in south London?'

'How do you know that?'

'Kiama,' he smiles. 'That boy loves to gossip, especially if you ask him the right questions.'

It's a weird thing to say. It implies that he's stayed interested in her all these years, but of course not, it's just Lewis rolling out his usual chat.

They walk on together and it's weird, too weird.

'I wish I knew what to say to you,' he says quietly, 'I never got a chance to say sorry. How you got caught up in the middle of everything, that whole situation.'

'Yeah, I know, Lewis. I wish none of it ever happened, but it did, so… '

He stops walking. 'No, I don't regret what happened with Emma.'

It shouldn't hurt her to hear him say it, but it does.

'Not for a second, because without her I wouldn't have Kiama.'

'Oh, of course. I didn't mean that. I meant more—'

'I wish we could have met each other at a different time. Don't you ever think about that?'

'No,' she lies. She thinks back to when she first met him at the club and how she waited for his call for weeks, only for him to get interested again when he was with someone else. He was a player then and is probably the same now.

'Would you give me your number if I asked you for it now?'

It's still a joke to him, it makes her furious. 'No.'

'Why not?' he laughs.

'Because I'm an adult and I have adult relationships. I'm not interested in playing games, waiting around for some guy to call me.'

'That was years ago.'

'So, what's changed? You seem like the exact same Lewis to me, flirting and trying to charm me.'

'Yvie, I'm nearly thirty-three. I've sorted myself out.'

'Well done,' she throws her hands out. Why is she acting like this? Like she cares so much? But the truth is the situation really hurt her. It also hurt her friendship with Emma. The secret forced a distance between them. Sometimes Yvonne put it down to her working while Emma didn't, or

Emma becoming a mother while Yvonne was enjoying the kind of freedom that came with having a well-paid job and no real responsibilities. But deep down the secret about Lewis was a big reason too.

'I'm sorry,' he says. 'I'm sorry for what happened between us. I know you don't believe me but I really did lose your number and I really did go back to The Troika the following Friday to look for you. But you weren't there. I had no way of getting back in touch with you. What did you expect me to do? Wait around? And we talked about this already.'

'You think I still care that you never called me?'

'I'm not sure. You're definitely still mad at me, I can see that. Tell me what I'm apologising for?'

She's surprised by how candid he looks, like he really can't understand why she doesn't have the time for him. 'You liked the idea of having both of us on the go.'

'That's not true. As soon as I saw you again I knew I had to break it off with Emma. I knew I wanted you. But I didn't know how to go about it. You act like I planned this all out. Like I knew you two were friends and that she was going to get pregnant.'

'You liked the idea of having us both,' she says again, because it's the truth, that's what this whole thing was about, his ego. 'Even when you knew Emma was pregnant you were still suggesting we stay together.'

They step away from each other as a group of tourists come close, moving between them, in the sluggish way of those both drunk and lost.

'You're full of it. And even now, you're flirting with me, as if anything could ever happen between us.'

Lewis leans against a shop window, 'But I can't help flirting with you.'

'No, of course you can't, because you're a player.'

'No, because I like you.' He folds his arms. 'I think there's still something there.'

She grinds her teeth together and through them says, 'There isn't. There really isn't. Especially, after everything that happened. Also, I've been listening to Emma moan about you for the last seven years.'

'You should hear what I say about her,' he laughs.

But this is awkward. She's used to being on Emma's side, to hearing about how 'Dickhead' was late to collect Kiama for the weekend or hadn't paid enough money into her account that month. Yvonne learnt fast that the only way she could deal with hearing about Lewis all the time was to block him from her mind, to listen to Emma and picture someone other than the man in front of her now, the one who still makes her feel this way.

She looks down at the ground and tries to remember how she ever got over Lewis. There was a lot of crying, a lot of feeling sad and numb but there was also the great distraction of her career and holidays and meeting new people. Then there was Emma, her best friend, a new mum. And of course, there was Kiama.

'You have a child with my best friend,' she says. 'That's complicated, Lewis.'

He stares at her for a beat then nods. 'Complicated? Yeah, I guess so.' He pushes himself off the window and stands straight. 'But at least let me drive you home.'

She thinks of Jaden, going home alone. And here she is,

with another man, trying to mentally list all the reasons why she shouldn't get into his car. 'No,' she says, 'I don't think so.'

Lewis laughs. 'I don't see the issue with me dropping you home.'

'Because of what I *just* said.'

'But I'm not hitting on you. I'm talking about giving you a lift home. Or would you prefer the vomit comet?'

She laughs at him, 'I've not heard that in years.'

'Let me drive you home.'

What's the big deal with it? She would send Jaden a text message when she got in, apologising for wanting to stay out. She would go over to his place in the morning and take him out for brunch. She would finally agree to that holiday he had been pestering her about taking, just the two of them, somewhere fancy.

'Come on,' Lewis says, as he begins walking off ahead. 'It's cold.'

The walk to the car clears her head and as she sobers up she becomes more convinced that there's nothing wrong with accepting a lift home from someone she used to know.

Once inside, with the heating on and the seat so soft, she finds herself relaxing.

'Nice car,' she says as he flicks through the radio stations. 'Is it Mummy's?'

'You've got no manners.'

She laughs.

'It's mine. I had a good year at work so decided to treat myself. So, I know you're south, but where?'

'Clapham.'

'Clapham?' he screws his face up. 'What made you do that?'

'It's up and coming. And I could get a two-bedroom place there.'

'Whoa, you bought? What, a house?'

'Half,' she says, 'for now.'

'I'm looking to do the same myself.'

'You're back at your mum's?'

He drives on for a moment in silence and then looks at her. 'She needed a bit more help at home.'

'No, I didn't mean it like that. I wasn't judging you.'

'All my brothers are married and have their own families. So it falls on me, as the youngest, to drive her back and forth to hospital, to check up on her.'

'It must be a lot to deal with. I'm sorry to hear that.' She recalls Kiama making a Get Well Soon card for his nana recently. 'Is it her sickle cell?'

'Yeah, she's had some bad episodes recently. Danny wants her to move in with him and his wife, but they fuss over her too much. When I'm home I can keep an eye on her and she still feels needed because I'll never get too old for feeding and lecturing,' he laughs. 'Kiama too, she loves having him over.'

'You're a good son, Lewis.' She can do this, she can sit in his car and be civil with him. 'And how's your business going?'

He casts a quick glance at her, 'You mean the restaurant?'

'You're setting up a restaurant?'

'You really don't know anything about me, do you?'

'Why would I? You think Emma and I sit around talking about you?'

He laughs. 'No. But I assumed you would have asked, over the years.'

She remains silent.

'Guess not. I sell gym memberships, but could do it in my sleep. Danny wants to open a restaurant and I'm going to back it, so looking at premises right now, around Wembley. That's what we were talking about tonight actually. I wasn't even meant to meet up with him. I had other plans that got cancelled last minute. Weird, isn't it? That's my first time in that pub.'

She knows what he's getting at. 'It's a coincidence.'

'You and I, we have a lot of coincidences,' he looks at her again.

'Doesn't mean anything. I bump into people all the time, especially around Soho.'

Will she mention this to Emma? Send a text saying 'guess who I bumped into?' No, that would feel too much like walking into trouble. But why? There's no issue here. She's doing absolutely nothing wrong. She'll even tell Jaden, that an old friend dropped her home. Again, there's nothing wrong with any of this.

They drive onto Tower Bridge and he grunts, 'Can't believe I'm on the wrong side of the river. I'm starting to feel light-headed.'

She should have got a cab. This was silly, allowing him to drive all the way out here. 'You know what, Lewis? It's too far, drop me around here, I can get a bus straight to the end of my road.'

'I'm here now, in the dirty south, you see what I'm willing to put myself through for you?' He smiles to himself, knowing her request is empty, that's there's no way she would get out of his car to find a bus. 'Plus,' he says, 'I want to see your place.'

'That wasn't part of the deal.'

'So, what is?'

CHAPTER FIFTEEN

MANDAZI

October 2020

Kiama

The next morning Kiama sits out in the yard with the girls. He watches Delia stick on her fake eyelashes and wonders what time to wake Yvonne up.

The gate clanks open and they all turn towards it.

'Purity?' Kiama shouts.

She jumps slightly, caught off guard, then her face widens into her huge smile. 'He is here,' she sings. 'He's here, he's here.'

He crosses the yard to hug her. She barely comes up to his shoulder, he's not sure he remembered this about her but of course, he's so much bigger now. Her grey hair is plaited and wrapped around her head like a crown.

She pulls back and studies his face. 'So big. So big.'

'We drove *hours* to see you yesterday.'

She throws up her arms and claps. 'Girls, did he tell you how I used to watch over him when he was a boy? A small, small boy, but what is this?' She picks at a tuft of Kiama's hair. 'You look like a lion.'

'Oh, er—' he pushes it down but it only springs back up. 'I'm growing it out.'

'And where is Yvonne? She is sleeping, yes?'

'Yeah.'

'Air travel. It's no good for women, makes us tired. Let her sleep, Ki-Yama,' she says, and it makes him smile to hear her very particular way of saying his name. It used to bug him as a kid, but maybe she's actually saying it correctly and everyone else, including his family, have always said it wrong.

She takes his hand and leads him into the house. The girls follow.

'How's Toby?' Alice asks. 'Is it really malaria? So awful.'

Purity makes a tsk sound and grabs an egg from the spread of breakfast on the table. 'He is well. His parents are travelling here now to pamper him. I told them, please do not come, your boy is fine, just a little diarrhoea, but do they listen? No, they are behaving as if the boy is dying.' She leans in towards Kiama. 'It's like looking at your mother,' she says.

'Really?' he breaks away, her gaze too intense.

'Your eyes. You have your mother's eyes.'

But he knows he doesn't, it's just one of those things people are always saying because they think it makes him feel better.

The house girl pours coffee into plastic mugs and sets them down. Purity talks to her in Swahili indicating things around the house, the almost-empty jar of jam, the dust which gathers around the table legs and the wonky paintings on the wall. At least that's what Kiama gathers from her overly animated way of speaking and the few words of Swahili he catches. The girl looks tired but nods anyway.

'I hope it's okay us staying here,' Kiama says. 'We arrived so late and—'

'Ki-Yama,' Purity says softly, taking hold of his arm. *'Mwana mwema ni taji tukufu kwa wazazi wake.'*

His mouth falls open for he understands, yet it's not something he wants to hear right now.

She pulls her head back and drops his arm. 'You forgot?'

'No, I, er. I never really knew it,' he lies. 'The other kids always spoke to me in English.'

'But I spoke to you. I spoke with you every day and now you have forgotten.'

It's true, she would have him in the kitchen, reading recipes from the big Delia Smith cookbooks aloud. It's how he eventually got better at reading. He would read it in English and she would repeat it back in Swahili and then he would copy her. If he tried, he could probably describe how to make pasta in Swahili but little else, even Mum never spoke it that well. He remembers how she would insist on ordering in restaurants, even when the staff spoke English. 'They appreciate you trying,' she'd tell Kiama and it was true, waiting staff were forever congratulating her on making the effort, yet the wrong meal often came out.

'I'd love to learn again,' Kiama says. All it would take is for Purity to talk to him, just like she used to, then it would flood back in the same way other fragments of memory have been doing since he arrived. He takes his phone out, ready to pull up some old Delia Smith recipe and ask Purity to translate, but then remembers there's no connection here.

Delia snorts, 'Difficult, isn't it? Being offline.'

Maybe Yvonne was right, maybe he *is* addicted. He puts the phone on the table face down and picks up a coffee instead.

'Why have you come?' Purity asks as she removes the eggshell in one expert move.

The coffee burns his tongue and Purity waits for her answer. The girls too, their eyes turned towards him. 'To, you know, to see my grandparents.'

'Yes. Your grandfather, he is a good man. You must greet him for me.' She leans closer, eating her egg and waiting for him to say more.

'And I wanted to see some of the places Mum liked and took me to when we lived here.'

'Ahem,' she nods.

'I have photos of a school or orphanage she used to work at, I can show you. I'd like to go there too.'

'Ahem. Yes.' Small pieces of egg stick to her lips as she nods but Kiama gets the vibe she's not really paying him her full attention for she keeps glancing over to the house girl. He doesn't want to get out his photos now, to have these random girls looking at Mum and asking questions.

'You came to see your grandparents. What a good boy you have grown into.'

'And, of course, I wanted to spend time with you again. I was wondering if we could—'

But she cuts him off to shout something across the room. She was always like this, busy, conducting several conversations at the same time as making dinner and hanging up a wash. Maybe this is why it felt so jilted and quiet with his grandparents, it wasn't only because Mum was missing it was Purity too. Her energy buzzes through everything.

She rises and starts pulling open drawers from the cabinet and rustling papers. 'I had something to give you, Ki-Yama. Hold on. I will find it.'

'Are they photos of kid Kiama?' Delia says. 'I bet you were so super cute.' She stretches her arms above her head until her scrubs ride up and expose her stomach. Is she flirting with him?

A car honks outside.

'That's our ride,' Alice says. 'Purity, we need to go.'

'I am coming. I am coming,' Purity shouts.

Kiama stands too. 'You're going?' There's more than a mild panic in his voice.

'Yes. I have work to do at the medical centre.'

'I can come with you? I can help out?'

Purity reaches up and taps him lightly on his cheek.

'When will you be back then?'

She takes another egg and drops it into the pocket of her skirt. 'Later.'

'What, like lunchtime? Afternoon?' he looks at the girls for help, for a clear answer, but they're busy making up sandwiches to go.

'Evening? Dinnertime?'

'Yes,' Purity says, 'after.'

He follows them into the yard and watches the car as it drives off; Purity doesn't even wave to him. Is she serious? He came all this way to see her and then she just disappears after ten minutes and expects him to wait around all day for her. And it *will* be all day. Just like when he was little and a quick trip to the market turned into an all-day marathon of dropping in to see this person and that.

He goes back in the house, sits alone at the table and stuffs a slice of bread in his mouth. It's too quiet, the house girl simply nods each time he speaks and he almost wishes for Dad's music.

Finally, Yvonne comes down, her hair hangs wetly around her face and she looks cold. 'Morning?' she croaks. 'Did everyone leave?'

'Yeah.'

'Sorry, I didn't realise you would be eating alone.' She sits opposite him.

'Purity came back.'

Yvonne looks surprised. 'That's brilliant. Where is she?'

'She went with the girls to the medical centre. But said she'll be home later today. I don't know when though. Dinnertime. Whenever that is.'

Yvonne's face falls. 'Oh, I'm sorry. Still, at least you've seen her. And so nice of her to let us stay here.'

Though they both know Yvonne has hated every second of staying in this house.

'Shame I didn't get to see her too. Why didn't you wake me?'

'I thought you looked pretty Zopicloned out.' He distracts himself by knocking an egg on the side of the table. 'Do you want to eat?'

Her face screws up as she looks over the spread.

'Seriously, are you trying to fit into an outfit or something?'

She tuts and walks away, over to the sofas where she sits and combs out her hair. He feels bad for getting at her. It's not her fault. After all she's the one who travelled all this way with him, who agreed to take a week from her life to do this. It's Purity who couldn't even take a day off work for him.

'Sorry,' he says. 'Coffee?' He fills one of the blue plastic mugs and holds it out for her as she walks over. She recoils upon her first sip. 'Urgh, you said this was coffee.'

'It is. I didn't say it was good.'

The house girl comes in and Yvonne goes, 'Mmm' and gives her a thumbs-up.

Kiama picks up the envelope and removes the photos of Mum, going through each one again. There's not even a sign in the background, no house name or door number. It's going to be impossible to find this place.

The house girl comes over and taps his shoulder, 'Lari?' she says.

'Sorry?'

'The Lari orphanage. That is where I worked in the summer, before I came here. Your photos are very old.' She takes the lid off the coffee pot and refills it.

It wasn't exactly a guilt trip. But he did have to lay it on pretty thick in order to convince Yvonne to go. Especially when they heard Joe was too ill to leave the guest house and the only way to get to Lari was to walk into the centre of town and get a bus.

'It wasn't this cold in Nairobi,' Yvonne complains.

He had given her one of his sweatshirts to stop her moaning before they left Purity's house. 'Why didn't you pack properly?' he asks as he pulls the hood up for her. 'Did you buy into the idea of Africa always being warm?'

'You're such a smart arse sometimes.'

The market sellers are laying out their wares and shouting greetings to each other. Yvonne stops by a stall with printed

T-shirts covered in stupid slogans and images of David Bowie Starman and the poo emoji. She pulls one from the rail and smiles. 'Ah, my dream man.'

Kiama laughs at the sweatshirt. 'Obama? Really?'

'Of course.'

'Surprised. I didn't think black men would be your type.'

She puts it back and her cheeks go red, 'Obama is *everyone's* type.'

They walk on, through a small cluster of shipping containers. Most are already open and inside each sits a tailor, a welder or a mobile phone salesman. Eventually they come to a clearing where the buses are. The 'bus station' is completely chaotic, but they find a purple matatu with a cardboard sign in the window announcing 129 and climb on seconds before it pulls out.

Outside, a drizzle starts and the fields are lush and green in the way he remembers Kenya looking, which is nothing like the dry savannah images you always see on TV.

Kiama shows a man sitting in front the hand-drawn map and asks for directions. 'It is soon,' the man says before shouting something to the driver. 'Here. Here.' The matatu stops in front of a stall stacked with hundreds of tiny green bananas and they jump out.

'*Mzungu*,' the man shouts as the bus pulls away.

'Why do they think it's acceptable to do that?' Yvonne asks. 'I know I'm white. I don't need it pointed out. Stop laughing.'

'I'm not,' Kiama says, unfolding the map. 'This is my concentration face. Okay, I think it's this way.'

'You *think*?'

'No, I'm ninety-six per cent *sure* it's this way. I can't believe I'm using a paper map. It's like a puzzle.' He puts it back in his pocket so it doesn't get wet.

They walk up a slippery dirt road through thickening bushes, stepping to one side each time a car crawls up behind them. At one point a heavy truck nears and they both press into the bushes to avoid it.

'Jesus,' Kiama calls as he feels a blast of air from the vehicle.

Yvonne pulls him up onto the grassy verge, where their matching Converse get soaked straight through. They enter a small clearing with some shops and houses. In a butcher's window a quarter of a cow with a cloud of flies around it hangs from a hook. An old man in a grey apron shouts, '*Mzungu*,' from his doorway and Kiama bites his lip before calling back, 'That's inappropriate.' The shopkeeper gives a toothless smile and waves.

'Was your ex-husband black?' Kiama asks, keen to distract Yvonne from the fact that his percentage of knowing where they're going is now around the sixty per cent mark.

'What kind of question is that?'

He shrugs. 'Just wondering.'

He wishes Dad would have gotten married. It would be nice to see him settled down with someone, rather than still living like a teenager, going from woman to woman.

'So, where are we now?' Yvonne asks.

'I'm sixty-three per cent sure it's this way.'

'Kiama? You're joking?'

'Okay, maybe seventy.' A dog sniffs around their path and Kiama holds onto Yvonne's arm. 'I hate dogs.'

'Still?'

'Yeah, they stink.'

'I'd be more worried about how far we are from a rabies shot.'

The dog darts off after something in the trees and then Kiama spots it, just like the house girl described, two small paths cross each other and on one side there's the compound. Two children run from the behind the walls and wave them in.

A young man, a little older than Kiama, walks towards them and Yvonne explains that they have come to see some of Kindred Kenya's work. Again, she puts on that 'phone voice', and it definitely makes her lies sound more truthful.

They follow the man, Simeon, into a large yard, passing a cooking hut and an orange swing set, the seats all tangled and wrapped around the poles, black print along the side boasts, 'Donated by Laura Gordon'.

Kiama stares at the house and imagines Mum walking out of the door, baby on hip, just like in the photo.

'Kiama?' Yvonne says and he flicks his attention to her. 'You need to take your shoes off,' she says, nodding down to his feet.

'Oh. Sorry.' Inside a line of orange rubber matting runs through the middle of the room, and everything is dark and filthy.

'The children are at church,' Simeon explains.

'Please, sit down,' he gestures towards two foldout chairs by a barred window.

The walls are bare, apart from a hand-drawn alphabet frieze and a picture of Jesus Christ with his arms spread wide.

A girl of about fourteen, wearing a grubby white party dress, brings in a floral-patterned flask and three plastic mugs.

'You look very pretty,' Yvonne says to her. 'Is it your birthday today?'

The girl giggles and hides her mouth.

'No,' Simeon says as he takes a jar of Milo from a shelf and spoons it into the cups. 'This is Zipporah. She is always dressed like this. She likes to feel special.'

Kiama smiles at the girl but she only giggles again and runs off.

'It is such a nice surprise to have visitors,' Simeon says. 'Have you also visited the medical centres?'

'No,' Yvonne says, 'not yet. We were really interested in this place because we think a friend of ours volunteered here once, but it would have been a long time ago.'

They're interrupted by the sound of children, outside in the yard. They kick their plastic flip-flops off at the door and pile into the house. They wear a mishmash of old clothes, frayed blue school dresses, neon fleecy jumpers and football shirts. They all have a buzz cut and he realises he can't tell who's a boy and who's a girl. The older kids sit along the table and begin filling out their school exercise books while the younger ones chase each other about. The smallest kid, Jenga, climbs onto Kiama's lap to stare at the stud in his nose and inspect the tattoos which peek out from under the cuffs of his sweatshirt.

Kiama helps them with their schoolwork, draws pictures on demand and answers a hundred questions about the plane journey over.

'You like kids, don't you?' Yvonne asks.

'I *love* kids. I'm going to have four or five.'

Yvonne laughs.

'I'm not interested in this one child thing. I want them to have each other.' He sometimes imagines how much easier his life would have been had Mum and Dad had another child together. It would have taken so much pressure off, not being the only link between the parents who grated on each other or the grandparents who didn't know what to say. Even now, the idea of having someone else to remember Mum with would make life so much easier. But isn't that what he's doing with Yvonne?

'Kiama,' Simeon calls from the indoor kitchen area. 'Come here.'

They squeeze into the small space where Simeon is crouched down, a large bag of flour at his feet. 'Mandazi,' he says.

'Is that what you're making?' Kiama asks.

'No, *you* are. You can both cook, yes? Help me prepare it.'

'Actually, we need to get going soon,' Yvonne says.

A small white cloud puffs up as Simeon unrolls the top of the bag. 'Already? No, you must stay. You can help.'

Simeon fills two metal bowls with flour and tips water into each. 'Here,' he hands one to each of them. 'Who can make the best dough?'

Kiama makes a V sign with his fingers, pointing them at his eyes and then to Yvonne.

'There's no way you can cook,' she says.

'What are you talking about? You met my nana. Did she really seem like the kind of woman to raise a lazy man?'

'She pampered her sons. Lewis never lifted a finger at home.'

207

'Well, she was always working me. Cooking, cleaning, running errands. I'm the perfect teenager actually. I remember everyone's birthdays, always send a thank-you card, which is a pain with the amount of people who still sympathy-buy me a present every year.' He hands his perfect ball of dough to the children, who form it into little triangles which are spread across the table to prove.

Kiama rests his head on his palm and watches Zipporah as she waves her hand over the pan to check the temperature before dropping in a packet of lard.

'When I turned eighteen, I got a lot of cards and letters. From people Mum worked with, went to uni with, all these random people who would've never given me a second thought if my mum hadn't died. Even the drunk guy who lived downstairs from us in Stratford got in touch.'

But Yvonne never got in touch, not in ten years of birthdays. Maybe she forgot. Or maybe it was too painful. He wants to ask her why she disappeared on him. But even the idea of saying it out loud makes him feel kind of down.

'I'm sorry I never sent you anything,' she says.

He looks away and picks at the remnants of dough drying between his fingers. 'It's not a big deal. I'm not that into birthdays. Plus, no one wants to celebrate anything in January anyway.'

'I'm still sorry.'

He doesn't want to have this conversation now, maybe it's one that's not worth having at all. 'Anyway, what do we do next?' The table is covered in puffy little triangles of dough. 'Do we drop them in the pan?' he calls across to Zipporah. She giggles backs wordlessly. 'Why have we been put in charge of this? Simeon? What am I meant to be doing?'

Simeon returns from outside and through the thickening haze of smoke he instructs, 'Drop them, drop them in the pan.'

Kiama throws a doughy triangle in and a small splatter of fat splashes up over his arm. 'Sh—' he starts before catching himself. It stings but he feels it would be wasteful to stand at the cold tap and let the water run; there's no clean cloth either.

Yvonne frowns at the pink welt. 'At least it's an improvement on that tattoo.'

He kisses his teeth.

After, they help to clean the plates and play a few more games with the smaller children in the yard. But aware of the time and warned by Simeon about the irregularity of the buses they soon say their goodbyes. Yvonne makes it quick, a simple whip round of all the kids in which she tells them to take care and try hard in school. But Kiama's not as hard as her. He takes his time with each child, getting hugs and chatting. He can feel Yvonne shoot him a look as she waits by the gate, making small talk with Simeon.

Finally, he walks over, his favourite little one, Jenga, around his waist.

'I was just telling Simeon how much we enjoyed visiting today,' Yvonne says.

'Yeah. It's been amazing.' Kiama looks at Jenga who gives him a huge crusty-faced smile.

'So tell me,' Simeon says, 'when did your friend work here?'

'It was my mum actually. But it was ages ago, early 2000s. I've got photos.' He puts Jenga down and goes in his rucksack to get out the envelope. He wipes his hands along his jeans before taking out the photos and handing them to Simeon.

'Oh, the house, it looks different. Cleaner,' Simeon laughs. 'This is how I remember it.' He turns over the next photo, the one of Mum caught mid-laugh with a toddler's hand on her cheek. Kiama has decided this is his favourite, because she looks so pretty in it, and the way her T-shirt is bunched up makes it look like she's got a bump.

'Did you live here then?' Yvonne asks Simeon.

'Yes. I was one of the first children to live here,' he smiles and stops on a photo. 'This one is me,' he laughs. 'You have a photo of me.'

Kiama doesn't know what to say. He takes it from Simeon's hand and stares at it. This can't be true. That the little kid in the photo is now standing here in front of them.

Simeon laughs again and it's almost annoying, like he's got one up on Kiama because he spent time with her.

'That's incredible,' Yvonne says. 'Can you believe it? That's Simeon.'

But he doesn't want it to be Simeon in the photograph, Simeon having one of Mum's hugs, Simeon making Mum smile. It should be him. He puts the photos back into the envelope and zips them away in the bag.

'I'm sorry I don't remember your mother,' Simeon says. 'What happened to her?'

Kiama studies Simeon's sandals, how thin the soles look as if worn down, how the Velcro straps don't quite close.

'She died when I was eight.'

'Who raised you after you lost her?'

Kiama looks up. Simeon is only two years older than him,

but lines appear on his face with each expression. His life here must be hard and small, so small. Yet Kiama can't stop his feelings of jealousy.

'I moved back to England. My dad and nana brought me up.'

'Then you are lucky, that you had your family.' He reaches out to shake Kiama's hand. 'Will you come again? The children would like it very much.'

Kiama looks down at Jenga, who is now sitting on the ground, playing with the rucksack, running the zip back and forth.

This place has something and despite his confused feelings towards Simeon, being here is the closest he's felt to Mum since arriving. 'Yes,' he says, 'I would love to come back.'

Simeon closes the gate behind them, and they walk back down the grassy verge. Kiama feels that sensation again, similar to how he felt earlier today, when the truck was closing in on him, its heavy bulk getting closer and closer. But of course when he looks there's nothing behind him, only the house. They walk on a bit and this time the closeness of something heavy almost winds him. He stops.

'What's wrong?' Yvonne asks.

He can't walk anymore, can't move on. He leans forward and puts his hands on his knees, feeling like he's about to throw up. Sometimes it's the only thing that works.

Nothing comes.

He stands again, feeling the blood rush from his head. He turns back to the house and sees Mum standing by the gate, smiling as a little kid runs towards her and jumps in her arms. Then, he can see her everywhere. Running races with the kids across the grass, tearing a mandazi in two and giving the other half away, smoking behind the tree thinking no one can see her.

Yvonne puts a hand on his arm but he steps away from her.

'It's like she's here,' he says, shocked that he can't contain the thought, can't keep the hurt in his heart like he usually does.

But Yvonne doesn't judge him for it, she doesn't get that worried look like Nana used to whenever Kiama would bring up Mum, she just nods and says, 'I know. I can feel her too.' Then, she reaches up and puts her arms around him.

CHAPTER SIXTEEN

SEX ON THE BEACH

July 2009

Yvonne

Yvonne paces the kitchen. 'I hate the way they've laid this floor.'

'What's that?' Lewis calls over the music. 'Are you complaining again?'

'No,' she runs her fingers along a line of grout. She had hoped the colour would be lighter than this.

'It looks good,' Lewis says as he sprays down the already clean kitchen counter.

She studies the floor tiles again, it'll have to do, there's no way she's having the builders back to redo it.

'You're such a perfectionist,' Lewis calls as he switches on the mixer, adding to the noise of the flat. 'No wonder this place is taking so long to come together. If you were less picky I could do a bit of DIY for you.'

She turns the music down a notch, leans against his back and checks on the progress of his batter mix. 'DIY? You?'

'Yeah. You already know I'm good with my hands.'

'But you're slow. I've already been waiting on this breakfast for an hour. I thought pancakes were quick.'

'They are, but you keep distracting me. Plus, there's something not right about this hob. You need to get it checked out.'

'I'll add it to the list,' she says.

He turns the stereo back up.

'Can't we listen to something else?' she asks.

He smiles and sings along. It's almost endearing how bad he is. 'You've got a horrible voice, Lewis.'

He pours the batter in the pan and laughs, 'I can't be good at everything.'

It's become so typical of their Sundays, the long, lazy breakfast before he has to drive back to his mum's house in Harrow. It would be so much easier if they lived closer to one another, but at least this way when he comes over he usually ends up staying for a day or two, sometimes even three. They don't arrange it, it just happens. The same way they don't speak about what they're doing, how much they're enjoying being with each other again and how different it feels this time.

The door buzzes from downstairs. 'Ah, that must be my package,' she claps and runs down, more excited than anyone should be to receive a set of crockery, but when she opens the door it's not her order.

'Claude?'

Her brother walks in, still in his work clothes, tools in hand.

'What are you doing here?'

'The kids are at karate and Mum is with Mel and the baby, so I've got two hours before I need to be home. You're not going to make me take my shoes off, are you?'

'Er, no, but... '

He makes his way up the stairs before she can stop him, let alone think of a reason why he can't come in.

'I didn't know you were coming over,' she says following him up.

'I wasn't, but like I say, I've got two hours. And—' he stops when he sees Lewis. 'Hi.'

'Hi.'

'I'm Claude. Yvonne's brother,' he says, looking back at her.

'I'm Lewis. Yvonne's—' he too looks at her and grins in a way that makes her bite her lip, 'friend.'

Lewis steps away from the hob to shake Claude's hand. Yvonne catches her reflection in the window and her expression is somewhere between a wince and horror.

'Pancakes?' Claude says as he nods over to the darkening smoke.

'Shit,' Lewis runs over.

'You really should have text me first,' she says to her brother.

'Don't mind me, I'll go and crack on with things.' Claude heads to the bathroom.

'Shit,' Yvonne says.

Lewis pushes the kitchen window open wide and shrugs. 'If I'm honest, I'm surprised this hasn't happened sooner. Your family all live so close by.'

'Yes, but they know not to drop by like this.' She sinks her head into her hands. 'Shit. Shit.' How long will it take for word to spread around her whole family that a man, unknown to any of them, is at her flat on a Sunday morning? 'This is bad,' she whispers.

'Why? Just tell him not to say anything.'

'You don't know my family. They're powered by gossip.'

'Mine's exactly the same. But Danny's known about you

215

for a long time and he respects that it's off limits, for now anyway. I'm sure your brother will get it too. Tell him we've only just started seeing each other. That you don't want the whole family knowing.'

'I really didn't want this to happen yet.'

He pours another round of batter into the pan and tuts when it doesn't quite reach the edges.

Why is he being so nonchalant about this? But then, she can't always tell what Lewis is thinking and feeling, he holds everything in so well.

'Lewis? Say something. What should I do?'

He smiles slowly and says, 'Go and ask your brother what he wants on his pancake?'

'This isn't funny.'

'It would have been funnier an hour ago. At least now you've got your clothes on. Look, we both knew this would happen sooner or later. I don't get what's so bad about your family knowing you're seeing someone?'

'Because I'm the last single one. My mum's desperate for me to get married and have some kids.'

Lewis flips the pancake over. 'Marriage?' he says trying to keep his face neutral. 'I wasn't quite expecting that, but I guess we have known each other for almost ten years.'

She covers her face.

'People are going to find out one day, Yvie.'

She gets this, but didn't want anyone in her family to be amongst the first to know. At least not before Emma.

Yvonne goes into the bathroom where Claude sits on the floor pulling nails from the old bath panel. 'I knew there was something going on with you.'

She clears her throat. 'He's just a friend.'

Claude nods, 'Of course he is.'

'Okay, more than a friend.' She puts down the lid and sits on the toilet seat.

'How long you been seeing this one?'

'This one? You make it sound like I have loads of men on the go.'

'You only broke up with Jaden a few weeks ago.'

'It was the end of March.'

'And when did this guy appear?'

'The end of March.'

Claude laughs.

'I like him,' she says.

'I can tell. I can see it in how you're behaving.'

Yvonne closes the bathroom door. 'The thing is we've got history.' Perhaps this is what the relationship needs now, to be admitted out loud and shared with another person. Perhaps then she will realise that there's no need to be so secretive about things, so worried that they're doing something wrong. 'You know my friend Emma and her little boy, Kiama? I've brought him up to Mum's a few times.'

'The kid with the big hair?'

'Yes, well, Lewis is his dad.'

No, it definitely sounds wrong.

Claude stops what he's doing and sits back on his haunches.

'Of course, Lewis is not with Emma,' she says quickly. 'Never was really,' she adds before he can hit her with his full disapproval.

'They have a kid together,' Claude says.

'She was a student when she got pregnant. It was one of those things. They went out for about five minutes.'

'And Emma's happy with this, is she? You seeing her kid's dad? So messy, Yvonne.'

She's met up with Emma twice since, once for a quick lunch in Brick Lane the month after she started seeing Lewis. Then again last month, when she was convinced she would tell her, but as they walked around the Horniman Museum she realised it would be impossible to do so with Kiama by their sides. Yvonne will tell her, of course she will, but it needs to be the right moment.

'She doesn't know, does she?' Claude asks.

'No. Not yet. But I will tell her, I'll tell her as soon as—'

'It's *your* life.' He pushes the bath panel back into place and stands. 'But if you really thought she would be okay with this, you would have told her by now. This is rotten.'

'What?'

'Your bath panels are completely rotten.'

She stands opposite him and feels like the little idiot sister. 'You can stay if you want? Have breakfast with us. Meet Lewis properly?'

'Nah,' Claude puts his hand on the door handle and she stops him. 'I really like him.' She's looking for approval, for her brother who is the most wholesome, big-hearted of people to tell her to go ahead and fall in love with Lewis. But he simply nods his head and leaves.

'Why is he taking so long?' Emma snaps.

Keen to diffuse Emma's growing annoyance, Yvonne says, 'I think he's packing his pyjamas.'

Tonight will be the first time they've gone out together in ages. Yvonne booked a restaurant and spent ages choosing an outfit. She's rehearsed what she wants to say several times and even had a pep talk from Claude before she left the house.

'Kiama,' Emma screams into the hallway. 'Come on. I don't want Nana bitching at me again for not having you ready.' She turns to Yvonne. 'Are you sure this looks alright? I feel a bit frumpy. I never know what's in fashion anymore.'

'You look fine.'

Emma collects a few dirty plates and mugs from the coffee table then empties half a glass of water into a browning cheese plant on the windowsill. 'I really don't want Nana coming in to wait for him. The place is a mess.'

Yvonne peels a fork from a newspaper and fills the sink. Every time she comes here she promises herself she won't clean.

'I don't want to look *fine*,' Emma says as she pulls at the hem of her skirt; hopefully she realises that it's a little too short for her, that she doesn't need to show so much flesh.

'You look great.'

'I look shit.' She takes a jar of Nutella from the cupboard and eats two spoons of it. 'How dressy is this place?'

'It's a restaurant. Smart casual.'

'I love your necklace by the way, looks expensive. You always have such nice things.'

'Mum,' Kiama stands in the doorway, he's got on a crushed Brazil football kit with mismatched socks. 'I can't find any pyjamas.'

'Oh for fuck's sake, Kiama, don't wear that.' Emma chucks the spoon in the sink, which splashes Yvonne's top with soap suds. 'Why are you wearing that?'

'Cause it looks good.' He spins on the spot.

'It doesn't look good. Where's your bag?'

'Dunno. On the sofa, I think.'

Yvonne reaches over and tries to smooth down his hair, which is sticking up in a hundred different directions. 'Why don't you wear those black jeans I got you for Christmas? They must fit you by now.'

He clicks his fingers, 'Good idea.'

'He's always on his best behaviour for you,' Emma says. 'He even made a point of putting the toilet seat down before you arrived.'

'Aww, you've raised the perfect man.'

They both laugh as Yvonne searches around for a tea towel to dry herself, but there's nothing. She can never find anything in this flat. 'Em, what time is Julie coming to pick him up?'

'Fuck knows. I've never been able to work out what time zone she lives in.'

'Kiama, do you want me to pack your bag? So you can go and get changed?' Yvonne asks.

'Yes please,' he says in triumph as he finds the bag. He throws it to her; it contains a few items of scrunched clothing and some paper. Kiama always has bits of paper. His room is littered with them, drawings mostly, of animals, cars, buildings.

'Does he take his toothbrush with him?' Yvonne asks.

Emma flips the gypsy shoulders on her top up and then down while pouting. 'Wish I had something new to wear.'

'Em?'

'I don't know. Nana will buy him whatever I don't send anyway. Even the stuff I do send she tends to chuck and replace. Nothing's ever good enough for any of her boys.'

The piping on the rucksack is burst and the zip doesn't quite close all the way. Does Emma purposely send old stuff so it's replaced? There's a tattered school book in the bag, the cover part torn off and scribbled on.

'That's his homework,' Emma says as she opens Yvonne's make-up bag. 'Bet he's still not done it, has he? I sat with him for over an hour the other night, trying to explain it.'

Kiama comes back into the room, smartly dressed, even his socks now match. He taps Emma on the back and says, 'Ta-da.'

'Well done.' She pulls him over and kisses him on the forehead.

'You look pretty, Mum.'

'Do I?' She lights up. 'Thanks, babe.'

'Yeah, put some stuff on your face as well.'

Yvonne lifts the homework book up, 'Do you actually understand this?'

He climbs across the sofa and sits down next to her. 'Nope.'

'I thought you were getting more help at school?'

'Yeah, so did I,' Emma says. 'But just because he's got a diagnosis, it doesn't actually mean anything.'

Yvonne counts the teacher's frequent scrawl of the word 'Absent' across the book's pages. No wonder he doesn't understand his work, Emma blames it on his dyslexia but he's hardly ever in school. Yvonne puts the homework book back in the rucksack along with a pair of Spiderman pyjamas, the ones Kiama wore to hers the last time he stayed over. Even then they were too short for him. Yvonne had made a joke with Emma about it the next day, about the speed at which her baby giraffe was growing, she laughed but obviously never replaced the pyjamas.

A car horn honks. 'Right, that must be Nana. Hurry up.'

Kiama chucks a handful of pens and pencils into the bag.

The horn sounds again and Emma's phone rings once then stops. She goes over to the window. 'I can't believe he's giving me a missed call.'

'Who?' Yvonne hopes Emma hasn't invited along some random friend or new man, which would be so typical of her.

'It's Dickhead. He always gives me a missed call so we don't have to talk. He's downstairs. I really thought Julie was doing the pick-up today.'

Kiama jumps. 'Is it Dad? Yes. I'm going to the toilet first. Tell him to wait for me.'

'Look at this arsehole,' Emma says. 'He tells me he's got no money, yet he's driving about in an Audi TT. You'll need to take Kiama down. I'm so not in the mood to deal with Lewis right now.'

'He's seven years old, I'm sure he can walk down the stairs himself.'

'He can't. He's terrified of that drunken guy on the second floor.'

'So make Lewis come up and get him.' Yvonne regrets saying this instantly, picturing herself hiding out in the bathroom while Lewis and Emma chat tersely on the doorstep.

'No, I don't want him up here, peering in my flat. Judging me on not having dusted or some shit like that.'

Kiama comes out of the bathroom and grabs his bag. 'Come on, someone take me down.'

Emma takes his face in her hands and kisses him again, 'Have fun, okay? And remember what I said, don't tell Nana about my job, alright.'

'Alright Mum, love you, love you, love you,' he says quickly, giving her three kisses back.

Yvonne follows him out onto the walkway and wonders if she can get away with leaving him at the foot of the stairs. Lewis gets out of the car and looks up to the balcony. Shit.

'Yvonne?' Emma calls. 'Remind Dickhead not to touch my son's hair.'

Yvonne takes Kiama down, past the drunk on the second floor, who looks at him and says, 'Alright, sonny boy.'

'See,' Kiama stage whispers as he grabs Yvonne's arm, 'why is he always chatting to me?'

'Because he's a friendly old man.'

'He's scary. But if he ever touches me, I'll kick him in the balls and run.' Kiama demonstrates a karate move then runs ahead.

Outside Lewis leans against his car, with his arms folded. His lips tremble as he tries to hold in a laugh when he sees Yvonne. 'Special K,' he shouts. 'What is going on with this?' He rubs Kiama's hair and frowns.

'I'm growing an afro,' Kiama says.

'No, you're not.'

'But I can make it look good.'

Lewis jabs him in the ribs and Kiama does the same back.

'I'm taking you straight to the barbers'.' He puts his hand up and Kiama gives him a high five. 'Say bye to Auntie Yvonne.'

Auntie. She's been referred to as his auntie before, when she's had to collect him from school or sign him into football lessons. But in this context it makes her feel sick.

'Laters,' Kiama calls.

'Sit up front,' Lewis says, 'I left something there for you.'

What is this? Is Lewis putting on a show for her? For all the time she spends with Kiama, this is the first and only time she's ever seen him with Lewis. It's made things easier somehow, allowing her to put a huge distance between them both in her mind. She doesn't see Lewis as Kiama's dad, if she did, she might think twice about what she's doing.

'Don't call me that,' she says.

'What?' he smiles.

'Auntie,' she pushes the rucksack into his chest and he pretends to be winded, as if he's going to get a laugh out of her now. How can he think this is funny? It's meant to be the thing they've both feared all along, but apparently not for him.

'This is messed-up,' he says. She doesn't look at him, but hears the humour in his voice and that's bad enough. 'I had no clue you were going to be here today.'

'I told you I was meeting Emma for dinner.'

'Yeah, but I didn't know you'd be here, actually at the flat.' His eyes move up to the balcony behind her. 'Where is the Princess? Is she up there watching?'

'I don't know.'

'Should I come over tomorrow? Or did you want to go out?'

'Do we really need to arrange this now?' she asks, casting a quick glance behind.

'Guess not. You heard anything from your brother? I keep thinking about your face when he saw me,' Lewis smiles.

'I spoke to him. He's not going to say anything.'

'See, all that worry about nothing. Makes you think, doesn't it? That things are best out in the open.'

Yvonne says nothing, it's too awkward. She opens the

front car door, where Kiama sits engrossed in a magazine and a family sized packet of crisps. 'Kiama, put on your seatbelt. See you soon, okay?'

'Bye,' he says, not looking up. She shuts the door and turns back to Lewis. Is this what it would be like? Would both of them come to collect Kiama on weekends? It's a weird thought, one she doesn't quite know what to do with.

'Yvie?' Lewis says. 'Why are we making things difficult for ourselves? Just tell her.'

Yvonne bites her lip. 'I was going to. Tonight.' That was the plan, but now, she can't imagine doing it. 'Though, I don't think I can, not after this, after seeing you here.'

'You're telling me you're going to spend all night with her and not mention me?'

'Get over yourself Lewis.'

He laughs, 'I didn't mean it like that.'

She double-checks Kiama's window is up, 'I want to tell her, I really do. But then I keep thinking, it's still early days for us.'

'Early days? And what about the years before? You know how much time we've wasted?'

She thinks about all the other guys she's dated over the years, about the feelings she's had and the times she's thought that she was in love. But this is different; her feelings for Lewis are so strong, so uncontrollable. 'I'm going,' she says, then pulls herself away from him. It's the only way for now, until she figures out how to do this.

Inside the flat, Emma holds her gaze for a few seconds then smiles. 'What happened? Did he say something to you?'

'No,' Yvonne smiles back.

'You've probably not seen him since we were at uni. He's the same arsehole though, isn't he?'

Yvonne coughs, the confession suddenly stuck in her throat, the words failing to form.

'Anyway, I'm nearly ready,' Emma says breaking the moment. 'We can go soon.'

When she leaves the room, Yvonne doubles over with the relief of being able to exhale.

Emma had complained recently about how her idea of eating out was the café at the Tesco superstore. With this in mind Yvonne wanted to take her somewhere special, but now, sitting in the blue velvet booth of the restaurant, it feels like a mistake.

Emma twists at the necklace. It suited her outfit more than Yvonne's. But it will break if she continues to wrap her fingers in it.

'You look nice, Em. Stop fussing.'

She lets go and frowns at the menu.

'The risotto is great,' Yvonne says. 'I had it the last time I came.'

'Think I'll be having the bread and tap water.'

'I'll pay. Don't worry about it.'

The menu slaps down on the table. 'It was a joke. I *can* pay for my own dinner.'

But there's no way Yvonne's going to let Emma pay for this. 'I chose the restaurant, so I'll pay. Besides, we're celebrating your new job.'

The waiter comes over and Emma begins her routine of flirting, asking where he's from, what he does for fun outside of work, if he's single. It's embarrassing, but not in the way it used to be, when Emma would always end the night with a phone number or love bite, but because the waiter looks about nineteen and Emma, well, she's not even thirty but there's a weariness about her tonight. She's thinner than usual, and maybe it's because she layered on too much heavy make-up, or because her hair's gone back to black, but she looks especially pale and tired.

The waiter leaves the table and Emma laughs. 'There's something about these Eastern European boys.'

Yvonne shakes her head. 'He looks very young.'

'I'll take whatever I can get. I haven't been with anyone in so long. It's depressing. I think my hymen's grown back.'

'Emma, shut up.'

The waiter returns and puts the drinks down with flourish and Emma winks at him before he walks off.

'This isn't even what I ordered,' Yvonne complains.

'No, me neither. He is so dumb. All look and no substance,' she says while removing a lychee from her cocktail. 'All these pretentious restaurants are the same.'

'Do you want to go somewhere else?'

'We're here now. I know how you love these types of places.'

'You think I'm pretentious?'

'Yes,' Emma says firmly, 'I've always thought that, even when you were poor.'

Yvonne laughs, she relaxes, but the food is disappointing. Or maybe it's just that it's so hard to enjoy with Emma constantly bitching about the portion sizes and over-ordering because she doesn't want to go home hungry. At one point she even compares the pudding to that of her boarding school and declares the school's superior. By the end of the meal most of the food on Emma's side has been picked at, prodded and discarded.

'Why aren't you eating? This is why you've lost so much weight.'

'Have I?' Emma smiles. 'Thanks.'

'It's not a compliment. I've never seen you this skinny.'

'It's the stress, babe.'

It's all she's spoken about all night, her anxieties about starting work again after being a 'stay-at-home mum' for so many years, her parents' complete lack of faith in her, Kiama's continued struggles at school. Yvonne listens and wonders why they bother anymore. But perhaps, after she tells all about Lewis, Emma won't want to see her again anyway.

It's an uncomfortable thought. Is that really what she wants? For the friendship to end?

Emma looks up. 'Sorry. I've been going on and on, haven't I?'

'No, it's fine. I'm tired, that's all.' It's true, today has exhausted her. She doesn't have the energy for it now. 'We should get the bill?'

'Already? I thought we were going out proper?'

'I've got a hundred things to do tomorrow.' It's not the right time to talk about this. Maybe it never will be. Maybe something will happen and Yvonne and Lewis will be able to exist in a place where Emma need never know about them.

'Spare me, I get you're busy.' Emma grabs her bag and rattles around for her purse. 'Going halves, are we?'

'Oh, don't be like that. Stop it. Em.'

'You know us frumpy single mums don't get out much, so forgive me for boring you.'

'Don't give me that single mum routine. You're out all the time. Let's have one more drink?' One more and maybe Yvonne will get her confidence back.

Emma nods, 'Only if you're not too busy?'

'I'm going to the loo. Get lover boy's attention and order something strong.'

Yvonne looks at her reflection in the mirror. She doesn't want to do this anymore. She doesn't want to keep the secret. Emma doesn't need to know about the stuff which came before, the one-night stand she had with Lewis at twenty-one, or the summer she was interning and spent every spare moment she could up at his flat. All Emma needs to know is that they're seeing each other now, and it's going well, so well, apart from this one big thing.

As she comes back to the table Emma is going through Yvonne's handbag and picking out her phone. Yvonne's heart races, 'What are you doing?' she panics.

'Your ringtone is so loud.'

Yvonne grabs it and checks the missed call, an unknown number.

'It rang for ages. Who's so desperate to get hold of you at this time on a Friday night?'

'No one. It's no one.'

'Liar. It's half ten. *That* was a booty call,' Emma teases. 'Are you getting back together with Jaden? Has he been *sitting* on your desk again?'

'No. That was ages ago. I told you that was nothing.' Yvonne switches off her screen and puts it in her bag, covering it with a scarf, as if it makes a difference. 'What did you order? Sex on the Beach? I hate peach.'

'I didn't know it was made with peach.'

'But you do know what I like. I'm surprised they even sell these here, so tacky.'

'For fuck's sake, Yvonne, I'm sorry I didn't order a sophisticated enough drink for you.'

'Oh, give it a rest.'

Emma straightens in her seat and takes a sip of the drink before recoiling. 'Urgh, this is sweet.'

They both laugh and Emma pushes the drink away. 'Sorry, babe,' she says.

'No, don't be. It's just a drink.'

'I don't know why you still put up with me,' Emma says. 'I bore myself sometimes.'

They look over at the next table where a group of men laugh overenthusiastically at each other.

'So,' Emma says in a way that signals she's about to say something serious. Yvonne prays that somehow Emma knows all and is about to confront her, to save her from having to say the words herself. 'I've been thinking about Kenya.'

'Kenya?' It throws her completely. 'What about it?'

'About going back. About making a different life for myself. Showing Kiama something real.'

'You're talking about poverty. What is this thing with people wanting to expose their children to extreme poverty?'

Emma pulls the orange slice from the drink and bites it, leaving the rind. 'I want to show him a different kind of life.'

'You took him before. You said he complained the whole time about it being too hot.'

'He was only four then.' Emma closes her eyes. 'I wish I could go back.'

'Everyone wants to go back to being a kid again.'

'We've got nothing here.'

'That's not true. Kiama has everything here. His family. His school. His friends.'

'I need to change my life.' She wraps the necklace around her fingers again and this time Yvonne doesn't mention it. 'Would I be able to sublet my flat?'

'No.'

'Why not?'

'Because you can't sublet a council property.'

'*Everyone* does it.'

'No, they don't. Because subletting is illegal. And immoral.'

Emma tuts, 'Well, there's no way I'd give up my flat. You need to be an asylum-seeking mother of ten to get a council place these days. And I'm never privately renting again. Remember when I lived above the dry cleaner's? I'm still waiting for the cancer to kick in.'

'If you can afford to go to Kenya, then you can afford to give up your council flat.'

'Babe, I'm not going to be the first person in the world to rent out my flat while I piss off back to Africa, alright.'

Yvonne laughs then stops herself. 'You're not really serious about this, are you?'

Emma nods, slowly, like she's only just convinced herself.

'But where would Kiama go to school?'

Emma rolls her eyes. 'There *are* schools there.'

'What, some international school, with a bunch of spoilt expat kids? He'd end up with a weird American accent. Like you at university, *dude*,' she mocks and they both laugh. 'If you're fed up with London, at least try and move out to Surrey or something first. Not all the way to Africa.'

'Ignore me. It's the drink talking. We're both not really in the mood, are we?' Emma yawns and Yvonne knows for sure that the moment has passed. Emma has trumped her confession with her own plans. 'Let's call it a night,' Emma says. 'I'll let you answer your booty call.'

They pull on their coats and go outside. It's drizzling lightly and women who are overly made-up and under-dressed scatter about beneath umbrellas.

'Emma, I'm sorry about tonight.'

'Why?'

'Because,' she stares at her friend and wonders if she'll ever be able to do it, to tell Emma she's fallen in love with the man who's made her life so difficult. 'Because, there's stuff on my mind at the moment. So, I'm—'

'It's okay. I know you get stressed with work and your flat sounds like an endless fucking nightmare. Plus, I'm not much fun. Especially, compared to whatever hot new relationship you're in.'

'No, it's not that, it's—'

'I do know you by now, I can see it in your eyes.'

Yvonne allows her bag to fall off her shoulder.

'I'm not digging. Go, it's too wet to stand out here chatting. Why are you crying?' Emma asks cautiously. 'What's going on with you at the moment?'

Yvonne takes a huge breath. 'We've been together for a while. I wanted to tell you, but I was waiting for the right time and the months go by so fast.' Yvonne covers her face, relieved that it's all finally coming out.

Emma laughs, 'Babe, it's great you're seeing someone. Why are you getting so upset?'

'Because, I've wanted to tell—'

'I don't take offence if you don't constantly update me on every detail of your love life. I know we're both in different places.' She pries Yvonne's hands from her face and squeezes them and Yvonne has the sensation of something slipping through her fingers. Emma has misunderstood.

'I'm happy for you. Be happy, enjoy it. I'll meet him when you're settled. Invite me and Kiama over for lunch or something.' Emma hugs her before breaking away. 'Oh here, let me give you this back now.' She goes to undo the necklace but it's caught in her hair.

'Leave it. I'll get it the next time I see you.'

'Sure? Okay.'

They hug and it's long, too long. Yvonne squeezes her eyes shut and feels the rain on her face.

'Thanks for dinner.' But as Emma pulls away her eyes are pink, from the alcohol, from the weight of things unsaid. 'Text me when you get home, alright.'

Yvonne nods and watches as Emma jogs towards the bus stop to shelter from the rain. She feels like she just lost her best friend.

CHAPTER SEVENTEEN

CHICKEN...

October 2020

Yvonne

They don't speak on the way back. But it's comfortable, like one of the barriers between them has finally broken down. They get off the bus in the centre of Kikuyu and Kiama gets excited when he spots Chick Burger, the place the girls had told them about yesterday, the place he *'had to experience to believe'*.

'We haven't really eaten much today, have we?' he asks.

And as much as she's repelled by the look of it, she also knows there's no way they're leaving the town without him trying it.

Inside he spends ages perusing the menu above the counter, pointing out each misspelling and the blatant rip-off of KFC brand names.

'I'm going for the Zingey meal,' he says finally. 'Also, let's get normal fries and chilli fries.'

'I'm not hungry. Go ahead and order.' Yvonne takes a seat, faced away from the television mounted on the wall.

'Can you hear that?' he says as he joins her at the table, phone in his hand. 'This place not only has reception but also Wi-Fi. Thank God.' For a few minutes he reads through everything he's missed. On the next table over a pair of school girls share a portion of fries, they squirt a line of ketchup onto each one before eating.

'Why does everyone want to eat this kind of food all the time?' Yvonne asks.

Kiama puts his phone away. 'I'm so happy right now.'

'Yes, because you've caught up on what all your friends have been doing, eating and watching. You're a complete slave to your phone.'

'It's about so much more than that.' He scratches the back of his neck.

'I bet it's not.'

'Look, I know you think you're being mad alternative by living *off grid*, but you're missing out on so much.' He takes a photo of the laminated menu on the table and rubs his palms together as the tray arrives. 'The moment of truth.'

'Aren't you scared? Think of what's in that? What it's doing to your body.'

'Delia told me they make this stuff from baboon arse.'

Yvonne laughs.

'Now you want to try it?' He takes a bite.

'No, definitely not. You never stop eating.'

'What are you talking about? I've hardly eaten a thing since getting here. I'm losing weight.' He recoils to pull the gherkin out. 'Look,' he eyes the front door as two old men walk in and sit under the television, 'more white people.'

'So?'

'You're meant to nod at your own. Acknowledge them. That's what minorities do.'

'Oh shut up.' But then the men look over at her, and one says, 'Good afternoon.'

Kiama laughs.

'Why do you say stuff like that? You're half white.'

'So is your lover boy Obama, world still sees him as black. Though I've been feeling pretty white here.' He takes another bite and sighs. 'Well, it's no Five Guys.' He itches again. 'Feel like I've got a rash or something.'

Yvonne motions for him to show her the back of his neck. As he lifts his hair she sees a circle of red blemishes. 'Oh no. It's because you were carrying the baby on your shoulders.'

'Why? What is it?' he panics.

'You've got ringworm. Er.' She goes in her bag for the bottle of anti-bac hand gel. 'We're going to have to find a chemist.'

He tuts, 'So, it's not a big deal. Is it? What is ringworm? Can it get in my hair?'

'It's a viral infection. The baby must have it on his legs.' It makes her skin crawl.

'Jenga? Yeah, he had a rash, I think. We'll need to get him some medicine too then. Actually, we should stock up on stuff for the orphanage, let me make a list.' He takes out his phone and starts typing, 'Soap, plasters, toothbrushes. What else? What's the name of that pink medicine? Calpol? You think they sell it here?'

'Why? We're not going back to the orphanage.'

'Yvonne,' he says, 'the money my granddad was talking about, it's not only my compensation.'

'Okay.'

'It's also the money Nana put aside for me, so it's,' he pauses and looks around, 'it's kind of a lot.'

It's what she's waited to hear, ever since Neil's comments, but now Kiama's come clean, she's not sure what to say. And what does it have to do with buying plasters and Calpol?

'I got access to it when I turned eighteen and while it was never my reason for coming here, it is just sitting in my bank account. I can't stop imagining how far it would go in a place like this.'

'It's not that simple.'

'It is. It's so simple. I have it. I don't want it. The kids need it.'

'The kids? We've only just met them. We don't know the set-up there. How it's funded by Kindred Kenya.'

'I know there are fourteen kids in that house. That small, dirty house.'

'How much is it? No, actually, don't tell me.'

He shifts in his seat. 'It's enough to turn that whole orphanage around. But I don't want to be like that person who donated the swing set no one can afford to fix. I could work it out, so that each year a little more money goes to them.'

'I don't know about this, Kiama. You need to think about your needs first.'

'Why? I'm not starving. I've got a roof over my head.'

'Yes, your family home. But you can't live with your family forever. Why don't you think about putting it towards a property?'

'Property? No one of my generation has the money for that.'

'You do.'

'Yeah, for a deposit. But what happens month to month? I'll never earn enough to make payments.'

'Oh, don't give me that whiney Gen Z crap. Just stop buying trainers and ketamine.'

He lets out a burst of laughter before putting his poker face back on.

'Owning a property isn't that out of reach for you.'

'Yeah it is. Cause your lot bought them all up.'

'My lot? Excuse me?' She can't believe that she's part of the 'lot', the generation blamed for wrecking things for the one coming up after. 'I worked hard for it. I had no leg-up. I'm one of four children. My parents struggled for years, so they always encouraged me to go and get my own properties.'

He laughs, 'Plural, you know. How many *properties* do you own?'

'Three.'

He gasps. 'In London?'

'No. One's in Manchester. A student house.'

'See, you're the reason,' he points his straw at her. 'Greedy baby boomer.'

'I'm not a boomer. How old do you think I am? Technically, I'm a millennial.'

'A millennial? But you can't even use Twitter.'

She takes a chip and he smiles like it's a personal victory. 'You're making me stress eat.'

'Two properties in London,' he shakes his head at her. 'You're probably the richest person I know.'

'And you're probably the richest teenager I know.'

He stabs the straw in the milkshake, 'Don't tell me I can't change things.'

'I'm not. I'm telling you that you can't dump a load of money in Kenya to make yourself feel better.'

He leans back in his chair and throws the napkin on the tray.

'Kiama?'

'I hear you,' he sighs. 'I hear you.'

Outside the market stalls are being packed up, as the evening draws closer. The arrangement was that they meet Joe back at Purity's house for six and then drive onto Lake Nakuru. Yvonne hoped the plan would stick whether Purity was there or not. They had already spent a whole night and day off-track because of her; Yvonne wasn't keen to do the same again.

'Last chance to get your Obama sweatshirt,' Kiama jokes as they pass by the stalls.

'Ha ha.'

They stop outside a chemist and Yvonne runs in to get Kiama some cream for his ringworm, when she comes out he's frowning.

'What?'

'Can I ask you something?'

She hands him the small paper bag of cream and nods.

'If someone would have given Mum a ton of money when she was my age, what would she have done?'

Yvonne can picture Emma, flirting her way from booth to booth in the student bar, getting everyone to sign a petition or put money in a pot. She was always crusading for some cause or charity.

'Honest answer, please,' he says.

'Your mum would have thrown it at the first cause to catch her eye, dolphins, battered women, Bangladeshi flash flood victims.'

He smiles. This wasn't the desired reaction.

'After the Boxing Day Tsunami, she gave a month's wages to the Red Cross.'

'That's amazing.'

'No, it was reckless. She was broke and her parents had to bail her out. She ate boiled rice and ketchup for a week. Also, you're not your mum. This money is for you to start your life.'

'But I don't want it,' he says. 'I don't want to build my life on this money.'

'You're set on doing this, aren't you? Giving it all away?'

'Dad lost a lot of money a few years ago,' he says suddenly. 'He and my Uncle Danny almost went bankrupt on some restaurant franchise. And the trampoline park feels like it's heading for closure. So, I can't talk to my family about money. But you're obviously good with it. I'm asking you to help me. I need support on how to make a plan, how to allocate it properly. You must know how.'

'I'm not sure. It's not my area of expertise. Though, I think it's a great idea to pack up some toiletries and leave them at the Kindred Kenya offices. We should definitely do that.'

Kiama shakes his head. 'Whatever. I'll find someone else.'

They were starting to get close, he was opening up to her and now she's taking them back to square one. She's ruining things.

'Kiama, please wait.'

'Nah. It's fine, Yvonne. I've already asked too much of you by making you come here.' He takes a few steps backwards, his face set into a sulk.

'I'm sorry. But I'm being honest with you.'

'It's fine,' he calls over his shoulder as he walks off. It's almost amusing, this throwback to how he used to be, storming off when his mum refused to let him play on his PlayStation for hours or stay out late with his friends running about the local adventure playground. But he's not a child anymore; he can't kick off because she doesn't go with his every suggestion. And she won't let him emotionally blackmail her like this.

CHAPTER EIGHTEEN

... AND BEER

October 2020

Kiama

He's not in a sulk, he's angry. Yvonne makes out like she's here for him, like she came all this way to help him face up to something, but really she's just in it for some flashy holiday where she makes herself feel better. He knows she feels guilty about not keeping in touch with him after Mum died, of course he knows, he's even played on it a few times. But it seems like her guilt doesn't stretch enough to want to help out some orphans, or take the time to understand why *he* does.

Purity should be back at the house by now, but even if she's not, Kiama's decided he'll wait on her for as long as it takes. Maybe it shocked her to see him this morning, maybe that's why she was in a rush to get away. He's come to understand that people who knew Mum fall into two camps when they see him, either they're desperate to talk about her or the whole thing makes them so awkward they can't get away quick enough.

He hears someone call his name and looks around.

Yvonne stops too and looks up. 'There,' she says.

Delia hangs over the rail of a balcony above them. 'Enjoying the sights of Kikuyu?'

'Yeah. Something like that,' Kiama calls. 'Is Purity home yet?'

'No. Turns out Toby does have malaria so she's at the hospital with him. Sarah's not there either, the house is locked. Come up for a drink?'

'She locked the house?' Yvonne says. 'How can she do that? All our stuff is in there. I said we'd be back.'

It's the perfect situation. 'I'm going for a drink.'

'I don't think so,' she says.

Kiama scoffs. What's this about? Is she really trying to step into some kind of mum role? At what point did he suggest that's what he needs? It pisses him off.

He makes his way into the dark and dingy staircase. The walls are painted a deep red and covered in graffiti. He doesn't even really want a drink right now, but needs to kill time and won't have Yvonne dictate things to him. She follows behind and they both pause on the landing next to a door flung open, a single pungent toilet sits in the middle surrounded by sodden balls of tissue.

'Really, Kiama? You want to hang out in a place like this?'

He sighs and walks ahead, out onto the open-deck bar, where the music is loud and there's alcohol and company, other than Yvonne. Why does she even have to come with him? Why can't she go for a walk by herself or something? It's suffocating to have her constantly around like this.

'I'll order you a Coke,' Yvonne says.

'Why? Is me drinking another thing you don't agree with?'

'I'm just trying to help. I'm trying to—'

'Mother me?'

'No,' she snaps.

But he can't be bothered to argue with her. She needs to realise what she's doing and stop it. For him, there's nothing more off-putting than someone trying to take care of him. He'd made the mistake last year of telling a girl he'd started getting serious with how he lost Mum. It changed things straight away. She went from being up for partying with him all the time to wanting to talk constantly. It felt like she was looking to relate everything he did and said back to the fact he didn't have a mum.

They get their drinks and join the girls on tall white stools which overlook the market.

'How will we know when Purity's back?' Yvonne asks.

Alice waves her phone. 'Because she'll summon us for dinner.'

'She was really excited about cooking for you two tonight, I think she might even get out the good beans,' Delia teases.

It's nice to hear that Purity's spoken about him today, that it means something to her that he's here.

They all clink drinks and Kiama reels off his story about the orphanage, the kids and poverty, it sounds almost generic and he feels a little guilty. But what else can he say? He's hardly going to talk about Mum's connection to the place and the way he broke down a few minutes after leaving.

The girls nod along and every so often interject with stories about the hospital, the shortage of basic provisions, the lack of training, the surgeons forced to operate by torchlight. Yeah, it definitely feels wrong talking this way, it's like they've been shown something private and are now gossiping about it over drinks.

Yvonne stays quiet, though every so often she takes a sip of her drink and frowns. She looks so uncomfortable perched on the stool, her nose turned up like nothing is good enough for her.

A sharp pain shoots up Kiama's left arm again causing him to squeal. It started on the bus back. 'I think I've pulled a muscle,' he says when everyone looks over at him.

'Have you been doing any heavy lifting?' Delia strokes his arms and laughs. He could tell straight away she was that sort of girl, a flirt. Usually, he'd be well up for it, but the day has already been too exhausting, plus he can feel Yvonne's eyes on them both, judging.

'I love your tats by the way,' she says, 'how many have you got?'

Yvonne rolls her eyes. 'It's from all the swinging,' she says. 'You were lifting and swinging the children for about an hour today, children are heavy.'

Alice gets in a round of Tusker beers and Kiama drinks his quickly. He's never had it before, but both Granddad and Mum used to drink beer and the smell of it is familiar.

Delia hands Yvonne her phone, 'Will you take a photo of us, please? We need a *snap* of us.'

'Yeah, hashtag activism,' Alice says.

Yvonne puts zero effort in and when they check the single shot, it's blurry.

'So tell me,' Delia says, '*are* you Kenyan?'

It's a question he's been asked before, especially if someone picks up on his name. 'Nope. I'm English.'

'But you're mixed race?'

Kiama's rolls out his usual, 'My mum's white, my dad's black,' line but Delia carries on. 'So your dad's from Kenya?'

'No. My dad's from Harrow.' He picks up his bottle but finds it empty, so takes Yvonne's untouched one instead.

'Oh, so what's the connection to Kenya? Why did you live here as a kid?'

Yvonne yawns loudly and the girls turn to each other and laugh. Was she trying to help him out there or just being rude?

'I think we're keeping her up,' Delia says.

Kiama thinks of the photos he's seen of Mum and Yvonne on nights out, both of them in tiny little dresses and too much make-up.

'It's funny because if I hadn't seen all the photos of you and Mum at uni I would struggle to imagine you as a party girl.'

She looks at him briefly and smiles.

'Maybe she's a retired party girl,' Delia says. 'University in the Nineties sounded so fun. It was cheap back then too, like a grand a year. No wonder they just partied all the time.'

Yvonne stands up, 'I think we should go back now.'

She's doing it again.

'Actually,' he says, 'I think it's time to switch from beer. Get some tequila in?'

The girls clap and Alice heads to the bar.

'So Key-ah-ma,' Delia says. 'Why do you have such a Kenyan-sounding name?'

'Because my mum was Kenyan.' He usually misses out this part of the story, it's so much easier to tell people that he doesn't know where his name comes from.

'But, er—' Delia taps her lips with a finger.

'You're boring me with all these questions about my ethnicity.'

246

She strokes his arm. 'Sorry, but I'm curious about you.'

Yvonne cuts in, 'One more drink, then we're going.'

'Yeah, she's right,' Delia says. 'Even if Purity isn't back, Sarah will be, and she'll be rattling her chains, she always locks that gate dead on seven. When you arrived last night you only got let in because we thought you were new volunteers.'

'Surely, she won't lock up until we're all back,' Yvonne says. 'We're only running in to get our bags anyway.'

'I don't know,' Delia teases. 'Sarah's a stickler for the rules and the curfew is Kindred Kenya's biggest one.'

'Why's that?' Kiama asks.

'A few volunteer houses got robbed last summer. So they brought in curfews. We've been right outside banging away once or twice and Sarah's point blank refused to open the gate just to prove a point. We've ended up in the guest house more times than I care to remember.'

The guest house, that's the place where Joe is resting up. 'Thought you said it wasn't for westerners?' Kiama asks.

'No, it's not, it's a dodgy dump. But,' she adds with the kind of smile he recognises, 'we've had some fun nights there.'

'I'm not staying in a guest house tonight, Kiama,' Yvonne says. 'And neither are you.'

He's about to remind her how old he is, about how much travelling he managed to do safely without her by his side when his phone rings. 'It's a WhatsApp call. This place has Wi-Fi, why didn't you tell me?'

'Why'd you think we hang out here?' Alice says.

'Dad?' He wobbles as he gets down from the stool, surely he can't be getting tipsy after two drinks, but then he did down them pretty quickly. He tries his best to walk straight, knowing Yvonne is watching, stacking her case with reasons for them to move on.

'I could do with more than one text a day,' Dad says. It's good to hear his voice, even if it does sound angry.

'I've tried, but the reception out here is mad patchy.'

'Where are you?'

'In a bar?'

'A bar? With who?'

Kiama stops on the other side of the balcony and leans over the rail. 'Some girls.'

Dad laughs, he's always like this, proud at any hint of his son being on the prowl.

'Hang on, what? Local girls?'

He looks back at Alice as she sets down the shots. Yvonne looks furious now. It's hard to believe she's the same person he used to find on their sofa on Sunday morning hung over and groaning after sitting in with Mum drinking all night. But then Dad always says life beats you around a bit. Maybe that's what happened to her. Maybe there's other stuff she's gone through that's changed her.

'They're not local girls, Dad, they're English, well, one's Irish or Scottish, something like that.'

'Nice,' Dad says. 'Is Yvonne there?'

'Yeah, course. But she's in a bad mood.'

A roar goes up in the bar as the right team scores in the football game that plays on a TV in the corner.

'Kiama, can't you go somewhere quieter?'

Yvonne is standing up. Is she leaving? He hopes so. It would make sense for them to have a break from each other. The day has been intense. He wants to tell Dad about it, about seeing Purity and the orphanage and Jenga and Simeon and, what else, there's been so much. He suddenly feels too tired to talk.

'All I can hear is a wall of noise,' Dad complains.

'Sorry.'

'Go someplace else.'

'What?' There's no way Kiama can explain everything that's happened so far, he wouldn't know where to start.

Yvonne looks over at him and throws her hands up. Clearly she expects him to leave with her.

'I've got to go,' he says. 'The reception is really bad.'

'Hold up. Are you okay? What's going on?'

'I'm fine.'

'You don't sound fine.'

Dad always says how Kiama was born without the ability to hide his feelings.

'K?' he asks.

'Look, I'm drunk, that's all.'

There's a pause on the other end, then Dad says, 'Okay. Call me tomorrow. And be careful with those girls.'

'Course.'

'Love you.'

'Love you too. Bye.'

He leans over the balcony and exhales deeply before walking back to the girls and Yvonne with her fed-up expression.

'Are you seriously drunk on two beers?' Delia laughs. 'Such a lightweight.'

'No, I'm not drunk on two beers,' he lies.

'So look, Purity's not coming back tonight so we've decided

to be rebels and stay out. But Yvonne's going. I can imagine being out for the night with us lot isn't her idea of fun?'

'No. It's not,' Yvonne says.

Delia flashes a stretched smile and says, 'Tell it like it is.'

He thought speaking to Dad would lift him but it's made him feel worse, more confused, like he's keeping secrets and he doesn't know why.

'I'm staying too,' he says.

'Yeah,' Delia and Alice clap.

'Really?' Yvonne says, clearly pissed off.

'Yeah. But I'm not stopping you from going on to the hotel if you want.' Please go, he thinks, please see that I need a break from you, from it all.

'We said we'd stick together.'

'When did we say that?' Why doesn't she get it? 'Look, I'm not your chaperone, if you want to go, go.' He doesn't mean for it to come out so harsh, but maybe it's what she needs to hear, how she needs to hear it. 'I'll make my own way up to the lake in the morning after I've spent time with Purity, which is *what* I came here to do. But right now, I'm staying for a drink.'

'One more and you'll be hardly standing.' This time, *she* sounds harsh.

'I don't need to be parented by you, alright?'

'But you're acting like you do. What do you think this is? Your gap year?'

He laughs. 'Did you seriously just say that?'

'I'm here for you, out here, disrupting my life not because I want to, but because you asked me to.'

'You only agreed to this trip to feel better about yourself. But you didn't expect to be dealing with a real adult, did you?'

'Actually, I did, but you're acting like a child, throwing your toys out of the pram because I won't help you waste your money.'

'Ooh,' Delia says, 'don't think we should hearing all this.'

He had almost forgotten the girls were there.

'This isn't how your mum would have wanted you to turn out.'

It's like a fucking train hitting him. She really just said that.

'She would have hated to see that you're so,' she looks for the words, 'so, entitled and so bloody spoilt.'

'Shit,' Delia says, as Yvonne moves away from the table and into the crowd.

'That came out of nowhere,' Alice adds.

Kiama flops back on the stool, like he's been winded. But the shock doesn't last long before the anger sets in. How can she say that to him? How can she think that's alright? He pushes through the crowd and takes the steps two at a time till he's outside on the street.

She's already walking away.

'I can't believe you,' he shouts. It makes her jump and turn to face him. 'You came all this way to tell me Mum would have been disappointed in me. Entitled? Spoilt? That's what you really think of me?' Even if she does, how could she say it? It's such a betrayal.

'Kiama, wait. I didn't mean—'

'No, don't apologise, you're right, I am spoilt. My dad and Nana let me get my own way all the fucking time. So, I'm sorry if I'm not the best turned-out teenager you know.'

251

'It was a stupid thing to say. It came out wrong.'

He takes a step back but can't stop looking at her, this woman who knew Mum better than anyone else in the world. Did she even think about the impact of saying something like this? It's unforgivable. 'How can you tell me what I've become wouldn't be enough for her? Go, Yvonne, I don't want to spend time with you.'

'Please,' she starts. But he turns away, he doesn't want to see her face softening as she realises she crossed the line.

He heads back inside the stairwell. Now what? He takes his phone out and watches the little reception icon hover at four bars. He leans his head against the mucky red wall and considers calling Dad. But to say what? Dad is always saying how proud he is of him, and while Kiama appreciates it he also wants to know that Mum would have felt the same way. Now he knows she wouldn't.

But he is trying; no one showed him how to do this. There's no set of rules of how to behave after you go through what he did.

Purity, that's who he could talk to now. She knew Mum too, maybe she wouldn't agree with what Yvonne just said.

'Hey?'

Delia stands a few steps up. 'You alright, hun? Has she gone?'

He puts his phone away and faces her. 'Yeah. She's gone.'

'You look like you need a drink. A proper one.'

And here's another option, to get so drunk he doesn't have think or stress about any of this for the next ten hours. He nods and heads back up.

CHAPTER NINETEEN

THE LUCK HUT

August 2009

Yvonne

Yvonne walks around the flat updating her list of all the things that have gone wrong this week; the doors on the wardrobe which have been put in upside down, the dripping boiler and the alarm system that keeps going off at 1.58 a.m. Some days, the list is endless.

'I feel like this place is getting more dangerous every time I visit,' Lewis says as he ducks to avoid the wires that hang from the ceiling. 'Is it definitely safe to use the gas again?'

'It's perfectly safe now. I even have a certificate.'

'Really? Maybe you should get it framed; you can put it over one of the holes in the wall.'

'You're not helping at all.' She's able to laugh along, but it's become tiresome living in a partial building site. Though over the last few weeks things have bothered her less than they should and she knows it's because Lewis has 'unofficially' moved in. His mum had complained about him getting under her feet and he took on a contract at a new gym a ten-minute drive from Yvonne's flat, so it made perfect sense that he stay with her. It wasn't even discussed, it just happened. So when the heating doesn't work, he's right there next to her and when the alarm goes off at night it's him that goes outside to charm the neighbours and apologise. And while he keeps talking about buying his own place, a little flat back in Harrow close to his family, she hopes he never will.

She puts what is surely the hundredth frozen pizza in the oven and tuts. 'You know, there are things other than pizza I can eat?'

'Yeah, like chicken, lamb, beef—'

'Are we really having this conversation again?' she laughs.

'I even bought a bag of salad,' he says as he empties the rest of the shopping.

'A salad? That's unlike you.'

'You keep going on about being healthy. Plus, I'm getting love handles. How can I work at a gym and have no time to actually go to the gym?'

'You could have gone tonight if you wanted.'

'After the day I had, all I wanted to do was come home and eat pizza with you.'

Home. Is that how he sees it here? Is that what she is to him?

He slides his hand up the back of her T-shirt, but his hand is cold against her skin. 'Doesn't take much to make you shiver, does it?'

'I'm cold,' she says coyly.

His phone buzzes between them. They both laugh and he lets go of her to take it out. He frowns, causing the appearance of that one little line between his eyebrows.

'All okay?' She takes the bottle of Bell's whisky from the bag and looks for the glasses.

'Emma's been trying to ring me,' he says.

'Maybe Kiama wants to speak to you.'

'No, we spoke last Sunday.'

'So? Call her back. I do get that you two need to speak to each other.' It's the most she's ever said to this effect. But it's important, as they get more serious, that he appreciates how understanding she is of 'the situation'. He and Emma have a kid together, and she's completely fine with the idea that they need to communicate. Just as they always have.

They walk through to the living room and Lewis rubs his head. 'I don't think I can face her right now. She's only going to ask me for something.' He puts his phone down on the coffee table and takes the drink Yvonne's poured.

'Like what?'

'Money,' he says loudly. 'And I don't have it at the moment. She can wait.' Lewis sits on the sofa and pats the cushion next to him. 'Let's not talk about this.'

Whatever is going on between them is not her concern, she doesn't want or need to know about it. But as the phone vibrates on the table he shifts a little.

'Answer it, Lewis.'

He takes the phone off to another room and she switches on the television to block out his voice, but every so often she can feel the bass of it bouncing off the bare floors and walls in the bedroom. She watches the news, taking none of it in before smelling the pizza and running back to the oven.

'Shit.'

He comes out of the bedroom. 'Can't believe you're still burning those? Not like you haven't had enough practice.'

'And now I know my smoke alarms don't work either,' she says, plonking the pizza on a chopping board.

They both stare at it, the atmosphere thick with the interruption of Emma.

'How's Kiama?' Yvonne asks as she looks in the freezer for something else to make. 'I haven't seen him in a while. How's he getting on at school?' When she turns back to Lewis he looks surprised, has she done the wrong thing by bringing him up?

'He's good,' Lewis says, 'I guess.'

She wants to pursue this, to make it normal. He needs to know he can talk about his son with her and it's okay.

'Did he tell you about Mr Linton? Having a male teacher has really made a difference.'

Lewis gets the plates out of the cupboard.

'The last time I spoke to him he was obsessed with ancient Egypt. I've got a papyrus somewhere I said I would send him, but obviously I can't find it in this place.'

'How do you still know so much about him? I thought you and Emma didn't speak much anymore.'

'We don't.' She decides to stick with the pizza; cracking it in half and putting a handful of salad leaves on each plate. 'But the last time I phoned the flat, Kiama answered and we talked. This is such a crap dinner.'

She catches him frown.

'What? Are you mad about me speaking to Kiama?'

'No. But I don't understand how she stops me taking him at weekends and restricts me to this fortnightly scheduled call, yet you're getting all this time with him, knowing his teacher's name and stuff.'

'I told you, I called—'

'Once a fortnight,' he repeats. 'What kind of relationship can we have on that? I keep telling her to give him a phone. All the kids have phones now.'

'What does he need a phone for?'

'To talk to me. He doesn't need to take it to school, just a cheap pay-as-you-go thing he could message me on. That way I could keep a check on him. Make sure Emma is coping alright.'

'She does more than cope,' Yvonne snaps.

Lewis looks up. 'Don't try to switch sides now. You know she's struggling. My mum said the last time she went over the flat was a mess.'

'Emma's flat is always a mess, Lewis. That's nothing new. And it's no reflection on how she's *coping*.'

'And we both knew she was too lazy to keep up the job, how long did that last? A month? And then she's surprised there's not enough money.'

'I don't want to hear this,' she says calmly. 'This has nothing to do with me.'

But he keeps on.

'I'm the one paying for everything but it's still not enough for her. Just bought all the new school uniform and trainers and she's going on like I don't support her.'

There's more to raising a kid than buying trainers, Emma had said this once, as she held a new pair of Nikes Lewis bought for Kiama. £120 they cost, the same amount as Emma's rent arrears.

'£12 a session for this tutor. It adds up. Maybe if she didn't

257

allow him to take so many days off school he would be able to catch up a bit quicker.'

Yvonne raises her hands, 'Emma does her best. And she's alone. It must be hard.'

'She's not raising him alone, Yvie. I know that's what she likes people to think. But I'm there for my son. I support him. I've seen him almost every month since he was born.'

'Every month? Really? Well done, Lewis, what do you want? A medal?'

'Where the hell did that come from?'

She's never heard him raise his voice, he sounds like a different person. But she's not going to back down now. 'Emma's put everything into raising Kiama. I've seen it. I've watched her struggle for years.'

'You think I'm a shit dad?'

'No. No, of course I don't. The same way I don't think Emma is a shit mum.'

He looks away from her and his jaw flexes slightly. 'Now I know the reason we never talk about this stuff. I'm going.'

She follows him into the hallway and watches as he makes his way down the stairs.

'Lewis?' she calls after him.

He stalls slightly and she heads down, but he still pulls on his shoes and jacket. 'I'm not perfect, Yvie, but I thought you were on my side.'

'I can't take sides in this. She's my friend.'

'Your friend? Really? But you never see her anymore.'

'That doesn't matter. We've known each other for years; we've been through so much together. She'll always be a part of my life. Where are you going?'

'Home.' He drops his head and turns his car keys over in his hands. 'You need to think about this.'

'About what?'

'About if this is too complicated for you.'

She shakes her head, but he's right. How was she expecting this to work in the long-run without Emma knowing? The longer it goes on the worse the betrayal is.

'Can you really be with me, while still having this friend-ship with Emma?'

'I told you, I hardly see Emma anymore.' Yvonne thinks of this often, of how their friendship, which used to be so intense and fuelled by them constantly spending time together, has turned into something else, something distant and habitual. 'Emma doesn't have many friends; you know that, she's got no family here either. So sometimes she does call me and I call her.'

Lewis puts a hand on Yvonne's cheek and she leans into it. 'Maybe we were both naïve to think we could pick up where we left off eight years ago. That it doesn't matter I have a kid with one of your friends.' He drops his hand and it feels as if Yvonne's heart has started to fall through her body.

'What are you saying? That we should stop seeing each other?' There's a panic in her voice she can't hide. Never does she want to have to choose between Emma and Lewis, but if that's what it comes to, she knows right then who she would pick. She's not proud of it either, that she would choose a man over her friend.

'I don't want to worry that whatever I do and say in front of you will get back to Emma. Or that you're judging me as a dad based on my mistakes. I'm trying to be there more for

Kiama, but it's hard with Emma. I don't need to add more stress to the situation.'

He unlocks the door.

'Please, don't leave,' she says.

He stops and leans against the door.

'Lewis, please, I'll tell her. I promise, I'll tell her.'

Yvonne waits at the bottom of the stairs for Lewis. On the mat sits a few birthday cards from her brothers, nieces and nephews and a handmade one from Kiama. On the front he's drawn two elephants, their trunks intertwined. She imagines how long it must have taken him, sitting in that cluttered living room, surrounded by the sprawl of his papers.

'He's getting good at this,' she says.

'What's that?' Lewis asks as he comes down, sunglasses on despite the thick greyness of the sky.

'Nothing.' She closes the card and folds it in with the council tax bill, hoping he won't see it. 'Just some birthday cards.' It feels deceitful, but necessary. She has to set boundaries between her link to Kiama and Emma, and her relationship with Lewis. After their argument it was agreed that Yvonne would tell Emma everything and they would see how things went from there. While Lewis believes it will end their friendship, Yvonne is hopeful that over time Emma will get used to the idea and things will work out, eventually falling into something that works for everyone.

'You ready to go?' he asks.

'Yes, but you still haven't told me where we're going.' Last month she had seen the page open on his laptop of flights to Dubai and the dates selected fell over her birthday weekend.

But, she knew all the money he was making at the gym was being ploughed into the business he was trying to get off the ground with his brother. A trip like that would have been well out of his price range. So, she'd been obsessively dropping hints about how much she wanted to do a weekend away with him in the countryside, somewhere remote, somewhere they could spend a good block of time together, secluded from the world. She was relieved last night when instead of telling her to pack a bikini he watched the weather forecast and asked if she owned wellingtons.

He takes her hand, '*I will not cease from Mental Fight.*'

'What?'

'*Nor shall my sword sleep in my hand.*'

'Oh no,' she laughs while following him out to the car. 'Please, stop.'

'*Till we have built Jerusalem. In England's green and pleasant land.*' He chucks her bag in the back. 'Perfect weather for a weekend in the countryside.'

The drive is longer than expected and Yvonne spends much of it holding the TomTom, which keeps falling off the windscreen, and repeating all the instructions Lewis mishears.

Her patience runs thin as they drive through Oxford and she turns the music down. Lewis raises an eyebrow at her, 'I can't believe you did that.'

'It's too loud and it's driving me mad. Can't we listen to something else?'

'You really touched my radio. That's my deal-breaker,' he turns it back up, even louder.

'It's been five months, Lewis, five months of listening to nothing but this monotonous crap,' she shouts over the music.

He laughs and shakes his head. 'And what are you talking about five months?' he asks. 'Today's our half year anniversary.'

She doesn't even try to count back in her head knowing that while Lewis is the kind of person to forget what time of day he arranged to meet someone, he's obsessive about dates, recalling the years certain albums were released or football games were played.

'Half a year,' she says. 'Do I get a trophy?'

Six months to make up for all those they spent apart. The back story doesn't matter. In the future when people ask how they met she will simply say, 'at a club,' or 'from around Soho.' And the fact that he has a child with a friend of hers, an old friend, won't matter. Families are complicated these days. Maybe in time Kiama will visit them both. It could happen, will happen soon. She just has to deal with Emma first.

Eventually the road becomes a lane and they park by a wooden toadstool with a discreet sign which reads 'The Luck Hut'.

'Here we are,' he says. 'Welcome to The Fuck Hut, honey.'

'Don't call it that.'

'Sorry. It was a joke.' There's a slight chill outside and it's drizzling a little, as Yvonne knew it would be, but it's just weather, what does it matter? They're together, alone, and away from everything.

Inside the pale pink round hut, she sits on the sofa with a glass of wine while he explores the bedroom and bathroom, shouting through comments like, 'Free slippers, you think we can keep them?' and 'Molton Brown in here, no rubbish.'

She always used to think of Lewis as much cooler than her, more sophisticated and worldly, so it had surprised her when she began getting to know him again properly to find out he wasn't. But it was almost endearing to hear him emit a quiet whistle at the prices in a restaurant or say things like 'how the other half lives'. It was so far from the uber-confident player she was crazy about at twenty-one.

'This place is great,' he says. He lifts the TV remote from the table. 'Ah, it's got Sky too. Who cares about the weather? We don't need to leave all weekend.'

She grabs the remote from his hand and switches it off. 'We've not driven all this way to watch TV.'

'Course not. It's called The Fuck Hut for a reason.'

'Please, stop calling it that.'

'I'm kidding.'

Outside, the wind changes direction and rain pelts the window.

'I thought this was going to be romantic,' she says, slightly annoyed by him.

'Romantic?' he mocks. 'Is that what you want from me?'

She sighs, then picks up her bag and takes it through to the bedroom. There's a small box of Guylian Seashell chocolates on the bed, along with a teddy bear holding a heart.

Lewis puts his hands on her shoulders and turns her around. 'See, I *am* trying.'

'Yes, you are,' she laughs.

'What? Did I get it wrong?'

'No, you got it perfect.'

'But, you're laughing at me. What did I mess up? I asked the girls at work and this is what they said they'd like.'

'You asked the girls at your work? Those nineteen-year-old dolly birds who run the Zumba classes?'

He looks a bit hurt. 'I've never done this before. You're expecting too much of me too quickly.'

'Too quickly?' She picks up the teddy. 'We've not just met, have we?'

'No, we haven't. But I'm doing my best,' he says. And she believes it, because his word is still all she has.

They spend much of the day hunkered down in the hut, waiting for the weather to clear. In the afternoon Lewis drives to the nearest supermarket for food and brings back a bottle of whisky in place of champagne and a reduced lemon tart in place of a birthday cake, but it doesn't matter. She's happy to be here with him, even if he does spend too much time on his phone in the bedroom, talking to his brother about business. Yvonne, while keen to know the latest mess-up with her flat, refuses to answer when she sees her contractor's number flash on the screen and shoves her phone between the cushions of the sofa.

'I found another blanket,' she says as he comes back to sit with her, thankfully phone free.

'Sorry about all this,' he says. 'It's constant at the moment. Why can't things just go to plan?'

'Because that would be too easy.'

He scrubs his face with his hands and pulls the blanket over his legs. 'It's freezing in here.'

'It's not that bad.'

The rain batters the roof and he shakes his head. 'I can't wait till I can take you abroad, somewhere nice, rather than here.'

'I love it here.'

He looks out of the window, at the sheets of rain which put an end to their hopes of riding bikes into the forest. 'I want to be financially secure, to be able to spoil you. I don't want my girlfriend picking up the bill all the time.'

'Girlfriend?' she cringes at the word. 'Please.'

He smiles at her, 'What do you want me to call you? Lover? Partner?'

'Anything but girlfriend. I'm almost thirty.' She crawls on top of him and feeling how cold his hands are pulls the blanket around them both.

'Maybe one day I'll be calling you something else.'

This time it's her phone which distracts them, vibrating from underneath the cushion. 'Sorry.' She fumbles to silence it, but catches the flash of *Emma* on the screen.

'Whoa,' Lewis says. 'Your face. I said the wrong thing? I'm usually accused of moving too slowly but I think I just went way too fast?' He laughs nervously.

'No. No. It's not that.' She can't drop the name here, in this moment, in the middle of this conversation. 'Forget about it. No more phones. Both of us.'

He nods. 'Yeah, okay.' But he won't look at her. He grabs her by the hips and lifts her off. 'I'm going to run you that bath, okay?'

All she can do is nod and watch as he walks away.

Yvonne's phone beeps with a message, she picks it up.

Happy Birthday to the baddest bitch I know. Kiama wants to know if you got his card?

She texts back. Yes & I loved it. x Thanks x.

She should switch the phone off now, but before she can even complete the thought, another message comes through.

Meet when you're back? I have news!

Followed by, Shit just got real.

CHAPTER TWENTY

ELEPHANTS

October 2020

Kiama

The next morning Delia stomps ahead, while Kiama drags behind. She hasn't said a word to him since they left the guest house, but then, why would she? He didn't mean to be so honest with her, but it was a big mistake sleeping with her and he wasn't interested in anything else happening.

The gate at the volunteer house is already open, a line of damp washing hung up, anticipating a sunny day. Delia takes off her shoes then throws them one at a time onto the dusty pile by the door. 'I'm going to try and disinfect my skin so I don't get that shit,' she says pointing to the ringworm on Kiama's neck. All he can do is nod. Shit. He feels bad about this on top of feeling bad about everything else that happened yesterday.

'Ki-Yama?' Purity calls from inside.

He takes a breath and sits down on the ledge, not yet ready to go in and face another pissed-off woman.

Purity comes out and stands in the doorway, her long skirt hitched up at the knees, revealing ashy legs.

'*Habari Gani,*' he says. He pulls off his trainers and stands slowly in front of her.

She picks a small twig from his hair, 'Where did you sleep last night? In the bush?'

'The guest house.'

'The guest house?' Purity crosses her chest. 'Do you know prostitutes use those beds? Those sheets? It is not good.' She makes a tsk sound and waves him inside, 'Go, shower, you smell.'

Upstairs, Yvonne's bag has gone and her bed has been stripped. Maybe this is for the best, that they break away from each other. That she gets to stay at her fancy hotel up by the lake and he stays here, finding whatever it is he's looking for. Though, he's no longer sure what that is. Or maybe he is, maybe it was Yvonne's approval on how he turned out and now he hasn't got it, there's no point in him being here at all.

He takes a long shower, hoping it'll clear his head or at least stop it from thumping.

'I'm never drinking again,' he mumbles while brushing out his hair.

'Hi,' he says to Purity's back as she stands in the kitchen, but she doesn't flinch. He tries louder and she makes that sound through her teeth again; it makes him smile, this little tick of hers he had forgotten about.

'Are you clean?' she asks, not turning away from washing her vegetables.

'Yeah.' He wonders if he should take the question as an invitation to go over and hug her. No matter how busy Purity used to be around the house, she was always ready with the big hugs when he was a kid, she and Mum would often be sitting in the kitchen together with their arms around each other. But he doesn't feel right about trying to hug her now, especially with the ringworm. Delia made such a big deal out of it; you'd think he had measles.

He steps into the kitchen, 'Can I help you?'

She turns and stares at him, her eyes wide with shock.

'What?' He looks down at his T-shirt, expecting it to be stained or crushed.

'Why did you get all these tattoos? That is not good.'

He pulls at his sleeves and crosses his arms. 'I'm sorry about last night. I shouldn't have stayed out. It was rude of me. But we didn't know if you'd be back or not and I didn't want to come in too late.'

She takes a handful of peelings and throws them in a bag on the worktop. Is she mad at him?

'Purity?'

'Yes?'

'You sure I can't help you do something?'

'No. Go and sit down.'

But he doesn't want to sit alone in the living room, he wants to stay in the kitchen, to hang around her feet and read her recipes and get one of those big hugs. He loved his nana to pieces but it always felt like she used affection as a reward; she was never one for just giving out hugs, he always had to be doing 'the right thing' first. She wasn't like it with everyone though, his cousins didn't seem to be held up to the same standards as him. Yet, when it came to talking about favourites, Kiama was always named as Nana's. But of course, he deserved to be, because all his cousins had mums.

'Where are the photographs you showed to Sarah?'

'Of Mum?' he straightens up.

'Yes, bring them. I want to see.'

He takes the envelope from his bag but doesn't want to look at them himself this morning, to see Mum's young smiling face, to imagine a swelling under her T-shirt, a son who disappointed her.

'Show me,' Purity says, her hands damp from the vegetables.

Kiama holds them out in front of her.

'My girl,' she says, the water flicking from her hands as she claps them together, 'my beautiful girl.' Her eyes mist over and she drops them down to her food prep. 'I loved her from when she was a baby. From the very first day.'

Kiama understands then that Mum was Purity's favourite; she was the one who Purity raised from birth and was like another child to her, not him. He's simply a by-product that came to stay for a few months.

She lifts the edge of her skirt and wipes her face.

'It's weird that Yvonne had these photos for so long and never had a clue where they were taken. My grandparents didn't know either.'

'They never went there.'

'I'm not surprised. They're not even interested in me, never mind some random orphans.'

She looks at him as if he's spoken out of turn. 'They are good people. They were always giving things to the house when I worked for them. And Emma liked it there too, helping and visiting the children.' She stumbles as she bends to reach a large pot and Kiama lifts it for her. 'Where is Sarah?' she says. 'She should be working this morning.'

Purity's hands look old, wrinkled in a way her face isn't. What age is she anyway? And still working like this?

'You don't need to cook today,' Kiama says. 'We can go out to eat.'

'What, to a *restaurant*?' she spits it like a swearword. 'Where you do not know who is making the food, what they are putting in it, how they are washing their hands. Then you pay them for it.' She shakes her head. 'It is not good. Like these girls here,' she nods upstairs, 'always wanting to eat food outside, at Chick Burger. I tell them, eat the food I prepare, but no, they want to eat that monkey burger.'

Kiama laughs. Then they both turn as the gate clangs outside.

'She's back,' Purity says, 'your auntie. Go and greet her.'

From the doorway he can see Yvonne sitting on the step in a slice of sunshine. Her eyes are closed, her head tipped back. She looks blissed-out, but of course she does, there's nothing at stake for her. It's just a holiday where she can spend a bit of time reminiscing about an old friend.

She must feel his eyes as she turns before he can creep off back into the house.

'Joe's feeling better,' she says. 'He's going to drive up here in the next hour. To be honest, I think he wanted a night in a hotel away from his babies.'

Kiama doesn't move, what is she expecting? That he sit and joke around with her like nothing happened last night, like she didn't make him feel worthless.

'Please,' she says, 'come and sit with me for a minute. I need to talk to you.'

It feels good to have the sun touch his skin, especially after the lukewarm shower. He closes his eyes and allows himself to enjoy the feel of it along with the sound of Purity humming from inside. He opens one eye to find Yvonne staring at him.

'You took your nose stud out?' she says.

He sits forwards and touches the empty hole. 'I think it fell out at some point last night.'

Two small birds land in the yard; they sit on the rim of a plastic bucket and tweet back and forth.

'I had no right to judge you,' she says. 'I really had *no right* at all. I can't throw things around like that because you don't act how I expect you to.'

Is that what it is, that she expects him to be someone else? He prides himself on not being defined by having a dead mum, on not being completely messed up by what he experienced out here. But maybe it's not true. Maybe there is something wrong with him coming all the way here and then spending his time getting drunk with some random girls in a bar.

'Did you mean it?' he asks. This is her chance to take it back, even if she did mean it, surely she realises that it would be better to lie here and spare him.

'Of course not. I was fed up and tired and… ' she trails off. 'Yesterday was hard, seeing the orphanage and all those children. I've never seen that kind of poverty before. And then being with you,' she puts her head in her hands. 'I shouldn't have said what I did. I don't know what I was thinking. I wasn't thinking. And I'm sorry.'

The birds fly off.

'I don't know how to explain it, other than the last time I spent time with you, you were this sweet little boy obsessed with football and PlayStation.'

'You can't be mad at me because I'm not eight years old anymore.'

'You're right, you're absolutely right. I thought the hardest part about coming here would be reliving old memories. I didn't think much about how to relate to you, now that you're—'

'An adult.'

'Exactly. So, I'm sorry.' She takes something from her pocket and holds it out to him. 'Look. I've kept this for years.'

He takes it from her hand. 'It's a really ugly piece of jewellery.' It looks familiar, but not in a way that he remembers her wearing, it's far too cheap for Yvonne and Mum never really wore jewellery because she would always lose or break it.

'You gave this to me before you moved here.'

'I did?' He holds it up between his fingers; come to think of it, he does remember, he'd gone with Mum to the high street and picked it out for Yvonne because, 'you loved elephants, didn't you?'

'No more than the next person. But for some reason you thought I did so I sort of went along with it. All the drawings, the birthday cards, everything always had an elephant on it. It was cute.'

He hands it back to her. 'Why have you kept it?'

'I kept all the stuff you gave me. I was never one of those people into babies, but I adored you from the first time I saw you. You had these really odd-coloured turquoise eyes, and

Emma's funny little nose and big eyebrows. She kept saying how much you looked like your dad, but I couldn't see it. I could only see you.' She nudges his shoulder with her own. 'God, Kiama, she would have been over the moon with you, with how your turned out.'

'Don't say that. Everyone says that to me all the time. I don't need to keep hearing it.'

'I know everyone says it all the time, but I get to say it because I knew her better than anyone else.' She takes his hand in hers. 'And I know what you've been through. What you saw. And then for you to come back here, she would have been proud, Kiama, I know she would have.' Her voice cracks. 'And I know that if Emma had a big pile of money she would definitely want to give it to the orphanage. So if you still want help sorting out what to do with the money here, I'll help you.'

It's so much quicker in the car, less than twenty minutes and they are already pulling up the dirt track, close to the orphanage. Purity joins them and sits up front with Joe, they talk the whole time, both of them shouting over each other like they're getting into it but then cracking up laughing.

The children are outside the compound walls, spread across the fields chasing each other and kicking a ball around. The girls are excited to see Yvonne again and immediately run over to claim her for one of their games.

'You came back?' Simeon says.

'Yeah,' Kiama calls as Zipporah and her sisters pull him towards the skipping rope.

They're already so familiar with him, like he's part of the family. Maybe Simeon told them about Mum and they now see him as one of them, part of the club. It's something he's had a few times before, once at school talking to another kid and realising that he also lost his mum at eight years old. It was like an instant affinity and even though they were never really the best of friends they still send each other the occasional message.

'You need to jump in,' one of the girls shouts.

They swing the rope slowly at first and he pauses at the edge planning his move before jumping in and getting tangled straight away.

'It was my hair,' he shouts, 'let me try again.'

The children laugh and it takes him three more attempts before he manages to jump the rope.

Purity leans against the car with Joe and carries on her passionate argument and occasionally Kiama swears he catches a phrase or two he can understand.

Yvonne sits under a tree with a few of the younger girls. He's glad she apologised, but feels wary of her now. Even if he was acting like a dick, what she said crossed the line. Still, they've got a few more days together and at least now she's on board to help him with the money. What more could he ask for? It's not like he's after a new best friend or anything.

Realising that skipping requires way more skill than he has he gets out of the next round and walks over to Yvonne, falling down a metre away from her, hoping the long grass will obscure him from the kids and give him a break.

'Is skipping a good hangover cure then?' she asks.

He huffs. 'I literally can't jump anymore.' He sits up and faces the same way as her, towards the view of the fields. He's hardly taken any photos the last few days, too conscious

275

each time he gets out his phone of her making some snarky comment about his supposed addiction to it. But why does he care so much what she thinks? He needs to stop placing so much weight on her opinions.

He takes his phone out.

'What are you doing?' she asks.

'Sorry, but I can't miss this opportunity. This background is amazing.'

'Yes, I can see it right here,' she says, 'in real life.'

'But after I put a filter on it and, oh wait, I think I just took your new profile pic.' It's the perfect shot, he leans over to show her, but she recoils like she hates it.

'Please delete that.'

He looks again. 'Why? It's a great photo.'

'It would be if I had on some make-up.'

'You look nice.'

She laughs. 'I guess no one likes the way they look in photos.'

'I do.'

'Yeah, I bet. Boys your age are so vain. My nephews are always primping and pruning.'

He wonders if she gives them a hard time too, if they feel forever judged by her. 'Do you spend a lot of time with them?'

'Do you spend a lot of time with *your* aunties?'

'I only have uncles, remember.'

Jenga stumbles over through the grass and sits on Kiama's lap. He's pretty much the cutest kid Kiama's ever seen.

'You're getting attached,' she says.

Jenga yawns and leans back against Kiama's chest, he's like a little puppy. 'I want to put him in my rucksack and take him home. What about you?'

'What about me?'

'Don't you wish you could take him home?'

'You wouldn't believe how many of my colleagues warned me to not come back with a baby.'

'You wouldn't be the first white woman to do it.'

'That's offensive.'

He laughs then stops, hoping he hasn't really offended her. You never know with some women, it might be a sensitive subject.

'Spit it out,' she says.

'What?'

'I'm a single forty-year-old woman. I'm, unfortunately, very used to being asked.'

There's probably no right way out of this one. He sighs, 'Well, why didn't you have kids?'

'Because I never wanted them.'

'But you liked spending time with me. You said it yourself earlier.' *Adored him* is what she said.

'Yes, I loved spending time with you. But you weren't mine, were you? I didn't have to deal with you waking up through the night, though I often had to deal with your mum calling me the next morning and complaining about it. I didn't have to buy you school shoes and worry about you getting sick or falling behind in school.'

'Neither did Mum.' He laughs, because that's definitely the one thing he does remember, that Mum wasn't perfect. It wasn't just that she'd kick off when he mashed up a pair of school shoes, she'd also get angry when he simply grew out of them, like he was doing it on purpose. The homework thing is another clear memory, not the doing of it, but the arguments around *not* doing it. Even once Mum handed it back to his teacher at the classroom door and moaned that it was too difficult for kids his age. It was embarrassing. But he holds onto these memories as tightly as all the others because they show she was a whole person, not just the perfect, beautiful angel everyone refers to her as.

'Look, I'm a modern man,' he says. 'I don't believe every woman should be spawning.'

'What a beautiful word.'

'But I've always wanted to be a dad, can't wait for it.'

'For your five kids?'

'Exactly. So for me it's hard to understand why someone *wouldn't* want kids. Male or female. Especially someone like you; you're from a big family and I see how you are with the kids here. You seem pretty maternal.'

'I was never one of those women who knew for sure they wanted kids. The fact that it's not happened for me is okay.'

'But what about if you met someone? And they wanted kids. Would you?'

'No. I'm too old to start with all that.'

'Shame. I think you'd be a good mum.'

Peter runs towards them. 'Playtime is over, come and help us do our maths homework.'

Kiama checks Jenga's shorts are pulled over to cover the patch of ringworm on his thighs before lifting him onto his shoulders and walking back to the house. By the time they reach the door Jenga is asleep in Kiama's hair and Yvonne has to help take him down.

Zipporah, again in the wedding dress, brings through the floral flask and pours cups of Milo for the adults.

'Ki-Yama,' Purity says. 'You like it here?'

'Yeah.' But it's not strictly true. He doesn't feel the same happiness being here he felt yesterday, he feels sort of sad today, noticing how thin the kids are, how quickly they tire, how dirty the place is.

'It must be hard work,' he says, 'looking after so many kids.'

'No, the children look after themselves,' Purity says as she watches Zipporah stir the drinks. 'And there are volunteers most of the year. They help with homework and cleaning and some will cook too. And after they go, they always stay in touch. They send things, well wishes, clothes for the children, money, so much money.'

Zipporah's dress reminds him of his little cousins, always in the garden in full ball gowns and tiaras. Nana would chuck the dresses straight in the wash when they dirtied around the hems. But Zipporah's dress is several shades darker than Kiama's own white T-shirt and he wonders when it was last washed, or if she owns anything else.

'So, if Kindred Kenya sponsors this place and volunteers are always sending money, how comes it's still like this?' he asks her.

Purity puts her wrinkled hand on his. 'The children here are lucky. They have shelter, food, education. They are blessed.'

'What is that smell?' Simeon shouts into the room and all the children look up. He takes a deep loud sniff. 'Can you smell something?'

Kiama and Yvonne shake their heads.

'Dog shit,' Simeon says. 'Who has walked dog shit inside?'

Kiama flips up each foot to find his white socks are discoloured with red dust but free from dog shit.

279

Simeon lines the children up against the wall and orders each one to lift their foot as he leans in and snorts, trying to detect the source of the smell. Jenga attempts to squirm from his grip. 'You?' Simeon slaps his little thigh and Jenga yelps.

Kiama flinches, as much as his dad and uncles joke about how Nana used to whack them around when they were little, Kiama's never actually seen a kid being smacked in real life. It feels like it's something from another time, something that normal people just don't do anymore.

Zipporah comes in with a shallow filled bucket of water and begins to scrub at the floor. 'Good girl,' Purity says. 'You see,' she says to Yvonne, 'this girl is always the good one. Anyone would be blessed to have a daughter like her. But her parents did not want her.'

Zipporah pauses for a second; her eyes dart up towards Kiama before sinking back to the soiled floor.

'These children,' Purity explains, 'are brought to this house from God, in so many different ways. Each one a blessing.' She exchanges some words with Simeon, who pulls out a chair and sits between them all. He's only two years older than Kiama, yet here he is, looking after a bunch of kids.

Jenga wipes his eyes and Kiama signals for him to climb back onto his lap.

'Kiama is asking how all the children came to be here. Why there are so many,' Purity says.

Simeon reaches across to Jenga and roughly wipes the tears from the child's face. 'You see this boy,' he says, 'his mother left him to die, in a carrier bag, on the train line.'

Kiama slides his hands over the little boy's ears.

'And the sisters, they were left in a farmhouse. The father

was always working and when the farm hands came they acted on their urges with the girls. They will not be able to have their own babies because of what those men did to them on the farm.'

Purity makes her tsk noise and waves her hand in front of her face. 'Terrible. Terrible. And of course Peter,' she says, 'he lost his father the same way we lost Emma. Peter saw everything.'

Kiama removes Jenga from his lap and leaves the house. He walks around the back, careful not to slip on the muddy trail of water which trickles down from the outhouse. He slides down the wall to the grass, suddenly nauseous. But it's not from the hangover; it's from picturing Jenga in a bag, the sisters alone in a farmhouse, Peter being witness to his mum's killing. It makes him sick.

Yvonne follows him out; she stands above him but says nothing. He wipes his eyes with a sleeve but there are no tears.

'The photos of this place are older than me,' he says. 'How can it still look the same? After all these years, all these volunteers, all this money. How comes it's not any better? It doesn't make sense.'

Yvonne slides down next to him, and he can tell she's struggling not to touch the grimy wall or sit on the grass.

'But think of how many children have passed through here in those years? Children who otherwise would have nothing. No home at all. Think about Simeon, he's a skinny little toddler in those photos and now he's at university.'

'And what about Zipporah, scrubbing the floor while Simeon talks about her being abandoned like it's some everyday thing and Peter, sitting there doing his homework while Purity talks about his dead parent. At least when people talk about me like that they don't do it in front of my face.' His voice breaks and he looks down at the grass.

'They're telling us these things because they think it's what we need to hear, in order to help, so that we don't forget about them once we go home.'

She doesn't get it. No one does. 'But it's not right to say that stuff.'

'I'm not disagreeing with you.'

'Can you imagine what it's like to grow up around so much sympathy?'

'No. I can't.'

He tries to think of a way to explain it, the words needed to make her understand how people look at him sometimes, what it feels like when he knows they've been discussing the fact he watched his mum die when he was a child. The pity that follows. 'It's suffocating, completely suffocating.'

Yvonne squeezes his arm then stands.

'I think I was wrong about this place, Yvonne.'

She shakes her head, 'I don't think you were.'

'I can feel it.' He looks at the outhouse, the chickens running ragged and balding. 'Can you imagine what it would feel like to even give a £100 to this place? I'd constantly be wondering where it went, how the kids were getting on.'

'You're going to have that wherever the money goes. It's never going to be spent exactly how you want it to be. Unless you stay here and set up your own orphanage and you're not going to do that, are you? Makimei oversees two orphanages like this in the area. There are loads of children in need and you can't help them all.'

'But there must be something I can do, other than transfer

a ton of money and hope for the best. I wish there had been something Mum told me about this place, some clue of what she would have wanted for it.'

Yvonne laughs then, completely out of the blue.

'What?' Kiama asks, wondering if he said something stupid, 'Why is that funny?'

'It's not. I was thinking about something your mum said to me after she came out here. She always wanted to set up this project where the kids would get a rucksack filled with pencils and books so they could learn to read and write.'

Kiama smiles; that's it, why is she only telling him this now? This is huge. 'Such a good idea,' he says.

'But these kids are already at school, that's being taken care of. Your mum got stuck on the idea of putting therapists into orphanages. It sounded like such a stupid idea at the time.'

'Therapists? The kids aren't even wearing clean clothes.'

'I know and that's what I thought at the time too. But she was right. Kindred Kenya puts all this focus on volunteers who have medical training, but what if it trained up someone who knew how to talk to children who had been through trauma, children like—' she stops and looks down at him, nervously twiddling her fingers.

'Children like me?' he says.

She nods, he gets it now.

CHAPTER TWENTY-ONE

LEAVING PARTY

September 2009

Yvonne

Yvonne comes out of the shower as Lewis wakes up. He stretches and knocks the lamp off the bedside unit, sending a cloud of dust over the pillow. Work has been non-stop recently so when she has time off she doesn't want to spend any of it cleaning; she just wants to be with him. She leans over to kiss him, adjusting the lamp he put back on the unit.

'Control freak,' he says.

'Do you want a coffee?'

He shakes his head and lies back down. He's been so quiet the last few days. It feels like there's nothing she can do to bring him out of his shell, to get him talking.

'Is this too fancy for a picnic?' she asks holding up a floral dress, the one she wore when they went to Kew Gardens last month; that day was perfect and he kept going on about how beautiful she looked, but today he hardly even looks up.

'No. It's great,' he says.

For Yvonne, Emma moving away represents a kind of freedom, some distance from the dwindling friendship that's doing no one any good. But for Lewis, it means losing his son. He'd been so casual about it at first, discussing Emma's move back to Kenya like she was going for a short holiday. But as it's got closer and closer it's like he's starting to realise this is real and his only child is going to live in another part of the world.

She sits next to him on the bed. She wants to tell him that it'll be better this way, so much better. Emma will be happier, supported by her family, which in turn will be good for Kiama. Being out there will give him a greater quality of life, and he'll be able to have the kind of idyllic childhood Emma had, one of living in a privileged little bubble. And of course, for Yvonne and Lewis the move means they can start coming clean, telling their families. It will be out in the open and they can move forward.

Lewis stares up at the ceiling and as much as she wants to lie down with him, to hold him, she knows she can't; what good will come from her wallowing in thoughts of missing Emma and Kiama too? She needs to be strong today, for herself and for Lewis.

'We said we'd go out for breakfast,' she squeezes his leg, 'come on, get up. Please, it'll do you good to get out.'

He pulls himself to sitting and leans forward, but then drops his head in his hands. He stays like this and she puts a hand on his back then removes it. 'Lewis?'

'Okay, okay, I'm up.'

He goes in the shower and she walks about the flat, clearing away the glasses and empty wine bottle from last night. They didn't talk about it then, they hardly said anything, just sat side by side on the sofa drinking, like some sad old married couple, the tension growing between them until she gave in and went to bed alone.

Back in the bedroom he's out of the shower and ironing his clothes, his face is neutral apart from the occasional flex of his jaw, which she's come to recognise as him being stressed.

'What do you fancy eating?' she asks, keen to distract him from his own thoughts.

'Not bothered.' He lifts his T-shirt to the light and checks for creases.

'Let's go up to the veggie café.'

He shrugs. He's definitely not listening, as this suggestion usually triggers a whine from him.

'You know I'll need to leave here about noon to get up to Stratford. The tubes are off so it's going to take me ages to get there. I don't know why Emma didn't check first. They do plan these things in advance.'

But then, Yvonne had only received the email invitation to Emma's 'leaving party' last week. She couldn't work out if it was because the party had been such a last-minute thing, or if inviting Yvonne was an afterthought. They had seen each other so infrequently over the last few months. Yvonne had tried to keep the friendship going, she loved Emma and still wanted to spend time with her, but it had finally gotten to the stage where Yvonne couldn't stand it anymore, couldn't stand herself.

She checks her reflection, deems the dress too fancy for a picnic and pulls it off.

'Wouldn't it make sense if I drove you?' Lewis asks.

'Yeah, I'm sure that would go down well, us two showing up arm in arm.'

'I didn't mean that. I could drop you nearby and then come in later, separately.'

She shakes her head. That seems too devious, the idea they would conspire to arrive at the same place separately. It was already bad enough that they would have to perform in front of people today, to act as if they were distant acquaintances, rather than what they really were; a couple.

'I know Kiama wants to spend time with his friends,' Lewis says. 'I told him I'd be there at four.'

'Okay.' Yvonne pulls on jeans and a T-shirt. What does he expect her to say? It's already so confusing, she's not sure what to say or how to feel. At some point today she will have to hug Emma, her friend of eleven years, and say, 'Goodbye.' She will have to do this knowing that she's still keeping this huge secret from her.

'Is it okay if we don't go out for breakfast?' Lewis asks as he sits back on the bed.

'Of course.' Does this mean he wants to stay in and talk to her? To confide in her how he's really feeling? She sits on the bed and strokes his arm.

'But you should eat before you go,' he says. 'It'll probably be a liquid-only picnic. My mum offered to bring food but Emma said no, told her she was handling it herself. What does that mean? When has Emma ever handled anything herself?'

Yvonne drops her hand. It still grates on her, his bitterness towards Emma, his lack of faith in her ability to get anything right. She no longer challenges him on it; it's not worth the argument. But today is the last day of it, the last time she will have to stand by and hear him talk about Emma in this way.

He types a message on his phone and throws it down on the pillow.

'This is really happening, isn't it?' he says.

Yvonne stares at the small wrapped package on the dresser, the personalised set of pencils she bought for Kiama. The last time she took him out to the Childhood Museum he had moaned about never being able to get a pencil or magnet with his name on it. 'Emma, Emma, Emma,' he said, pulling all the pencils with his mum's name on them, 'but never any Kiama. Why did they give me this name? The kids keep calling me KiamaObamaRama.'

Yvonne laughs.

'What?' Lewis says.

'Nothing. Just thinking about something funny Kiama said to me the other day.'

'I can't believe she's really taking my son away.'

It hurts to hear it and Yvonne thinks of her guilt, of how she encouraged Emma to go. Lewis doesn't know about all of this, about the phone calls between them, the lending of money so Emma could book her flights without having to ask for her parents' help.

She looks back at Lewis and the sadness seems to radiate off him. She's never seen him like this before. 'You know what Emma's like,' Yvonne tries. 'She'll probably get bored and come back in a few months.'

'A few months,' he laughs, his face turned to the ceiling. 'When Kiama was about five, I messed up one too many times and Emma stopped me seeing him for a while.'

Yvonne remembers this, Emma's fury at Lewis for

repeatedly failing to pick up Kiama as promised on a Friday evening. Why is he bringing this up now?

'It was over two months,' he says. 'She completely removed me from his life, didn't answer my calls, wouldn't open the door when I went over. Then finally, when I saw Kiama again, you know what happened?'

She shakes her head, even though he doesn't look up at her. 'His feet had grown two sizes, his hair slightly changed colour and he'd moved from being obsessed with Hulk to Iron Man. That was two months, Yvonne.' He gets up from the bed and goes over to the window. 'Two months,' he says again, to himself.

She kisses him, cautiously, on the cheek. 'I'm sorry this is going to be difficult for you.'

But doesn't he realise that it's going to be difficult for Emma as well? Just like those two months were. Yvonne remembers going over to the flat one Saturday and seeing Kiama sulking about, angry at his mum for taking away his dad.

'But Lewis, she's talked about doing this for years.'

'Not to me she hasn't. Cause I would have talked her out of it.'

'Is that a dig?'

He doesn't answer straight away, but stares at the window frame, his eyes move along the new crack in the plaster he pointed out the other day. 'Why didn't you talk her out of it? Why didn't you say it was a terrible idea? She would have listened to you. She always listens to you.'

Yvonne sighs, there's no point talking with him about this, not now, while it's so raw. Also, what can she say? She's in the middle of it all and this seemed like the only option that worked for everyone.

She looks at him closely, this man she got after so long wanting. She's giving up her best friend for him. She's lying to her family for him. He's everything to her.

'Please, come for a walk with me?' she asks.

Lewis puts his hands over his face. 'I need some time alone.'

She sighs and leaves.

The party is at the park across the road from Emma's flat. It's sunny but chilly, and Yvonne finds she's not the only one to have misjudged the weather and come without a jacket. She sits on a blanket, along with some of Emma's friends from the school gates, drinking Asti from plastic flutes while wrapped in tartan blankets trying to keep warm. Each time the conversation trails off Emma pulls another bottle from one of the Aldi bags and busies herself refilling everyone's drink, but not her own. She seems distant, drifting off, allowing herself to be talked at by these women she always complains about. She catches Yvonne staring at her and smiles. 'Alright, babe?'

'Yeah. You?'

Emma moves closer and pulls the blanket onto her bare legs. 'I've hardly spoken to you.'

'I know, but it must have been full-on recently, getting ready to move abroad.'

'No, I mean today. Eshal's been chewing my ear off for the last forty minutes about her mother-in-law,' she whispers. 'Honestly, these women bore me to tears.'

'So why did you invite them?' she laughs.

'Cause they're the ones who planned it. As if I have time for this.'

That explains it, the drinks and food, the plastic flutes and organisation. It was all someone else's work.

Even up to a year ago something like this would have fallen to Yvonne to organise, not some random new friends. Emma loved parties but was terrible at organising them, prone to under buying food, forgetting to invite essential people and even once, for Kiama's fifth birthday, turning up with him two hours late. Yvonne smiles when she thinks about it now, because these are the stories they laugh about with each other.

'You're my only non-mum friend who showed up by the way.'

It had taken almost two hours to get here, swapping trains three times and then getting on a rail replacement bus which toured the dreggiest parts of East London. But Yvonne would do this every day for Emma, even if it was only to sit in a cold park with her.

Emma's legs look blotchy from the cold and Yvonne tucks the blanket around them more.

'This is so the wrong temperature for this shit,' Emma says.

The mums laugh wildly at something and attempt to 'clink' their plastic champagne flutes together. Yvonne wishes none of them were here, that she and Emma could hang out alone together one last time. She looks at her friend and wonders if either of them are doing the right thing.

Emma catches her staring but says nothing, just smiles and wiggles her eyebrows until Yvonne laughs.

'Babe,' she says, 'you look how I feel. Stressed.' She puts

her head on Yvonne's shoulder, 'I should have spent longer thinking about this.'

Yvonne bites her lip and shakes her shoulder gently till Emma puts her head up. 'You were always going to do this.'

Emma nods, 'Yeah, you're probably right. Kiama's going to love it there. All that outdoor space,' she says convincing herself. 'The school has loads of clubs as well, he can finally get into sports properly.'

'Exactly. He'll love it.' There's an image of Kiama Yvonne has been building ever since the Kenya move was first mentioned. In it, he's older, happier, more confident. No longer this overly emotional little boy being ping-ponged between parents. It makes her feel good but also there's a kind of sadness that comes with the realisation she won't see him grow up. 'Where is Kiama anyway?'

Emma checks the time. 'Good point. Nana took the kids to the adventure playground ages ago. She could have had a heart attack in a basket swing for all I know.'

'Julie's here?'

'Yeah. She's trying to spend every last minute with him, she's been round my flat four times already this week. Plus Dickhead is coming later to pick them both up,' Emma rolls her eyes.

'I still have so much of your stuff in my storage unit,' Yvonne says, desperate to get off the subject of Lewis before it even starts. 'You said you were going to move it somewhere else.'

'I don't have time for that,' she waves a hand. 'Chuck it.'

'No. I can't do that. It's your photos, your books and your weird collection of plant postcards.'

'Oh my botanical postcards, keep those, please, they'll be worth money one day.'

Julie comes back with the kids, Kiama and a gaggle of awkwardly sized eight-year-old boys, loud and demanding. They throw themselves on the blanket and immediately start to grab at the food, like they've never eaten.

'Hello,' Julie says, as she sits down, in Emma's place, next to Yvonne. 'I'm Kiama's nan. Though, we have met before, haven't we? At one of Kiama's birthday parties?'

'Yes.' She takes the woman's hand cautiously.

'I didn't realise that you and Emma went to the same university. She was telling me the other evening how long you've been friends for. You probably know my son as well then, don't you?'

Yvonne's mouth falls open. 'Kiama's dad? No, not really.'

Julie squints at her, 'Didn't you come to my house once? For a barbecue?'

'Erm, maybe, yes, but that would have been with Emma. I don't know Lewis, not really.' She's lying. This is awful.

'He's got so many friends, I can't keep up. But every year I do the barbecue and all my sons can invite whoever they want. Sorry, can you grab me that bottle of water, please?'

Yvonne reaches over and fills up Julie's plastic flute.

'Pills and Asti is a bad mix,' she says as she takes two tablets. 'Painkillers. I've got an ache starting up in my back. That'll teach me to go on the slides, won't it?' she laughs.

It feels deceitful, listening as Julie feigns good health. Especially as Yvonne knows how many times Lewis has driven her to the hospital these last few months. Yet she looks well, far from the frail, sickly woman Yvonne often pictures. Though she never gave much thought to meeting Julie or any of Lewis's family, how could she, when she was always the secret? How would it work? That one day she'd walk back into that house in Harrow in her new role as Lewis's girlfriend. Lewis had said it would matter very little, but she's not so sure.

'Will you go out and visit them?' Julie asks.

'In Kenya?'

'Yes.' She has the same big earnest eyes as Kiama.

'I haven't thought much about it.'

Kiama kicks her drink over as he tries to reach some crisps. 'Sorry, Nana.'

Julie grabs a handful of napkins and begins to mop up the spill. 'This boy is so clumsy,' she says and then grabs his cheek.

'Stop it,' he moans.

She lets go and attempts to stroke down his hair, which today is out in a little afro.

'Nana?'

'Yes, sweetheart,' she says kissing his head as he slides down next to her.

'Do you have any money on you?'

'Have you said hi to your auntie Yvonne yet?' Julie says.

He leans over and waves at her. 'Hi, Yvonne.'

'Hi, Kiama. Did you have fun at the adventure play-ground?'

'Not really, I was too hungry to enjoy myself properly.'

'What do you need money for?' Julie asks as she pulls out her purse.

'An ice cream?'

She hands him a £10 note and he smiles before nudging

a friend and running off towards the ice cream van at the park's gate.

'Can't believe he's going,' Julie says. 'Going so far away.'

'And will *you* visit?'

'I'm already looking at flights,' she whispers. 'Though I want to give it some time. Let them settle in. Don't want Emma feeling like I'm checking up on her. But I will need to see my boy soon.'

They watch as the boys do a cautious slow walk back, holding their bright blue ice creams in one hand, cans of Coke in the other. They sit on the edge of the blanket and alternate between mouthfuls of each.

'Why is she going?' Julie asks. 'Why would she do this? It's completely ridiculous.'

Yvonne shakes her head; she doesn't want to speak for fear of what she'll say. Julie has this thing about her, this warmth which makes you trust her. Emma often said the same thing, that every time Julie would visit in those first few months after Kiama was born, Emma would confide in her and cry her eyes out. It didn't matter that she was Lewis's mum.

'Emma's your best friend. You must know why she's doing something so extreme? It's not normal to pick up your family and leave like this. Especially to go there.'

'But Emma's from there. Her family is in Kenya. Her parents.'

'And what about Kiama? *His* family is here. His dad, me, all his uncles and cousins.'

Lewis is always telling stories about his family, about his brothers, nieces and nephews. But it's hard to picture Kiama as being part of this, because Yvonne can only ever see him as an extension of Emma.

'I have six grandchildren, I try not to meddle in their lives,' Julie says, 'but him,' she nods over to Kiama, who now sits cuddling into Emma as she convinces him to leave the park, 'he's the one I worry about.'

'Why?'

'You know why. You've seen him grow up. He struggles with so many things.'

Yvonne nods, she understands. But that's exactly why the move will be good for him.

'Emma's a good mum,' Julie says. 'I know she tries, but it's hard for her being on her own. I won't defend my son. He's never put enough effort in with any of it. And he shouldn't be letting them go.'

'Right, everyone,' Emma shouts, 'we've decided to drop the pretence of a picnic to relocate to the nearest pub.'

Kiama pulls from her grip and strops. 'I don't want to go,' he shouts.

'But it's cold.'

'I'm not cold. I'm baking.'

The uneaten food is chucked, the blankets shaken of crumbs and rolled up. It's a relief to be off the grass and away from Julie and her talk. Kiama is getting riled up now and Emma looks distressed by him.

'Kiama,' Yvonne says as she hands him a blanket, 'carry this and stop sulking.'

'I don't want to go to the pub,' he says. 'We always go to the pub. We wanted to go back to the adventure playground.'

Some of his friends wave him off, as the group starts to part ways. Yvonne worries he'll start crying in front of everyone so she makes him walk over to the bins with her, where she keeps him for a few minutes, distracting him with questions about who his friends are until he calms down.

They join the others as they walk up to the high street towards The George. 'It's not even that cold,' he mutters again behind Emma's back. 'I'm hot.'

'Too hot for a hot chocolate?' Yvonne asks him as they go inside.

The group settle into a large booth at the back of the pub, Yvonne gets the first round in, more Asti and big bowls of chips for the remaining kids. Then she and Kiama stay at the bar for hot chocolates. His eyes light up as it's set down in front of him, frothy and covered in mini pink marshmallows.

'Yes, marshmallows,' he says, 'I'm never allowed them.'

'A little sugar won't kill you.'

'No, it's not the sugar, it's because they're made from pig snouts and stuff.'

'Shit,' Yvonne says as she attempts to pick them from the creamy top.

'No, no stop it,' he covers the drink with his hands.

'Don't tell your mum, she'll go mad.'

'I know how to keep a secret. Dad lets me have them for breakfast.'

How is he already this big? It stumps her. He was a baby so recently.

Some hot chocolate spurts across the bar as he blows it with too much force. 'Yvonne, will you come to Kenya?'

'It's a long way to go.'

'But you have to. Because I know you love elephants and in Kenya there's this amazing elephant sanctuary where they take the babies that don't have mums anymore because the poachers got them. So then, these humans look after the elephants. They give them milk from baby bottles, but like gigantic baby elephant-sized ones.' He looks up at her and nods, 'It's true.'

'Sounds wonderful.'

'And when you visit you can bring me a ton of KitKats because I heard they don't sell them in Kenya.'

'Ah, okay, is that the deal then?' She wraps her hands around her own mug of hot chocolate, knowing she won't tell Lewis about any of this conversation. He still reacts oddly when she talks about Kiama, as if it's too close for him. 'Are you excited?'

'Yeah,' he says. 'My new school has a swimming pool. That's amazing. My school here doesn't even have a climbing frame.'

Emma comes over and puts her arms around him. 'What are you drinking?'

He puts both hands over the rim of the mug, 'Orange juice.'

She squeezes the tops of his arms, 'You're a bad liar and you have a milk moustache.'

'I think Kiama can pull it off,' Yvonne says.

Emma wipes his face with an old tissue from her pocket. 'Did you give your?' She wiggles her eyebrows at him until he smacks his forehead. 'Ah, the present.' He runs back to the booth to get his rucksack.

'What is it?' she asks Emma.

'Wait and see.'

He comes back holding a little H. Samuel box which he proudly puts in Yvonne's hand.

Emma signals over his shoulder and stifles a laugh. 'He chose it himself.'

'Open it,' he says as he reaches forward and removes the

lid for her. Inside is a cheap silver chain with an elephant pendant on it. 'You like it?' he smiles at her.

'Yes,' Yvonne says. 'I love it.'

'Try it on.' He takes it from the box and starts to fiddle with the catch. 'I can't do it.'

Yvonne takes it and puts it on, making an effort to look pleased.

'Whoa,' Emma says, 'that is so Yvonne's style.'

'Thank you so much, Kiama.' She gives him a hug.

He turns to Emma and says, 'See, I told you she likes necklaces. I think the chips are coming, I'm going to get some.'

Emma twiddles the pendant. 'All these years and I never knew you loved elephants so much.'

'I don't and I don't know where he got this idea from.'

'You must have said something before. Probably some passing comment he's run with. You know what he's like.' She looks into the empty mug of hot chocolate. 'I saw you talking to Julie in the park. Was she asking you to convince me to stay?'

'Kind of.'

'She won't give up. I give her a month before she books flights to come over. Babe, you have to visit us too. Realistically, none of these other bitches will come out. You're my only friend with disposable income.'

'Thanks.'

'I'm serious. I love you. Kiama loves you too. We are going to miss you so much.'

Yvonne tries to shut the emotions down, 'You're getting soppy.'

'I know. Because I'm drunk and I'm leaving.'

Yvonne turns away, knowing if she looks at Emma's face she'll definitely start crying. 'Come on, let's go and have a drink with your boring friends.'

Emma is handed a drink as they arrive back at the table, she says thanks and announces, 'You guys, Yvonne is my oldest friend. She was the first person I met at university. The first person I told when I found out I was pregnant.'

Yvonne slides in the end of the booth. She doesn't want to start crying here in front of all these women she hardly knows.

Emma sits on Yvonne's lap and puts her arm around her. 'I'm serious. I'm going to miss you. I know we don't see each other lots but I couldn't have done this without you.'

Yvonne wipes a stray tear from the corner of her eye because despite everything, she's really going to miss Emma. 'Stop it.'

'I love you,' Emma says, 'from the bottom of my heart,' she pauses and looks off. 'Oh fuck. Is it already past four? Dickhead's here.'

Kiama stands on a chair and knocks against the glass, 'Dad?'

Emma sits down on a free stool and holds her glass out, 'Someone fill me up quickly, please? I'll need it to deal with him.'

Lewis walks over to the table and says hi to everyone. Yvonne can feel the women glare at him. They've probably been told nothing but bad things about him, about how he's a deadbeat dad who doesn't help out financially.

'Dad, you're so late. Where have you been?' Kiama says as he tries to eat the rest of the chips quickly.

'I'm not late. Nana said she would call me when you were done playing. You ready to go now?'

Julie gathers her things, says bye to everyone and takes Emma in her arms, while Lewis looks on.

Eshal leans into Yvonne's shoulder and whispers, 'Now we see where Kiama gets his looks from.'

Emma overhears and flips her middle finger up.

'Kiama, say bye to everyone,' Lewis says.

He makes his way around each of the women saying goodbye, getting more and more awkward as they grab him for hugs and try to take a few last photos of him and the other kids together.

Lewis looks over at Yvonne, and she turns away quickly, hoping he doesn't notice that she's been crying. Only when she's sure he's not looking in her direction does she watch him. How he takes Kiama in an affectionate headlock and walks off with him. Emma follows too, outside to where his car is parked across the street, the music is playing loud enough they can hear it inside the pub. His brother, Danny, waves as Kiama comes over.

Lewis and Emma talk, their expressions neutral and their body language completely unreadable. What are they saying to each other? It feels so wrong, because throughout all these years, Yvonne's never actually seen the two of them talk, not since the barbecue at Julie's house before they graduated. Lewis leans in and hugs Emma. When he releases her, she wipes her eyes before heading back into the pub.

CHAPTER TWENTY-TWO

THE PLACE

October 2020

Kiama

They give up on visiting Lake Nakuru altogether and return to Nairobi that afternoon. They find a new hotel, one less fancy than the first but a palace compared to the guest house he stayed in last night. Again, they get rooms next door to each other and settle in. The sheets are turned down and a bath towel twisted into a creepy-looking giraffe sits at the end of Kiama's bed.

He opens his rucksack and the smell of Kikuyu drifts out, of dust and dirt, of the reused oil from Chick Burger. He hadn't noticed it smelling so strongly when he was there. His Converse too, which were pale blue when they left Heathrow are now stained with the red dust of the countryside and soiled from walking in the damp muddy verges of Lari.

He had told Yvonne he'd let her know when he was ready to go out, to return to the place where Mum died all those years ago. Doing this was his original reason for coming here. He had read a book about people returning to the sites of their trauma and it helping them get over things. He likes to believe that once he sees the place again, like actually stands there and allows the memories to come back, everything will make sense and he'll be able to move on.

But now, he's terrified. What if he can't deal with the memories it brings back or worse, what if it brings back nothing and he feels numb?

He picks up the hotel phone. 'Dad?'

'Oh, I'm special enough for a call now, am I?'

'How you doing, Old Man?'

Dad sighs. 'You promised you would call me yesterday. Yet, here you are, a day late.'

'Sorry. Things have been a bit… ' He doesn't really know what his excuse is. He knew where the reception spots were around Kikuyu, he should have made the effort to go to one. But it felt kind of freeing, to be away from Dad's interrogations for a while, at least while his head was spinning with everything about the money and Yvonne.

'I assumed you were still out drinking actually? Or with one of those Irish girls you were talking about.'

Kiama snorts, but he didn't call for this kind of conversation, he needs to really talk. 'Dad? We're going there today.'

'Today?' He's got his attention now.

'Yeah. And I'm scared.'

'I understand. Of course you are. It's okay that you're scared.'

Kiama opens the bedside drawer and pulls out a copy of the bible. It looks completely untouched, the spine isn't even cracked. 'What happens if I don't feel anything? Or if I feel too much and freak out?'

'I wish I was there with you. I shouldn't have let you do this on your own.'

'I'm not on my own.' And it's true that he doesn't feel alone in all this. Even though being with Yvonne has turned out to be more difficult than he imagined and Purity's welcoming of him fell short of expectations. For the first time he doesn't feel like he's dealing with this by himself. He could never explain it to Dad though, because Dad's always been there for him, he just isn't very good at dealing with anything to do with Mum and her death.

Kiama puts the handset on his shoulder and flicks through the bible before chucking it back in the drawer.

'Special K?'

'Yep.'

'You don't have to—'

'It's what I came here for.'

'But if it's going to make you feel a way you don't want to feel then—'

Kiama laughs, 'Literally every feeling I've had here is something I could have done without. This won't be any different.' He sighs. 'But I feel kind of stupid about laying flowers, like I know I do it at the grave, but do you think it's okay that I don't do it here?'

'Course, son. Do what you feel. When are you going?'

'Soon.'

Dad is silent.

Kiama studies the blemish on his arm from the hot oil. The skin looks stretched and red. It makes him cringe but a small part of him also wants to take a safety pin and pop it.

'I think you're really brave,' Dad says.

Kiama kicks the towel giraffe off the bed with his foot. 'I'm not.'

'Yes, you are. I'm proud of you.'

He can't hear this right now, not before he's even done the thing he's being congratulated on. 'I've got to go. I'll call you when I get back, okay.'

'I've heard that before.'

'No. I promise.'

'Okay, son. Love you.'

'Love you.'

He hangs up and lies back on the bed, waiting for bravery to kick in.

An hour later they head out onto the busy streets. It's a nice area, full of bars and shops. He had read an article about it online before he left, about how it's the 'Brooklyn of Nairobi', an area that was once undesirable but is now filling up with young professionals, the new Kenyan middle class. But expats have always been in the area, he remembers being at the shopping centre quite regularly with Cynthia, eating lunch in the food hall at the weekends and getting the food shop from the big Nakumatt.

'You remember the way?' Yvonne suddenly asks him.

'I memorised the map before I left.'

Maybe it was a strange thing to do, but he had looked at it so many times on his phone over the last month, trying to piece together where everything was, where things happened.

They walk along a shopping street towards the centre and he stalls.

'This is it,' he says. 'This is where the ambulance was.'

Yvonne was with him inside it. She sat across from him while the paramedic lifted each of his feet, inspecting the damage from the glass. He's never forgotten the glass; it's the thing that's stuck in his mind the clearest all these years. Even back home, seeing a broken car window makes him sick, it's like he can feel it embedding in the soles of his feet all over again.

The shopping centre is across the road, but neither of them attempts to cross.

'Don't you remember the ambulance?' he asks her. 'This was the view from the back of it, this street.'

She shakes her head.

How comes she doesn't remember? 'It was right here.'

'I'm not sure, Kiama. Why does it matter so much?' she asks.

'It doesn't.' He didn't mean to raise his voice. He takes a step back and looks across the road. The worst part was leaving, the ambulance driving off without her, without Mum. They should have let him stay with her.

He leans forward and puts his hands on his knees. How is this meant to help? Coming here and feeling like this? He wanted to feel some kind of relief but instead he feels like he's being drained, as if all his energy is running from his body and he's about to keel over.

Yvonne puts a hand on his back and its weight makes him feel even worse. He stands and wipes his eyes on his sleeves. 'I don't think I can go there,' he says, 'I came all this way but don't think I can do it. I don't want to. I really don't want to.'

'It's just a place, Kiama. You don't have to do anything.'

He rubs his face again and says, 'I've had enough.'

CHAPTER TWENTY-THREE

CHEETOS

October 2020

Yvonne

She waits for him to knock on her hotel door, laptop in hand, desperate for someone to watch TV with and keep him distracted from his own thoughts. But he doesn't and by nine o'clock she starts to worry. It's hard to know if she should leave him alone, if that's what he needs. She paces the room until finally deciding to check in on him. She grabs a bottle of whisky and listens outside his door, relieved to hear talking inside, a muffled TV perhaps, before knocking.

'Hey.' He opens the door wide enough for her to enter.

'Hi.'

He flops on the bed and pauses whatever is playing from his laptop.

The window is open but the room smells like the dry oil from Avon he sprays onto his skin, the one he said his nana swore kept the mossies away when they went to Barbados.

His eyes are still red but don't look so swollen anymore, but it's the most tired she's seen him since they arrived.

'Fancy a drink?' she says.

'Really?'

'Yeah. You don't have to, but I think I need one.'

He nods at the bottle of whisky in her hand. 'When did you even buy that?'

'At the airport,' she sits on the bed opposite him, 'I'm not a fan of hotel miniatures. Right, I know you've got some Cokes stashed in here somewhere?'

'Coke?' he asks in shock.

'Yes, as in cola.' She laughs at him.

'Oh. Well, I never know with you.' He grabs a carrier bag from the floor and hands her two cans of Coke.

She wants to ask him how's he's feeling, if it helped to stand there earlier and cry for his mum. But how can she?

'This is pure weak,' he says upon tasting the drink.

'That's a full measure.'

'After today you ought to be pouring me a full cup.' He holds it out and she tips another finger in. They drink in silence.

'What were you watching when I came in?'

'I wasn't watching. It was a podcast about toxic masculinity. I don't even need to see your face right now to know you're about to laugh.'

'I'm not,' she says, but the effort to keep her face straight makes her cheeks wobble. 'It's another one of those things everyone is talking about and I don't really get it.'

'Toxic masculinity?'

'No, podcasts. They're just badly produced radio shows.'

'No, this one is really good. I'm going to send you a link. Even Dad listened to it.'

'And what was his reaction? Did he beat his chest and run back to his cave?'

Kiama laughs, 'What is it with you and him?'

'Nothing,' Yvonne says quickly, embarrassed that she said anything at all. 'I just remember him being quite an alpha male.'

'My cousins are the same. Then there's me.' He laughs and takes two packets of Cheetos from the carrier bag and throws one over to her.

'Hmm, but I wouldn't say you're quite free of Lewis's traits either.' It's dangerous ground and she needs to get off it. 'Do you want to talk about—'

'No,' he snaps, his big eyes flick around the room before stopping on her, 'I definitely don't want to talk about it.'

She nods, relieved that they don't have to pick apart the afternoon right now. She wasn't sure how it would make her feel being there again; she was almost surprised when she felt so little. But it was his reaction which hurt, the way he broke down on the side of the street, it was horrible to watch and know that he was reliving the worst few hours of his life. Then, as they walked back to the hotel he went completely silent and into himself. It reminded her of him at the funeral, of a little boy lost.

'I've been looking online a bit,' she says, 'and I've got some ideas about how we can get a therapist to join Kindred Kenya; I don't think it'll be that hard or as expensive as I originally thought.'

'I feel relieved that someone else knows about the money. I should have told you at the start. But I've always been discouraged from talking about it.'

'Why?'

'Because it makes people uncomfortable, the idea of someone so young coming into money. I once overheard my teachers talking about it and it freaked me out. I didn't want anyone to know about it. I didn't even want to know about it.'

He puts music on the laptop.

'I read an article online a few years back about compensation for victims of crimes abroad and all the comments were people bitching that the money should go to the NHS instead, like it's a direct competition or something.'

'That's ridiculous.'

'I know. But I always think of that. How important it is that I do the right thing with this money.'

'It's your money. You should do whatever it is you want with it. Whether it's for Kindred Kenya or if you want to pump every penny into relaunching your nu-jazz DJ career.'

'Cheers to that,' he holds up his glass. 'Oh, I'm running low. Top-up?'

'I'm not sure about that, we've established you can't handle your drink.'

He pouts a little before finishing off what he has.

'So, what are your plans for when you get back home? Are you thinking about college?'

'I'm fed up of talking about myself. You talk.'

'About what?'

'I don't know,' he says with a mouthful of cheesy puffs. 'Like, what's the best play you've seen this year?'

'Oh, you're a comedian now?'

'To be fair, it's all I know about you. There must be more

to your life than walking around hills and buying up all the property.'

'What do you want to know?'

'Well, what happened to your husband?'

'You say it like an accusation. He moved back to Sweden.'

'Sweden? I went out with a Swedish girl once. She was hard work. Were you with this Swede when I still lived in London?'

'No. We met about a year after.'

Kiama clicks his fingers, 'No, you were with a chef. We ate at his restaurant, it was the first time I ever had a profiterole.'

She rolls back on the bed laughing, 'Daniel Jordan? I can't believe you remember him? You were about six.'

'I'm not saying I remember him, I remember the profiterole. And there was another guy, think he was from up north, he had a sheep dog called Rocko and it used to stink.'

'What?' She thinks back but of course she knows who he's talking about. Another miss, one of the first relationships she thought was serious. 'Will Britton?' she covers her face with her hands and laughs into them. 'Were you taking notes?'

'Has there been anyone serious? Apart from the Swede? I don't even know his name.'

'Ben, his name is Ben. We got married very quickly. It was intense and messy and,' she sighs, 'one of those things. But we've managed to keep it civil. I still see him once or twice a year. He's getting remarried this Christmas, he invited me.'

'Really? Weird.' Kiama drops some crisps on the bed then dusts them off with his orange fingertips. 'So Swedish Ben, eh? He was *the one*?'

She raises an eyebrow at him.

'The one that did it for you? The Jay-Z to your Beyoncé?'

'You're an eighteen-year-old boy, what do you know about "the one"?'

'Nothing. I'm asking for an education.'

'No, Ben wasn't the one. That was a different guy.' She refills their cups, her own with a measure big enough to get through this conversation. 'You don't marry that guy, Kiama.'

'So, there's no one right now?'

'No, not right now. I'm too busy with work.'

'Don't you get lonely?'

'Are you asking me about sex?'

'Whoa, whoa! I didn't say anything about that.'

'Oh don't be such a prude, you started the conversation.'

'Yeah, asking about a *significant other*,' he puts emphasis on the description, 'who you go antique shopping with. Who sits next to you when you watch one of those boring plays you've been going on about. I'm not asking about that other stuff. Jesus.'

'You think you're so liberal but you can't handle the idea that someone over eighteen still has sex.'

'Please stop.' He puts his hands over his ears. 'I'm not comfortable with the idea that anyone has sex.' He leans on the bed and changes the playlist on the laptop.

Her head starts to feel heavy. 'I can't believe you're acting so prim when you've already spent a night in a hotel with a girl. And to think my first impression when I saw you again was how camp you looked,' she teases, because really it's not what she thought at all when she first saw him.

He kisses his teeth, 'That's not very woke of you, Yvonne. You think all gay men wear pink tops and earrings?'

She laughs at him, then tops up his drink one more time. 'Shame though, Emma would have loved to have a gay son.'

'You're weirdly not the first person to have said that to me,' he yawns.

She wonders if his memories of Emma are mixed with those from other people. All the hundreds of stories that get pressed on him by those who think they're doing him a favour, adding to his limited memories.

'Oh gosh,' Yvonne holds her head. 'I haven't eaten enough today to drink like this.'

'When do you ever eat enough?'

She sits up to check how much they've had from the bottle, but her head spins and she sinks back down. 'Whisky is not my friend. I don't know why I always drink it.'

'It messes me up too. You should see my dad on it. He can sink half a bottle and not even slur.'

'Yeah, but he's had years of practice,' Yvonne laughs.

'Mum used to like a drink too, didn't she?'

'Oh yeah. We were bad when we got together, we'd—' she stops.

'Don't start self-censoring,' he says with excitement, 'I want to hear some good stories. I never get to hear anything scandalous about either of my parents.'

'Really? Even your dad?'

'Especially him. You know how low the bar is set for single dads? Most women think he's God's gift.'

'I don't know about that, but he's always been able to put away the drink and remember everything the next day. I've seen him spend a whole day in the pub drinking then come home and tile a bathroom. And you're right, he never slurs, I remember

313

once he was so drunk but holding a whole coherent conversation with you on the phone. I was sitting there listening while he explained algebra to you, but like I say, he's had practice.'

Kiama laughs and then stops short, 'Hang on, when was this?'

'What?'

'You said my dad was tiling a bathroom? At your place?'

Yvonne realises her mistake. 'No, not my bathroom.' How to get out of this? 'Yours. Your mum's.'

Kiama shakes his head, 'But he never came up to our flat. And you were with him when I called? Was this when I lived here?'

The silence stretches long and wide. What is he thinking? Which part is he working out?

'I can't remember. It was ages ago.'

'Were you and Dad friends?' And there's no real suspicion in his voice, his face is still open and curious.

'No. I wouldn't say that.'

'But you saw him after we moved here? You met up and got drunk with him?'

'No. Not really. Or maybe once or twice.'

'When was the last time you spoke to him?'

Her palms sweat, she feels her heartbeat. 'We spoke on the phone, right after I met you.'

Now, Kiama's face changes, it hardens, he sits up. 'You didn't tell me that. He didn't tell me that either.'

'I was trying to reassure him. He was worried.'

'Why?'

'Because,' she puts her glass down, 'it's Kenya. It scares him.'

314

'But why did neither of you tell me?'

The music cuts off as he slams the laptop lid shut.

'Is there something you're keeping from me?'

'Nothing that matters.' When she next looks at him, his expression is unreadable.

'I'm tired,' he says, winding the wire around his speaker and putting it back in his bag.

She stands, 'Okay. I'll leave you alone. Goodnight, Kiama.'

CHAPTER TWENTY-FOUR

WHITE PASHMINA

March 2010

Yvonne

Emma plucks a strand of hair from Yvonne's head. 'Babe, you're going full on grey.'

'Stop preening me,' Yvonne whacks her away. 'I've been going grey since I met you.'

It's an old joke, but it's true that Yvonne's first grey hair was found after meeting Emma at the Freshers' Week.

A short barman clears their empty glasses. 'Would you like anything else?'

'Same again please,' Yvonne says, 'she's paying.'

He nods and turns to the wall of spirits, happy to have something to do. The hotel bar, which is dimly lit and expensive, even for Yvonne's taste, is mostly empty at this time of the afternoon.

'Why are we here?' Yvonne asks. 'It's so formal. Surely, this isn't where you usually drink?'

Over the last six months there have been phone calls and emails, but Yvonne still feels like she knows so little about Emma's new life here in Nairobi.

'I *usually* drink in my bedroom alone at night.'

'What happened to the dream of live-in babysitters?'

Emma sighs. 'When I first got here my parents were so happy for me to go out, every night they were like "go and make friends", "enjoy your life", "we'll watch Kiama", but now when I propose a night off, my mum looks at me like I've suggested she be my surrogate or something. And my dad, well, you've seen what he's like, a fucking tyrant.'

Yvonne's been in Kenya for less than twenty-four hours but has already witnessed three arguments between Emma and her dad. The last one just after breakfast, when he claimed Emma had put a scratch on his new Land Rover. He had even gotten Yvonne involved asking her if she remembers Emma 'driving carelessly' on the way back from the airport the night before. Yvonne wished then that she *had* booked that hotel after all. But it was Emma who convinced her to stay with them.

'I'm surprised you're still living with them,' Yvonne says. 'I never thought the plan was for you to stay there so long. In their house. Surrounded by all their hoary shit from England.'

Emma laughs. 'I know. But until I sort my visa out I can't legally work. Plus, it's great not having to worry about bills for once.'

Two Kenyan businessmen with shirts stretched over wide bellies call the barman.

'I thought this place was *the place*,' Emma says. Her face scrunches as she takes note of the bar's clientele, mostly rum-and-Coke businessmen. 'I don't really do the expat scene here. I don't know where everyone hangs out. Ah, I can see another grey. I think it's the light in here.' She leans towards

Yvonne's head then pulls back as the drinks are placed down. 'Why don't you go with it? I can imagine it would really suit you and that you'd pull off grey as well as everything else.'

Yvonne pulls a few strands in front of her face. 'I'm not even thirty, I don't want to be grey.'

Emma narrows her eyes.

'What?'

'You're looking good, babe. But that's what money does, right?'

'I've been taking care of myself. Eating properly, doing Pilates. But you look good too.' It's true, Emma's changed in the time she's been living in Kenya, she's tanned and slightly more filled out, in a way that does suit her. 'You look happy here. Happi*er* than when you were in London.'

'Well, that's not hard, is it?' She lifts her glass for clinking and says, 'To Kenya.'

The drinks are going down too easily and it's not even four o'clock. Also, the jet lag is kicking in. Emma suggests switching to Tusker, a local beer which she swears you can drink all day and not get drunk on. But Yvonne tries a sip and puts her bottle back on the table. This isn't why she came all this way, to sit across from Emma and act like there's nothing of significance to say.

She and Lewis had argued about it, he didn't understand why she couldn't tell Emma over the phone, as if it was something that could be dropped in the middle of a conversation. He said that her going there added to the weight of the confession.

'So, are you going to tell me?' Emma wiggles her eyebrows and pokes Yvonne in the ribs. 'Tell me, tell me.'

'Tell you what?'

'Who your new man is?'

It knocks the breath out of her. 'What makes you think I have a man?'

'Because you look like you do. Cheerful. Relaxed. Well-sexed,' she laughs.

'You are still so inappropriate.'

'Well-sexed was actually me toning it down, it's not what I really wanted to say. I'm glad though, you seemed quite serious about the last guy, but when you never mentioned him again I assumed things ended badly.'

This isn't the right setting for this conversation, it's too intimate and fun, like they're about to share some girl talk rather than the secret likely to blow their friendship apart. Or is Yvonne being melodramatic? Maybe Emma won't care that much. Maybe it's something that when she knows, she'll feel was obvious anyway, that it makes sense.

Emma pushes the bottle towards Yvonne. 'How drunk do I need to get you before you tell me?'

Yvonne pushes it back. 'It's too early to get drunk. Plus, I thought we were going shopping later. I already promised Kiama I'd get him some new bits. So annoying how nothing I brought for him fits. What are you feeding him out here? I really don't think I should have drunk so soon after taking those antimalarials, I'm starting to feel nauseous.'

Emma rolls her eyes and downs both drinks.

'So, are we calling a cab then because you're probably over the limit now?'

'Babe, this is Nairobi. Drink driving is the least of anyone's worries.'

'And if you scratch your dad's car again?'

'He deserves it. But look, you can't be this boring all week.' She takes out her purse and for the first time in years, picks up the bill. She must notice Yvonne's reaction because she turns and explains, 'It's Neil's card.'

They collect Kiama from school and walk to one of the shopping centres in the expat distract near Emma's home. It's a more casual crowd than the hotel bar, mostly young couples and families. Yvonne insists they visit the top-floor car park where there's a Maasai market taking place.

'You do know most of this shit is made in Taiwan,' Emma says as she holds up a wooden bowl painted with zebra stripes. 'Such a tourist trap.'

'Great, because I *am* a tourist.'

Kiama sits on the ground next to one of the stall holders and slams around on a selection of *djembes*.

'Don't even look at me like that,' Emma warns him. 'There's no way I'm buying you a drum.'

'I'll buy it for you before I leave,' Yvonne says as she counts the number of beaded bracelets she's bought. 'My nieces love stuff like this. They're so easy to buy for.'

'How many kids have your brothers got now?'

'Too many.'

'Kiama, come on, let's head downstairs.'

He gives the stall holder a five high and trails behind them as they walk down the orange staircase back into the air-conditioned comfort of the centre.

'Last chance for the toilet?' Emma says as they pass through the second floor.

'Mum. I don't need the toilet every minute, okay.'

'You've had about two litres of Coke. Don't ask me to stop on the way home.'

'Maybe *you* need the toilet,' he says. 'You smell like beer.'

She grabs his face and kisses it, to which he squirms away.

They head down the next flight and walk into the food court on the first floor, now filling up with families for an early dinner. Kiama runs off to get an ice cream from a place he declares 'the world's best'.

Emma massages her temples and pulls a bottle of water from her bag.

'See,' Yvonne says, 'afternoon drinking is always a bad idea.'

Emma finishes the bottle and shakes her head. 'I feel fine. But I need to eat something. Are you okay to head back soon or did you want to buy more African stuff?'

'African stuff?' Yvonne laughs. 'No, let's go. I'm tired. Where's Kiama?' She turns around and notices him standing by a Dixie cart filled with rolled down bags of nuts and dried fruit, he's chatting and laughing with the owner. 'Who's that man he's talking to?'

'Oh, that's the nut guy he likes,' Emma says casually.

'Oh yeah, the nut guy, him.'

'You know what Kiama's like, he makes a friend wherever he goes.'

'Yeah, I've noticed. And is it always men? Do you think it's something to do with missing his dad?'

Emma flicks her head up. 'I can't believe you just psycho-analysed him like that. He's only chatting.'

'I didn't mean anything by it. I meant more like, well, I was thinking about my brothers and my dad. How much they look up to him, crave his attention even now. I'm thinking about you more, how it must be hard for you to—'

'To be both mum and dad, yeah it's hard but I think I'm doing an okay job.'

Yvonne's glad Kiama is out of earshot, listening to the nut guy talk while eating his ice cream as fast as he can.

'Besides, look around,' Emma waves her free hand about. 'Kenya is full of inspiring, strong men for Kiama to look up to.'

Yvonne turns her attention to looking for these men. The security guards in light green shirts eating sweetcorn from Styrofoam cups, their guns hung casually by their sides; the skinny teenager in a fast food chain uniform, chatting up a pair of tall Nordic-looking girls; the men in white shirts having a loud debate in Swahili.

'The men here outweigh Dickhead by a mile. It's a cultural thing.' She lowers her voice as Kiama walks back over, crunching at the wafer cone.

'Mum, do you have any more money?'

'No,' she answers sharply and zips her bag up.

'What do you want?' Yvonne knows she will answer yes to whatever he is about to ask.

He scratches at his plaits. Emma's always prided herself on being able to cane row afro hair but it looks messy and fluffy. It's one of Lewis's main complaints whenever he's sent photos of Kiama, his unkempt hair and how he appears constantly sunburnt. 'I'm cold now,' he says. 'I think I need a hot chocolate.'

'You should have brought a jumper; you know what the air-con is like in this place. And no, we're not stopping for hot chocolate.'

Yvonne shrugs apologetically at him. He throws his head back and huffs, before walking off again, his flip-flops slapping the orange tiles as he goes. She finds herself looking for evidence that he's happier here than in London, something tangible to report back to Lewis, to reassure him that it's okay his only child is growing up in another part of the world.

'Does he miss him?' Yvonne asks.

'Of course he does. But they speak on the phone. And without having a kid to care for Dickhead can finally fuck around in peace, can't he?'

Yvonne bristles. 'You always make him out to be such a womaniser. But, say if he changed? Met someone? Settled down? Would that make a difference?'

Emma's eyes harden, 'Make a difference to what? And he's always meeting someone. But we both know what the problem is with him, don't we?'

'What?'

'That he's not yet managed to find someone who fancies him more than he fancies himself. Plus, he's hardly a catch, is he? Kiama told me he's back living with his mum, poor Julie she can't get rid of him.'

But the reality is he spends almost every night with Yvonne, at her place.

'The property prices are crazy at the moment,' Yvonne says. 'I can't believe how much the flats on my road are going for.' She had looked recently and wondered if it would make sense to find somewhere bigger and closer to Harrow so Lewis wouldn't be so far away from his family.

Emma unfolds a shopping list. 'And I bet he's still working at that leisure centre. Crap job.'

'Actually, he's quit. He wants to focus full time on the restaurant business.'

'What business? Where are you getting all this from?'

Yvonne feels herself blush, she could blame it on Kiama, say he told her, but what would be the point in that? She's walked into it now. It's time.

'These ones,' Kiama calls. 'Can I get these shorts, please?' He presses his hands against a display window, a white plastic mannequin in red board shorts stares back. 'Please?' he calls again.

A shadow of something creeps over Emma's face, recognition. Could it be? Yvonne feels her neck become clammy under the white pashmina she bought to guard herself against the chill of air-con.

'Babe,' Emma says, 'come here.' She takes two steps and reaches up. 'You've still got the price on.' The paper tag snaps as she pulls it from the pashmina.

The muzak fills the space between them. Then Yvonne says, 'I need to tell you something.'

Emma looks at her now, her green eyes glassy.

'About Lewis.'

They stand like this, this close for what feels like a minute or two, but surely it's only seconds, seconds in which Emma works everything out. She cocks her head to the side and starts to say something but stops.

'About me,' Yvonne adds.

Emma folds the paper tag several times in her hands.

'I wanted to tell you before you left, but I, but we, well, we didn't think it was anything. That it was serious. So we waited. And then, and now, I'm here and you should know.'

Emma takes a sharp step back. 'I don't get what you're telling me.'

'It's him, Emma. I'm with Lewis.'

Emma shakes her head marginally and a little smile of disbelief flashes on her face. 'You can't be. That's ridiculous. It's too close. You can't.'

'I'm sorry, it just sort of happened. We bumped into each other last year.'

The colour drains from her cheeks. 'Last year?'

'Yes. But nothing happened straight away. We didn't think there was anything. That it was anything at all. So, I didn't tell you, I didn't tell anyone, but... '

'How can you do this?'

It's a tone she's never heard Emma take.

'I don't understand how you can do this. How you can stand in front of me and say this. Like's it's okay. Like it's normal.' She laughs. 'With Lewis? For fuck's sake, Yvonne, tell me you're joking?'

'I'm sorry. I really am. I didn't want it to happen.'

Emma looks over Yvonne's shoulder and frowns, 'Kiama,' she calls, 'stop running off.'

Yvonne turns to see him back pedalling, stopping as one of his flip-flops falls off.

'So, what now?' Emma asks. 'He has a son, remember that?' she says viciously.

'It doesn't affect that, his relationship with Kiama, my relationship with Ki... '

'Of course it does. Of course it does. What did you think, that we'll explain to him how you're no longer my friend, but his stepmum?'

'That's ridiculous. I'm still your friend.'

'I don't want him thinking relationships are interchangeable like that.'

'Em, please. I didn't want to hurt you. I love you.'

'Then how could you give him the time of day when you've seen how he's treated me all these years? How could you think any of this was okay?' Her voice breaks. 'I bet I could guess when this started too. I bet I know.'

Yvonne shakes her head and thinks of how long she's kept the secret.

'Easter.'

So, she did know, something slipped, something got through. Yvonne racks her memory, trying to pinpoint what it was that gave her away.

'I'm right, aren't I?' Emma says. 'I'm right.'

Yvonne nods. There's no point going back through the whole story, not now, maybe not ever.

But Emma won't stop, 'Ask me how I guessed?'

Yvonne shakes her head. 'Let's talk about this later.' She looks at Kiama, still unaware, balancing on one leg as he inspects his sandal for something.

'No, I want you to ask me how I guessed.'

'How did you guess?' she says under force, each word hurting.

'Because every time he's with someone new he loses a little bit more interest in being a dad. So, thanks for that.' She turns on her heel and heads down the escalator, rushing past shoppers towards the double doors which lead to the car park.

'Fuck,' Yvonne puts her fingers in her hair. There was so much build-up to this, so many years of holding it in and then in a few minutes it's all over with. Except it's not, because she's here, in a foreign country, with another six days stretching out in front of her, days in which she has to get Emma to understand.

Kiama hops over. 'My flip-flop broke. Where's Mum?'

'Oh, she needed something from the car.' Her voice sounds empty and it feels like she's not really here. 'Give it to me,' she says for a distraction. She focuses on trying to push the rubber thong back through the sole, but the hole's been made too big. 'This isn't going to work. You need new ones.'

'But these are my favourites. Nana got them for me. They make them in Brazil out of car tyres.'

'I'll get you another pair.'

'When? Now? Cause I can't walk like this,' he demonstrates hopping around in a little circle.

She could do that, walk about the shops with Kiama and pretend as if nothing happened. Maybe eventually Emma would calm down and join them. Except Emma has the money, Yvonne hadn't thought to bring a small handbag with her and earlier put her purse and phone in Emma's bag. 'Your mum has my money.'

'Ah,' Kiama shouts, 'my trainers are in the car, let's get them.' He hops towards the escalators then stops to look back at her and waves. She takes his wrist to steady him as they step on then off, her anxiety growing as they push open the doors into the grey low-ceilinged car park.

'I don't remember where we parked,' she says.

'Mum always parks in the same place. Blue zone. This is annoying.' He pulls off the other flip-flop and hands it to her. 'I'll wash my feet when I get home. Don't tell Cynthia, she hates it when—'

A man shouts, he's Kenyan but the words are English, something like, 'Don't try, don't fight.'

It shocks Yvonne into stillness. Kiama pauses too and looks back at her. The man shouts again, this time she doesn't catch the words. There's another voice, different, and angrier, yelling. Yvonne grabs Kiama by the T-shirt and pulls him back. A bunch of keys falls on the floor, then there's a scream, a woman. A shot is fired and Yvonne drops, pulling Kiama with her. Glass smashes. Another shot.

She can't tell if it's near or far, the acoustics of the space confuse her. On the ground in front there's nothing unusual, concrete, wheels, a few stray pieces of litter.

An exit door opens and men in light green shirts run in. They're uniformed? Security? Safety? They shout something in Swahili. An engine starts and the sound of the radio momentarily blares then shuts off. The car disappears leaving the smell of burnt rubber and Bonfire Night. Silence.

Kiama rises from the floor and Yvonne reaches out to grab him but his T-shirt slips through her fingers. For a moment she's paralysed and muddled, cold and sweating, unable to get up.

She hears Kiama scream for his mum.

Then again, but this time it sounds blurry, as if coming from under water. It propels her up and she staggers over to where his cries are coming from. The empty parking spot, marked with black skid marks and a carpet of broken glass.

Kiama kneels by the side of it while Emma lies in front.

CHAPTER TWENTY-FIVE

AWOL

October 2020

Yvonne

She returns to her room and talks herself into believing that she said nothing incriminating. But deep down knows and can feel that Kiama's worked it all out. She lies on the bed and waits for her head to clear so she can think of what to do next.

It's embarrassing how after such a short time here with him she had allowed herself to imagine that she was now back in Kiama's life for good. As they drove into the city this morning they had shared banter in the back of Joe's car and she thought, this is it, I've made amends. She had jumped ahead, and thought about the advice she would give him, the books she would send, how she would be the sole reason he decided to give college another chance, to consider university. She had pictured herself at his graduation, feeling the same pride Emma would have felt. She even had the boldness to imagine the work they would do together, using his compensation to put a therapist in front of all the traumatised children across Kindred Kenya's orphanages. Something huge to make up for all the years she missed from his life. She alone was going to fill up the gaps Emma left.

But now, none of this will happen because of some humiliating old secret she's allowed to resurface.

Yvonne looks through the contacts in the Nokia phone and stops on David, the generic name she chose to hide Lewis's number behind in case of what, she's not sure, but this was always the problem with their relationship, it only existed hidden behind something else. She picks up the hotel phone and calls him. He answers after two rings. 'Kiama?'

'No. It's me.'

The last time she called him from Kenya was when she had to tell him that Emma was dead. Lewis had said nothing then, but she'll never forget the way he exhaled with relief when she told him Kiama was unhurt.

'Has something happened? Is Kiama okay?'

'He's—' but she's unable to speak.

'What?' The shock of his raised voice makes her want to sink deeper into the bed, to disappear. 'Where is he?'

'He's fine,' she snaps back. 'He's fine. He's safe. But Lewis—'

'Yvie,' he asks, calmer now, 'what's going on? You're freaking me out.'

'He knows about us, he knows we were together.'

'You're drunk?' he says. 'You got drunk and told him? I can't believe you. What did you say?'

'Nothing. But he knows. He doesn't know it all but—'

'So keep it that way.' There are a few moments of silence, then he says, 'You're overreacting. We'll say it was a fling, back at university.'

'No. He knows it was more recent than that. That we were seeing each other when he was here.'

'How? What did you say?'

'I'm not sure.'

'What did you tell him?'

'I don't remember,' she shouts.

They both pause. Yvonne's head feels as if it's full of swirling liquid. 'I wish it was just a fling,' she says. 'I wish it was some shitty one-night stand that I told Emma about. She would have laughed. She would have thought it was hilarious. I don't even remember why I kept it a secret.' She thinks about this often, how she sat across from Emma in the pub, drinking shitty beer and listening as she talked about how much she liked Sweetboy76. Yvonne kept quiet when what she should have said was, 'I know him too and I slept with him last term.' But instead, she stayed silent, for years. If only she had told her sooner, then Emma wouldn't have been so upset, she wouldn't have been so furious, she wouldn't have run off to the car park that day.

'She still would have gone to Kenya,' Lewis says. 'Whether you told her nineteen years ago or ten years ago. You can't blame yourself for her being out there.'

'But I do. And that's why I wanted to make it up to Kiama so badly.' She turns the receiver away so he doesn't hear her sniff into the pillow.

'Where is he now?' Lewis asks.

'He's in his room. He doesn't want to talk to me. But I need to talk to him, I need to explain.'

'No, leave him. When he's fired up, there's no talking him down. Wait till the morning.'

'And what am I meant to tell him in the morning?'

Lewis stays silent then says, 'Tell him it was nothing.'

Nothing. But surely that's another lie. Lying is what's got them here.

Lewis sighs on the other end. 'You sound a mess. Get some sleep.'

She's woken by the sound of a hoover in the hallway outside. Through sticky eyes she sees the late hour and groans as her head pulses. Why didn't he wake her? But then, she remembers.

Slowly she rises and finishes what's left of the water by the bed. It's time to put things right, to condense a huge old lie into something flippant and unworthy of even wasting effort talking about. She showers and dresses quickly, edging out of her room and wincing at the bright light of the hallway.

'Good morning,' the maid says as she gathers a bale of white towels from a trolley.

Kiama's door is open. The bed is stripped and a clear carrier bag by the entrance is filled with his rubbish; a shampoo bottle, scribbled on pieces of paper and several empty packets of crisps.

'Excuse me,' the maid says as she stands next to Yvonne in the doorway. 'Do you need help?'

Yvonne steps inside and looks around the room. He's gone.

'Ma'am?' the woman asks her forehead etched in concern.

'Sorry,' Yvonne says, 'sorry, I made a mistake.'

Yvonne sits across from Purity at the dining table. She and Kiama had planned on returning to Kikuyu today, to visit a local ancient forest which Delia described as 'Insta worthy' and of course, to visit the orphanage one last time to make a final decision. But he wasn't there. He wasn't anywhere and it worried Yvonne.

'I'm so stressed,' she says. How many times has she said this, thought this, already today?

Purity indulges her. 'He is fine.' She refills the blue plastic coffee cups.

Yvonne knows all this caffeine must be causing her to feel worse, more jittery and anxious, but she can't help it. She needs something to occupy her hands and to keep the hangover at bay.

'Should we call Simeon again? Maybe Kiama went straight to the orphanage.'

Purity shakes her head. 'You believe he will go there alone? I am not sure he could find it again.'

'He did it before. We got a matatu.'

Purity laughs. Why does the idea of Kiama disappearing concern her so little? Doesn't she realise how serious this is? The fact that he just walks out of his hotel room and tells no one where he's going?

When Yvonne arrived earlier today she went straight to the house expecting him to be there, but no one had heard from him, even Delia pouted like she'd already forgotten who Kiama was. Yvonne had then made Joe drive her by the guest house, the chicken shop and even the bar, where she crossed the fingers on one hand as they walked up the dirty red staircase hoping to find him, perched on one of the stalls drowning his sorrows with Tusker beer. But it was all in vain. The barman remembered Kiama clearly as 'the tattooed boy with all the hair' and promised to pass on a message if he saw him again. She even called Neil, who laughed and asked if perhaps Kiama had chosen to spend his last few days in Kenya 'finding himself on a safari'.

The longer they looked the more convinced Yvonne became that he had left the area altogether. Over breakfast the other day he had spoken again about Mombasa, the place where he and Emma spent their only beach holiday together.

'But say if he's gone home?' she asks Purity now. 'Decided he's had enough and gone back to the UK?' She rubs her eyes and her head thumps from the whisky, from the stress.

'Why would he run?' Purity asks, her attention half on Yvonne, half on picking the seam from a piece of clothing.

'Kiama's angry with me. Last night, he found out something I didn't want him to know. Something about his dad and me, something that happened a long time ago.'

Purity lifts the material up and Yvonne sees now that it's a skirt. 'A secret?'

'Yes.'

She shakes her head. 'Secrets are not good.'

'I know. But this trip was meant to be about his mum, about Emma, not about me and his dad. Not about something stupid we did a decade ago. Though now, that's probably all Kiama is thinking about. It's probably all he'll remember from being here.'

'Do you think this will fit Alice?' Purity asks. 'The girl is so thin. I said I would make her a skirt. She wanted traditional Kenyan, but I do not know where she bought this material. From China maybe.'

Purity's lack of concern is almost reassuring, it reminds

Yvonne that there's nothing really that terrible about an eighteen-year-old boy going AWOL for a few hours.

But then the afternoon slides away and the evening creeps in.

She sits on the ledge in the yard, listening to local voices as they pass by on the other side of the gate. Delia and Alice return from work, and as if sensing the strain of the situation, ask few questions about what has happened and lend Yvonne their phones to try and get through to Kiama. His phone is switched off but the girls encourage her to leave messages on each of his social channels.

Eventually, an hour past curfew, Joe is given leave and the gate is locked. Purity shrugs apologetically as she puts the padlock on the door. 'Here,' she says to Yvonne as she presses the bunch of keys into her hand. 'You can open it when he comes back.' The unspoken assumption being that Yvonne will not move from this spot until Kiama shows up.

CHAPTER TWENTY-SIX

FORGIVENESS

October 2020

Kiama

He doesn't want to deal with this; he wants to be somewhere else entirely. He wants to be drunk at a bar in Barcelona, listening to some local girl warble on about Post Malone and the politics of Catalonia which he can nod along with and pretend like he understands. He wants to be home in Harrow, being dragged out of bed to help his nana do the garden. But most of all he wants to be eight years old and back at that beach bar in Mombasa, eating masala chips and drinking tamarind juice with Mum.

He had switched off his phone as soon as he left the hotel yesterday morning. Then, without a clear plan he grabbed a bunch of leaflets in the lobby before getting a cab to a local city zoo. There he spent the day walking around on his own, eating ice cream and watching the captive monkeys be taunted by the wild monkeys, who climbed all over the outside of the cages.

'There's no way I'm letting that school drag you into central London to stare at a bunch of locked-up animals all day.' Word for word, that's what Mum said the day he brought home the permission slip for the school trip, right before she ripped it in two and added, 'We'll bunk off and stay home instead.'

She never even asked him if he would have liked to. He was so angry then, angry at her for not giving him the chance to take part and angry at himself for wanting to go so badly. He knew it was wrong that animals were locked up in zoos, but how else would he ever get to see them in real life?

'In Kenya the animals are free,' she said, 'it's the only way to see them.' And she was right. The first time Kiama saw a giraffe roaming freely in the national park is a moment he'll never forget.

He's not sure why he chose to do something so depressing when he was already feeling down. By the afternoon, he considered going back to Purity's for a final trip to the orphanage, but then thought of Zipporah's dirty dress and the sound of Simeon's hand against Jenga's thin legs. He knew he didn't have the strength for it, especially to go alone, without someone by his side.

So instead, he found a bar, full of tourists, students and expats, and drank.

He dreads switching his phone back on, mainly for the wrath of his dad, so is surprised to see just one text from him asking for a call. Does he know? Did Yvonne tell him what happened? Kiama doesn't know how often they speak. Maybe she's been updating him on every little part of this trip all along. It's jarring to think about.

When he finds reception he books an earlier flight to Mombasa and sends Joe a text explaining that he'll need to be picked up from Purity's house in Lari. He can't leave without saying goodbye to her.

He doesn't read any of the thirteen messages from Yvonne, but hits delete on each one. There's nothing she could say now that he wants to hear. He can't trust her anyway. Ever since they met she's been keeping things from him, rewriting their history to fit with what suits her. He laid himself out to her as well, showed her all his insecurities, let her see him when he was broken and down. And then, she's not even who he thought she was.

Kiama pulls the hairband off his wrist and pulls his hair off his itchy neck. He hopes the girl, whose name he can't remember, didn't notice the circle of red spots on his skin there, he did have a cream for it but left it somewhere at the volunteer house.

The girl was most probably too drunk to notice anything, as was everyone by the time they fell out of the bar to head to hers.

She comes out of the bathroom with a glass of water and walks around the living room surveying the human dregs from last night.

'I need to get home,' he says.

'Oh, okay then,' she sounds relieved he's leaving. 'Where are you staying?'

'Kikuyu,' he answers.

She makes a face and wipes her head with the back of her hand. 'All the way out there? Well, I'm not driving you.'

'I didn't ask you to. But could you call me a car, please?'

'Sure. It's going to cost a lot though. Especially at this time of the morning.'

He shrugs. 'Whatever, as long as it's someone trustworthy.'

The car drops him to the gate and waits outside for payment. As he steps out he feels the chill he's come to recognise as being particular to Kikuyu. The gate is unlocked and he slides it open, but the clank is loud. Purity comes into the yard, her hair loose and messy, her skirt tied in a large knot. She doesn't step forward to hug him but unleashes a mixture of Swahili and English. And as much as he expected this, it's difficult to handle it being hungover. Purity takes his chin in her hand and pushes his face from left to right. 'This is not good,' she says, surveying the bruise on his eye.

Yvonne stands behind on the ledge, he hadn't even considered that she would be there and as much as he'd like to never communicate with her again, he realises he needs her now. 'I haven't paid the cab,' he says.

She goes back inside the house leaving him in the yard with Purity. He wonders what Purity thinks of him. Purity who spends most of her days in an underfunded hospital or dump of an orphanage, Purity who thinks it's extravagant to eat out, Purity who called a boy pampered because his parents flew to be by his hospital bedside.

Yvonne returns and gives a handful of notes to Purity to sort out with the driver.

'What happened?' she asks him. 'Were you robbed? Attacked?'

'I got into a fight,' Kiama says.

'Did they take anything? Did you call the police?'

'No. It was my fault. It's fine. I'm fine. Just really tired.' Again he feels it, that deep kind of tiredness, the one which makes everything feel like it's too much. He moves to walk past her but she blocks him. 'Can I sleep?' he snaps.

'We need to talk,' Yvonne says softly, keeping her calm, but of course she does, that's her thing. Come to think of it, she was always like this. They'd go over to her flat for lunch and Mum would kick off because he knocked a drink over the cream carpet or got a bit of felt-tip pen on the coffee table. But if Yvonne was angry she never showed it. She never showed anything. And what was the thing about elephants, why did she let him believe she loved them, getting him to draw her pictures and acting like she loved that ugly necklace when she didn't even like them? It makes him wonder what else she's been hiding.

He heads inside the house and towards the stairs. She follows him but stops at the foot. 'Can we talk? Please?' she calls. As if he's in the mood for this now. 'Kiama?' she tries again.

He storms back down and towers over her on the step above. 'Why? Are you finally going to fill in the blanks for me?'

'What do mean?'

'You know what I mean. I have part of the real story now, don't I? But what's the rest? What's missing?' There has to be more, he thought about it all yesterday, about how she and Dad ever got together in the first place? How long they were together? If Mum knew? When they broke up and why? There's so much that doesn't make sense to him.

'I want to tell you everything,' she says. 'I'm ready to tell you everything.'

Then, there's the big question, the one it hurts to even

think about, but he needs to know. 'Was your relationship with my dad the reason we moved here?'

'No,' she says. Then why does she look so guilty? 'Emma wanted to come back here for ages. It was her home.'

'And did she know?'

'No. Well, yes. I tried to tell her.'

'How long did you see each other for?'

But this time, she doesn't answer straight away, because she's thinking about it, she's trying to come up with an answer that won't piss him off.

'Let's sit down,' she says. 'Let's talk properly.'

'No. I don't want to sit down with you.' His patience wanes, this was a bad idea. 'Just tell me. How long were you with him?'

'It was off and on.'

'How long?' he shouts, because how else can he get her to answer him.

'For a few months, then you came here, so all together it wasn't even that long.'

It's clear now, why Mum chose to pick up their whole life and move away, it's because her only friend had gone behind her back, because someone she thought she knew turned out to be something completely different. 'This is why we ended up in Kenya?'

Yvonne shakes her head.

'You came all this way here with me, giving me these speeches about Mum like you were her friend and the whole time you had this? Why didn't you tell me?'

'I don't know. I'm sorry.'

'This is where it comes from,' Kiama says, 'this guilt you

341

have.' Because of course that's what it is. What other normal person would agree to a trip like this? To putting their own life on hold to travel so far with someone they don't even know?

Only someone who had a guilty conscience, someone who was trying to make up for something shitty they had done before. She's guilty and not only about betraying Mum, but about leaving him too.

'I've wondered about it,' he says. 'Why you kept away from me all this time.'

'That's not it. Let's talk about this properly, when you're calmer.'

'No, I'm not waiting anymore. How many more years do you need?'

'Ki-Yama,' Purity steps between them on the stairs and takes his arms, '*Mwana mwema ni taji tukufu kwa wazazi wake*.'

It makes him so angry he wants to scream at her. 'Will you please stop saying that to me?'

But she repeats it and the meaning becomes clearer to him, she's giving him a message and he can't ignore it. He can feel himself losing it, the tiredness, the emotions, the come down from the tiny pill which last night made him feel so great.

'*Mwana mwema ni taji tukufu kwa wazazi wake*.'

He covers his face, not wanting to put himself out there again by crying. Then, Purity's hands are on his arms, directing him up the stairs and away.

He wakes up in his original room, the one he shared with Yvonne on their first night here. Her stuff has gone, but he knows she's downstairs, waiting for him, ready with her stories and excuses. It's what he's asked for, the whole story. And this is probably his only chance to hear it, because once he gets back home, he never wants to hear anything about Yvonne or Kenya ever again.

Purity has left his bag by the door and he manages to sort himself out a little, having a shower to wash away the smell of the club and the girl he slept with last night. But in the mirror he still looks wrecked, in need of a shave, plus the bags under his eyes are huge and dark and the bruise around his eye has turned a greenish shade of purple.

There's another text from Dad, but the message is still the same, Call me when you get this. He's not ready to think about Dad, about his part in all of this, the secrets he's kept. There's only so much he can be angry about at one time.

At the top of the steps he stalls, closes his eyes and tries to picture Mum. What she would advise him to do now, how she would feel about this. But it's hard, so hard, because even though she was his mum, the closest person to him for those first eight years, it was *only* eight years. Sometimes it feels impossible to know what she was really like. How well did he know her really? All he has are his memories and the things people like Dad and Yvonne tell him, and now he knows he can't even trust them.

Yvonne sits at the dining table, a book and a cup of coffee in front of her. He doesn't acknowledge her, but goes straight to the kitchen where he boils a pan of water and makes a sandwich.

Eventually he goes back through and sits opposite her, but can't bring himself to look up at her directly, scared of what emotion will arise. He still feels anger, but there's also sadness and a feeling of being let down, massively disappointed.

'You went out last night?' she asks. 'In Nairobi?'

He tries to focus on his sandwich, but it's not enough, so rubs at the red smudge of the club stamp which remains on his left hand. 'Yep.' The bread lodges in his throat and the coffee is too hot. It's all hard work. He doesn't even have the energy to eat. He drops his hands either side of the plate and Yvonne puts her hand over his. 'Do you want to come for a walk with me?'

He pulls away. Does she really think he's going to make it that easy for her? That a bit of affection and a walk is all he needs right now?

'Kiama, we need to talk.'

He eats the last of his sandwich with effort, half hoping she'll leave the table, but she doesn't give up. 'I don't need to talk,' he says eventually, but it doesn't sound convincing, because of course it's the one thing he needs right now more than anything else.

'No. Okay, well, I do. I'll talk,' Yvonne says.

He looks up at her and nods.

They walk along the dirt road outside Purity's house, following the path up to where the houses become thinly spread. They pause in a large field which overlooks the town. Below are a few blocks of flats and the roofs of the messily placed houses. In the middle sits an old-fashioned white wooden church Kiama hadn't noticed before, how comes? Perhaps he's been so busy looking for reminders of Mum that he's failed to really look at the country she loved, to see it for what it is, rather than just the place that took her away.

He stops and stares, making an effort to take everything in before sinking down on the grass. Yvonne follows.

The sound of singing drifts up on the breeze, there must be a service taking place in the church below. It looks so out of place here, like it's been plucked from the Deep South of America. He wants to share this with Yvonne but instead bites his lip.

'How's your head?' she asks.

He looks down and shakes it, 'Been better.'

'I was worried.'

'So, what's new? You're always worried. Must be exhausting.'

'I know you're angry. But you shouldn't have put yourself in danger like that. I was terrified.'

But this is the thing; everyone around him does whatever the hell they like. Mum pulled him from his life in London when she wanted a change, Yvonne ran a mile when it suited her, Dad picks and chooses what he tells him about the past, yet he's the one who's left, expected to be extra careful and to think of everyone else's feelings all the time.

'Where did you sleep? Or did you stay out all night?'

He sighs, are they really still talking about this? 'There wasn't any danger, Yvonne. I went to a bar then went back to some girl's house for drinks with a couple of British students.'

'You've got a black eye.'

'I got punched because I drank someone else's drink.'

'And your money?'

'I lost my wallet because I was too high to look after it.'

He pulls his knees in towards himself and lays his head on them for a few moments.

'When you got in touch with me,' Yvonne says, 'I felt like it was my chance to put things right. I've always felt guilty about how I encouraged your mum to come here. And of course, I've felt guilty about not seeing you grow up.'

'Wow, that's probably the most truthful thing you've said to me this whole trip.'

'I want to tell you everything, I really do.'

'But?'

'But it's not all my story to tell.'

She's exhausting, even now, trying to dart around the truth. 'But you're here, Yvonne. You're here and Mum's not. So tell me.'

'I met your dad before Emma met him. On a night out. We slept together, a one-night stand, like you do at that age. But then months later he showed up at our student house. He was seeing Emma and I didn't know.'

A coincidence, one he didn't know about, but it doesn't tell him anything really.

'Harrow's small. There was one bar. And me and your mum, well, we had the same taste in men.'

'Pff,' Kiama scoffs. But if he wants the story, this is part of it. 'Why didn't she break it off when you told her?'

Yvonne closes her eyes. 'Because I never told her, because I could see she was falling for him. I didn't want to hurt her. After we left university I started working all the time and your mum made a new bunch of friends. We didn't really spend time with each other anymore and I assumed the friendship was over. I started seeing Lewis and even though I knew he had broken your mum's heart, well, I guess I was falling for him too. This sounds so terrible,' she says. 'I planned to tell her, I really did but—'

'But what? You liked the secret or something? Sneaking about?'

'No, she was pregnant with you. She wasn't sure if it was Lewis's baby at first.'

Now *that*, he didn't know.

'So we stopped seeing each other. Then, years later, when you were about seven, we bumped into each other again. This time we were older, and we got really serious really fast. He moved in with me but we still kept things quiet, even your nana didn't know. Then you both came out here. I knew I had to tell her, face to face, I owed it to her. Plus, I missed her, I missed you both.' Yvonne stops and wipes her eyes with the back of her hand. 'But we never got to talk about it. Not properly.'

That's enough, he doesn't want to hear about the conversations they had when Yvonne was here in Kenya. 'I can't believe you lived together.' He thought he'd worked it out, that they were just being sneaky, that Yvonne was one of those women he used to hear his nana and her friends bitch about, the kind that only liked a man when he belonged to someone else. But it doesn't sound like that's what it was.

'I still don't get it. You two lived together but no one knew about you. So, what was it?'

She takes a breath, as if getting ready to compose a lie. 'It was complicated.'

'*Complicated*,' he tuts, 'I can tell. You said you would talk. So talk.'

'It was real. We were so into each other, so in love. To the point we were stupid and didn't think about who we would hurt.'

The church doors fly open and people in brightly coloured outfits stream from it, many of them hold balloons, their talk and laughter drifts up in pieces.

'Do you still love him?'

'I haven't seen him in a decade, so no.'

'That's the truth?'

'Yes. I swear. He called me after you and I first met and of course I called him yesterday morning in a complete panic. But no, I haven't seen him.'

A cheer rises up from the congregation and the balloons float into the air. One gets stuck in a tree and a little kid attempts to jump up and reach it, but even from here Kiama can see she's got no chance of reaching it.

'When I first went back to London one of the hardest things was that there was nothing left of Mum,' he says. 'Nana made sure I was in school pretty much straight away after the funeral. So it was all new friends, a new area. I even had new clothes, because so much of my stuff was left here. I didn't have anything from my life before.' He picks at the welt on his arm, which is now dried and darkening. 'I wish you would have stuck around, Yvonne. You were one of my only links to her.'

'I'm sorry. I never thought of that.'

'It's too late now anyway.'

'You're leaving, aren't you?' she asks.

He pulls out his phone and glances at the screen. 'Joe's driving me to the airport and I'm going to Mombasa. I can't deal with this,' he says. 'I feel like I should be picking sides or forming allegiances and I don't know how to do that, how I'm meant to feel about any of this.' He plucks a handful of grass and repeats, 'I can't deal with it.'

'I'm sorry it's turned out like this.' She looks at him then, her expression serious as if there's something else she wants to say, but she doesn't and he can't be bothered digging. Not anymore. He's done.

As they walk back down the hill together Yvonne turns to him and asks, 'That thing Purity said to you earlier, what does it mean?'

It's annoyed him from the start that of all the phrases to remember this was the one he knew instantly. He recalled Purity saying it to Mum often.

'Is it something about your mum?' Yvonne asks. 'You don't have to tell me if you don't want to.'

'It means she would have been proud of me. That I would be the crown of honour she wore.'

They glance at each other and carry on walking.

Joe sits outside the house in his car with the seat right back as he sleeps in his suit. He jumps as Kiama raps the window. 'You're early.'

The window goes down, 'I needed to escape my children.'

'Well, I'm packed. Give me five minutes to get my bag.'

Purity is already there in the yard, with Sarah behind, pulling Kiama's rucksack.

'My boy,' she says. She takes his cheeks in her hands and smiles. Maybe he was wrong about her, maybe she did more than just tolerate him because he was the offspring of Mum.

'Go well,' she says, 'and greet your father.'

'I will.'

She hugs him hard and he knows he'll never see her again. But it feels okay.

He tries not to look at Yvonne but when he does, she takes it as an opportunity to engage him. 'This is really quick,' she says. 'I wish you would stay, at least another day.'

He feels that tiredness again, but this time knows what it is, it's grief. It pulls at his chest and attempts to drag him down to the ground and it's not only grief for Mum, but for this place, for Purity and even for Yvonne. All these things he's now ready to move on from.

'What's the point?' he asks.

But she doesn't have an answer for him.

Joe pops the boot open and Kiama chucks his bag inside. 'See you, Yvonne.'

He gets in the car and watches her shrink in the rear-view mirror.

CHAPTER TWENTY-SEVEN

LAST TANGO

April 2010

Yvonne

They shaved off Kiama's cane rows for the funeral. Yvonne's not sure if it's this that makes him look so different, so much older, or if it's the shirt and smart trousers. They're at Julie's house; the one Yvonne came to with Emma for a barbecue when they first finished university. It's eerie how little has changed. The same car sits on the drive and inside the hall is still lined with family photos, though there are more now, mostly of kids. Even the kitchen is the same, filled with trays of food and stacks of plastic cups and plates, ready for guests, as if it's been stuck in time for nine years. But of course it's not the same.

Yvonne manages to smile at Kiama as he comes into the kitchen, 'You looked very grown-up today.'

He nods blankly and walks over to Julie by the fridge. She reaches out to adjust his collar. 'Do you want to take this off now?'

'I thought you said I had to look smart.'

'Yes, for church. But we're home now.'

Home? Yvonne hadn't even thought about this place as

Kiama's home, but of course it is. Over the last few months Lewis had been pretty much living with her in Clapham, much to his family's confusion. He said they all knew he was with someone but respected his privacy, unlike her own family. Lewis had promised to introduce her once she got back from Kenya. It seems like a plan from a different world now, another time completely.

Kiama's legs look long and thin in the black trousers, could it be that he's lost weight? Or is it that Yvonne's not used to seeing him dressed like this? The pale blue shirt doesn't quite fit and the collar especially is too big.

Earlier, she heard Julie explain to a friend that she bought everything large so he could keep it for when he starts school after the Easter holidays. The time period for his grieving already set in stone.

He continues to stand there by the fridge, unmoving as adults bustle around him. But he's always been one of those children in the kitchen with the adults; *big ears*, Emma used to say. You wouldn't even know he was there sometimes until he piped in with a comment or laugh as you gossiped about people.

'Why don't you go out in the garden with your cousins?' Julie suggests.

After the church ceremony, the children had been bribed with colouring books and crisps and sent outside, an uncle directing them to the end of the garden where they sat within the tall grass around the greenhouse, trying their best to stay quiet and respectful.

'Oh look,' Julie says as she leans over the kitchen sink.

'Your cousin Ray is out there too. You've not seen him ages. Go on, go and get some fresh air.'

Kiama's little face falls as he turns to leave the kitchen.

'Hold on,' Julie calls, a slight panic in her voice, as if he were going somewhere other than the garden. She grabs a bottle of sun cream from the top of the fridge and beckons him back to her. She had complained earlier about how tanned Kiama was, and despite the day being cool, she slathers the cream on his face thickly, leaving him coated in a white shine.

'There you go,' she says and kisses him on his newly shaven head.

He walks out and Julie waits till she can see him through the window, as he pads down towards his cousins and uncle before she sighs with relief. 'I keep saying and doing the wrong thing.'

'No,' Yvonne says. 'He needs to be distracted. It's good for him.' It's good for her as well, since arriving at the house this morning Julie has kept her busy with a hundred different jobs from grating cheese for macaroni, to finding appropriate napkins, to opening and replying to each sympathy card.

'I only feel at ease when he's close,' Julie says. 'I don't know how I'm going to do it when he goes to school.' She sets another block of cheese in front of Yvonne. 'You hear about things happening in schools, don't you? Bullying. Grooming. Some nutter bursting into a classroom and—' she stops and pulls on her rubber gloves.

Yvonne walks over to the sink, 'He'll be okay.'

Julie turns and hugs her and Yvonne feels warm bubbly water from the Marigolds drip down the back of her shirt. 'I'm so glad it was you,' Julie says. 'I'm so glad you were there to keep him safe, to bring him home.' They pull apart. 'Sorry, look what I've done. You're soaked.' She grabs some kitchen roll and they both dab at the shirt, before wiping their eyes instead. Yvonne didn't think it was possible to cry this much in one day. But it's felt good to let it out, especially after the last few weeks of feeling so completely blocked and numb.

'Mum, have you—'

Yvonne flicks her head around in response to what she thinks is Lewis's voice, but it's not. They all sound the same, the brothers. Ever since she arrived it's been disconcerting, to constantly hear Lewis.

'Sorry to interrupt,' Danny says. 'You alright, Mum?' He puts his arm around her but she snaps back to *being fine*. 'What are you looking for?' she asks, while plunging her hands into the sink.

'My phone charger. Oh, it's still plugged in.' His eyes settle on Yvonne. 'How are you holding up?' he whispers. It seems so genuine, but he's the one, the only one here who knows the truth about her and Lewis. What must he think?

'I'm okay.'

He squeezes her shoulder and says, 'Be strong, okay.' Then pulls the plug and leaves the kitchen.

Julie slides the door shut behind him. 'I don't want Kiama seeing us crying.'

The two women sit at the table, look at the mountain of grated cheese and laugh.

'How many more people are you expecting?' Yvonne asks.

'Not enough to eat all this. I'll take it up the church later, there's always someone in need of food.'

'I guess so,' Yvonne says as she eats a pinch of cheese. 'Kiama seems so vacant today, so quiet. How has he been?'

'Tired. But then he doesn't want to sleep at night. We put him in the room and he keeps getting back up. I've been told that's normal.'

'And physically? His feet?'

In Kenya, Yvonne had overheard the police tell Neil and Cynthia how Kiama had survived 'without a scratch', as if he was spared, some miracle, but it wasn't true. His bare feet were ripped raw from the broken glass he ran across in the car park. But it's the mental trauma which worries her, how does an eight-year-old recover from seeing what he did?

'The scars are going down well,' Julie says, 'it's a hard area to heal, especially when you're walking on it all the time. Lewis is a bit of a mess though.'

'Lewis?' Yvonne's head shoots up, surprised to hear his name. 'Because of Emma?'

'No, because of Kiama, of how close he came. It's been a wake-up call. I don't think he'll ever let Kiama out of his sight again, which is not a good way for a boy to grow up.'

'I've hardly spoken to him,' Yvonne says. 'I don't know what to say.'

'You don't need to say anything. Just be here.'

Yvonne sits on the sofa as the music gets louder and the talk gets further and further away from Emma. Of course people are sad, but most of those in the room today only knew Emma as Kiama's mum, or as Lewis's demanding baby mother. So this send-off is really more about showing solidarity with Kiama than it is about mourning Emma.

It hurts Yvonne that she wasn't at the ceremony Cynthia and Neil held in Kenya, but she couldn't face staying on there, to spend any more time in that house with their silent sorrow.

Yvonne walks out to the hall to get away from the noise and finds Kiama, sitting on the steps with a pair of orange Converse in his hands. 'New shoes?' she says. 'They're so bright.'

He fiddles with the laces. 'Dad said I didn't need to wear black ones.'

He slips one on and folds the laces continuously.

'Do you want me to retie that for you?'

'I can tie it up myself,' he snaps. 'I just forget sometimes.'

'It's okay.'

'No, it's not. I'm almost nine.' But he can't do it. He kicks the shoe off and lets it fall to the floor.

'Do your feet hurt?'

'Only if I do lots of walking.' He stares up at her with his big eyes, and she looks for traces of Emma, for something to hold onto. But all she sees is a sad little boy and it breaks her heart more than anything else has today.

'You've been wearing flip-flops for half a year. Of course you've forgotten how to tie up laces. It's nothing to be embarrassed about.'

She picks up the shoes and pulls his feet onto her knees. 'Okay? Not too tight?'

He nods, 'Thanks.'

'You're welcome. Here,' she puts her arms around him and pulls him close. They sit like this until a figure comes to the door and the bell rings. Then, that's it, for the rest of the day she only sees him in small snatches, being passed around and hugged. He's not used to all these people, all this fuss. Why don't they know this about him? Why won't they leave him alone? It's hard to watch and after a few hours she decides to leave, gathering up her bag and jacket but then hovering around, wondering how to get Lewis's attention. There's so much they need to talk about and of course now isn't the right time or place for it, but she needs to connect with him somehow, to let him know she's here and ready to talk.

He's in the living room, where he's been for most of the afternoon. He sits in the middle of the sofa with Kiama pressed next to him, his little head on Lewis's shoulder. It's the clothes; she thinks again, as to why Kiama looks so unfamiliar today, that and the haircut. She can't imagine ever looking at him again and not being overwhelmed by the urge to lift him into her arms. She feels sorry for him and she feels guilt. Does Lewis feel it too? It was their fault after all, why Emma was running away.

Lewis looks up at her and stares, he's completely unreadable. She takes a step forward and he shakes his head marginally before looking back down at his son.

A week passed and Yvonne kept busy at work during the day and in the evenings completed all the tiny jobs around the flat that Lewis never got round to. Despite her brother's advice she tried several times to instigate a meeting with Lewis, but each time he answered her call he said they needed to 'wait' before cutting the conversation short. Wait for what? They didn't need to wait anymore. They needed to get on with their lives, to build something strong and stable for Kiama. She hadn't worked it all out yet, but it made sense for them to tell everyone the truth, that together they were strong and that as a three they could get through this.

When he finally called her over she felt nervous as she sat on the tube up to Julie's house, wringing her fingers and wondering what the plan was. Had he told his family about them already? Or would they do it together? Maybe some huge confession wasn't the best way forward, perhaps it would be gentler to have her increasingly around, then it wouldn't feel like such a shock for people to see them as a couple.

Lewis opens the door and briefly hugs her. She steps in behind him and pauses by the living room, where the curtains are drawn but the TV is on, the bright colours of a kids' film light up the room. It's on mute and Kiama lies on the sofa.

'He's asleep?' she whispers. 'It's only five, is he feeling okay?'

Lewis signals for her to leave the room and follow him through to the kitchen. There's no one in there, the garden is empty too; it's too quiet for a house which is usually filled with so much activity.

'It's Danny's birthday, so everyone is out for dinner,' Lewis says, picking up on her expression.

'Why didn't you go?'

'Didn't feel like taking down the mood. Drink?'

She nods.

He brings down two tumblers from a cupboard and pours whisky into each.

'I would have asked for coffee,' She's not sure why she's trying to lighten the mood, to pretend that it's a normal visit and everything is okay. 'So, he's sleeping a lot then?'

Lewis sits and puts an arm on the table and leans his head on it. 'Not really. But I let him sleep whenever he can. He was up again last night. For hours.'

'Oh.' She takes her glass.

'He's okay falling asleep most nights. We do the whole routine with him, you know, like he's a toddler, bath, book, bed for eight o'clock. My mum reads to him, she sits with him till he falls asleep, it's the only way.'

Lewis doesn't sound like himself. Is it because she's never heard him talk about Kiama in this way, fatherly, worried, caring? And if so, why should it make her feel uncomfortable to finally see this side of him?

'He wakes up screaming,' Lewis says, 'every night without fail, sometimes at two in the morning, sometimes four. I've started going to bed at eight as well, because I can never get back to sleep once he wakes up like that. I end up lying awake the rest of the night watching him for signs it's about to start again… so I can stop it, before he goes through it.' He dips his head. 'At first I kept trying to work out what it was that was waking him up and why at those particular times. But there's no link.' He looks embarrassed, as if he'd tried to correlate the time difference and time of Emma's death to see if it was the same. He takes a drink and she mirrors him.

'I didn't know,' she says. 'Has he spoken to anyone?'

'Yeah, umm, the child psychologist has seen him. And when he starts school they'll give him counselling. But, I don't know, Yvie. I don't know if he's okay. How can he be okay after seeing that? He's too young to see something like that. He doesn't understand it.'

'Children are resilient.'

'No. This isn't some small domestic upset he's seen.'

'I know, Lewis, I was there. I'm struggling as well.' She sounds so selfish. It shouldn't be about her. It *isn't* about her. She pushes the glass away. 'And I shouldn't be drinking.'

'No. Neither should I. But it helps sometimes, right?'

She wants to crack, to break down and fall into his arms, it's all she's wanted these last few weeks, to be with him, to feel him surround her and be safe.

'When are you going back to work?' he asks.

'I'm already back. I needed to keep busy. That's what works for me.'

'And your family? They're looking after you?'

It was her parents and Claude who'd picked her up from the airport when she'd first returned home. At first she thought it was unnecessary, that she was well enough to get a cab. But once Kiama went with Lewis and Julie, her unravelling began. She remembers how her brother held her hand the entire journey back, how she was confused when they took her to her parents' place, rather than her own home. Her mum ran her a bath and Yvonne lay in it until the water turned cold. That's all she remembers, that and sleeping.

'My family,' her voice cracks, 'yes, they've been great.'

'I'm glad you're not alone.'

'But I am. When are you coming back?'

He gets up and throws the rest of his drink in the sink. The smell bounces around the room. He puts the lid on the bottle and returns it to the cupboard.

'Lewis?'

'I need to sort my head out, Yvie.' He looks tired and worn. It's the oldest she's ever seen him look. 'I'm sorry,' he says.

'Sorry for what?'

The smell is nauseating.

He doesn't return to the table, but stands with his hands in his pockets, his jaw flexing slightly while he thinks of what to say next. 'We can't do this anymore. It's not going to work.'

What is he talking about?

'I've got to raise my son.'

'We're in this together, Lewis.'

But he shakes his head. 'No, we're not. I need my family right now and I can't lie to them.'

'Then, don't lie to them. Tell them. We'll deal with whatever comes next together.'

'I'm worried about you being here even now. About Kiama seeing you and if it'll trigger something in him about what he saw.'

'That's ridiculous.' And hurtful. 'If anything, it will help him to have someone to talk to about what happened.'

'I'm worried about you being around. I'm sorry but it's the truth. I need to protect him. I don't need the added stress of our relationship on top of everything else. It's just me and Kiama now. He needs me. He's falling apart and I need to fix him.'

Yvonne shoves her chair back and moves closer, 'He needs us *both*. We can do this together. We can get through it together.'

'We pushed her to go there,' he says, causing Yvonne to stop in front of him. 'Both of us did. It's our fault he was put in harm's way. That he witnessed what he did.'

'Don't say that. We never knew what would happen.'

'We did. You said it yourself, how dangerous the city was.

How much you didn't even want to go out there, yet you pushed her to go, you pushed and pushed. Because it suited us and now she's gone.' He wipes his face and then his voice changes. 'Kiama needs me and that's what I need to focus on. I can't get distracted by anything else.' He looks at her, and there's no room for doubt in his expression. 'I'm sorry, but it's over. It has to be.'

CHAPTER TWENTY-EIGHT

HOME

November 2020

Kiama

A Tribe Called Quest plays in the kitchen. Kiama grabs his coat from the bannister and quietly creaks the front door open, but Dad hears and calls him through. He puts his coat on before squeezing past the boxes marked 'Xmas Decs' and into the doorway of the kitchen.

Dad holds a ball of tangled fairy lights in his hands. 'You off out?'

'I'm going round Trina's.'

'Again?'

Kiama nods. In the last month she's been the one person he's found he could talk to. It was easy telling her about Mum and Kenya and Yvonne and Dad. He loved the way she listened to him without bringing in the dramatics and he realised he liked her more now than when he kissed her drunkenly at Yates's after work in the summer.

'You been spending a lot of time with that girl.'

'Yeah. She's nice.'

'So, what's going on with you two? Are you sleeping with her or—'

'Boundaries,' Kiama shouts, but Dad just laughs. 'What are you doing with all these boxes?'

'I've been trying to untangle these lights for ages. You're good at stuff like this.'

'Am I?' Kiama asks.

Dad's expression drops, he *is* trying, but it's constant and a little jarring. Kiama sighs and walks over. Dad goes to hand him the lights but pulls back. 'Are you expecting a cold snap?'

Kiama huffs and pulls off his jacket, catching Dad's half smile as he hands the lights over.

It's going to take time to fully get back to normal, to how they used to be. The first few days home were the worst. It felt like the whole experience had finally caught up with him and coming off that plane and into the same arrivals hall he probably walked into when he was eight years old broke him completely. But he didn't want Dad's comfort; he didn't want anything from him.

Kiama even refused to get in the car at first, but it was so stupid, he knew, deep down, that he was too tired to do anything other than be driven home. They didn't talk about any of it at first, then one evening it started to come out. Slowly at first, with Kiama sharing stories about learning to skip with the kids from the orphanage, about Delia freaking out over his ringworm and about getting punched by some obnoxious Kiwi backpacker in a bar. It reminded him of when he first came back from Barcelona, of how he'd ramped up the stories for comic effect. But this time the laughter stopped abruptly on the first mention of Yvonne and Dad waited for Kiama's lead.

'Why didn't you tell me?' he asked finally.

Dad picked up his glass to find it empty. 'When was I meant to tell you? You were a kid. You had other stuff going on. Then, you were grown and it didn't seem like it mattered anymore.'

'But when I met up with her? When I first started talking about going back to Kenya?'

'I've had you in this little bubble all these years. I wasn't ready to let you see what I was before.'

'Before what?'

'Before I became your dad. I wasn't around enough, so when your mum wanted to take you away, what could I say? I always felt guilty like it was my fault you lost your mum, because if I wasn't so busy with a woman, neither of you would have been there in the first place.'

A woman, that's how Dad always described his partners, it felt like they never moved past this title to become anything else. Even when he was with Anya for those two years she was still just 'a woman'.

But when he told his side of the story about the relationship with Yvonne, Kiama felt he picked up on something he missed the first time around. They didn't break up because Mum died; they broke up because they didn't want to complicate things for him growing up.

It's hard to know you're the reason that a couple split. He keeps thinking about it, about if they'd still be together if Mum hadn't died. Would they have been happier in their lives if they had each other?

'So, Special K,' Dad says. 'You think we should get a real tree this year?'

'It's November,' Kiama says.

Over Sunday dinner last week the whole family had come together and decided to make a huge deal out of Christmas this year, to celebrate big in order to honour Nana. Kiama remembers the first one after Mum died was big too. He'd only ever spent Christmas Eve with Dad before then and found the whole day too noisy and intense, with no TV on and constant laughter around the table. It wasn't that he didn't enjoy it, it just wasn't the same as it was with Mum back in the flat, where she'd chuck a string of fairy lights around the big cactus in the living room and allow him a mince pie for breakfast.

'I know how you love Christmas,' Dad says. 'We might as well make an early start on decorating.'

Kiama sits on a stool and tugs at the lights. 'Jesus, are you really playing *Midnight Marauders* again?' The more he fiddles with the lights, the bigger the knot becomes. 'Piece of crap,' he mumbles.

Dad raises an eyebrow at him. 'They're fine, untie it slowly.'

The music is too loud, annoying. Q-Tip's droning on but Kiama knows better than to ask for something else. It wasn't even like Dad tried to convert him to like hip-hop anymore; he simply didn't care what anyone else wanted to hear.

The lights get tangled beyond saving and Dad starts spraying down the counter with that bleach spray Kiama hates the smell of.

'Alexa, turn it down,' he calls.

'Don't address my woman.'

Kiama often jokes that Alexa is the only female voice in

the house, but it's actually quite depressing. He stands up and drops the lights in the pedal bin. 'Done with this.'

'What's wrong with you?'

'I'll get new ones, it's almost Black Friday.'

'No, what's wrong with your mood?'

'I was going out,' he offers.

'Well then, go out.'

But the sight of Dad, flicking through old Christmas cards, is too depressing. 'And what are you doing tonight?'

Dad crosses his arms and nods back through the door at the Christmas boxes.

'It's November,' he cries, 'come on, Dad, you're not going to sit in decorating the house all alone, are you?'

'No. I'll wait for you. I just wanted to see what was in the boxes.'

It's too much pressure. Kiama doesn't want his dad sitting around waiting for him to do stuff with. It's too much responsibility. It was easier when Nana was alive, at least then he was kept busy. There were women then too, even the ones that didn't stick around for long saw to it that Dad was occupied and not rattling around the house compulsively cleaning.

'What are you doing? Go out. Go see Trina. But don't come back here without bringing me some new lights, you hear?'

Is this really enough for him?

'Isn't it time you started getting back out there?'

'What? Where is this coming from?'

'I'm worried about you.'

Dad snorts. 'Why?'

But Kiama doesn't know what to say really, how to tell

Dad that it's okay, that he doesn't have to dedicate his life to looking after him anymore.

'You can't just drop that in the conversation and go silent. What are you worried about?'

'I'm worried about you staying in this house. About you being here alone if I go off travelling again. About you getting bored and getting old.'

'Behave yourself.' He rips some of the cards in half and chucks them in the recycling bin. 'You don't have to worry about me.'

'And I'm worried about this intense relationship you have with Alexa.'

They both laugh.

'I've got more than enough stuff to be getting on with. I've got a house to sell, a business to save, a son who's eating me out of house and home. You really think I have time for the additional stress a woman brings? At least I assume you're talking about a woman?'

'Yeah, I am,' Kiama says. 'Can't you feel your biological clock ticking?'

They've had so little banter in the weeks since he returned it feels good to talk like normal again, to jibe each other and laugh. 'Seriously though, what are you looking for?'

Dad leans against the counter and folds his arms. 'What makes you think I'm looking?'

Kiama thinks again, he knows what he wants to say, but isn't sure if he's brave enough to come out with it. 'Okay, let me ask you another way, what are you *waiting* for?'

'What do you mean?'

'You know what I mean. Don't make this more awkward for me than it already is. You know who I'm talking about.'

CHAPTER TWENTY-NINE

BLACK FRIDAY

December 2020

Yvonne

In that first week back home, Yvonne plodded through each day of work on autopilot. No one really asked her much about Kenya other than if she had any photos of safari and if she found Nairobi as dangerous as everyone said it was. There was also a sense a genuine disappointment from her idiot intern that she hadn't adopted a baby and it made her think of Kiama and his jibe about her bringing an African orphan home.

At night she fell asleep quickly, but would wake several times at odd hours, remembering the same vivid dream, of Emma in Kenya, picking tea leaves by the roadside and wearing a gold crown.

Emma. It was strange how Yvonne missed her more now than ever before. She had felt so present in Kenya, so by Yvonne's side. It was amazing to have, after all this time, someone she could talk about Emma with. Kiama never bored of hearing about his mum and it was a relief for Yvonne to be able to bring up Emma at any time and not have to worry about making anyone awkward. She wasn't just a dead friend from years ago with Kiama, she was Emma the person, full of life and off-colour remarks. That's why it hurt coming back, because it was like losing her all over again.

She hadn't heard anything from Kiama and respected him enough to not make contact. But in moments of weakness she looked him up online and scrolled through his photos, his various nights out, festivals, meals, girls and hairstyles. He looked like anyone else his age and continued to post as if nothing had changed. Maybe it hadn't for him, his life was unusual anyway. But for her, everything was different.

Night after night she spent hours online researching orphanages and programmes, charities and fundraising. She wasn't sure what she was looking for. She set up a generous monthly online payment to one of the big children's charities in Kenya and hoped this would appease the deep feelings of guilt she had, but it didn't. It didn't even make a dent. So, she got back in touch with Makimei and discussed how much it would cost to have a counsellor on his staff, someone who could go around the orphanages under the Kindred Kenya umbrella and work with children like those they met in Lari, children who had seen horrors which were never spoken about unless it was to get westerners to open up their purses.

But still, it wasn't enough, the trip had highlighted a hole in her life, something was missing and she couldn't fill it up by doing a few bank transfers. There had to be something else.

And then, he got in touch.

*

The first flurry of snow usually signals a complete shutdown of the London transport system and Yvonne tries not to get her hopes up. He probably won't be able to make it into central, even if he tried. But come five o'clock, he's there, outside London Bridge station, a thick scarf around his neck, a carrier bag by his side. Taller than she remembers and Kiama was right, Lewis has put on weight.

Her heart thumps.

He smiles as he spots her, but holds back, not jumping in with the usual kiss on the cheek or hug. It's been too long for that. He stops a few feet in front. 'Hey, Yvie.'

'Hi, Lewis.'

He pulls his shoulders up to his ears and shivers. 'It's freezing. Let's get inside somewhere.'

They walk into the nearest pub. Originally, he had suggested dinner, but she didn't want to commit to spending that much time with him. She's not even sure why she agreed to meet him at all, but he had insisted on talking through everything, having a sort of debrief on the trip. Plus, three weeks on she still hasn't heard from Kiama and is curious to know how he feels about things, if he was happy.

Despite the weather the pub is busy, filled with after-work drinkers, shoppers and people tutting into phone screens as they watch their trains being cancelled.

'What do you fancy?' he asks.

'A coffee, please.'

'A coffee?' he repeats. 'You driving?'

'No, but I'm cold.'

He orders while she goes off to find a table at the back.

He looks disappointed as he sets down the two mugs. 'When did it become socially acceptable to drink coffee in pubs?'

'Not everyone wants to drink all the time. And it's a family place. It does food,' she adds pointlessly as she picks up the menu.

'I thought you didn't want dinner?'

'No. I don't. I'm just saying.'

They stare at each other for a bit, assessing what ten years looks like on the other person's face.

'How is he?' she asks.

'Kiama? He's okay. For once he's not bouncing around trying to do a hundred different things. He's kind of, umm, still. Does that make sense?'

'Yes, but it doesn't sound like him.'

'Exactly. But it's good. He's thinking about what he wants to do next. With his life. With the money. I know he told you about it.'

She nods slowly.

'I think maybe he was disappointed, because he went out there convinced he would figure out what to do with it. But it only made him more confused, seeing all that poverty, all those needs. That orphanage you went to. It really affected him.'

'I know.'

'And was it definitely the same place?' he asks. 'The one Emma volunteered at?'

'Yes. Crazy, isn't it?'

'Yeah,' Lewis takes a breath and sighs. 'It was always kind of in the back of my mind that he'd want to go back there one day, to Kenya. I'm glad he got it out of his system.

I think it helped him.' He raises his mug then shakes his head, disappointed. 'I really wish I ordered a real drink.'

'Why didn't you?'

'Because you're not drinking.'

'So?'

'So, I'm following your lead.'

They both make moves to drink their coffees, but they're too hot. Neither of them knows what to say next.

'Kiama's teetotal,' he says.

She smiles. 'Since when?'

'Since you got him paralytic on whisky.'

She puts her mug down. 'That's not what happened.'

One side of his mouth goes up, he's teasing her. 'Last month vegan, this month teetotal.'

'He definitely wasn't a vegan in Kenya. He was eating monkey burgers and all sorts.'

Lewis laughs. 'You know what these Gen Z kids are like. They don't stick to anything. What? Why is that funny?'

'Because you sound old.'

'I *am* old.' He leans back in the chair, and a small smile crosses his face, 'I'm forty-five next year.'

'Really? Is that all?'

He turns his head and laughs. 'I almost forgot what you're like.'

'It's been a while.'

He looks outside at the snow, at a group of young girls in hijabs as they pose and take selfies with all their shopping bags. 'And why have they got to take photos of everything all the time?' Lewis says.

'I can't believe you've turned into a grumpy old man.'

'This is what sitting in a pub drinking coffee does to me.'

Yvonne stares at him, and is terrified by the idea that she could fall so easily in love with him again, for what would be the third time.

'Emma was always taking photos. She loved those single-use cameras you'd get from the chemist. But she lost so many of them before getting them developed. I was grateful at the time, because it was mostly pictures of us drunk. But now, I really wish I had all those photos.' She's rambling, desperate to keep talking, to keep her mind on something other than the old feelings which are resurfacing.

Lewis leans forwards. 'You miss her, don't you?'

He's never asked this before. No one has. 'So much,' she says. 'Especially now, since coming back from Kenya. She's on my mind a lot.'

He nods. 'I understand. I didn't before, you know, it was easier for me if I pretended you two weren't really friends. But I get it now.' He looks down at the table.

'I found myself constantly looking for her in Kiama. In how he looks, how he behaves. But there's so little of her there.'

'You're kidding? I think he's like her in so many ways. Where'd you think he gets those lofty morals from?' Lewis laughs. 'And this obsession with seeing the world and trying to save everyone in it. That's not from me. And the messiness,' he throws his hands up, 'if you were to see this boy's bedroom, that's definitely from his mum.'

'I guess so,' Yvonne says, unconvinced.

'But, most kids are nothing like their parents. And Kiama's just pure,' he looks around for the right word, 'Kiama.'

She laughs, 'Yeah, well, he's pretty confident, that's definitely from you.'

'I think you mean humble, don't you? That's the word you're looking for?'

She covers her smile, they shouldn't be doing this, flirting like they're carefree and on their first date. He must feel it too, as he looks away, back out onto the snowy streets. She drinks the shitty coffee and looks over enviously at the wine glasses on the table opposite.

'Can you believe that The Troika still exists?'

'The bar?' she asks.

He nods. 'I drive past it on my way to the trampoline park. That place has outlasted every single one of my relationships.' He takes a sip of his coffee, his eyes on her the whole time. What is he expecting her to say? She can't reminisce about this stuff with him.

'Freaky Fridays,' he laughs. 'I bet you wish you never went out that night?'

'I don't know what to say that.' There's no right response, to any of these things. And this is without them even addressing any of the big issues.

Sensing her discomfort, Lewis pushes his chair away from the table. Maybe he's feeling it too, maybe he's about to leave. She looks up at him as he pulls a blue carrier bag from the floor. 'I almost forgot,' he says as he dumps it between the mugs. 'This is for you.'

'What is it?' She takes it, dreading some twee reminder of their youth, of Emma. 'Kiama says it's yours.'

Something she left in Kenya. She opens the bag and unfolds a large grey sweatshirt. 'Oh my God,' she laughs.

'What? What is it?' Lewis looks. 'Obama?'

She's laughs so much and before she knows it, there are tears too.

'I don't get it,' Lewis says.

She holds the jumper in her hands, looking at Obama's smiling face backed by the stars and stripes. The cotton smells of Kenya, of market mornings and burning coal. She can imagine Kiama so clearly, browsing tourist tat in Mombasa and thinking of her and she can't help but confess, 'I miss him, Lewis. I really miss him.'

Lewis makes a face which causes the appearance of that one little line on his forehead. 'So, call him.'

'I can't. He hates me.'

'He doesn't hate you.'

Yvonne pulls a tissue from her handbag and wipes her eyes; she's momentarily embarrassed by the amount of make-up on it, proof that even though she swore she wouldn't, she did make an effort for him today. She blows her nose and tries to compose herself, but it's no good. She pulls on the Obama sweatshirt.

Lewis smiles at her. 'Now I'm looking at it, I think Kiama has the same sweatshirt. He has a bunch of things like that he wears *ironically*. Freddie Mercury, Ronald McDonald. But look at you; you look like you're wearing it out of pure love.'

She strokes the plastic print on the front and smiles. 'That's because I am.'

'Call him, Yvie. Call Kiama. He wants to speak to you, I know he does.'

'Really?'

He nods. 'Yeah. Don't leave the ball in his court.'

She scrunches up the damp tissue and throws it back in her bag. That's done then, the expertly put on make-up, the carefully chosen outfit. What made her think she would be able to keep her guard up with him today?

'How was he with you when he came back?'

'He was pissed,' Lewis says quickly. 'But I think I didn't get the full brunt of his anger as he wore some of it off when he was in Mombasa. By the time he got home he was more just exhausted and confused. He started by telling me little bits about the orphanage and some girl he slept with,' Lewis grimaces.

'He told you about her?'

'Yeah, he pretends like he wants boundaries but tells me everything eventually. Even the stuff I'd rather not know about, like him buying pills off some stranger in Nairobi.'

'I didn't know that.'

'But the big things, they took a little longer to get out of him. Like how let down he felt by his grandparents and even Purity. I knew that was going to happen. Kiama's so used to being the centre of everyone's world, I think it shocked him to be around people who weren't ready to drop everything for him.'

'That's understandable.'

'Then, slowly, he started asking me about you.' Lewis glances at her then away. 'He had a lot of questions. But I told him everything. At least, I thought I told him everything but then even today, before coming here I realised that maybe I hadn't.'

'What do you mean?'

He shakes his head. 'Nothing. It doesn't matter now.'

Afterwards, they walk through the browning sludge towards the station. The snow has stopped falling yet there's a sense of mild panic amongst the commuters, who are almost racing with each other.

'Which way are you going home?' she asks.

'I go to Euston then get the fast train home,' he pulls the tube map from his pocket, 'it's the black line, right?' She hears Kiama laugh about using anything other than a smart phone to access a map.

'Is that wrong? Is it not the black line?'

'No. I wasn't laughing at that.'

The crowds push around them, and they step to the side of the pavement.

'Thank you,' he says, 'for meeting me.'

She nods. There must be something to say, after all these years, everything they've been through, there must be something else.

He looks around and in a direct copy of Kiama says, 'Jesus. I always forget how busy London is.'

'It's the biggest shopping day of the year. I'm surprised you didn't try to drive in.'

'I thought about it,' he laughs. 'Wish I did now. The trains are going to be packed, aren't they?'

'Afraid so.'

'Maybe I should wait a bit. Let rush hour finish.'

She nods, 'That's a good idea.'

'Do you want to get a drink with me?' he says quickly and then looks sheepish. 'Sorry. I shouldn't have asked.'

Neither of them says anything. She takes a breath, ready to answer but then he laughs and says, 'I still can't help myself, Yvie.'

'We just had a drink. Didn't we?'

'We had a *coffee*,' he corrects. 'I don't think that counts.' He crosses his arms in front of his chest and tilts his head to the side, in a manner of his she recognises, but it's slightly more cautious now, less cocky than it was back then. He doesn't seem so sure of himself anymore, about his clout over her. Again, he looks at the train station and hordes of people.

'Okay,' she says.

'What?'

'Let's get a drink. A proper one this time.'

'Are you sure?'

Then, for the first time in over twenty years, she takes Lewis's hand without any guilt and they head back to the pub.

ACKNOWLEDGEMENTS

Thanks to my agent Eve White, I knew from the start I was lucky to have you and as this journey goes on I just keep having this confirmed. To my editor Manpreet Grewal, I don't know how you do it, but you're simply outstanding, thank you for everything.

To the HQ dream team, you all epitomise enthusiasm, brilliance and hard work, especially Lisa Milton, Lucy Richardson, Janet Aspey and Rebecca Fortuin. Also shout-out to all my fellow HQ authors, I've loved sharing this journey with you.

Homecoming was such an intense challenge to write and I don't think I could have done it without the feedback from my first readers Kevin Linnett, Alexis Rigg, Gill Haigh, Paul McMichael, Veronika Dapunt and Jo Haas.

Thank you to James Wambua for graciously checking my Swahili and to Maryam, the unofficial Head of the Litty Committee, for schooling me on being an eighteen-year-old. Any mistakes in language are my own.

I'm so grateful to have a family who are supportive of

my writing, which at times can be the most draining of side-hustles, so thank you to Patrick and Annabelle.

A final thank you to The Society of Authors for their generous grant which allowed me to complete this novel.

Read on for an extract from Luan Goldie's emotional debut *Nightingale Point*, longlisted for the Women's Prize for Fiction 2020.

SATURDAY, 4 MAY 1996

The evacuation began this morning. No sooner had the bins been collected than the hundreds of residents from the three blocks that make up Morpeth Estate began streaming away in their droves.

Bob the caretaker sat in his cubbyhole on the ground floor, telling anyone who would listen that 'it's only a heatwave if it goes on ten days'. But no one listened, instead they asked when the intercom was getting fixed, if he knew the lifts were out and what he was planning on doing about the woman on the third floor who kept sticking a chair out on the landing. Moan, moan, moan.

Bob stubs out his cigarette and looks up at the grey face of Nightingale Point, smiling at the way the sun illuminates each balcony, every single one a little personal gallery, showcasing lines of washing, surplus furniture, bikes, scooters, and pushchairs. Towards the top a balcony glints with CDs held by pieces of string; a few of the residents have started doing it and Bob doesn't have a clue why. He must ask someone.

I

Mary is amazed at how well it works. Who would believe that hanging a few CDs on the balcony stops pigeons from shitting on your washing? She had seen the tip on *GMTV* and immediately rushed to the flat next door to ask Tristan for any old discs. His music was no good anyway, all that gangbanging West Coast, East Coast stuff.

Mary wraps a towel around her hair. Her husband could show up any minute and the least she can do for him, after being apart for over a year, is not smell of fried fish. She switches on the TV, but the picture bounces and fuzzes. She doesn't even try to understand technology these days, but heads next door to get Malachi.

Malachi sits behind a pile of overdue library books and tries to think of a thesis statement for his *Design and the Environment* essay that is due next Friday, but instead he thinks about Pamela. If only he could talk to her, explain, apologise, grab her by the hand and run away. No, it's over. He has to stop this.

Distraction, he needs a distraction.

On cue, Tristan walks over with *The Sun* and opens it to Emma, 22, from Bournemouth.

'Your type?' he asks, grinning.

But Malachi's not in the mood to see Bournemouth Emma, or talk to Tristan, or write a thesis. He only wants Pamela.

Tristan sulks back out to the balcony to read his newspaper cover to cover, just as any fifteen-year-old, with a keen interest in current affairs, would. After this he will continue with his mission to help Malachi get over Pamela, and the only way to do it is to get under someone else. Tristan once heard some sixth-former girls describe his brother as 'dark and brooding', which apparently doesn't just mean that he's black and grumpy, women actually find him *attractive*. So it shouldn't be that hard to get him laid.

There's a smashing sound from the foot of the block and Tristan looks over the balcony.

The jar of chocolate spread has smashed everywhere and Lina doesn't have a clue how to clean up such a thing, so she walks off and hopes no one saw her.

Inside the cool, tiled ground floor of Nightingale Point, the caretaker shakes his head at the mess. 'Don't worry, dear, I'll get that cleaned up. Don't you worry a bit.'

'Thanks,' Lina says. A small blessing in the sea of shit that is her day so far. She hits the call button for the lift but nothing. 'Please tell me they're working?'

The caretaker cups his ear at her. 'What's that, dear?'

'The lifts,' she says.

He fills his travel kettle and shrugs. 'I've logged a call but it's bank holiday, innit.'

Lina pushes on the heavy door to the stairwell and sighs as she looks at the first of ten flights of stairs. 'By the way,' she calls back at the caretaker, 'I think there's kids on the roof again.'

Pamela loves being on the roof, for the solitude, for the freedom, and for the small possibility that she might spot, walking across the field below, Malachi. She has to see him today and they have to talk. Today's the day; it has to be.

At the foot of the block the caretaker tips a kettle of water over a dark splodge on the floor and gets his mop out. Just another mess to clean up at Nightingale Point.

CHAPTER ONE

Elvis

Elvis hates to leave his flat, as it is so full of perfect things. Like the sparkly grey lino in the bathroom, the television, and the laminated pictures tacked up everywhere reminding him how to lock the door securely and use the grill.

'Elvis?' Lina calls. 'You want curried chicken or steak and kidney?'

Elvis does not answer; he is too busy hiding behind the sliding door that separates the kitchen and living room, watching Lina unpack the Weetabix, bread and strawberry jam. She unscrews the jar and puts one of her fingers inside, which is a bad thing to do because of germs, but Elvis understands because strawberry jam can be so tasty.

This is the nineteenth day of Lina being Elvis's nurse. He knows this as he marked her first day on the calendar with a big smiley face. There are fourteen smiley faces on the calendar and five sad faces because this is when Lina was late.

She puts the jar of jam in the cupboard and returns to the shopping bags, taking out a net of oranges. Elvis hates oranges; they are sticky and smelly. He had asked for tomatoes but Lina said that tomatoes are an ingredient not a snack and that oranges are full of the kind of vitamins Elvis needed to make his brain work better and stop him from being a pest.

Lina's face disappears behind a cupboard door and Elvis watches as her pink coloured nails rap on the outside. He likes Lina's shiny pink nails, especially when her hair is pink too.

'Elllviiiis?' she sings.

He puts a big hand over his mouth to muffle the laughter, but then sees Lina has removed the red tin from the shopping bag – the curried chicken pie. He gasps as he realises he wants steak and kidney.

'Bloody hell!' She jumps and raises the tinned pie above her head, as if ready to throw it. 'What the hell you doing? You spying on me?'

'No, no, no.'

'Elvis, why are you wearing a sweatshirt? It's too hot for that.' She slams the tin down on the counter.

'Steak and kidney pie,' he tells her. 'I want steak and kidney pie. It's the blue tin.'

'Yeah, all right, all right.'

'Can I have two?' he tries, knowing his food has been limited. He is unsure why.

'No, Elvis, that's greedy. Now go. Get changed. You're sweating.'

'Get changed into what?' he asks.

'A T-shirt, Elvis. It's bloody baking out; go put on a T-shirt.'

Elvis goes through to his bedroom and removes his sweat-shirt. He stands for a moment and looks over his round belly in the mirror, moisture glistening among the curly ginger hairs

5

that cover his whole front. When he takes off his glasses his reflection looks watery, like one of his dreams. He then pulls on his favourite new T-shirt, which is bright blue and has a picture of the King on it. It also has the words *The King* in gold swirly writing. He smiles at himself before going to the living room to sit on his new squashy sofa.

Elvis listens carefully to the steps Lina takes to make the pie: the flick of the ignition, the slam of a pot on the gas ring. Then, the sound he likes best, the click of her pearly plastic nails on the worktops. He loves all the flavours the tinned pies come in and he likes the curried chicken pie most days, but today he really does want steak and kidney.

'Right, master, your pie is on the boil,' Lina says as she walks into the living room. 'Nice,' she says, acknowledging his T-shirt.

'Are we going to the bank holiday fair?' He had seen posters for it Sellotaped up on bus shelters and in the windows of off-licences: *Wilson and Sons Fairground on the Heath, 3–6 May. Helter Skelter, Dodgems, Ghost Train!* He really wants to go.

'Yeah, maybe when it cools down a bit.' Lina flops on the sofa next to him and picks up the phone. 'Go.' She waves him away. 'Why you sitting so close to me? I *am* entitled to a break.'

But Elvis is comfy on the sofa and he has already sorted the stickers from his *Merlin's Premier League* sticker book and watered his tomato plants on the windowsills. He has already carefully used his razor to remove the wispy orange hairs from his face as George, his care worker, had taught him, and rubbed the coconut suntan lotion into his skin as he knows to do on hot days. This morning Elvis has already done everything he was meant to and now he wants to eat his steak and kidney pie and go to the fair.

Lina has his new special phone in her hand. Elvis loves his phone; it is his favourite thing in his new living room, after the television. The phone is so special that you can only make a call when you put money inside and you can only get the money out with a special key that George looks after. Beside the phone sits a laminated sheet with all the numbers Elvis will ever need: a little drawing of a policeman – 999; a photograph of Elvis's mum wearing the purple hat she reserves for church and having her photograph taken – 018 566 1641; and a photograph of George behind his desk – 018 522 7573. Elvis is trying to learn all the numbers by heart but sometimes when he tries, he gets distracted by the fantastic noise the laminated sheet makes if you wave it in the air fast. Next to the phone is a ceramic dish shaped like a boat that says *Margate* on it. The dish is kept filled with change for when Elvis needs to make a call.

He watches carefully as Lina feeds the phone with his change and starts to dial, her lovely pink nails hitting the dial pad: 018 557.

'Go and sit somewhere else,' she snaps.

But there is nowhere else to sit apart from the perfect squashy sofa, so Elvis goes into the kitchen where he can watch and listen to Lina from behind the door. In secret.

'Hi . . . I'm at work. Elvis is driving me nuts today,' she says into the phone. 'He keeps bloody staring at me . . . Yeah I know . . . Tell me about it . . . Ha ha. Yeah, true true . . . ' She slides off her plimsolls and pulls the coffee table closer, putting her little feet up on it. 'But you know what my mum's like, always busting my arse over something: look after your baby, wash the dishes, get more shifts. I thought the whole point of having a baby was that you didn't have to go work no more . . . Exactly . . . Especially on a day like this. Bloody roasting out.'

Even from behind the door Elvis can see that the nails on Lina's toes are the same colour as those on her fingers, but shorter. The colour looks like the insides of the seashells Elvis collected at Margate last summer. He likes Lina's toes; this is the first time he has ever seen Lina's toes. He likes them but knows he is not allowed to touch them.

'Can I have a biscuit?' Elvis asks as he comes out from behind the door, now peckish and unable to wait for the pie to boil.

'Hang on. What?' Lina rests the phone under her chin like one of the office girls at the Waterside Centre, the place where Elvis used to live before he was clever enough to live by himself in Nightingale Point.

'Can I have a biscuit?' he asks again.

'I'm on the phone, leave me in peace.' She tuts then returns to her call. 'But look, yeah, I'm coming to the fair later. Soon as I'm done with the dumb giant here I'll be down . . . I'll get it; pay me later.' Lina slides the rest of the money from the ceramic boat into her pocket.

Elvis pictures the laminated sheet of Golden Rules that hangs in his bedroom. Rule Number One: Do not let strangers into your flat. Rule Number Two: Do not let anybody touch your private swimming costume parts. Rule Number Three: Do not let anyone take your things. Lina is breaking one of the Golden Rules. Elvis must call George and report her immediately.

Lina picks up the laminated sheet of phone numbers and uses it to fan herself. It makes her pink fringe flap up and down, and Elvis wants to watch it but he also knows that he must report her rule break. George once told him that if he could not get to the house phone and it was an emergency, he could go outside to the phone box to make a call. The phone box, on the other side of the little field in front of the estate, is the second emergency phone. Elvis must now go there. He leaves the living room and slips on his sandals at the door. *Jesus sandals*, Lina calls them, but Elvis does not think Jesus would have worn such stylish footwear in the olden days. He opens the front door gently, quietly enough that Lina will not hear. Then, and only because he knows he is allowed to leave the flat to use the second phone for when he cannot use the first phone, Elvis steps out of flat thirty-seven and heads into the hallway of the tenth floor.

CHAPTER TWO

Mary

Ever since Mary woke up she has been feeling uneasy. And as the mother of two, grandmother of four, nurse of thirty-three years and wife to a fame-chasing husband, Mary knows what uneasy feels like. Her elbow has been twitching and she can't shake the feeling that something is wrong. Something is coming.

She opens the pink plastic banana clip and allows her long greying hair to fall about her shoulders. Everything is cooked and cooling but she now needs something else to occupy her mind, to stop herself from worrying.

She covers the last plate – vegetable spring rolls – and stands within the tiny space of bulging cupboards and greasy appliances as she looks for a place to lay them. The worktops are already loaded with plates of food; each one gives off a different fried smell from under sweating pieces of kitchen roll.

'Ah, too small, too small,' she mutters. But no one could accuse Mary of failing to make the best use of her space. In each corner of the lino two-litre bottles of Coke are stacked like bowling pins; on tops of cupboards tins upon tins are stashed, heading slowly towards their expiry date; and on a small shelf above the fridge sits no less than seven boxes of brightly branded breakfast cereals. She buys them for her grandbabies. Though after a long shift on the ward she loves nothing more than to peel off her tights and eat two bowls of Frosties while lying on the sofa listening to *The Hour of Inspiration* on Filipino radio. Mary shuffles around some things, swears to finally get rid of the dusty sandwich maker and to stop buying five-kilo bags of long grain rice.

Her elbow. Twitch twitch twitch.

'Stupid old woman,' she mumbles. She knows she is being ridiculous, worrying too much about everything and nothing. She makes a mental list of her worries and tries to remember what the doctor on *The Oprah Winfrey Show* said to do with them.

'You think of a worry, you cross the street,' she says as she pictures the studio audience of determined, applauding, crying American women.

Mary thinks of each worry: talk that teenagers are gathering in the swing park at night to watch dogs fight; the cockroaches that continuously plague her kitchen; the smell of gas that sometimes lingers on the ninth floor; the woman from the top floor who was robbed of her shopping money last week as she got in the lift. It's a long list.

'Cross the street, cross the street.' Mary waves her arms as she imagines each worry float off behind her. But then larger worries, those that are more likely to happen, these are things she can't dismiss as easily, namely the imminent arrival of her estranged husband, David. Fifteen months he had been gone and then a call from Manila Aquino Airport two days ago: 'My love, I am coming home, but I am on standby. You know what these airlines are like: locals back of the queue.' She has heard this from him before, claims of him booking a ticket, being at the airport, getting on the next flight. Even once a call to say he had been diverted to Birmingham and would arrive the next day. She had wrung her fingers with anxiety for almost a week until he finally landed on her doorstep – their doorstep – with an excuse she now struggles to remember. For David, there is always some excuse, some distraction, some offer of money he can't turn down. Whenever he is due to return home the world is full of people desperate for a poor Johnny Cash tribute act. Or maybe he is with one of his many floozies. Mary has never gotten over her own brother's accusation that David had 'a floozy waiting at the side of each stage'.

'Cross the street,' she says more weakly as she pictures David's travel-weary face, greasy rise of hair and fake Louis Vuitton suitcase. 'Cross the street.' She cringes as she imagines David pulling her in for an obligatory married couple kiss. 'Cross the street.'

'Talking to yourself again, Mary?' Malachi waves a hand as he enters the kitchen.

She felt bad for pulling him away from his studies, but also pleased for an excuse to check in on him and his younger brother Tristan. When had she turned into such a meddling old woman?

'I've fixed the TV,' Malachi says.

Mary takes the two small steps needed to cross the kitchen and throws her arms around his middle.

'It wasn't even broken.' He shakes free from her arms and wipes the small beads of sweat on his dark brown skin. 'Your aerial was unplugged. Tell the kids to stop playing behind the TV.'

Mary nods, knowing she will never tell her grandbabies any such thing – those perfect little girls would have to throw the TV out of the window before she dare aim a cross word at them. Each time they come to stay they leave her exhausted, and the small flat trashed, yet she can't wait till they come again.

'Why don't you open a window in here? It's twenty-four degrees already.' Malachi leans over the sink and pushes on the condensation-streaked glass. It screeches loudly as it gives way, allowing the heat from outside to do battle with the steam from Mary's cooking.

'I have the vent on, see.' She indicates the tiny, spinning, dust-covered fan. 'You look tired,' she says gently, keen not to nag the boy. 'Too much study, study, study.'

He looks up at the window and undoes the top button on his shirt. Mary does not like the way he has taken to wearing collarless shirts; she watches *MTV* sometimes, and knows this is not a fashion among young people. She notices too, as he goes under the sink, that his trousers – muted green cotton with a sharp crease down the middle – are for a much older man.

'What you looking for?' she asks as he rummages around her collection of multi-buy discount cleaning products, fifty pack of sponges and long abandoned, but not yet disposed of, cutlery holders and soap dishes.

'You need to oil your window.' He twists the nozzle on a rusty can of WD-40.

13

'Don't worry about my window.'

He stops and looks down at her. His almond-shaped eyes search for something.

'What?' She touches her face, wondering if a stray Rice Krispie is stuck on her cheek.

'You're saying *I* look tired. You all right? You look a bit . . . frazzled.'

'I worked forty-eight hours already this week – what do you expect me to look like? Imelda Marcos?'

Malachi blesses her with one of his rare smiles and then positions his knees into the two small free spots on the worktop. He seems more sullen than usual.

'Are *you* okay?' Mary asks as he squirts the window frame.

'Yep. I'm always okay. Just hot and this smog, it plays havoc with my asthma.' He jumps down and stares blankly across the kitchen.

Mary knows he's still hung up on the blonde girl from upstairs. 'Well, I'm glad you're not still sad about whatshername.'

'I have a hundred other things to think about,' he snaps.

She was the first girl of Malachi's Mary had ever met. He even brought her over for dinner once, one wet afternoon where they sat, with plates on their laps, eating chicken bistek.

'Some things are not meant to be. I could see it from the start,' Mary lies, for all she saw that afternoon was Malachi buzzing around the girl like she was the best thing since they started slicing bread. 'I always know when couples don't match. I even said it about Charles and Diana, but did anyone listen to me?'

'I really don't want to talk about this.'

Mary throws her arms up. 'Me neither. Goodbye, Blondie. Plenty more pussy in the cattery.'

He wipes his face to hide his embarrassment and she's pleased to see the tiniest of smiles emerge on his sad face.

'Why'd you make so much food?' he asks.

'I told you, I need to work every day next week so I'm stockpiling. Like a squirrel.' She wraps an old washed out ice-cream tub with cling film and hands it to him. 'This is for your tutor.' She had been sending food parcels to anyone related to Malachi's education since his first semester of university. Anything to boost the boy's chances. 'The rest is for your freezer.'

'Thanks. I appreciate it.'

'And I appreciate if you put on some weight. What is this?' She pinches the flesh of his side.

'Ow.'

'Heroin chic!' she announces. 'I saw it on *GMTV*. Teenagers with bodies like this.' Mary holds up her pinkie finger. 'No woman wants that, Malachi. You need to eat properly.'

She had looked in Malachi's and Tristan's fridge a few days ago and saw nothing but a loaf of value bread and jar of lemon curd. The freezer was even worse: a half empty box of fish fingers and two frosty bottles of Hooch, which Tristan explained were 'for the ladies'. If their nan knew they were eating so poorly under Mary's watch there would be murder.

'Freezer, you hear me? Tell your brother he can't eat, eat, eat all in one sitting. And why has he got zigzags shaved in his hair? Does he think he's a pop star or something?'

'You know what he's like. He's a little wild.'

'He can't afford to be *wild*.' Mary tries to put the word in air quotes but uses eight fingers and makes a baby waving motion. 'Too many riffraffs around here going wild like this.' She makes a stabbing gesture and tries to look menacing, but her only reference point is *West Side Story* and she makes a dance of it.

Malachi puts a hand under a piece of kitchen roll and drags out a bamboo skewer of prawns. Mary slaps him.

'Did you hear me say help yourself? Does this look like the Pizza Hut buffet to you?'

'You just told me I need to eat.'

'Not prawn. Too early for prawn.' She turns her back to him as she rewraps the skewers. His eyes burn her; she must explain her snappy mood. 'I need to leave my spare keys with you in case David gets in early. He's on standby for a flight so could be here tonight, tomorrow or next week. Oh God.' The reality of him arriving hits her again. It sends her elbow into overdrive.

'David?'

'Yes, David, my husband. Remember him?' There's a hysterical edge to her voice. She puts a hand on her forehead to save herself as Oprah has taught her. 'I don't even want to talk about it.'

'I didn't know David was coming back.'

'No. But we didn't know Jesus was coming back either.'

Mary takes her nurse fob watch from her pocket – a present from David on one of his rare jaunts back home. An obscure-looking Virgin Mary with oversized arms ticks around the clock, hung on a thick, gold link chain. Well, it was gold once, now it's more silver, the shine, like everything else to do with David, rubbed away by the sweat and grime of real life. Quarter to twelve.

'Mary?' Malachi waves his arms to get her attention. 'Hand me these keys then. I need to get back home.'

Mary nods as she looks in the junk drawer, rifling through papers, wires and replacement batteries for the smoke alarm until she finds the spare keys. Tristan had once attached a plastic marijuana leaf to them thinking it was funny. Mary had given him a lecture about the dangers of drugs but never bothered to remove the key ring.

She fusses with the catch on the watch as she pins it to her uniform, swearing to get it fixed. 'You want some tea before you go?' she asks Malachi.

He spins the keys around a long finger. 'No, thanks. Too hot.'

'You call this hot? It's thirty-five degrees in Manila today.' She lifts the kettle and gives it a shake before she flicks the switch.

'Right,' Malachi says. 'I better get back to my books.'

He sulks off and she rolls her eyes at his constant grumpiness. But as she hears the front door close she stops cold. The twitch becomes a scratch. Something is wrong, for her feelings never are. Today, something horrible will happen.

CHAPTER THREE

Pamela

There is not a stitch of breeze on the roof of Nightingale Point. Today, up here is just as suffocating as being in the flat with Dad. Pamela places her new running shoes on the ground and holds onto the metal railing; her long rope of blonde hair falls forward and dangles over the edge. The sunrays hit the nape of her neck and she feels her skin, so dangerously pale and thin, begin to burn. She shifts her body into the shade of the vast grey water tanks and imagines the water as it rolls between them and into the maze of pipes around the block's fifty-six flats. Pamela loves the roof. Since she returned to London a few days ago it's become the only space Dad does not watch over her. Sometimes she wishes she was back in Portishead with her mum, just for the freedom from his eyes. But in a way being there was worse, because it meant Malachi was over a hundred miles away rather than two floors. At least here there is a chance she will see him, run into him in the lift, or bump into him in the stairwell.

Blood runs into her face as she leans further over the

railings. Her head feels heavy. She wonders, not for the first time, how it would feel to fall from this spot, to flail past all fourteen floors and land at the bottom among the cars and bins. It would probably feel like running the 200 metres. Air hitting your face and taking your hair, your lungs shocked into working harder than you ever knew they could. Pink and yellow splodges dance in front of her eyes as she lifts her head. It's coming up to noon, only halfway through another monotonous, never-ending day.

She assumes it's other teenagers that repeatedly bust the locks on the door that leads up to the roof. They leave their crushed cans of Special Brew and ketchup-smeared fish and chip papers across the floor as evidence that they are having a life. She often fantasizes about coming up here at night, catching them in the throes of their late-night parties, tasting beer and throwing fag butts among the pigeon shit with them. If only Dad would let her out of the flat past 6 p.m. No chance.

The sky appears endless. Unnaturally blue today, almost unworldly, not a blemish on it apart from the single white smear of a plane.

Does she need to run back? Has it already been twenty minutes? She doesn't care. What does time matter if you're all alone? What difference does any of it make if you're about to throw yourself from the top of a tower block? She takes three deep breaths but knows that she doesn't have the confidence to do it. But the thought alone makes her feel like she has some edge on Dad, something that she *can* do without his permission.

In front of the estate people are living their lives: a child runs, the drunks drink, some girls sunbathe in pink bras and denim shorts, and a lone large figure in billowing purple crosses the grass at speed. Pamela tries to picture who the bodies are, how they would feel if they witnessed a girl fall from the building, their faces upon discovering her body bashed at the bottom. They would be traumatised, she thinks, for a while at least, and then her death would become another estate anecdote. *The tale of the broken-hearted teenager with the strict dad.* It would become just another story to get passed around the swing park and across balconies, along with tales of who is screwing who and which flat plays host to the biggest number of squatters.

Pamela wishes she could go for a run. She needs to clear her head. Surely Dad will let her out.

'Please, one hour out,' she rehearses. It sounds so feeble out loud, so knowing of a negative answer.

Her running shoes swing by her sides as she pads across the greyness in her socks. She steps over the glossy ripped pages of a magazine; a girl in a peephole leather catsuit stares back at her. The door bounces against its splintered frame as Pamela enters the building. Her world starts to shrink. With each step down to the eleventh floor the brightness of the unending blue sky disappears and the stairwell begins to close in on her. The concrete walls suck the air away until there is only the suffocating stink of other people's lives.

'Do you think it will be okay if I went out today? Maybe. Perhaps.' Her voice echoes eerily; she feels even more alone. 'I'm thinking of going out today.' This time with more confidence. But what's the point? He will say no. He will never trust her again.

She opens the door onto the puke-coloured hallway and the shouts and music of her neighbours. Outside flat forty-one she stops and rests her head on the security gate, takes a few breaths and then pulls it open. She looks down at the letterbox and for a moment feels like she has a choice. She could still go back to the roof. But, as always, the choice is taken away from her as the lock clicks from within and the front door swings open.

Dad fills the doorway; a fag hangs from the corner of his mouth. 'You're pushing your luck, girl.' Patches of psoriasis flame red on his expressionless face. He's put back on the same sweat-stained yellow T-shirt and army combat trousers from yesterday.

'I was getting some air.' She pushes past him into the dim, smoky living room.

He follows her, sits on the sofa and pulls his black boots on. 'Air?' He methodically ties up each of the long mustard laces. The woven burgundy throw falls from the back of the sofa to reveal the holes and poverty beneath it. 'We got a balcony for that. I don't wanna start locking the gate, Pamela, but if you're gonna be running off every opportunity—'

'I didn't run off. It's a nice day. I was on the roof.'

'Well, I've heard that before. You can't blame me for not trusting you.'

She rearranges the throw and stands back. She only wants an hour outside, just enough time to clear her head. So much can change in that time; like the day she first met Malachi. Dad had given her an hour then too, explained how grateful she should be for it. 'More than enough time to go round the field and straight back home.' She grabbed that time, and even though he was watching her from the window, she felt free as she ran loops around the frosty field.

The drunks, immune to the freezing temperatures of the morning, watched from their bench as she ran past them several times that hour. 'You should be running this way, blondie,' one called, while shaping his hands in a V towards his crotch on her last lap. They all laughed and she ran faster. She could always go faster and with time ticking she needed to get home before Dad came out for her. She cut onto the grass, slipped and fell awkwardly. It hurt straight away. Her ponytail caught the side of her face as she turned to check if the drunks were still laughing at her, but they hadn't even noticed her fall. The dew began to seep through her leggings and she tried to stand, but buckled immediately with the pain.

'Hey,' someone called. 'You okay?' A tall man came running towards her and put out a gloved hand. 'You really went down hard there.'

'Yeah.'

'Here, let me help you.'

As he helped her to a bench she tried to concentrate on the hole in his glove to stop herself from blushing.

'You really do run out here in all weathers, don't you?' he asked.

'Sorry?'

'I live up in Nightingale Point. I always see you out here.'

He had seen her before. How had she never seen him? She tried not to stare, or lean into his arms too much.

Tristan Roberts came over too. He was from her school, one of those loud, obnoxious boys everyone seemed to know.

'Oh, shit, did you break your leg?'

'No, she ain't broken her leg. This is my brother.'

They looked nothing alike.

'Ain't you cold?' Tristan pulled the drawstrings on his hoodie tighter. 'Running round out here? That's long.'

She could see Dad coming across the field now, his face red from fatigue and panic.

'I'm fine, really. Thanks. I need to get home.' She tried to rise but the pain shot through and she winced. He grabbed her again; the pain was almost worth it.

'Get off her. Pam.' Dad was closer. 'Pam, Pam.' He pushed past Tristan and put his hands either side of her face. 'I knew I should have been watching you. What happened?'

'She's all right, man, she just tripped, innit,' Tristan said.

'Who are you? Why are you two even near my girl?'

'Dad, stop it. Tristan goes to my school.'

Tristan looked confused. He obviously didn't recognise her. It confirmed she had no presence at her new school; she was nobody.

'I'm Malachi. We live in the same block. We were making sure she was all right. That's all.'

'Well, she's fine 'cause I'm here now, ain't I?' Dad snapped. 'Come on. Let's get you home.' His grip on her arm was tighter than it needed to be. She could see Malachi noticed it too.

'This looks bad, Pam. Don't think you'll be running again for a while.' Dad looked relieved, happy because injuries meant she had no reason to go out.

Even now, with the injury long healed, he still won't let her out, but then he has other reasons for wanting to keep her inside the flat these days. She pulls the curtains open and the room brightens, but even the sun's glare is not enough to chase the perpetual gloom out.

Dad inspects his roll-up for life before roughly squeezing it onto a saucer. It's from her nan's set, cream with tiny brown corgis around the edge, once used for special occasions but now reduced to holding ash.

'I'm going to the bookies,' he says. 'Will be back for dinner. We'll heat up that corned beef.'

'They're fighting again,' she says.

'Who?'

'Next door. Can't you hear them?'

They stop for a moment to listen to the searing soap opera from flat forty-two that plays itself out so regularly. It sounds particularly theatrical today. What is the woman shrieking about this time? She always seems to be arguing with her teenage daughter over something. Pamela longs for that kind of relationship, one so freely volatile that you could scream and shout at a parent, rather than stand there and soak up their disappointment.

'They been at it all morning,' he huffs. 'Their voices go right through me.'

Pamela tries to block out the domestic so she can focus on Dad, her own situation. She tries to assess his mood by the way he clears his throat and collects his wallet. She wonders at her chances of success and waits to pick her moment.

He looks straight at her. 'Why you dragging those about?' He nods towards the pair of pink and lilac trainers in her hands.

The tip of her ponytail tastes chemically; he always buys the cheapest shampoo.

'I won't go anywhere other than around the field. I promise.'

'You've only been home a few days. You expect me to let you start running wild again?' He holds his anger in so well, but she can see it behind his eyes, ready to pop like glass. 'No chance. You're staying in.'

'You know it rained the whole month I was at Mum's. I haven't been out running in ages.'

He shakes his head again.

'I want to go round the field a few times. It's the middle of the day,' she tries. 'You can watch me from here.'

'Told you. I'm going out.' His keys jangle as he taps his pockets and walks away, her chances dissipating.

'What about swimming? Can I go to the pool?'

He laughs. 'Yeah, right, the pool. Why? You arranged to meet someone there, have you?'

'No. Dad, please.' She follows him into the hallway, not content to let it end there. She knows she's already in trouble anyway. 'So you expect me to stay in all day listening to that?'

The walls leak more cries from the quarrelling neighbours.

He checks the handle on his bedroom door: locked. 'You can use the phone. Call one of your mates for a chat.'

'I don't want to chat. I want to go out. I want to run.'

He stops by the front door and gently takes her plait in one of his hands. 'No.' So calm. So fixed. 'I don't trust you out the flat. In fact, I don't even know if I trust you to be alone *in the flat*.' He lets the long plait fall and kisses her on the head.

'What do you mean?'

'Well, how can I be sure that the minute I go out your little boyfriend won't come running up?'

'Because I don't have a boyfriend anymore. Remember?'

He holds her gaze but what can he say? He knows he ruined it for her; he ruined everything.

'Dad?'

He turns to face her, keys now in his hands as he opens the front door. 'Yeah? Come on, Pam, what you wanting now?'

I hate you. 'Nothing.'

The door closes and she listens for the Chubb lock, but hears no footsteps. He's still outside; maybe he will change his mind and give her permission to start living again. But then, seconds later, there is the distinct clank of the security gate and the crunch of it being locked: the confirmation that she will spend today locked inside her home. Trapped.